CALL OF WIZARDRY

COMPANY OF STRANGERS, BOOK 6

MELISSA MCSHANE

Night Harbor Publishing

Map by Oscar Paludi

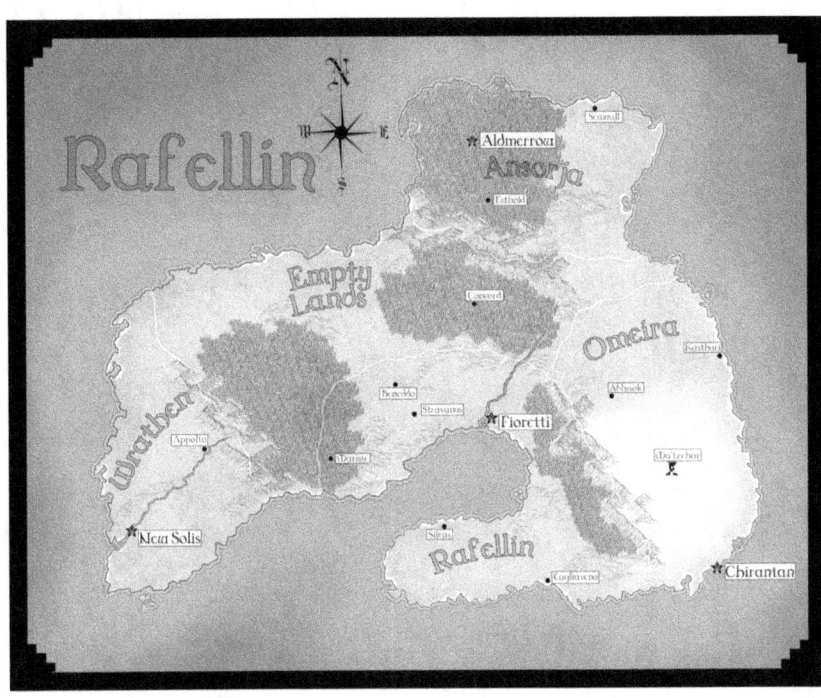

This book, and the Company of Strangers series, is dedicated to all role-playing gamers everywhere who ever said the words "Let me tell you what my character did."
This is our story.

1

The familiar brown brick of the three-story houses along the gently sloping street welcomed Sienne home. It was early evening, when the cool breezes off the harbor blew away the heat of the true summer day, and the long, slanting rays of the setting sun pointed the way to Master Tersus's back door. Their warmth soothed Sienne's aching back, sore from her having lain propped on her elbows for ten hours on her flying carpet.

She could have *ferried* herself and her companions back instantaneously, but the joy of flying had captivated her enough that she didn't want to give it up, regardless of the pain. And it was far superior to riding. Ten hours on horseback would have been painful in a different way. It also would not have gotten them nearly so far. They'd made the entire journey from Chirantan in Omeira to Fioretti in that ten hours—a journey of more than a week by ship or twice that overland by horse. Sienne rubbed her lower back. Such lightning travel was worth a little pain.

"Are you all right?" Alaric asked. He walked beside her, toting both their rolled-up carpets. They weighed practically nothing because they floated whether they were rolled or flat, but they looked heavy, and Alaric had pointed out that no one would believe someone her size could carry a carpet that big.

"Just sore," Sienne said. "Aren't you?"

"A little stiff. Next time, we should take more rests."

"I concur heartily with this decision," Perrin said from behind them. He sounded so relieved Sienne pinched her lips against a smile. Perrin hated heights more than she did, and he'd looked so chagrined that morning when Alaric declared they would fly home Sienne could guess how he felt.

"We might not need to, if Sienne can find *transport*," Dianthe said. "Kitane's eyes, but I'm hungry."

"If we have luck, Leofus has supper still," Kalanath said. He sounded as fresh and unwearied as he had when they'd said goodbye to his parents that morning.

"Let's not count on it," Alaric said. "Sienne, will you get the door?"

Sienne hurried ahead to open Master Tersus's back door, then stood aside for the others to enter with their awkward burdens. She paused for a moment when they'd all passed her to look out over the street that sloped downhill before her. It smelled of dozens of different evening meals that blended together into the scent of hot meat and salt potatoes and, from somewhere nearby, a hint of chocolate. That might be Leofus's cooking. He'd been experimenting with the unusual southern delicacy when they left.

The warm evening light turned the paving stones more golden than usual, burnishing them to a bright radiance. Sienne heard laughter from across the street where one of the neighbors was having a party, judging by the extra lanterns strung around his front door and leading around the side of the house. She breathed in a sigh of contentment. Home. They were all safe, no one had died in Omeira, and their quest was all but complete now that Alaric was a full Sassaven unicorn, and she...

She closed the door and went into the bath house to wash her face. The carpets' magic included an invisible shield that protected their riders' faces from wind blasting them at gale force speeds, but Sienne still felt grimy. Dozens of invulnerable magic lights shed a cold white light over the sink and the pump and the porcelain tub for a rather more thorough cleaning. The whitewashed walls peeled at the corners from the damp, making Sienne itch to pull strips off the walls.

She scrubbed and splashed herself clean, then dried off with the cloth hanging from the wall. Then she used a small magic to heat the water the cloth absorbed, making it evaporate and drying the cloth. Three days ago she wouldn't have bothered because it took her so much time. Now she did it in seconds. Just another way in which she'd been altered by the ritual that had changed Alaric. It exhilarated and unnerved her.

It had been an accident. The ritual had been intended only to unlock Alaric's full potential. They hadn't realized it worked both ways, affecting the one performing the ritual as well as the one undergoing it. Now Sienne no longer needed a spellbook to cast spells, and her magical reserves had increased so dramatically she didn't know what they were anymore, and her so-called small magics were enormous by comparison to what they'd been. She felt like a stranger to herself, and she felt more complete than she'd ever felt before. Strange contrasts. If she looked in a mirror and found her hair had gone as blonde as Alaric's, she wouldn't be surprised.

The door opened. "Looks like we had the same idea," Alaric said, entering the room. Sienne stepped back to give him room at the sink. "Leofus is putting a meal together for us. Complaining noisily the whole time, of course, but if he weren't glad to see us, he wouldn't do it at all."

"I didn't realize how much I missed home until we got back." Sienne thought about leaning against the wall, but remembered in time how damp it always was.

"Me too. I'll be glad to sleep in our own comfortable bed." He held out a hand for the cloth, and Sienne tossed it at him with her small magic called invisible fingers. He dried off and tossed it back to her, and once again she dried it, marveling at how easy it was.

Alaric reached for her hand and drew her close, putting his arms around her. "On the other hand," he continued, "we don't have to sleep."

Sienne ran her fingers over his strong chin and the curve of his neck. "I've been thinking about a back rub since we left the Bramantus Mountains behind."

"Mmm. Yours, or mine?"

"Both, so long as we're naked for it." She pulled his head down for a kiss. He smelled deliciously of pine forests and the heady musk of the unicorn, and his lips were firm and warm on hers.

"I thought you were hungry," Dianthe said from behind them. Sienne, startled, jerked away from Alaric and was brought up short by his encircling arms. Dianthe smirked. "Dinner's ready. Though if you want to keep on with what you're doing, might I suggest the bath house isn't the best place for it?"

"Suggest away," Alaric said, and kissed Sienne once more before letting her go.

Leofus was still complaining when they entered the kitchen and took their usual seats at the table. "No warning," he said, "no advance notice at all, it's like you don't appreciate my genius, don't know what you'd do if I just up and refused to wait on you all—"

"Thank you, Leofus," Sienne said. "I'm amazed you were able to put together a meal this good without any notice." The table was covered with remnants of past meals, cold roast chicken and sliced ham and the tag end of a pork roast, hardboiled eggs already peeled, sliced cooked carrots and baked potatoes still in their jackets, sautéed squash emitting aromatic herbed steam, and a tureen of dumplings floating in golden chicken gravy.

"Don't take advantage," Leofus warned, gesturing with his ubiquitous spoon, but he was smiling.

Sienne sat next to Alaric and heaped her plate high with chicken and squash. "I like Omeiran food, but there's nothing to beat home cooking," she said. Leofus beamed.

"Let's talk about tomorrow," Alaric said. "Sienne has to meet with this—what was her name?"

"Carys Bettega," Sienne said. "Ghrita said she's a retired scrapper wizard who might be willing to sell me some spells. A scrapper is likely to have *transport*, and if I can get that, it will change how we go to Beneddo."

"But we *are* going, correct?" Perrin said. He hadn't taken large portions of anything, and Sienne noticed he'd only picked at what he had taken.

"Of course," Alaric said. "The next step is to make sure your family is still safe, and see what progress Sienne's brother has made on their problem."

Sienne nodded and said, around a mouthful of tender squash, "Alcander will have a plan by now. I'm sure of it."

"When I spoke with Cressida this morning, she indicated all was well," Perrin said, "but I...would like to see for myself."

His uncertainty surprised Sienne. Perrin had spoken with his former wife Cressida almost every day since they set off for Omeira, and Sienne had been sure they were working out their differences and moving toward a much desired (on Sienne's part, at least) reconciliation. Perrin loved Cressida still, and Sienne thought Cressida returned his feelings, so if they could just sit down in the same room for ten minutes and talk things through...but now Perrin sounded doubtful in a way he hadn't throughout their journey. If he was having second thoughts, Sienne didn't know what to do.

Outside, a dog howled, a low, mournful sound like the cry of a lost soul. Leofus groaned and muttered, "Not this again."

Alaric turned toward the window. "Again? Has this been going on long?"

"Four days," Leofus said, scowling. He held his spoon, dripping with chicken gravy, like a spear. "Howls like the undead every night around this time. Some stray dog, like as not, though it might be someone doesn't want to lay claim to the beast and get the neighbors in an uproar after him."

Alaric looked thoughtful. "Odd. I could swear..." He shook his head. "At any rate, we need to stop in Beneddo sooner rather than later."

Dianthe nodded. "We can be on our way day after tomorrow,

either by carpet or by *transport*. Or—I suppose Sienne could use *ferry*, take us one by one."

"We'll need to travel overland once we reach Ansorja, so I don't want to leave the carpets behind," Alaric said. The howl cut across his words, fainter this time as if the dog had run away. "But we have plenty of options for that. At any rate, tomorrow Sienne hunts for spells, the day after that, we go to Beneddo, and then, once we know where things stand with Perrin's family, we'll leave for Ansorja."

His final words fell like shards of ice into the sudden silence, broken only by the sound of Kalanath steadily eating his way through the last of the roast. Sienne laid down her fork and knife and pushed her plate away. "And then we confront the wizard," she said. "Are we ready for that?"

"We still don't understand how the unbinding should work," Dianthe said, "and we aren't sure about whether it makes more sense to try to do that, or just kill the wizard and hope that breaks the binding."

"I'm inclined to the latter," Alaric said. He wiped his mouth with his napkin and dropped it on his empty plate. "Subduing the wizard long enough to perform the unbinding could be dangerous."

"But what if the binding persists after his death?" Sienne asked. "That would leave the Sassaven—the adults, anyway—trapped in something they can never break."

"We'll have time in Beneddo to finish working out the details," Alaric said. "I don't want us rushing off without a plan. There's no hurry."

"I am glad of this," Kalanath said. "I do not wish to face this wizard with no plan. It is not what I see."

Alaric frowned. "Did you have a vision?"

"Last night," Kalanath said, nodding. "But I do not say because I do not understand it. I think about it while we fly."

Sienne wasn't used to her friend being so open about his ability as *devesh*, the holy child of God, to have prophetic dreams. His time in Omeira, and his growing relationship with the father he never knew, had changed him.

6

"I see us flying," Kalanath went on, "flying like birds, I mean. And we fly over forests and mountains to a tower. It is too tall—no tower is so tall without falling."

"That sounds like the wizard's tower," Alaric said. "It really is impossibly tall."

Kalanath nodded agreement. "We fly, and fly, but the tower's top is always out of reach. So we fly to the ground and search for an entrance, but there is none. And in my dream I know it is because we must have a plan."

"The wizard's tower is solid stone. No stairs," Alaric said. "There's what we call the walkstone in the base. It's an artifact that transports you to the top. I think I remember how to activate it."

"And we have to worry about the Sassaven attacking us," Dianthe said. "Hard to figure out a strange artifact while a mob is nipping at our heels."

Alaric yawned and stretched. "I'm too tired to think about this now. Let's sleep on it, and discuss it in the morning."

Sienne gathered up her plate and Alaric's and scraped the bones into the scrap bucket. "Thank you again, Leofus," she said as she handed him the plates.

"Taking me for granted," Leofus muttered, but he was smiling.

Alaric trailed Sienne up the stairs to the third floor. The third floor had once been servants' quarters, back before Master Tersus had bought the place, and the bedrooms were plain and plainly furnished. Sienne pushed open the door of the room she shared with Alaric and winced at the heat radiating from it. "I wish I'd left the window open a crack before we went to Omeira," she said.

She crossed to the window and got it open with some shoving. Cool evening air breezed past her, bringing with it the smell of the distant harbor, brine and hot tar and a hint of cinnamon. She inhaled, closing her eyes. It reminded her of their sea voyage and how beautiful the waves were.

The bed creaked, and she turned to see Alaric sitting on it, removing his boots. She'd cast *fit* on the bed weeks ago, enlarging it and its bedding enough that Alaric's feet didn't dangle off the end. He had his attention on his boots and his brow was slightly furrowed. "Something wrong?" she asked.

"Hmm?" Alaric looked up, one boot in his hand. "Just thinking about getting into the wizard's tower."

"I thought you said you were too tired to think about that."

"I am. But my brain didn't get the message." He set his boot down and tugged off the second one. "This isn't going to be easy. Avoiding the Sassaven, subduing the wizard, performing the right ritual...there are still too many unknowns."

Sienne sat beside him, sending up her own creak. "We'll figure it out. There are still things we have to do before we can make any concrete plans. If I get new spells tomorrow, that could change things."

Alaric put his arm around her. "How likely is it that this Carys Bettega will want to deal with you?"

"Ghrita thought she'd at least be willing to meet with me. She said Mistress Bettega collects scrapper stories, like as a historian or something. But she's not with the university, so I don't know exactly what that means. If she's not willing to sell or trade, she might know others who would be. I feel confident I'll get something out of meeting her."

"We could come with you."

"I thought about that, but the rest of you will do better to prepare for the journey to Beneddo. Besides, I don't want to overwhelm her." Sienne rested her head on Alaric's shoulder and felt his arm tighten around her. "This is nice."

"I had in mind something a little more intense than 'nice.'" Alaric's hands went to the hem of her shirt. "Unless you're too tired."

"I hope I'm never too tired for that," Sienne said.

Outside, the dog howled again, mournful and loud. Sienne, leaning in to kiss Alaric, found his lips unresponsive. His hands rested unmoving on her hips. "What's wrong?"

"I don't know." He blinked and looked at her. "Nothing. That howl...it sounds familiar."

"All dogs' howls sound the same to me." She kissed him again, and this time he returned her kiss, slow and sweet. She loved his kiss.

The howl went up again, and Alaric stiffened. "I swear I've heard that before," he said. He stood and went to the window. "I don't see anything. I—"

The unseen dog howled again, closer this time. Alaric swore and turned away. "Sorry. That howl is going to drive me mad." He crossed to the door without stopping to put on his boots.

"Wait for me," Sienne exclaimed as he strode out of the room. She hurried after him, the floorboards warm against her bare feet.

Outside, the noise of the neighbor's party drifted toward her on the wind, which had picked up since they returned home. Snatches of laughter, and the music of a fiddle and flute, filled the air with a carnival sound. The howling had stopped. Alaric rounded the corner of the house into the small garden, no more than fifteen feet on a side. Yew hedges taller than Sienne could see over bordered the garden on three sides, with the fourth side being the kitchen wall. Kalanath practiced his fighting routines there in the morning, and Sienne had often watched and admired his flowing, graceful movements. At the moment, it was dark and still.

Alaric said, "I need light."

Sienne made half a dozen magic lights with a thought and sent them spinning into the air to illuminate the garden. Their white light cast strange shadows over the hedges, throwing each tuft of needles into stark relief. The branches needed to be trimmed back; their bushy limbs looked like they were reaching for Sienne with prickly fingers. Sienne looked closely at their bases. Nothing moved. She and Alaric were the only creatures in the garden.

"Maybe it ran away when it heard us coming," she said.

Alaric nodded. "Maybe." He had a distant look in his eye, as if he were thinking hard. Then he shook his head. "It was probably nothing."

Another howl swallowed the word "nothing," longer and louder than before. "Around front," he said, and ran from the garden. Sienne followed him, carefully avoiding the small rocks of the gravel path.

Alaric stood at the edge of the street, looking east toward where the houses rose along the steep incline. Lights burned behind windows and in front of each house—it was each householder's duty to maintain a lantern to light the street—some white with magic, some warm and yellow with real fire. The sound of the party was louder now, and Sienne could barely make out the booming voice of Master Innes, calling for more wine. If not for that, the street would have been its usual quiet, peaceful self.

Sienne looked westward, toward the bottom of the street where it curved away to the north and toward the harbor. The small round paving stones were slick when it rained in winter, but at the moment they were dry and not at all treacherous. Cypress trees grew where the street curved, planted years ago by some overzealous property owner who wanted the neighborhood to look more prosperous than it was. Sienne's eye lingered on the base of the left-hand tree. Was it her imagination, or were the shadows there deeper than they should be?

She opened her mouth to ask Alaric what he thought, and the shadow detached itself from the tree and flung itself toward her.

Sienne gasped and said, "Alaric!" Instinctively she flung up her hands and chanted the spell *force* even though the shadow was moving fast enough it would reach her before she finished.

Alaric grabbed her and slung her roughly out of the way, interrupting her spell. She took a few stumbling steps to regain her balance and saw the shadow was a dog, a lithe black creature built like a greyhound. The dog's mouth was flecked with foam and it growled deep in its throat as it ran. It ignored her and went for Alaric, who crouched, hands at the ready to wrestle the animal to the ground. Sienne took a few more steps to the side and once more began casting *force*.

The dog launched itself at Alaric's throat, knocking him over. Alaric got his hands around its throat, holding its head with those sharp teeth away from him. The dog went still. *Alaric,* it said in a voice that echoed in Sienne's head.

2

Alaric released the dog and pushed himself into a sitting position. *"Leaf,"* he said in Sorjic. *"What are you doing here?"*

Sienne spoke Sorjic well, but the dialect Alaric used was unfamiliar, with emphasis on the wrong syllables and a funny drawn-out sound to the A's and O's. She had to pay close attention to understand him.

Alaric, the dog repeated in the same language. Its accent matched Alaric's. *You were gone long. Took ship, and I could not follow. I waited here in hope you would return.*

"That doesn't explain why you left the valley. How long did it take you to get here?"

I do not know time. A few seasons. It was winter when I left. Leaf butted its long head under Alaric's hand, and he scratched it idly. He looked more stunned than Sienne had ever seen him.

"Alaric," she said, "you know this dog?" Questions about why the dog could talk would have to wait.

"Pekkanen," Alaric said. "She's Pekkanen, not an ordinary dog."

"Loyal," Sienne translated. "I can see she's not ordinary. Dogs don't generally speak. Did she come all the way from Ansorja?"

"It seems so. *Leaf, what happened to bring you here?"*

Your sister Genneva. The wizard took her for his host.

Alaric's hand stilled, and his whole body went rigid. "*Impossible.*"

Not impossible. He thinks she is a liability. Wayward daughter of a rebellious breed.

"Because I left," Alaric breathed. "I ran away, and he thought that meant any of my mother's children might be ...tainted. *What happened to Karlen?*"

He is well. He is one of the Niskanen.

Alaric's eyes narrowed. "*I wish I could say that surprised me. But he wasn't damned for my sins?*"

No. And your mother has not been punished. The wizard does not know who your father is.

Alaric's shoulders relaxed. "*But Genneva...how long ago?*"

Before I left.

"*That could have been as much as eight months ago.*" Alaric looked up at Sienne. "This changes everything. Wake the others. We need to talk."

———

FIVE MINUTES LATER THEY SAT AROUND THE KITCHEN TABLE AND watched Alaric pace. He looked like a caged animal, something that might break free at any moment. Sienne clasped her hands tightly together in her lap. He hadn't said a thing since asking her to rouse everyone, and the wild look in his eyes frightened her. Leaf lay on a blanket in the corner, her oversized head on her paws. It only looked oversized, Sienne realized, because she was so gaunt, her fur matted and her paws filthy. She certainly looked as if she'd run a thousand miles to find Alaric.

"I can't remember how much I've explained about the wizard who created the Sassaven," Alaric said. "You know he's over five hundred years old. I think I told you how he makes himself immortal."

"He takes the heart of a unicorn and swaps it with his," Dianthe said. "It keeps him young, right? And makes him invulnerable. We have to destroy his heart to kill him."

"Right." Alaric stopped pacing and drummed his fingers on the windowsill. "His own heart is so corroded and evil it corrupts the host over time. They only survive for a year, maybe fifteen months if they're strong. Then the wizard does it again. And this time, he chose my sister Genneva."

No one spoke. Sienne hesitated to ask the obvious question, saw Dianthe looking at her as if to urge her to speak, and realized she would have to be the one to bring it up. "Were we...planning to kill the host, then?" she said. "Isn't that how we destroy the wizard?"

Alaric stopped fidgeting and turned to face her. "We aren't killing my sister."

"But is there an alternative?"

"We'll force the wizard to reverse the exchange of hearts. Then we'll kill him." Alaric's eyes blazed pale blue in his sunburned face.

Sienne glanced at Dianthe again. Dianthe jerked her head minutely in Alaric's direction. Sienne inwardly groaned. So she was the sacrificial goat because she was sleeping with him. Wonderful. "That sounds...difficult," she said. "I mean, if it was going to be hard to get him to hold still while we work the unbinding, it will be almost impossible to compel him—"

"It's what we're going to do. Only almost impossible is good enough for me."

"What do you mean, 'what we're going to do'? Shouldn't we discuss this?" Sienne felt like a fly pinpointed by a glass lens, Alaric's intensity a light focused on her that scorched her skin.

"You think my sister's life is a matter for discussion?" Now he sounded dangerously calm, as if a storm were brewing inside him.

"We don't want Genneva to die," Sienne said. "But we can't just fly off to the rescue without a real plan. It would be suicide."

Alaric slammed his fist against the wall and swore. "I've just told you the plan. Since when are you so cowardly?"

Sienne shoved her chair back, standing in one swift, angry movement. "That's not a plan. That's *idiotic*. We don't know anything about the wizard's capabilities, we don't know how much he knows—for all we know, this is a ploy to draw you back to the valley and kill you. You're letting your personal feelings blind you to reality."

"Am I?" Alaric roared. His face was white with fury. "I guess this is what it always was—my problem, not yours. Is this how all of you feel? Only interested in my quest so long as it didn't involve any real danger?"

"We've put our lives on the line for you more times than I can count!" Sienne shouted.

"This is getting us nowhere," Perrin said. He sounded calm, but his hand where it rested on the table was closed into a white-knuckled fist. "Can we not discuss—"

"There's no *time* for discussion," Alaric said. "I have no idea how long it took Leaf to get here. Gen may only have weeks left. We have to act now, or everything we've done is wasted."

"I thought we were doing this for all the Sassaven, not one woman," Sienne said.

Instantly, she knew it was a mistake. Alaric turned a furious glare on her, took a step forward, and she couldn't help herself— she cringed, old memories of his hand around her throat coming back to fill her with fear. She made herself stand straight and face him.

Alaric didn't seem to notice her reaction. "She's the one I care about," he said in a low, terrible voice. "I'll save her or die trying."

"Dying is what you'll do if you do what you propose," Sienne said.

He looked at each of them in turn. "So that's how it's going to be, is it?" he said. He almost sounded calm. "Fine. Cower here if that's how you feel. But I'm leaving for Ansorja in the morning." He turned on his heel and stomped out of the kitchen. Moments later, the back door slammed.

Sienne sank back into her chair and covered her face with her hands. "Thanks so much for helping," she said bitterly.

"Would it have made a difference?" Dianthe said. "You're the only one he listens to when he's got the bit between his teeth. And he knew how we all felt."

"He is afraid," Kalanath said, "and that makes him angry, to be powerless. I remember when he is controlled by the carver wizard. He does not like being not in control of himself."

"We cannot let him go," Perrin said. "He will die for nothing. But I have no idea how to prevent him leaving, unless we hide the carpets. And that would be a mistake."

"It would tell him we think he's a child," Dianthe agreed. "He needs to cool off. Maybe by morning he'll be ready to see sense."

He always was impetuous, Leaf said, startling them all. *Ready to take risks. It is why he leaves the valley.*

"Is that...the dog?" Perrin said. "She speaks Sorjic?"

"Alaric said she was Pekkanen," Sienne said. "He didn't say what that means." In Sorjic, she added, *"Alaric isn't usually like that. I guess he's changed over the years."* Or maybe he hadn't changed much, given his display of anger and impatience.

You speak oddly, Leaf said. *I can barely understand you.*

"The valley has been isolated for more than five hundred years. Languages change in that length of time."

Dianthe rose and went to kneel beside Leaf, gently examining her paws. "She needs food and water," she said. "Not much, or she'll vomit. She looks near starved."

Perrin nodded and got up. He took the remnants of the roast chicken from the cupboard and cut the meat away from the bones. "Such devotion, to make that journey," he said.

"And following an eleven-year-old trail, too," Sienne said. To Leaf, she added, *"How did you know where to find Alaric? Is that part of what makes you Pekkanen?"*

I have known him since he was an infant, Leaf said. She nibbled on a hunk of chicken. *He is himself. That persists.* Her mental voice wasn't impeded by her mouth being full.

"I don't understand what you mean."

An intangible breeze brushed her, like the memory of wind. It carried with her familiar scents of pine and rich humus and a deep, heady musk. The scents took shape in her mind, impossibly visible as the outline of a large man. *It is him. I would know him anywhere. He left his mark all along his trail, and it is not a thing that disappears like scent.*

"*Can all Pekkanen do this? What are you?*"

Leaf sighed. *We are the wizard's greatest failure as the Sassaven are his triumph. We could not contain the magic to be what he wanted. Now he despises us. We hide from him because he sometimes kills us when he is in the mood.*

"*I remember now.* The Pekkanen are what the wizard created first," she told the others. "You know, how he tried to combine dogs and humans, but the dogs weren't big enough, so he used horses instead? I didn't realize the dogs were still around." She didn't think they were a failure at all, if they were intelligent and capable of tracking someone years after they'd passed. One more reason the wizard needed to be defeated.

That thought sent a pang through her heart. Alaric wouldn't actually go through with his crazy not-a-plan, would he? He wasn't a fool. But he was devoted to his sister, and maybe that was enough to override his good sense. *And enough for him to threaten you?* her inner voice said. He'd said he never wanted her to look at him in fear. Maybe that only mattered when he wasn't angry enough.

"So what do we do?" Dianthe said. "We can't let him go alone." She filled a shallow bowl with water and set it beside Leaf.

"But we also cannot accompany him on this mad venture," Perrin said.

"If we had another plan, something more rational, maybe he'd listen." Sienne cupped her chin in her hands and sighed. "The problem is that Alaric is usually the one who comes up with our plans."

"We are not stupid," Kalanath said. "We can use our heads and think."

Dianthe nodded. "All right. I think we can all agree that we should save Genneva if we can. So what do we need to accomplish that?"

"A way into the valley, and then into the wizard's tower, without being spotted," Sienne said, ticking the point off on one finger. "Something to immobilize the wizard while we do the unbinding. And a way to force him to reverse the transfer of hearts."

"It is the last I do not think we can do," Kalanath said. "He will say, there is no reason, it will kill me, and I do not have an answer for that."

"We can't use reason, that's true," said Dianthe, "so what else is there? Magic?"

"I don't know any magic for," Sienne began, and let her voice trail off. "But there is magic for that. *Dominate*."

"The charm spell?" Perrin said. "You said it was forbidden."

"It is. But there are people who know it. It's not a lost spell like *ash*, just one you can be seriously punished for just for having it in your spellbook."

"Sienne," Dianthe said, "you can't be serious. How would you even go about finding it? No one's going to admit to having it."

"I don't know. I'm just saying it's the only way I can think of to force someone against his will." The words tasted like bile. She'd seen *dominate* used before, on Alaric, and it had been such a terrible violation he'd had trouble overcoming the memory. And here she proposed using it herself. Against someone evil, true, but somehow she didn't think that made doing what was essentially evil all right.

"Is it something you *should* do?" Perrin asked, as if he could read her mind. "Charm spells are forbidden for a reason."

"I don't know," Sienne said. "Maybe it's irrelevant. Like Dianthe said, the odds of me finding it are slim. I don't know that we should base a plan on it. But I really don't see any other way of freeing Genneva."

Silence fell, interrupted only by the sound of Leaf slurping up water. "What about getting into the valley?" Dianthe said. "What if the wizard sees us coming?"

"He cannot scry us out, as that is a priest's magic," Perrin said. "As is the magic that sets off an alarm when something crosses its boundaries. It is unlikely he can see beyond the limits of his natural eye, unless he has a spyglass, and that has its own limitations."

"He'll be able to see magic like I can," Sienne said. "But not at a distance."

"So he'll depend on the Sassaven to relay what they see," Dianthe said. "Which means we'll need to stay out of sight of them. Damn, but I wish I knew more about the binding. Like, do they have to tell the wizard everything, or only respond to his direct questioning?"

"Alaric would—" Kalanath's words cut off mid-sentence. "It is hard planning without him."

"Let's just act as if Alaric is willing to listen," Dianthe said. She didn't sound very certain. "Alaric can tell us what the Sassaven are bound to do, and we can work out how to get around them. Then there's the...what did he call it?"

"The walkstone," Sienne said. "If Alaric can't, I can probably work out how to operate it. I'll just need time."

"So we'll need to evade the Sassaven long enough for someone to make the walkstone work," Dianthe said. "And it seems like all we need to subdue the wizard is one good *force* bolt to the face."

"But we don't know how to perform the unbinding," Sienne said. "Jenani told me that meant reversing the original binding, and we know what that is, but I'm not sure how much we can trust what it said, given that it tried to kill us."

"It did not need to lie," Kalanath said. "Lying did not make it more powerful against us. I think it speaks truth."

"And that solution makes sense," Dianthe said. "What I'm concerned about is that we'll need a chain to break as part of the ritual, and we don't know if that has to be a particular chain the way the coming of age ritual needed a particular goblet and knife."

"That's something we could work out on the way," Sienne said.

"We will not fly again, will we?" Perrin said, sounding almost plaintive.

"If Alaric would get his head out of his ass for half a breath, he'd see waiting a day for me to try to find *transport* is the smart thing to do," Sienne said, feeling anger rush through her again at Alaric's bull-headedness. "Have Perrin scry out a location, I'll *jaunt* there and get enough of a sense of the place for *transport*...it would take us half an hour at most. Even the carpets aren't that fast."

No one spoke. Sienne didn't need their words to know what they were all thinking: more than anything else, this plan depended on

Alaric being willing to see sense. Finally, Dianthe said, "I think that's the best we can do for tonight. We shouldn't wait up for him, though. He'll just feel attacked and won't listen."

"*Do you need anything else, Leaf?*" Sienne asked.

The Pekkanen shook her head. *Sleep will be good, now I have found Alaric,* she said. *I have not slept well in many seasons.*

"*You should come upstairs. There's an empty bed—it will be more comfortable than the floor.*"

Leaf stood, her legs shaking. Perrin lifted her into his arms. "Does she mind being carried?" he asked Sienne. "Perhaps I should have ascertained this before picking her up."

Having established that Leaf didn't mind being carried, Sienne led the way up the stairs and supervised Leaf's installment on Alaric's old bed. The Pekkanen was asleep almost before Sienne pulled the door to without latching it.

She trudged to her own room. Dianthe stopped her when her hand was on the knob. "It will be all right," she said, hugging Sienne. "He's not stupid. He'll be back."

Sienne nodded. Now that her anger had passed, she felt cold inside, and as empty as if her shouting had hollowed her out. She sat on the edge of the bed and stared at her hands. They'd never spoken so harshly to each other before. He'd never physically threatened her before—all right, he hadn't threatened her, but his verbal aggression had felt like a blow to the face. A few tears dripped onto her hands, and she wiped them away. She hated fighting with him, even when she was in the right. Maybe she hated it more when she was in the right, because she never knew what to say.

She undressed and put her clothes away, folding them neatly into the clothespress. Her eye fell on her dancing dress, hanging on a peg on the wall. The sight made more tears fall. Suppose he ran off and was killed? It was stupid to think of how that meant no more dancing, it was so frivolous, but the only reason he danced was because he loved her, and that reminder was too much for her bruised heart to bear. She sat on the bed in her nightdress and wept silently until she ran out of tears, then dried her face and waited for him to return.

She nodded off twice and nearly fell off the bed, but she couldn't bear to sleep before he returned. If he returned. To stay awake, she read some of the book she'd borrowed from a shelf downstairs. It was boring, but it gave her mind something to do that wasn't dwelling on Alaric and the awful things he'd said.

She'd almost given in to despair and gone to sleep anyway when she heard his heavy footsteps on the stairs. Fear and misery shot through her like a *force* bolt to the chest, electrifying her blood and waking her fully. Would he even come to her? The last time they'd fought, he'd gone to his old room rather than face her. This time, she didn't think she could bear to confront him. Of course, Leaf was in his old room, so maybe he wouldn't want to disturb the Pekkanen. Or maybe he wouldn't care; maybe he meant to sleep on the small, cramped bed alone.

The door opened. "You're awake," Alaric said. He shut the door behind him and stood looking at her, his face impassive.

"I couldn't sleep," she lied. "I didn't want to go to bed after...you know. Fighting."

Alaric sighed and ran a hand through his hair, scratching his scalp. "There's nothing more to say. I'm not going to change my mind."

She felt tears come to her eyes again and blinked them away. She'd sworn never to manipulate him with tears. "We talked about it after you left," she said. "Alaric, we want to help. We just don't want to do it in a way that will get us all killed."

"I've led this team for over a year," Alaric said. "I've kept everyone alive all that time. Why have you suddenly lost faith in me?"

His eyes looked hollow and bruised, and for the first time since she'd known him, she saw doubt there. "Why have you suddenly stopped caring what we think?" she shot back. "This team isn't you telling us what to do, it's all of us working together to achieve something. How dare you suggest we don't care about your quest after everything we've done to accomplish it?"

Alaric closed his eyes and bowed his head, the very image of a man praying for strength. "I trust you all," he said, "but you don't understand. All this time, Gen's been the one I thought of when I imagined my people being free. She helped me escape—helped me plan for this future. I *can't* let her down, Sienne. I won't be able to live with myself if she dies when I had a chance of stopping it."

"Then let us help you," Sienne exclaimed. "We want to do this the right way—the way that means nobody has to die needlessly. Give me time to find *transport,* at least, and maybe some other spells that will let me face the wizard on equal terms. As equal as we can manage, anyway." She drew in a deep breath. "But if you can't do that...I'm going to Ansorja with you in the morning."

His eyes flew open. "What happened to all that talk about certain death?"

Sienne rose and took a few steps toward him until she was close enough she had to tilt her head to meet his eyes. "I love you," she said, "and I couldn't bear it if you died alone. So I'm going with you."

He was silent for a moment, his blue eyes fierce on hers. Then he gathered her into his arms and held her close, as tenderly as if she might break. "I'm sorry," he whispered. "Forgive me. I never meant to hurt you."

She put her arms around him and rested her head against his chest. "You scared me," she said, and felt him tense.

"I know," he said. "I saw you flinch, and I was so angry I didn't care. Not until later, when I came to my senses... I should never have done that. I was so afraid you'd hate me for it."

"I don't hate you. And I was angry, too. I'm sorry."

He let out a low chuckle. "We were hard on each other, for two people in love." He kissed the top of her head. "I don't think I've let my emotions get the better of my common sense in years. I'd forgotten how it feels to be so out of control."

"I understand."

"Do you?"

"We were all more afraid for you than angry. So yes, I understand."

Alaric let out a deep sigh. "I am more blessed in my friends than I deserve." He released her and began taking off his clothes. "Let's go to bed. I want to hold you while you sleep and be grateful you still want me to."

Sienne's heart felt lighter than air. "I will always want you to hold me. Always."

They snuggled together in the big bed, with Alaric's breath tickling the back of Sienne's neck. "I love you," she whispered. "I hate it when we fight."

"You always say that, sweetlove," Alaric murmured.

"Because it's always true. I'm afraid someday we'll say things we can't come back from."

"That's never going to happen," Alaric said. "It's not in your nature to be so cruel, and I watch my tongue because I live in fear you're going to wake up one day and realize you'd be better off with someone else."

She rolled over to face him. "Are you serious?"

"Partly serious. Different races, different social classes...by all logic, you and I should not be together. Every day you're with me feels like a miracle."

His candor made a shiver run through her. She put her arms around his neck and drew him close. "I'm not going anywhere. Promise."

"I'll hold you to that," Alaric said, and brushed her lips with a kiss.

3

Dianthe, Kalanath, and Perrin were at the breakfast table when Sienne and Alaric descended the next morning. "I want to apologize," Alaric said before anyone could speak. "I let my emotions get the better of me, and I was stupid. I'm sorry for how I behaved."

"Thank Kitane you're still here," Dianthe said. "We were worried you might actually leave without us."

"We understand your feelings," Perrin added. "And we have discussed more possibilities, if you are willing to listen."

"I'd say 'of course I am,' but after last night nobody believes that's a given," Alaric said. He helped himself to sausage and a few slabs of ham, nodding to Leofus, who regarded him warily. Sienne wondered how this all sounded to the cook, who hadn't been present for the big blowup. She scooped porridge into a bowl, added a lump of sugar, and took her seat next to Alaric.

Perrin took a long drink from his coffee cup and sighed in pleasure. "We have some questions," he said. "We have deduced that the wizard's information on what happens in his valley comes from his Sassaven eyes. What we do not know is the nature of the binding. Are the Sassaven compelled to go to the wizard with information immediately as they gain it, or must they only share that information when directly asked?"

"Mostly the latter," Alaric said. "We try to stay out of the wizard's way because he tends to forget things that aren't either directly in front of him or a current part of his breeding program. Most Sassaven won't volunteer information—it's the only way they have to defy his control. But there are a few who are scared, or want to curry favor, and they will immediately tell the wizard anything they think he needs to know. And then there are the Niskanen. You'd call them enforcers if the binding didn't make it so there's nothing to enforce. They keep the peace between Sassaven and take the wizard's orders throughout the valley. They speak with his voice. I was afraid of them as a child because so many of them enjoy the power they wield over the rest of us. They're the ones who bring word when a Sassaven has been chosen for the breeding project, the bastards."

"Leaf said your brother Karlen was one of them," Sienne said.

Alaric grimaced. "I wish I could say that surprised me. Karlen loves telling people what to do, not because he's a bossy prig—though he's that, too—but because he believes rules make people safer. It made growing up with him unbearable, especially since for most of my life I was a lot smaller than him and he could force me to obey or eat dirt."

"I am trying to picture you small enough to be overwhelmed," Perrin said with a grin.

"Heh. I remember the day I finally overtopped him," Alaric said, grinning back. "I was fourteen and I'm afraid I goaded him into a fight I knew I could win. Before that I was short and chubby."

"*That,* I can't imagine," Sienne murmured.

"At any rate, we'll have to worry about the Niskanen, because most of them think like Karlen, and we can't tell which ones might be sympathetic to us just by looking." Alaric bit into a sausage and chewed as fiercely as if he could defeat Karlen that way.

"I can probably keep us hidden, if I know the terrain," Dianthe said, "and Perrin can scry out the valley and show us what places to avoid."

"That will be easy enough, provided Averran is on our side—and I believe he is," Perrin said.

"And if you can't remember, I might be able to work out the walk-stone," Sienne said. "If I know what an artifact does, figuring out how to operate it becomes a lot easier. But if I can't guarantee that, I can think of a few other ways we can enter the tower. At worst, I cast *float* and we climb up its outside."

"Let's hope we can use the walkstone," Alaric said. "So, that gets us through the valley and into the tower. It occurred to me that Sienne could knock the wizard out with *force* and subdue him that way."

"We thought of that, too," Dianthe said. "And we can perform the unbinding ritual, so long as we have the right chain."

"It was always the same chain when he bound a Sassaven," Alaric said. "I don't think there was anything special about it. But the important thing is that it will be in the tower, so when we need it, it will be on hand."

"That brings us to reversing what he did to Genneva," Sienne said.

Everyone fell silent. Alaric looked like he wanted to speak but didn't know what to say. Sienne cleared her throat. "There's only one way to compel someone to do what they don't want to do."

Alaric's head came up. "You mean *dominate*. Sienne, you can't do that."

"I know it's a long shot, but if I can find it—"

"I mean you *shouldn't* do that. Just because the wizard is evil doesn't mean we should stoop to evil in return. *Dominate* is…I don't want to talk about it." His face was paler than usual, and he held his fork halfway to his lips as if he'd forgotten it was there.

"If it will save Genneva, I'm willing," Sienne said.

Slowly Alaric set down his fork. "You," he said, then seemed to run out of words. Eventually, he said, "I'm not deserving of friends like you."

"We do not deserve each other," Kalanath said, "but it is not about deserve. It is the gift we give. And receive."

"Wisely put," Perrin said. He poured himself another cup of coffee. "I do not think we should depend on *dominate*. However, Sienne should meet with Carys Bettega today."

Sienne held her breath, waiting for Alaric to repeat his insistence on leaving immediately. But he said only, "That makes sense. Sienne, when will you go?"

"In an hour, when the day isn't quite so new." Sienne scraped the last of her porridge out of the bowl. "I hope she'll see me without advance warning. I didn't have time to ask for an appointment."

"You're sure you don't want us to come along?" Dianthe said.

Sienne nodded. "The rest of you can plan for the journey. Even if I get *transport*, that's less effective for wilderness locations because... it's hard to explain. My teachers said you need a unique location to *transport* to, and trees and valleys all look alike on the level *transport* operates on, so cities are easier. Anyway, that means I'll only be able to get us as far as Esthold, and we'll need to go overland from there. So we'll need Ansorjan coin to buy supplies."

"Let us worry about that," Alaric said. "You worry about being so charming this Bettega woman will open her spellbook and let you dive right in."

"Wouldn't that be nice?" Sienne said with a laugh.

———

THE AQUILA DISTRICT WAS A STUDY IN CONTRASTS, ITS OLD, SOMEWHAT decrepit houses at odds with the well-scrubbed streets and newly installed drains. Some construction indicated at least a few of the owners were interested in bringing their homes up to date, but for the most part the buildings, three or four stories tall and only one or two rooms across, had the comfortable, lived-in look that characterized an old, established neighborhood. Most of the houses had hanging plants in pottery bowls next to their doors, ivy or petunias or geraniums, giving the plain tan bricks splashes of color. It wasn't as pretty as Master Tersus's neighborhood, but it had its own kind of charm.

Sienne strolled down the street with her spellbook clutched firmly under one arm. She wasn't worried about theft, but she superstitiously feared she might set it down and walk away without thinking about it now that she didn't technically need it. Children raced past her, chasing a ball and shouting at each other. What would that be like, growing up with virtually no supervision? And yet they had parents, or someone, who looked out for them and made sure they were clothed and fed. Someone who provided the ball, for that matter. She knew better than to romanticize their childhood, but she couldn't help wondering how her life would have been different if she hadn't been born Sienne Verannus.

Carys Bettega's home was another one of the identical tan brick buildings in a row near the end of the street. The façades had been unified sometime in the last five years so the row presented a solid front, with no divisions between the individual houses. All the doors were painted the same color, a dull green that managed to clash with the bricks, but the small four-paned windows in the upper stories were blotches of random color from their curtains and gave the buildings more of an individualistic feeling.

Sienne trod the three steps up to number five's door and rapped on it. People passing stared at her as if she'd done something outrageous by putting herself even those three short steps above the paving stones. She smiled pleasantly at them, and they turned away.

A key turned in the lock, and the door eased open. A boy perhaps ten years younger than Sienne said, "Are you here to see Grandmama?"

"My name is Sienne Verannus. I was wondering if Mistress Bettega might give me a moment of her time?" She knew she sounded overly formal, but it wouldn't hurt to come across as a serious student of magic.

The boy's eyes went wide and his mouth fell open. "Verannus? The duke?"

"Yes. I don't mean to intrude, but I—"

"It's no intrusion." The boy opened the door wider. "I'm Milo Bettega. Please, come in...I'm sorry, I forgot your name already. I mean, I remember the Verannus part, of course I remember that, the duke's daughter—"

"I'm Sienne. Thanks."

The narrow corridor beyond the door wasn't wide enough for both of them to walk side by side. Sienne trailed along behind Milo and admired the portraits on the walls. Most of them showed a strong family resemblance to Milo, though they were in a bland enough style that even though the clothing styles changed, she couldn't be sure if the woman she kept seeing was Milo's mother, or grand-mother, or aunt, or even older cousin.

One picture depicted four people, three men and a woman, dressed in the fashion of forty years ago, formal and stiff-looking. The woman had very black hair in a braid pinned around her head, much the way Dianthe habitually wore hers. The men all had short, utili-tarian haircuts that to Sienne screamed "scrapper." She lingered a few steps to look at it, but hurried her pace when Milo turned to see where she was.

Two doors opened off the hallway, one to either side, and stairs as narrow as the hall led up at the far end. They creaked as Milo trotted up them, forcing Sienne to hurry along behind. Though the stairs went all the way up to the top of the house, Milo left them at the second floor landing, which let off on a hall just as narrow as the one below. There were two doors on the left and one on the right, all of them painted a flat white that matched the walls, which were devoid of pictures and made the hall feel wider than it was.

Milo opened the right-hand door, saying, "Grandmama, this lady is here to see you."

Sienne followed Milo through the door. The room beyond was flooded with light from two of the small, four-paned windows whose diaphanous midnight blue curtains were drawn back and held in place with silver cords. The room was long and thin, and Sienne suspected it ran the entire depth of the house, front to back. Book-cases flanked the windows at one end of the room, where an armchair matching the curtains and a small table sat.

A fireplace, empty at this season, lay opposite the door, its wooden mantel stained a dark cherry color and rubbed until it gleamed. At the far end of the room from the bookcases stood a larger table surrounded by four wooden chairs with embroidered cushions. Sienne immediately felt she would like the owner of this room. Whoever she was, she knew what she liked and surrounded herself with it.

An elderly woman sat in a chair drawn up before the empty hearth. Her hair was mostly gray, with a few black streaks through it, and the wrinkles of her face said she'd had a long, interesting life that had left its marks on her. She'd been reading when they entered, and now she took a peacock feather that lay on the arm of her chair and marked her place before setting the book down where the feather had rested. "A visitor, eh?" she said, her voice as hoarse as if she'd just finished a coughing fit. "Milo, you know better than to bring uninvited strangers up."

"But she's the duke of Beneddo's daughter, Grandmama," Milo said. "You'll want to see her."

Carys Bettega looked Sienne up and down. "But why would *she* want to see *me*, I wonder," she said to the air.

"Ghrita Chakhorkurda mentioned you," Sienne said. She hoped she hadn't mangled Ghrita's surname too much. "She said you were a scrapper wizard once. I'm a scrapper looking for spells, and I hoped we might be able to come to an agreement."

The old woman's eyes narrowed. "Milo, fetch coffee," she said. She indicated an armchair facing hers as Milo left the room. Sienne sat and arranged her spellbook in her lap. Carys eyed it and smiled.

"A scrapper's spellbook," she said, sounding contemplative. "It's been a long time since I routinely carried my spellbook with me. It brings back memories."

"How long were you a scrapper?" Sienne asked.

"Twelve years. I know, that's a long time," Carys said as Sienne tried to control her astonishment. "I had a good team. We gained and lost members over that time, but it always felt like family. It fell apart maybe three years after I was invalided out." She gestured to her legs, which looked normal to Sienne aside from being completely motionless, without even the minutest shifting or tensing of muscles. "But three of us survived to have lives beyond scrapping. I call that marvelous."

"It is marvelous," Sienne said. "I've never heard of a scrapper team lasting so long."

"You have to have the right mix of personalities. How long have you been a scrapper?"

"Fourteen months. It's how long my team has been together, too."

"So you're no longer fumbling about trying to work together. I take it your team is working well?"

"We've come through so much together. I hope we have many more years in us."

"I hope that for you, too. And that you don't have to replace anyone, though that's unlikely."

Sienne shivered. Carys's casual words felt superstitiously like a warning. "I can't imagine replacing any of my friends."

"Neither could I." Carys was looking at something past Sienne's right ear, probably the past from the way her brow furrowed. Then she blinked, and turned her attention on Sienne. "So. You're looking for new spells."

"I am. We're facing a tremendous challenge, and I'd like to be as prepared as possible."

The door opened, and Milo backed in bearing a huge silver tray with a matching coffee pot and an assortment of cups and bowls. With the grace of a man twenty years older, he poured coffee and handed cups to Carys and Sienne. Sienne poured in plenty of cream and a chunk of sugar and stirred. Carys took hers as black as Perrin did.

"Anything in particular?" she added when Milo left again.

"More powerful targeted spells than I currently have. Defensive spells to back up Perrin—he's a priest of Averran. *Transport*, if you have it." Asking about *dominate* was probably too much for this casual acquaintance.

"A priest of Averran? They aren't usually scrappers."

"He fell into the work when there wasn't anything else he could do to support himself. Now I think he likes it."

Carys nodded. She held out one hand. "May I see your book?"

Sienne removed the harness from around her shoulders and handed it over. Carys turned the pages, giving each one her full attention. "A lot of confusions early on," she remarked. "Were you at Stravanus?"

"I was."

"I'm surprised you were able to survive as a scrapper. Most confusions aren't much good against monsters."

"I had a few other spells. And a lot of help from my companions. And luck."

"Indeed." She turned a few more pages. "And you said you've been a scrapper fourteen months? How many spells did you have before that?"

"About a dozen."

Carys riffled the unbreakable pages, counting, and whistled in appreciation. "You've been busy. And successful, to afford this quantity of spells."

"Some of them we found." She didn't mention the wizard necromancer she'd inadvertently killed, or the spells she'd taken from his book.

"Even so." Carys went back to reading. "*Castle, fury, shout...*I'm not sure what I can do for you that you don't already have."

Sienne swallowed her disappointment. "Oh."

The old woman glanced up at her with a keen eye. "Tell me," she said, "how to use *castle* as an offensive spell."

Sienne blinked. "Ah...well, I've done it to move an enemy away from a defenseless ally, but I've always thought it would work in reverse—to bring someone, maybe a wizard or an archer, from where they're attacking at a distance to close enough my companions could hammer them."

"What's the most creative magical attack you've ever made?"

"I don't know if it's the *most* creative, but I once disarmed an enemy wizard by casting *grease* on his spellbook. And later, when the grease had evaporated, I used invisible fingers to open the latch of his book and snatch all the spells out. They went all over the room." She decided not to mention she'd stolen three of his spells before that, just in case Carys wasn't as friendly as she looked.

Carys laughed. "I've done that, too," she said, "unlatched a spellbook. I don't know why it doesn't occur to more people, though I suppose it's fairly rare to be fighting other humans rather than monsters." She sobered. "What about casting a spell that might catch your companions in its effect? How do you deal with that?"

"Teach them to duck, mostly. But that's when I switch to a targeted spell like *force*. It's easier with *shout*, because that spell spreads out in a plane, but even with *fury*, if they're paying attention, they don't get hit."

"Though having to pay attention means dividing their attention."

"Right. Which is why I use *force* or *burn* instead."

"Smart." Carys nodded. "Are you sleeping with one of your companions?"

Sienne, wary, said, "What makes you ask that?"

"It's inevitable, when you're as close as you are to your companions, that more profound emotions emerge. I'm wondering if you've acted on them."

Sienne wanted to tell the old woman it was none of her business, but Carys's expression didn't seem condemnatory. "I...yes. Alaric is my lover."

"And that's not a problem?"

"No. It was more of a problem when we were still dancing around the issue of being attracted to each other and being afraid to act on it. Alaric is our leader and I think he worried about...oh, favoritism, or the chance he might do stupid things to protect me. But he does stupid things to protect all of us. And we've never let it interfere with work. We don't sleep together when we're in the wilderness, for example."

"That's an interesting solution. Linus and I...well, I was our team's leader for nine of those twelve years, and I was with Linus for eight. Our relationship was tempestuous, and it drove at least one companion away, but I couldn't give him up. It sounds as though you're more well-adjusted than I was." Carys smiled, her mind once again wandering down memory lane.

"So...you stopped because you were injured?" Sienne asked, feeling Carys had grilled her long enough and was due some questioning of her own.

"I did. Broke my back fighting a pod of chimeras. Serran—he was a priest of Kitane—he had some powerful healing blessings, but nothing short of a miracle can repair damaged nerves, and Kitane apparently thought my scrapping career should be over." Carys didn't sound bitter, just matter-of-fact. "I came home, settled down, had children—thank Kitane my injury didn't interfere with that—and went into business teaching young wizards the four spell languages, with some basic transform work on the side. Mostly the decorative arts, altering colors for women redecorating their homes, that sort of thing."

"I haven't thought about what I'll do after our scrapping days are over."

"Based on this, you have a solid grounding in all four spell languages. You could teach. Or... actually, you have more transforms than I ever did, so that's another option."

"I love transforms. I wouldn't mind helping people with bad vision or hearing—I've done that before."

"Yes, that's better and cheaper than a divine healing, if less permanent. Or you might find there's something you want to do that has nothing to do with wizardry."

That seemed unlikely to Sienne, but she'd learned never to assume she knew the future. "It will depend on what Alaric wants to do, too."

"So your relationship is permanent."

"It is."

"I hope it lasts, then. Linus and I had wonderful sex, but we didn't have anything but scrapping in common. I'm not happy he died—in fact, I mourned him desperately for a long time—but in the long run, it's better I married Mercario. So I wish you and your young man the best."

"Thank you." Sienne drained her coffee cup and set it back on the tray.

"So." Carys put down her own cup and folded her hands in her lap. "What did you intend when you came here?"

"I was hoping you had spells I could purchase, or trade if you prefer. But Ghrita didn't tell me anything but that you used to be a scrapper, so I'm not sure what I have that *you* want."

"You're right. Much of what you have is useless to me, so trading is not an option." Carys propped her chin on one hand. "And, to be honest, I don't really need money. But...well. Can you bear it if I tell you an old scrapper's story?"

"I'd hoped you would, but I didn't like to ask."

Carys smiled. "Back in the day—this would have been, oh, forty or forty-five years ago—dueling wasn't illegal. No, that's not true, it was illegal, but the queen didn't crack down on it. Those old Fiorus monarchs were lazy and self-serving, and bestirring themselves to stop wizards dueling was too much like work. I understand King Derekian is nothing like them."

"He's not."

"This—really?" Carys's eyes gleamed. "You speak as though you know him."

"We've met. He doesn't like me and my team much. I think he sees us as a recurring impediment."

"That's a story I'd like to hear later, if you don't mind. But I was talking about dueling. Wizards fought over the slightest provocation, on the off chance of incapacitating their opponent long enough to steal a spell or three. I admit, I was hotheaded, and I entered my share of duels. Won, mostly, and my team was always there to protect me if an enemy wizard came a little too close to doing serious damage."

"That sounds dangerous."

"That's why I liked it. But there was one time...I was twenty-two, I'd been a scrapper for three years, and I thought I was at the top of my game. We were staying at an inn and there was a man there, a wizard, maybe ten years older than I and...oh, the most disreputable sort you can imagine."

"And you dueled?"

"He didn't want to. I thought that meant he was weak. At the very least, afraid of me. But I finally goaded him into going out back, where we wouldn't be disturbed. And it took him less than ten seconds to knock out my entire team and paralyze me. I think I might have singed him with *scorch*, but that was all. I thought we were all dead. He—I remember this so clearly—he sat on a log on the frost-rimed grass and stared at me for twenty minutes until *shout* wore off, playing with this long knife that gleamed like silver in the moonlight."

Her calm voice combined with the vivid details of the story made Sienne shiver. She wanted to ask a dozen questions, but kept silent, fearing to interrupt.

Carys smiled. "When I finally started to twitch, he sat me up and took out his spellbook. 'You're brash, and stupid,' he said, 'and I used to be like you. I ought to take your book and make you start over. But I think you'll remember this better if I use a carrot instead of a stick.' And he told me he'd give me any three spells from his own book, no conditions attached. It was the last time I ever dueled."

"Amazing," Sienne breathed. "He didn't ask anything from you?"

"No. Not even a promise to stop dueling." Carys used her hands to shift her body slightly. "There have been three—no, four scrappers before you who've come looking for a trade or a sale. Two of them I sent away with nothing. The other two, I let them take what they wanted. I'll offer you what I gave them: anything you think will help you, you can have, no restrictions. I want to see you and your companions succeed, and it sounds as though you're already a solid team. This might give you a bit of an edge."

Sienne let out the breath she was holding. "That's...incredibly generous. But you already said you didn't think you had anything I'd want."

"I said I don't know what I can do for you," Carys said with a smile. "But you're clever. I think it's a question of what you'd make of what I have." She pulled on a bell rope hanging near the fireplace, and a few seconds later, Milo entered in a way that suggested he'd been listening at the door. "Milo, bring me my spellbook," she said.

Milo nodded. He cast a quick glance at Sienne before going to the bookcases and pulling out a book fatter than its neighbors. "Thank you," Carys said when he handed it to her. "Please clear the tray."

When Milo had once again left, Carys handed the spellbook to Sienne. It was bound in flexible red wood the same color as the mantel with a couple of black ravens painted on it. "Fashions have come back around," Carys said when Sienne traced the outline of the ravens. "We neither of us suffered through that awful craze for embellishing spellbooks with bones or gems that only fall off or get broken."

Sienne nodded and opened the spellbook. Carys's spells were arranged at random, which meant she'd likely put them in as she got them. It was how Sienne did it, and she'd always felt it marked a true wizard not to waste time organizing and reorganizing spells as you added more powerful ones. She turned a few pages. Carys had specialized in transforms early on, basic spells like *sharpen* and *break*, moving up to *cat's eye* and *gills*—nothing Sienne didn't have.

She turned a few more pages. Confusions, a few summonings, an evocation or two. She closed her eyes briefly and tried to remember the spell she'd just read, but found the memory slipping away from her. So, did that mean she still had to have a spell written in her own blood to be able to truly memorize it, or was it the act of writing that turned muscle memory into true memory? She read on. More powerful spells... "All the *wall* spells," she said. "Two *barriers*. And— you do have *transport!*"

"I do," Carys said. "Is your team small enough to use it?"

"Yes, just." She turned another page. "I've never heard of *rainbow*. It's not a confusion?"

"Oh, you'll want that one. I'll teach you to use it. It was always one of my favorites."

"You must have had the most interesting life." She gasped. "Dear Averran. You have *seeming!*"

"I take it you know that spell?"

"We had it sort of used against us once."

"I find few people really understand how powerful a weapon a confusion can be. But you're Stravanus trained, so it doesn't surprise me that you do."

Sienne closed the book. "This is a tremendous gift you've given me. Thank you."

"Just remember this. You'll be in a position to pass the favor along someday. I hope you'll use it wisely."

Sienne's brain buzzed with the spells she'd read. "Will you demonstrate *rainbow*?"

Carys held out her hand for the book. "It really shouldn't be done indoors," she said, "but there's not a lot in here that can be hurt by *rainbow*. It's meant to affect living creatures. Not that I'll cast it on you or Milo, but I think you can see the effect well enough if I cast it on my table. Move your chair."

She waited for Sienne to shift the chair a foot to the left so Carys could have a clear view of the table, surrounded by chairs. "The thing about *rainbow* is its somewhat random effect. If you read it straight off, with no pauses, the ray it produces flashes through six colors—hence the name—and does something different depending on what color it is when it strikes its target. It also strikes unerringly whatever you intend to hit."

"I thought rainbows had seven colors."

"As if anyone's ever seen indigo." Carys snorted amusement. "But if you emphasize one of the syllables, you can control which color the ray is. That gives it a shorter range, and less power, and you have to aim carefully, but sometimes you don't want to depend on chance." She spoke the syllables of *rainbow*, its harsh, acidic accents painful to hear, and at the end a coruscating beam of colored light shot away from her to score a shallow gouge across the table top. Sienne realized she was grinning like a madwoman and made herself stop.

"If you brought supplies, I'll help you scribe these now," Carys said. "I'm sure you're busy."

"Not too busy for this," Sienne said. She opened her pack and removed paper and a vial of blood ink she'd prepared earlier, along with a handful of pens.

Carys turned pages in her spellbook and cast *float*, then pushed herself across the room to sit at the table. "I'm very adept at *float* after all these years," she said. "Good thing, because I still hate being dependent on others to lift and carry me. Even my husband, may he enjoy God's rest, couldn't keep me from resenting it."

Sienne settled in next to Carys and spread out her supplies, pouring the blood ink into a shallow dish and aligning the first page just so. "Let's start with *seeming*," she said.

An hour later, her hand ached from writing, but she had five new spells. She sorted through them. *Wall* of earth, the only useful magical defense against a *force* bolt. *Transport. Rainbow. Seeming.* And *glow*, which made a body shine with light. She had no idea what she'd do with it, but it had caught her imagination. And Carys had smiled when she'd chosen it, which suggested it was a good idea.

"Thank you," she said again as she put the pages into her spellbook and tidied away her supplies. "Do you...maybe this is an intrusion, but could I bring my team to meet you sometime? You must know so much about scrapping, and have so many stories—but I don't want to encroach on your time."

"I'd love to meet them," Carys said. "Talking about the old days... people always say it's like feeling young again, but the truth is I don't feel any older inside than I did when I was nineteen and just starting out, whether or not I talk about it. But no scrapper ever stops thinking about scrapping, and I'm just as interested in hearing your stories as you are in hearing mine. So yes, bring them around."

"We're headed for Ansorja soon, but maybe when we return." Saying the words made Sienne conscious again of how dangerous this job was, how likely it was that they might not all return.

"Something's troubling you," Carys said. "What is this job, that it makes you look so worried?"

Sienne shook her head. "I can't tell you the details," she said, "but it's dangerous."

"All the most worthwhile jobs are," Carys said. "Good luck to you."

"Thanks," Sienne said. "I think we'll need it."

4

S ienne lifted the last of the rolled-up carpets to the top of their lopsided pyramid and steadied it so it didn't roll off. The debate that afternoon about whether to take the carpets to Ansorja had ended with Alaric saying, "They can't carry much luggage beyond one or two small bags, not enough to supply us on the overland journey. And we'd have to fly much higher than before to get above the forests, because trying to navigate between the trees would slow us considerably. I hate to admit it, but I think we have to leave them behind." Perrin was quicker than the rest to agree.

She thought about casting *seeming* to conceal the carpets, but there was no point, given that Master Tersus never interfered in their rented space and Leofus didn't pry. She just wanted an excuse to use her new spell...and maybe that was a good enough reason. She opened her spellbook to *seeming* and began reading aloud, committing the syllables to memory as she did.

A blue haze rose up around the carpets, fogging her view of them. It thickened as she continued, taking on the colors around it: the deep green of the sofa, the lurid pink and blue of the ugly carpet that would never wear out enough to be replaced, the deep brown of the floorboards peeking from beneath the carpet. More shades of brown appeared, hard and angular and obscuring the ugly carpet.

She spoke the last syllable of the spell, and the haze pulsed once, then solidified. The carpets vanished. In their place was a short stack of wooden crates running the length of the sofa. The room even smelled of raw wood. Sienne stretched out her hand and patted the air. Her fingers sank into the topmost crate's lid, disappearing beneath *seeming,* and she could feel the smooth surface of the topmost carpet curve beneath her fingers. She realized she was grinning like a fool and made herself stop.

Only Dianthe was in the kitchen when she returned to it and dropped heavily into her chair. The sun had set, and the sky outside the window was blue-black interrupted by the dark shapes of the yews. Dianthe was counting out coin into five piles. "Did you get a good exchange rate?" Sienne asked.

Dianthe nodded, not interrupting her counting. "Good enough I won't complain." She pushed one of the piles toward Sienne. "Your emergency money."

"Thanks." Dianthe would handle most of their money, but after a memorable day in the western dukedom of Marisse in which Perrin had been separated from the others without coin, they never went on a job without making sure everyone was provided for.

Sienne slipped her handful of silver and copper coins into her purse. "I've never been to Ansorja. It's too bad we won't have time to look around, because Esthold is supposed to be beautiful."

"I've never been farther north than Concord. The journey is perilous if you're on your own, and once Alaric and I teamed up, he didn't want to go north. Makes sense." Dianthe made her somewhat larger bag of money disappear. "And we're going to bypass all that."

"I hope it works. I've never cast *jaunt* using a scryed image instead of a place I know well." Sienne stretched out her legs. "I know it works in theory, but it's not the same as doing it."

"I'm not worried." Dianthe chuckled. "I never thought I'd be so blasé about magic. Could you have imagined we'd be at this point a year ago? And Alaric...well. You already know."

Footsteps sounded outside the kitchen. "What about me?" Alaric said. He sat in his chair at the head of the table and scratched his head. "Am I in trouble?"

Sienne took his hand. "We were talking about how far we've all come from where we were a year ago."

"That's true. And tomorrow we'll be in Esthold and setting off on the next part of this adventure."

Kalanath entered and propped his staff against the wall. He looked a little sweaty from his evening exercise. "I like it when we say it is an adventure," he said. "It is better than saying maybe death."

"More positive," Dianthe agreed. "Where is Perrin?"

"Talking to Cressida upstairs," Alaric said, "at least that's what he said he was going to do. He wanted to explain why our arrival in Beneddo would be delayed."

"I hope everything is still all right," Sienne said. "We did say we'd go there as soon as our job in Omeira was finished. This feels like going back on a promise."

"Perrin was the first to say we needed to put this quest ahead of his family problems," Alaric said. "And your parents will protect the Deluccos."

Sienne once again refrained from pointing out that they didn't know if they'd even survive this adventure. "I know. It's not rational."

Feet thrummed rapidly down the stairs, making Sienne turn toward the door. A moment later, Perrin appeared. His long, dark hair fell across his face, and he was breathing rapidly. "They have taken my children," he said. "This afternoon. Cressida is frantic. Sienne, I must go to Beneddo at once."

Sienne felt superstitiously as if they'd made it happen by talking about how everything was all right. "Perrin—"

"I am sorry, but this cannot wait." Perrin gripped the door frame as if he might tear it from the wall. "I cannot abandon Cressida. You will have to go to Ansorja without me."

"What?" Dianthe exclaimed.

"We need to talk about this," Alaric began.

Perrin cut him off. "Do not *dare*," he said in a low voice, "to tell me this is less important than your own needs."

"I wouldn't," Alaric said, unmoved by Perrin's anger, "but you don't have to face this alone. We want to help."

Perrin closed his eyes. "I do not see how," he said. He opened his eyes and looked at Sienne. "Can you take me there?"

"I grew up in Beneddo. I know it better than just about anywhere," Sienne said. She stood and offered him a hand, but pulled it back when he would have taken it. "I think we should all go. If there's anything we can do, there's no point wasting time going back and forth. And I can practice *transport*."

Perrin nodded. "What do we do?"

"Everyone join hands—no, actually, not all. Alaric, put your hand on my shoulder. I need a hand free for the spellbook." Sienne took Dianthe's right hand in her left and cradled her spellbook in the crook of her right arm.

"What about Leaf?" Alaric said. "She's still upstairs."

"We'll be back for her—for everything—eventually," Sienne said. "This is complicated enough I don't have time to figure out how to bring an animal along." She willed the book open to *transport*. Steeling herself against the sharp syllables, she began reading.

Immediately, she tasted blood from dozens of tiny cuts the spell inflicted on the inside of her mouth. She swallowed and kept reading. As she did, she felt her mind absorbing the spell, writing it on her memory. She brought to mind memories of her bedroom in the ducal palace, how she'd grown up there, how it had been the home she returned to once a year when she was fostered at the school at Stravanus. It would be crowded with all of them in it, and she added that observation to her memory, picturing herself and all her friends standing in a circle on the hearth rug.

She spat out the last blood-flecked syllables and closed her eyes. A terrific jerk dragged her sideways, as if there were a hook embedded above her navel. She took two stumbling steps, gripping Dianthe's hand and her spellbook tightly, and opened her eyes. Her familiar bedroom surrounded them, the hearth empty and cold, the lavender canopy over her small bed fluttering in the wind produced by their appearance. It was all so familiar, the bed and the book-shelves and the little armchair where she'd spent so many nights reading when she was supposed to be asleep, that her heart gave a hiccup of pleasure.

Perrin released Alaric and Kalanath and made for the door. "Per-rin, wait!" Sienne cried out, but he was already gone. "He doesn't know where to go."

"Neither do we," Alaric said. "Where might Cressida be?"

"Guest quarters, on the third floor," Sienne said, "or she might be with my parents in their private drawing room."

"Let's try that first," Dianthe said. "I can't imagine your parents letting her be alone after this."

Sienne led the way down the long hall half-paneled in cherry-finished oak. The walls were white above the dark paneling, making the hall feel more open than it was. Ahead, golden sunlight from the setting sun bathed the landing where stairs went up and down. Beneddo was far enough west that sunset hadn't reached it yet, though the light had a dim twilight quality that made Sienne feel like squinting.

Beyond the stairs, the hall continued, lit only by another window at the far end. Unlike the clear window overlooking the landing, it was made of stained glass in shades of ruby and amber that made the light look like blood. Perrin had stopped halfway to it and stood embracing Cressida, his arms tight around her, his hand cradling the back of her head with such tenderness it made Sienne forget to breathe. Cressida's face was buried in his chest, and her shoulders shook with sobbing. Perrin inclined his head to hers, and his mouth moved in speech too quiet for Sienne to make out.

Dianthe put out a hand to stop Alaric when he would have advanced. "Wait," she said quietly. "They need to be alone."

"We can't just stand here," Alaric said.

"Sure we can."

They waited in uncomfortable silence until Cressida raised her head and nodded. *Kiss her*, Sienne willed Perrin, but he only smiled and wiped away her tears. That was enough.

Perrin released Cressida, though she didn't move very far away, and turned to look at them. "It is not too late," he said. "My father himself came to the house and demanded the children's return. He had legal documents properly signed, and the duke and duchess were helpless to prevent it. But that was only three hours ago. They have not left Beneddo. We can get the children back."

"We can?" Dianthe said. "That doesn't sound promising. And where would they go? They can't come back here."

"We can figure that out later," Alaric said. "Right now we need to retrieve the children before Master Delucco returns to Fioretti. Taking them from his house would be much more difficult. Do you know where he's staying?"

"Wait," Dianthe said, "just wait a moment. You realize this is legally considered kidnapping, right? If we're caught, the law won't care that we're righting a wrong."

"Dianthe is correct," Perrin said. "I cannot expect you to put yourselves in legal jeopardy. This is my problem."

"I didn't say we wouldn't do it," Dianthe said, exasperated. "I'm just pointing out that we have to protect ourselves in ways we don't normally need to. We'll need disguises, for one, and we—Alaric, we really do need to know where we're taking the Deluccos, because that has to be part of the job. They can't come north with us."

"Why not?" Sienne asked.

Everyone but Cressida looked at her as if she'd lost her mind. Cressida looked confused and a little frightened. "Well, they don't speak the language, for one," Alaric said, "and for another, we're headed into terrible danger and I don't want children along to complicate matters."

"But there's an Ansorjan community in Fioretti," Sienne said. "An enclave, really. There has to be something similar for Rafellish in Esthold—it's nearly as big as Fioretti is. And Master Delucco will never think to find them there. They can wait for us—they'll be perfectly safe."

"That assumes I will be going with you to the wizard's valley," Perrin said. "I cannot accompany you. My family needs me."

Sienne, her mouth open to forestall more objections, found herself with nothing to say to that. An uncomfortable silence descended. Sienne, catching Alaric's eye, could guess what he was thinking: without any one of them, their chances of succeeding dropped to almost zero. Without Perrin and his blessings, they might as well not make the attempt.

"Perrin—" Dianthe finally said.

"I know," Perrin said. He wasn't meeting anyone's eyes. "But I have a duty I have neglected for far too long. I am truly sorry."

"I don't understand," Cressida said. "If it is a...a job, a scrapper job, you cannot postpone it?"

"Not for more than a few days," Alaric said. "But...if that's how it has to be, Perrin, we understand."

"But we can't—" Sienne exclaimed, and Alaric silenced her with a swift glare.

"Let's focus on retrieving Delphine and Noel," he said. "Cressida, do you have any idea where Master Delucco went?"

Cressida shook her head. "I do not know Beneddo well enough to guess where he might stay," she said, "though I do not believe it is with a private individual. He does not have friends who might put him up. So it will be an inn, and likely an expensive one."

"I have two scrying blessings to seek out a location," Perrin said. "It will be difficult, but I believe I can scry out where the children are, or at least one of them. The difficulty is in identifying where in the city the location is. But it is worth the attempt."

"Once we know that, I can examine the building and work out the best approach," Dianthe said. "Then it could be as simple as renting a room in the place and sneaking around after dark."

"I just need to know which room they're in, and I can *transport* them back here until we decide where to go next," Sienne added.

Cressida drew in a breath. "I begin to believe you might actually succeed at this," she said.

"Not to jinx our efforts, but this isn't the most complicated job we've ever taken," Alaric said. "Sienne, where can Perrin go for some quiet?"

"At this hour? The library," Sienne said. "I'll show you where it is, and then I want to talk to my parents."

The library was on the ground floor, a room twice the size of Leofus's kitchen without windows to interfere with the maximum use of bookshelf space. Lamps glowed on all four walls and at the shining mahogany table surrounded by matching chairs. It would have looked intimidating if the chairs and table hadn't had nicks and black marks from generations of Verannus offspring kicking them idly during lessons. Sienne's attention was drawn to the armchairs upholstered in dark green velvet. She'd spent so much time draped sideways over the armrests, reading or working small magics. This room was as much a part of her childhood as her own bedroom.

Perrin made for one of the armchairs and dropped into it. He tore a blue-smudged blessing from the ragged riffle of papers and examined it. "I shall need quiet for this, but you need not leave," he said. He addressed them all, but his eyes were fixed on Cressida, who looked uncertain. Slowly, she sat beside him in the other chair.

"I'll be back," Sienne said.

She ran back up the stairs to her parents' drawing room, the outer room in their suite. Her father was sitting at the writing desk when she entered, and her mother stood by the empty fireplace, her hands clasped before her. They both looked up when Sienne entered. "Oh, you're here!" her mother exclaimed, and hurried forward to hug her. "How did you know?"

"Cressida told Perrin. We came as fast as we could." Sienne hugged Papa and breathed in the comforting woody scent that would always remind her of him.

"I thought such a journey was impossible for you," Papa said.

"I...have a new spell." Sienne still hadn't decided what to tell people about her newfound abilities—or whether to tell anyone at all. "What happened?"

"Lysander Delucco found a corrupt judge willing to sign off on his foul decree." Papa released Sienne and resumed his seat at the desk.

"I almost refused to allow him entrance, but that would have put us and the Deluccos in contempt, and I judged we didn't need any complications in this mess."

"Pontus is writing to the king," Mother said. "We insisted Master Delucco leave his warrant with us as proof of his rights, which means we have the name of the woman who signed it. That and the warrant itself is evidence enough that Master Delucco bent the law to take the children."

"Alcander is preparing to go to Fioretti to meet with Derekian," Papa said. He blew gently on his letter and folded it. "He's been busy. He met with a group interested in repealing the very aspects of law touching on Perrin's situation, and they've made it their landmark case. And he also discovered that the judge who signed off on Perrin's disinheritance and his annulment is the same woman who signed the warrant to take the children. Now it's just a matter of time."

"So long as Master Delucco doesn't make the children disappear," Mother said.

"How can he do that?" Sienne asked. "*Why* would he do that?"

"Because he is a rat bastard who sees his grandchildren as pawns rather than people," Mother said, startling Sienne with her choice of language. "I spoke with him when he arrived on our doorstep this afternoon. I am convinced he cares for them only so far as he can use them to hurt his son. If he can't win this case, he will make sure Perrin and Cressida never see their children again."

"Then we can't just wait for Alcander to settle things with the king," Sienne said.

"No," Papa said. "And that's the last I'm allowed to say on the subject. If *someone* were to rescue those children from Master Delucco, I can't know anything about it." He winked at Sienne.

"Of course," Sienne said. "And I came here alone. To lend Cressida moral support. Naturally I would never participate in illegal doings with my powerful and endlessly flexible magic."

"You've turned out just as we always hoped you would," Mother said, hugging her again. "How are your friends? And Alaric?"

"We're all well. We'll have to come for a real visit soon. I want you to know them better."

"I want an opportunity to tell stories of your childhood. I'm sure Alaric will appreciate that," Papa said.

Sienne rolled her eyes. "I can't stop you telling the pastry story, can I?"

"But 'Dumpling' is such a sweet nickname, Sienne—"

Sienne groaned and let herself out.

When she returned to the library, she found the others gathered around the mahogany table. Sheets of paper were spread over its glossy surface, one of them a map of Beneddo Sienne recognized as having drawn herself before she went away to school. "Did you find him?"

"We did," Alaric said, "and we are working out the best route to the place."

"The inn is located here, in what I believe to be a well-to-do section of town," Perrin said, tapping the map with a pencil. "Perhaps you can give us assistance?"

"I know where this is," Sienne said. She took the pencil from Perrin and drew a line through the city. "I don't know exactly which building it is—I've been gone too long for that—but you're right, it's a wealthy part of town. It shouldn't be hard to locate."

"Unfortunately, it's wealthy enough that none of us look like the kind of patrons they usually serve," Dianthe said. "So we'll have to sneak in after dark. It's less optimal, but between *imitate* and *float* and maybe *jaunt*, we shouldn't have a problem."

"Maybe not," Sienne said. "If all we need is someone who looks wealthy, I have a solution for that." She grinned. "And it won't even require *imitate*."

5

Sienne had to use *fit* on her gown to get it over her head. It was embarrassing. She hadn't put on that much weight in the last year and a half, had she? She'd expected her own old wardrobe, left behind in the ducal palace when she ran away to Fioretti, would still fit her. But no, after an awkward struggle during which Dianthe didn't laugh as hard as she probably could have, Sienne resorted to the spell and worked her way into the silver and cream confection.

She'd forgotten how uncomfortable formal gowns were, with their long skirts and tightly laced bodices. There had been a brief moment, pre-struggle, in which she'd considered bringing some of the gowns back to Fioretti with her. Alaric certainly got the most smitten look in his eye when he saw her in something other than her typical scrapper attire. But five minutes of wearing the thing had changed her mind.

Now she stood in the library and cast *shift* or *imitate*, one by one, on her companions. No need for *voice,* as it was unlikely anyone would recognize them by their voices, but between the confusions that made them look nothing like themselves and the wardrobes borrowed from some of her parents' servants, they were perfectly disguised. Alaric was six inches shorter, and both he and Kalanath looked like Rafellish men; Dianthe and Perrin resembled the owner of Alaric's favorite tavern in Fioretti and her husband. Sienne had altered her own features only slightly, resisting the urge to look like herself and overwhelm the innkeeper with his proximity to nobility. But that meant risking someone asking why the duke's daughter wasn't staying with her parents. So *shift* it was.

"All right," she finally said. "Remember prolonged contact with someone else will increase the chance they'll see through the confusion. It's why I made you change clothes instead of using *imitate* to alter what you're wearing—fewer things to fool onlookers into believing. But it's unlikely anyone will feel like hugging you."

"I think I'm rather fetching, don't you?" Dianthe said with a grin.

"I'm never going to get used to this," Alaric said. "Now, Sienne is Genevra Mossino, we're her servants, and we're too snooty to talk to anyone. Perrin will negotiate for her room, and Sienne and Dianthe will go straight there. Kalanath, you don't speak at all—we can't do anything about your accent. The men will watch outside for trouble, and after dark Dianthe will locate the children, and Sienne will *transport* them back here to the ducal palace. Then the rest of us will take the carriage—you're sure your parents don't mind us taking it?"

"They don't know and they don't want to know. I chose one of the unmarked ones and I'll cast *mirage* on it to keep it from looking conspicuous."

"Then we'll take the carriage back to the palace and work out from there where to take Cressida and the children." Alaric eyed Perrin. "And Perrin."

"Pray, do not look at me that way," Perrin said. His mouth was set in a stubborn line. "You know it is the right thing to do."

"Of course," Alaric said. "We'll need to move fast, because as soon as Master Delucco discovers the children are gone, he'll come straight here. Any questions?"

"Will it take long?" Cressida asked. She was sitting on the armchair nearest the fireplace with her hands clasped tightly together. "I do not wish to be impatient, but I will have to wait, and I... would like to know what to expect."

"I can't be sure, because finding the children will take time," Dianthe said. "Before dawn, certainly. Don't worry, Cressida. We'll get them back to you."

Cressida nodded. "Then...I would like to speak to Perrin alone, if you don't mind."

Alaric nodded. "We're ready when you are," he told Perrin, and shepherded the rest into the hall.

"I hope they're kissing," Sienne said as soon as the door closed. "What? You know they want to. It's so hard to watch them together when they so clearly don't know how to apologize to each other."

"We can't interfere," Dianthe reminded her. "It's up to them."

"That doesn't stop me hoping." Sienne hitched her bodice into a more comfortable position. "What are we going to do?"

Nobody asked what she meant. Alaric said, "Convince him of what needs to happen. Find a place for his family so secure he won't feel bad about leaving them."

"But where?" Dianthe asked. "We can't take them back to Fioretti, and they can't stay in Beneddo."

"I still think a Rafellish enclave in Esthold is the best option," Sienne said.

"But if we do not return, they are trapped," Kalanath said.

"If we don't return, what are the odds Master Delucco will ever stop looking for them, legally or not? They might have to live out their lives in Ansorja no matter what."

The door opened, and Perrin emerged. He didn't look like someone who'd been kissing his true love. "I am ready," he said. "Let us go before I realize we are all insane."

The black carriage, open to the sky and drawn by four matched chestnut horses the color of Sienne's hair, was already plain enough she didn't think they needed *mirage*. But she'd learned in fourteen months of scrapping that the thing you didn't think you needed always turned out to be the thing that saved your life. She cast the spell without resorting to her spellbook, which she'd left behind in her bedroom. Wizards drew attention, and it wasn't the kind of attention Sienne needed that night.

With the carriage now sky blue, Sienne sat beside Dianthe as they rattled through the streets of Beneddo. Across from them, Perrin sat stiffly, not meeting her eyes. She suspected he felt guilty at abandoning them. How unfortunate that his guilty feelings hadn't prompted him to follow through on his commitments to his team. Though...was it really right to expect him to ignore his family's needs just as he was on the verge of regaining them? Sienne felt a surge of annoyance toward Lysander Delucco. The horrible man had the worst timing.

Alaric drove the carriage as if he'd been doing it all his life, though Sienne knew he'd had exactly fifteen minutes' instruction before taking the reins. She was grateful they were driving a very direct route to the inn and not anything complicated. She risked a glance at Kalanath, hanging on behind. He didn't look worried or nervous. Maybe she was the only one concerned about the complexity of this plan. Complex plans were the worst. They never went the way you wanted them to.

They curved around the great roundabout at the center of Beneddo, with the towering bronze statue of Kitane Sienne's mother had commissioned when Sienne was eight. She'd had to stand with her mother and siblings—there had only been five of them at the time—and wave at the crowds and bow her head for the invocation. The statue never failed to bring back memories of that day. She suppressed the urge to give it her traditional wave; after all that, she felt as if it belonged to her.

Past the roundabout, stone houses three or four stories tall lined the streets, gradually becoming wider and more separated from each other until they were mansions whose glass windows caught the last rays of the setting sun and glimmered like mirrors. Then they were past the mansions and into another business district, one so upscale the shops didn't have signs with pictures of what could be bought inside, just brass plaques with the shop names inscribed on them in curling script. Sienne hated shops like that. They were so exclusive, in the original sense of excluding others. She much preferred the sprawling market of Fioretti, where you could buy anything at all and nobody was turned away unless they didn't have coin.

The carriage slowed. Sienne made herself look unconcerned the way a woman of her apparent social status would, but she surreptitiously examined the inn they pulled up in front of. It filled the space where two broad thoroughfares met, its ground floor of granite blocks uninterrupted by windows, its upper stories half-timbered in a style Sienne recognized as "trying too hard to look antique." She judged the inn to actually be no more than ten or fifteen years old. The beams were stained almost black, the plaster walls between them painted a stark white that looked even whiter by contrast, and the shutters flanking each narrow window were too wide to be anything but decorative. It was exactly the sort of place someone like Master Delucco would patronize.

Alaric brought the horses to a halt with a quiet "steady, there." Perrin stood and exited the carriage, striding up to the front doors as if he really were the servant of a great lady. Sienne gripped Dianthe's knee when she would have risen to follow. "We wait for him to return," she whispered. Dianthe nodded.

They waited a long while. Sienne's nerves twanged with every passing minute. So many things could go wrong. *Shift* had failed, and the innkeeper had balked at serving someone who'd been in disguise. It had failed just as Master Delucco was passing, and he'd recognized his son and had Perrin taken into custody. They'd gotten the wrong inn. They'd gotten the *right* inn, but Master Delucco had left already, taking Noel and Delphine with him. Her thoughts went round and round like spinning tops, dizzying her.

Finally, Perrin emerged from the inn and slammed the door shut behind him. Sienne's heart sank. He walked like someone intent on destroying anything in his path. Stomping up the carriage steps, he threw himself into his seat. "Drive," he told Alaric.

"Drive where?"

"Anywhere. We must talk, and it should be away from this place."

The carriage lurched into motion, forcing Kalanath to make a grab for a secure handhold. "I should have expected this," Perrin said. "It is exactly what he would do."

"What?" Sienne demanded.

Perrin scowled more fiercely. "He has bought out all the rooms in the inn for the night. For his comfort, so he is not plagued by strangers coming and going. I argued with the innkeeper for nearly twenty minutes and was continually rebuffed. No amount of money would persuade him to change his mind."

Alaric swore. "Now what?"

"We go back to the second plan," Dianthe said. "We reconnoiter and we sneak in. But we'll need to change clothes."

"Go back to the stables, and I'll meet you there with clothing," Sienne said. "We'll leave the carriage and *transport* somewhere close to the inn." She spoke the syllables of *jaunt* and was yanked sideways to her old bedroom.

Alaric and Kalanath were still wearing their own clothes, so Sienne gathered up her things, Dianthe's, and Perrin's and stuffed them all into a knapsack she unceremoniously dumped out on her bed. Cinching the buckles tight, she picked up her shoes and Dianthe's—Perrin was already wearing his—and tucked them under her chin. Then she made her way through the house, avoiding the places people might be, and out the side door to the family garden.

It wasn't as nice as the big gardens at their country estate, her father's pride and joy, because Pontus Verannus never had time for anything but business when he was in town. But it was still beautiful, with short hedges of tiny round-leaved shrubs lining the paved walks and a range of flowers that bloomed from first summer to the beginning of winter. Right now, the azaleas were coming into bloom, and they filled the air with a robust sweet-spicy scent. Their bright colors were visible even in the dimness of evening, though they would be more beautiful if the garden were lit as it sometimes was, when there was a party or just when Mother felt like spending an evening outdoors.

Sienne crossed the garden, juggling the shoes, and nudged the garden gate open with her toe. Beyond it lay the vast field between the house and the stables, its grass kept short by the horses and a miniature flock of sheep. Unlike the dark hedges, the grass was pale under the night sky, a still ocean of motionless waves. Lights burning at the corners of the stable roof beckoned her onward, and she half-ran, half-trotted across the field toward them.

She didn't know the stables well enough to *jaunt* to them, but the smell of dozens of horses all in one place was so memorable she wished *jaunt* depended on senses other than sight. A lone stable hand swept the hard-packed earth of the stable floor; he glanced at her once, then turned back to his work. Clearly she wasn't as interesting as whatever he was sweeping up. Sienne set her burdens down and waited, leaning against a stall door. Its occupant stuck his nose over the door and snuffled the side of her head. She laughed and petted its soft cheek. "What's his name?" she asked the stable hand.

The boy glanced at her again. "Sweet Running," he said, in a voice as indifferent as his gaze.

"Sweet Running, eh?" Sienne petted him again. "I miss my horse Spark. She couldn't come on this trip, but I'm used to having her around. I wonder who rides you? You're big enough you could carry Alaric."

She heard a rattling noise, and the sound of horses' hooves, and turned in time to see the blue carriage draw up at the far side of the stables. Sienne gave Sweet Running one last pat and grabbed her burdens. "That was fast."

"Too fast," Dianthe said. "We nearly tipped over twice." Her face was paler than usual, and her hand shook on the carriage door.

"The important word there is 'nearly,'" Alaric said. He hopped down from his perch and beckoned to the stable hand, who dropped his broom and came running. "Get changed. We'll help settle the horses. Sienne, do you have a place in mind for *transport*?"

"I do," said Sienne.

———

THE ENORMOUS BRONZE STATUE OF KITANE LOOKED EVEN TALLER WHEN you were right up close to the base. Sienne let go Alaric and Dianthe's hands and craned her neck to see Kitane's face. The avatar in her warrior guise looked stern, as if she knew what they had in mind and didn't approve. In life, Kitane had always faced challenges head-on, none of this sneaking around; that was something the avatar Lisiel would have thought appropriate. "We're saving two lives," Sienne whispered. "You ought to understand that."

"Did you say something?" Alaric said.

She shook her head. "The inn is about ten minutes' walk from here. Dianthe, what comes next?"

"I'll go ahead," Dianthe said, "and work out where to conceal the rest of you. There are enough people on the street still—" she gestured vaguely around herself—"that you won't draw attention. Not like we just did."

Sienne blushed and looked around. She was used to Fioretti, where there were enough wizards that people appearing from thin air didn't draw more than a few curious glances. Some people were still staring at them and pointing. "Sorry," she said. "I wasn't thinking."

"It's all right. Nothing to be done about it now." Dianthe examined the street in both directions. "We'll just have to brazen it out. Walk like you're out for an evening stroll, and if you don't see me by the time you reach the inn, keep walking." She strode off down the street, more briskly than she'd suggested they walk, and turned a corner that put her out of sight.

Alaric glanced around them. "I think we should definitely start moving. Those people are going to remember us, and I don't want anyone thinking we're worth following."

"I *said* I was sorry."

"That wasn't a criticism, sweetlove. But if you can think of any more misdirection, now would be a good time for it."

Sienne considered her options: *mirror*, that created three identical copies of herself, or *mirage*, to make it look as if they were going two different ways. "I can't think of anything that wouldn't just draw more attention to us," she said. "Like Dianthe said, we have to brazen it out. So...let's walk."

She paid close attention to everyone around them as they strolled off after Dianthe. No one seemed to be following them, but she didn't have Dianthe's keen sense of her surroundings to perceive someone tailing them. She thought about taking Alaric's arm to add to the appearance of a couple of friends out for a casual stroll, but decided against it when she thought about *imitate* being accidentally dispelled through that contact. So she walked, and listened, and tried not to fret. The air was full of the scents of flowers and horse manure in the streets, normally a relaxing smell, but one that at the moment reminded Sienne of how ordinary this walk wasn't.

They drew closer to the inn, and Dianthe didn't appear. Sienne felt as if the tall stone houses and shops leaned in over her, watching her and whispering to each other about what she was doing there. Carriages containing men and women out for an evening's drive passed close by them. It was just her imagination that the passengers stared closely at Sienne and her companions, that they could not only see through *imitate* but knew the spell was present, that all of them suspected what Sienne was up to... She let out a deep breath and told herself to relax. Nobody knew what they intended, and everything was going to work out well. *Just like it already has*, she thought, and made herself focus on the next step. Which wasn't going to happen unless Dianthe showed up.

The inn was only a few dozen yards away. They were going to walk right past it. Sienne had to breathe deeply again and remind herself not to grab Alaric's hand.

"Over here," Dianthe whispered, making Sienne jump. They were passing a shop with one of those depressingly elegant brass plaques that read *Heristo's*, as if that told anyone anything about its wares. Dianthe beckoned to them from the deep shadow between Heristo's and the next shop. She stood at the entrance to the alley after they'd all scurried in, watching the passersby. "All right," she said. "No one's paying attention to us. It looks like you left any unwanted attention behind."

"What did you learn?" Alaric said.

"There aren't any guards posted," Dianthe said. "This area is too well-trafficked and too wealthy for casual theft, which is what guards are good against. The problem is, that means someone knows there's no conventional defense against a good thief, so there will be more precautions inside. That makes this more complicated. Not impossible, just complicated."

"Do you know where my children are?" Perrin demanded.

"I know where they aren't. Master Delucco wasn't sufficiently paranoid to light every room to disguise which ones aren't in use. There are two rooms on the third floor, northwest corner, that were both lit until five minutes ago. Now only one of them is. I'd bet the children are in the first room, and Master Delucco is in the second."

"That seems a safe bet," Alaric said. "Do the windows open?"

"No. But they don't have drapes. Easy enough to see out, or see into." She looked at Sienne.

"*Float*, and *vanish*," Sienne said, "and I'll climb up the outside of the building until I can see in, then *jaunt* to get in and out again. I hesitate to call it easy, because anything could happen, but...it seems easy."

"Then we'll wait here while Dianthe shows you which room," Alaric said, "and come rushing to the rescue when everything goes south."

"Wait," Perrin said. "I think..." He pulled out his riffle of blessings and selected one with a rosy smudge on one corner. "I have one more communication blessing. I think I should invoke it on Sienne, so we will have contact in that small way."

"Like the one you use with Cressida?" Sienne asked. The idea made her nervous. They'd used a similar blessing months ago, linking all their minds, and it had been uncomfortable and awkward, if effective.

"Yes. But it allows one only to hear the other's coherent thoughts. It will not grant us the ability to perceive each other's unconscious thoughts or feelings. The effect is rather like hearing someone speak very close in one's ear." Perrin held the blessing midway between himself and Sienne.

"All right," Sienne said. "That makes sense."

Perrin bowed his head and muttered an invocation under his breath. The paper burst into rose-pink flames that licked over Perrin's fingers without burning him. Sienne immediately felt a swelling, tight sensation in her ears, as if she'd flown too high too fast on her carpet. She swallowed, and her ears went *pop*. A dull ringing sensation took the place of the swelling, and then Perrin said, *Can you hear me?*

She was looking right at him and his lips hadn't moved. "Yes," she said, then repeated *Yes* with her thoughts alone. Perrin nodded.

"I will feel more confident knowing you are not entirely alone up there," he said.

"Me too, actually," Sienne agreed. She chanted out *vanish,* and the world took on a brief rainbow sheen before settling back to normal. Looking down, she saw nothing where her feet and legs had been. "I wish I could see myself," she complained. "This is unsettling."

"For us, too," Alaric said. "Good luck."

Sienne nodded, remembering too late that she was invisible, and said, "Dianthe, I'm following you, but don't move too fast."

Dianthe slipped out of the alley and walked leisurely toward the inn, not paying any attention to it. Sienne followed as closely as she dared. It had a vaguely menacing air about it that was probably Sienne's imagination, come back to complicate her life again.

Dianthe rounded the corner and continued past the other side of the inn. All the windows were dark but one, and that one was brightly lit as if several lanterns burned there. The lights were the pale yellow of real fire and not the cold white of magic lights, but Sienne didn't know if there was any significance to that. It probably meant Master Delucco didn't have a wizard in his train, or it might just mean he didn't like the starkness of magic lights. But it was too late to worry about that now.

Dianthe stopped beneath the lit window, shaking her foot. Then she removed her boot and turned it upside down, shaking it as if to dislodge a stone. "The window to the right of the lit one," she whispered. "Good luck."

Sienne hurried over to the inn's stone foundation and assessed the wall's climbing potential. The ground floor, as she'd already noticed, was made of large stones that wouldn't allow much purchase if she were really going to climb it. The gaps and bulges between stones were big enough for her to push off after casting *float*, though. The beams of the upper stories crisscrossed each other in interesting patterns and would be even easier to use to work her way around to the correct window. She recited *float* and felt her feet leave the ground. Pressing herself flat against the wall, she reached for her first handhold.

It was easier than she'd imagined, though some of that was her experience maneuvering with *float*. She carefully pulled herself from crack to beam, moving slowly though her heart urged her to hurry. Hurrying only bounced you off surfaces harder than you wanted, potentially sending you floating away from your perch and into the air where you'd dangle like a helpless starfish, groping at air. Doing it while invisible made it doubly difficult because she couldn't see her own hands and had to depend on her fingers' sense of where they were. Inch by precious inch she climbed, breathing slowly and steadily as she ascended.

She had no idea how long it took her to reach the window, but it couldn't have been more than ten minutes. Better than she'd hoped. She clung to the window frame and peered inside. The rising moon dimly lit the interior, and Sienne held still and waited for her eyes to adjust. Gradually, shapes swelled into view. Two beds, both occupied. A small table beneath the window, with a vase of dying flowers on it —that was close enough she might have touched it if the glass weren't in the way. A clothespress. And something else, something like a—

Sienne's heart lurched. Someone sitting very still on a chair near the door. Someone whose eyes glinted in wakeful alertness in the darkness. Someone watching the Delucco children while they slept.

6

Sienne commanded her heart to slow down. Whoever the watcher was, he couldn't see her, and if he had, he would have raised the alarm. She continued to observe him. He was a dim shape, no more distinct than the children sleeping in their beds, but he had short hair cut in a masculine style, so she felt confident of his gender. His arms were crossed over his chest, and his legs were stretched out: alert, but not tense. That struck her as bad for her plan.

She withdrew from the window, leaned back against the wall, and thought *There is someone in the room with the children.*

A pause, then Perrin said, *Can you snatch the children before he reacts?*

No. Transport *takes too long to cast. I need him out of the room.*

Wait a moment.

Sienne wished she could hear the argument no doubt going on just then. *Don't let anyone set fire to the inn,* she thought. *We're not criminals.*

The pause that followed told her someone had suggested it. *We will not,* Perrin finally said. *We have a plan.*

Do I need to do anything?

Be prepared to take the children the instant their guard leaves.

All right. What's the plan?

I intend to walk in there and demand the return of my children.

Sienne gasped. *You can't do that!*

It is not illegal. My father will enjoy gloating. And I intend to make enough noise to draw that man out of the children's room. If not, the others will start a fight.

That's a terrible plan.

It is better than arson, don't you agree?

She didn't know what to say to that. *I'm ready when you are,* she said.

Perrin didn't reply. She decided not to say anything more for fear of distracting him. True, there was nothing illegal in his asking to see his father or demanding the children's return, but Sienne knew enough of Master Delucco to know he was capable of hurting Perrin when he got him alone and in private. *O Averran,* she prayed silently, *he's your servant—please see him through this.*

Distantly, she heard the inn door open, and after about a minute, it closed again. *I am inside,* Perrin told her. Once more she heard only the sounds of carriages passing and the melodic trill of a fiddle from some tavern a short way down the street. Then the guard stirred, sitting up and turning his head to look at the door. Sienne held her breath. *That's right, get up and investigate,* she mentally urged him.

What was that? Perrin asked.

Nothing. Sorry. She chewed her lower lip in agitation. The guard leaned forward, resting his elbows on his knees, but didn't stand. She heard nothing more from inside the inn.

He is infuriating, Perrin said. *But not infuriated. Do not be afraid, whatever you hear.*

That made her more afraid than ever. The guard sat up again, alerted by some sound Sienne couldn't hear. One of the children stirred—Sienne couldn't tell which—and she heard a muffled sound that might have been the guard telling the child to go back to sleep. Sienne hoped the noises would wake both children. *Transport* would be easier if they were conscious.

She heard shouting from nearby—from inside, not outside. She couldn't make out the words, but the first voice was joined by a second, and both sounded furious. The guard stood and went to the door, but hesitated before opening it. Then he walked to the window and looked outside, not just at the street below, but to both sides. Sienne held her breath, though it was impossible he could see her. This close, his face was visible, and she shuddered at how hard and cruel it looked, with a long, sharp nose and thin lips. It was a wonder the Delucco children had been able to fall asleep with someone like that hovering over them.

The guard gave one last, long look at the street below, which was empty of passersby. Then he strode to the door and flung it open. Delphine sat up and said something that was muffled by the glass. The guard replied in harsh tones Sienne also couldn't understand. He glared at Delphine while she cringed, and Sienne thought about *force*-blasting him. Then he slammed the door behind himself.

Sienne chanted *jaunt* almost too fast to be effective and felt the eerie sensation of being pulled through the wall and into the room. Delphine was still sitting up, and Noel was stirring. "Don't scream," she said in a low voice. "It's Sienne Verannus. I've come to take you home."

"What?" Noel murmured. Delphine, despite Sienne's warning, let out a tiny shriek.

"Take my hands—oh, here they are, and don't worry, I'm just invisible," Sienne said. She grabbed Noel's somewhat sticky hand—how did children always manage to get sticky no matter what they'd been doing?—and Delphine's warm, nervously sweaty one. "Hold each other's hands, and *don't let go*, all right? You'll be with your mother soon."

"But—" Delphine began.

"No talking! Do you want that man to come back?" Sienne began speaking the sharp syllables of *transport*, hoping they wouldn't be interrupted, hoping the children would hold on to her and to each other. Her heart was going fast enough to choke her, not something she needed when she had to speak clearly.

The door flung open again, and the hard-faced guard stood

silhouetted against it. Sienne got a good look at him; he looked stunned at what to him looked like the Delucco children with their arms outstretched for a hug. It was all the distraction Sienne needed. She spat out the last syllable and the spell jerked her sideways—

—and into the Verannus library. Sienne released the children's hands.

"*Mama!*" Noel shrieked, and Sienne turned in time to see both children fling themselves on their mother, who had begun to rise from the armchair and was knocked back into it by the force of their greeting.

"Sienne," Cressida said, "where are you? Where is Perrin?"

"I'll be back," Sienne gasped, and *jaunted* back to the closest place she could think of, which was also the most dangerous—the bedroom she'd just taken the children from. With Perrin in some unknown danger, and the rest of her friends Averran knew where, she didn't have time to waste going to the statue and running to the inn from there.

Lights filled the room, blinding her. She stepped back to press herself against the window. "—and your filthy co-conspirators," Master Delucco snarled. He was a handsome man in his sixties, with silver hair disordered around his face as if he'd been fighting.

Two burly men, one the guard who'd been watching the children, held Perrin up between them. Perrin sagged as if his legs wouldn't support him. His dark hair fell around his face, and his left eye looked bruised. "You do not think I would risk losing my children forever by stealing them?" he said. His voice was steadier than the rest of him. "I have no proof they were ever here. What have you done with them?"

They're safe. I'm here, in the room with you, Sienne thought.

Perrin didn't react. "You have overstepped yourself," he continued, "and I will—"

Master Delucco slapped Perrin hard enough to make his head rock back. "You continue to defy me?" he shouted. "Faithless, treacherous whelp! It's past time I taught you your place." He worked his belt free from his trousers. "Hold him fast. I want him to feel every stripe."

The two men wrestled Perrin around to face the wall. *Perrin!* Sienne thought.

Fury, Perrin thought. *Stop them all.*

But it will take you as well!

Do it, Sienne!

Perrin started shouting vicious swear words Sienne didn't realize he knew. It took her a moment to understand he was providing cover for her spellcasting. Swiftly she chanted the harsh, acidic syllables of *fury*, praying Perrin knew what he was about. Master Delucco raised his arm for the first strike. Sienne spoke faster, conscious of the need for perfect timing—too fast, or too slow, and the spell would slip away and she'd have to start over.

Master Delucco's arm came down. Perrin cried out in agony. The last syllables of *fury* sped away from Sienne's lips. Six yellow bolts of magic energy erupted from her to strike the four men, with two bolts grounding themselves harmlessly in the ceiling and wall. All four men collapsed, twitching, into unconsciousness.

Sienne dropped to her knees beside Perrin, though she knew *fury* didn't do permanent damage. Where were the others? She'd never wished for that group thought-sharing blessing so hard as she did just then.

Footsteps pounded along the hallway, and Alaric came to a panting halt inside the door. "Sienne? Where are you?"

"Here." With a thought, she dismissed *vanish*. "We need to get out of this place. They'll be unconscious for a while, but—"

Alaric bent and heaved Perrin over his shoulder. "Hold hands," he said. "I can't balance him for more than a minute."

Dianthe and Kalanath peered in around Alaric's bulk. "Well, that's one solution," Dianthe said, whistling in appreciation.

"Talk later," Alaric said, grabbing Dianthe and Kalanath by the hands. "Move now."

Sienne fumbled for her friends' hands and cast *transport*. Moments later, they arrived in the library, startling Cressida into a shriek that turned into weeping when she saw Perrin. "What happened?" she exclaimed, brushing his hair away from his face.

"He distracted Master Delucco so I could get the children away," Sienne said. "He's just unconscious—he made me cast *fury* on him to keep Master Delucco from beating him."

Cressida's mouth fell into an O of astonishment. "Father Delucco never sullies himself with physical violence," she whispered.

"I think Perrin pissed him off royally," Alaric said. "At least, that was his plan."

"But he—" Cressida's words cut off abruptly as she seemed to remember the children were present and listening avidly. "What do we do now?"

"How long do we have?" Alaric asked Sienne.

"I'm not actually sure anymore how long it takes *fury* to wear off," Sienne said. "A minimum of twelve hours." She prodded Perrin with her toe. "But that means he'll be out that long, too. And we need him to decide what we'll do next."

"No," Cressida said, "we don't."

Sienne looked at her in surprise. There were tears in Cressida's eyes, but her voice was as firm as her chin. "You said you were going to Ansorja, or would have done had our affairs not interfered," Cressida said. "Then that is what we will do. We will go to—Esthold, is it? and find a safe place for me and the children to stay while you accomplish whatever you intend. And Perrin will go with you."

Sienne glanced at Alaric, who looked like he'd been struck by *fury* himself. "Perrin won't agree to that," he said. "He'll want to stay with you."

"But you need him more than we do," Cressida said. "It is past time I started taking responsibility for my children's lives. We will be safe in Esthold, and when you return...then Perrin and I have things to discuss."

Sienne could tell when Alaric reached the conclusion she had, which was that arguing with anyone who looked as stubborn as Cressida did was pointless. "All right," he said. "Let's everyone get some sleep, and we'll leave in the morning, since it looks like no one will chase us tonight."

"Thank you," Cressida said. "For everything. Will you bring him to...to my room? I will not feel comfortable if he wakes unexpectedly and is alone."

Sienne thought about reassuring her that it was unlikely Perrin would be conscious before dawn, but decided not to interfere. Alaric picked Perrin up like a long-limbed baby and maneuvered him through the library door and up the stairs to Cressida's room. When they'd said goodnight to the Deluccos, and were standing together in the hallway, Sienne said, "Are we sure we want to stay here overnight? Master Delucco may be out of it for a while, but he has servants."

"None of whom will want to act on their own initiative, unless I'm wrong and Master Delucco is a kind and generous human being," Alaric said. "And finding an inn, let alone a Rafellish enclave, in Esthold at this hour is going to be tricky. Better we approach the city by daylight."

"I won't argue," Dianthe said. "Mortal terror makes me sleepy."

"Was it that bad? I couldn't hear anything," Sienne said.

"We followed Perrin into the inn, after he drew off all the guards and servants," Alaric said. "We heard him taking a beating. I don't think Master Delucco did all of it, but even if he did, he's no weakling for all he's sixty and more years old. Perrin insisted we not interfere until he knew you had the children away safely." His face went grim. "I'm not ashamed to say I'd be just as happy if Lysander Delucco never woke up."

"Alcander will fix the legal side of things, so they can be a family again and Master Delucco won't have power over them," Sienne said.

"And then we'll dissuade him from pursuing any...extralegal options," Dianthe said with a bloodthirsty grin.

"That's a good long way off, though, and right now I can only think about sleeping," Alaric said. "Not to mention we didn't bring any of our things. Is everyone packed? And—damn. I forgot about Leaf. She'll be wondering what happened to us."

"All these rooms on this level are empty guest suites," Sienne said.

"Go ahead and settle in, and I'll fetch our things and Leaf. Then we won't have to go back to Fioretti in the morning."

She stayed long enough to see where everyone went, then cast *jaunt* and silently went through Master Tersus's house gathering people's packs and Kalanath's staff. Leaf was asleep on Alaric's old bed, but woke when Sienne entered. *Are you going somewhere?*

"We're leaving for Ansorja in the morning. It's...a long story. Will you let me carry you while I jaunt to where Alaric is?"

I do not know jaunt. You sound as if it is unusual.

"It is, a little. I'm a wizard, and jaunt is a transportation spell."

The Pekkanen cringed away from Sienne. *You are a wizard? And Alaric—his smell is all over you. I do not understand.*

Sienne hitched up Dianthe's pack where it slipped over her shoulder. "Alaric and I are lovers. And he trusts me. I know it must seem odd, when that wizard is your enemy, but I'm nothing like him."

Lovers? Leaf sat up. *You are not Sassaven.*

"I know. It's not what you expect. But I love him, and he loves me."

He has a duty to his people. You are not it. The Pekkanen's matter-of-fact tone stung, and Sienne had to bite back a harsh reply. There was no sense yelling at Leaf for something Sienne knew in her heart was true, even if Alaric had chosen differently.

"You'll have to talk to Alaric about it," she said instead. "Now, can I carry you? It will only be for a minute."

She juggled her load and the awkward dog, who felt like a knobbly bag of bones, but eventually got everything balanced and cast *jaunt* to the Verannus library once more. Putting Leaf down a little faster than was strictly polite, she hitched up the bags again and made her way up the stairs to the third floor, going slowly so Leaf could keep up. The Pekkanen walked stiffly, like a dog twice her age —apparent age; if Leaf had known Alaric since infancy, she was more than twenty-five years old. It wouldn't surprise Sienne if Pekkanen lived as long as humans.

By the time she reached the top of the stairs, she felt more weary than she had in days, and was grateful for Alaric's decision that they stay the night. She delivered her friends' belongings to them and then sank onto the bed in the room Alaric had chosen. "I'm tired enough I don't care if anyone knows we're sleeping together," she said. Leaf gave her a disapproving look. Sienne resisted the urge to stick out her tongue.

"Don't your parents already know that?" Alaric said, stretching out beside her.

"Yes, but the nobility like to keep up appearances—oh, I don't know why it matters. We love each other, we're not married, and that's nobody's business but ours." She unbuttoned her shirt and pulled it off over her head before remembering that Leaf was watching. Blushing, she put on her nightdress as rapidly as possible, then lay down in the curve of Alaric's arm.

She watched as Leaf settled down on the rug before the fireplace. There was so much she didn't know. How much dog was still in the Pekkanen? Did they eat the sort of thing dogs usually did? Was a hearth rug sufficient bedding for them. "Are you comfortable, Leaf?" she asked, then repeated herself in Sorjic.

This is enough. Far better than most of where I have slept these last seasons.

"*You disapprove,*" Alaric said. Sienne, confused, turned to look at him. He was regarding Leaf with a steady, unblinking gaze.

She is not Sassaven.

So, they were going to have this conversation with her in the room. "I should go," Sienne said, but Alaric's arm tightened over her and made leaving impossible.

"*I make my own choices. I always have,*" Alaric said.

You have a duty to your people. And you always wanted children.

"*I want Sienne more. If I can free my people from the wizard, I consider my duty fulfilled.*"

Your mother will be disappointed.

"*That's a low blow, Leaf. She can hardly expect me to be unchanged by living among humans all these years.*"

Viveka—

"*My cousin has nothing to do with it.*"

She waited for you.

Sienne moved involuntarily. He had a cousin who waited for him? Even she could tell Leaf meant some kind of romantic entanglement with this Viveka. "*She wasted her life if she did,*" Alaric said. "*I might never have come home. I might not have* survived *to come home.*"

If you want to throw your life away—

"Stop right now," Alaric said. "*You're being overdramatic, and worse, you're being ridiculous. Who I love, who I make a life with, isn't throwing my life away. Sienne intends to help me defeat the wizard and save Genneva. She is deserving of respect.*"

Leaf sat up and growled, her lips peeling back to reveal sharp teeth. *Genneva is lost. You cannot save her. It has been too long. That is my fault.*

"*It's not too late. I won't let her down.*"

Then you are as much a fool as you ever were. Leaf rolled over to face the empty hearth, as clear a gesture of dismissal as Sienne had ever seen.

Sienne looked at Alaric. His gaze was focused on something in the distance, and his arm across her weighed her down. "You're not a fool," she murmured, low enough that she didn't think Leaf could hear. "We'll save Genneva and free your people. I know it."

He glanced down at her, his eyes coming into focus. "You believe that?" he said, his voice as quiet as hers. "Because I'm no longer sure."

Sienne put her hand on his cheek and made him look at her. "You've gotten us this far," she said. "Don't give up now. I believe it. I believe in *you.*"

His eyes lost a little of their distant expression. Then he bent to kiss her, his lips firm and passionate, his hand rising from her waist to caress her cheek. It made Sienne forget Leaf was in the room, forget everything except his hand touching her, his lips on hers. He kissed her again, longer this time, and when he finally pulled away from her, said in the same low voice, "Marry me."

Sienne sucked in a sharp breath. "*What?*"

"It doesn't have to be tonight, or even anytime soon. Just—I want to be your husband. I want the world to know what we are to each other. Marry me."

Her heart beat hummingbird-fast in her ears. "I—" She threw her arms around his neck. "Aren't you even the least bit superstitious about this? We're heading off to possible death...suppose God sees this as an opportunity to make our lives desperately tragic?"

"I don't think God thinks that way, sweetlove." He kissed her again, lightly this time. "But this is my way of promising you that we *will* come back from this. I was going to wait until it was all over, but then I realized—there's always going to be one more job, one more flirtation with mortal danger, and if I wait for all of them to be over, for the perfect moment, I'll miss out on it entirely. So..." He took her hand and rubbed the back of it with his thumb. "This wasn't the reaction I hoped for."

Sienne smiled. "Really? What were you hoping for?"

"Oh...for you to leap into my arms, shouting yes, and then tearing my clothes off and having your way with me."

"With Leaf in the room?"

"Pekkanen don't care about human sexuality. It doesn't embarrass them."

"Well, it embarrasses me."

Alaric nodded. "Well, if that's how you feel...it's not like we need to be married..."

Startled, Sienne said, "What do you mean?"

"It's not what you want. I understand."

"Of course it's what I want!" Her arms tightened around his neck.

Alaric arched an eyebrow. "You didn't say yes."

"Didn't I?" She reviewed the conversation in her head and blushed. "I guess I didn't. Ask me again."

He smiled. "Sienne, will you marry me?"

She drew him closer. "I will. Forever and always."

Alaric cast a glance at the hearth. "Leaf is asleep."

"And we're both exhausted, Alaric."

"I'm never going to be *that* exhausted." He slipped a hand down her back to pull her close. "And who knows when we'll have the chance again?"

"When you put it like that," Sienne said, "how can I say no?"

7

Sienne woke the next morning to Alaric rolling out of bed and opening the door to let Leaf out. Sleepily, she wondered where the Pekkanen would go to relieve herself, but decided she didn't care enough to pursue the question. Alaric, rather than returning to bed, shook her shoulder. She blinked up at him. "It's after dawn," he said. "We should check on Perrin."

Sienne rose and collected her scattered clothing. "I forgot last night that he needs to pray for blessings so he'll be able to scry out a location in Esthold for me to *jaunt* to. His father might be here before we can get away."

"Your parents won't let Delucco in," Alaric said, pulling on his trousers. "They have no idea where we are, and likely don't know where the children are, either. They'll stall him long enough. Don't worry."

Sienne's stomach chose that moment to rumble. "I suppose we can't go down for breakfast."

"Dianthe will sneak in and fetch something. We'll have a proper meal in Esthold."

They crossed the hall to knock quietly at Cressida's door. No one answered for a long time. Alaric raised his hand to knock again, and the door opened, revealing a harried-looking Cressida. "He is awake," she said. "Perhaps you can convince him to see sense."

Perrin reclined on the bed, his head propped on several pillows. His black eye had spread and turned a glorious dark purple. "Was this your idea?" he asked Alaric, his voice hoarse. "This madness?"

"If you mean taking your family with us to Esthold, no. It was Cressida's plan," Alaric said.

Perrin attempted to sit and groaned, falling back against the pillows. "Abandon my wife and children in a strange city where they do not speak the language and have no means of support?"

A little thrill went through Sienne to hear him refer to Cressida as his wife again, but Cressida didn't react as if it thrilled her too. "I have already said I am not afraid," she said. She sounded tense, as if this argument had been going on for some time. "Esthold is a civilized place, is it not? And I am certain you will provide for us for the time you will be gone."

"It's nearly as big as Fioretti," Alaric said, "and far more modern than the capital at Aldmerrow. They would be perfectly safe in the Rafellish enclave."

"Which we do not know exists!" Perrin shouted.

"All right," Alaric said, unmoved by his outburst. "What was your plan?"

Perrin fell silent. "Marisse," he said. "Sienne has been there before—she can *transport* us there. We will disappear into the city."

"That is an excellent plan," Cressida said. "Save for the small matter that it will prevent you going with your companions."

Perrin closed his eyes. His lips pressed tightly together as if he were biting back words. "I will not leave you again," he said, opening his eyes and looking at Cressida. "You do not know the journey we intended to embark upon. It is extremely dangerous—"

"And will be more dangerous for them if you do not accompany them," Cressida said. She sat on the edge of the bed and took Perrin's hand in both of hers. "They risked themselves to rescue our children. You work well together—I have seen it myself. Am I correct that you intend to go with or without Perrin?" she said, turning to face Alaric.

"Yes," Alaric said. "We can't wait for your situation to be resolved. I'm sorry."

Cressida shook her head. "You need not be sorry. Perrin will go with you, and when he returns, we will discover what Alcander Verannus has done in our absence. And all will be well."

"Cressida," Perrin said, "you—"

"You are not the only one who prays, Perrin Delucco," Cressida said sharply. "I feel certain this is the path Averran has chosen for you. The path he put you on eighteen months ago when he set that disreputable Evander Galli before you." She smiled, a rueful expression Sienne wished she knew the cause of. "Do not deny God's word when She goes out of Her way to present it to you."

Perrin again struggled to sit up, and this time he succeeded. "An excellent notion," he said. "I must pray for a scrying blessing to send Sienne and the others on their way. I will ask Averran what he thinks of your plan. And when he concurs that it is madness, will you leave it and do as I ask?"

Cressida's lips twitched upward at the corners. "If you do not fear the answer you will receive, I hardly think I should stop you."

Perrin rose as if he ached everywhere and walked across the room to a chair near the window, lit by the soft light of dawn. He dropped heavily into it and rested his hands on his knees. Closing his eyes, he drew in a slow, deep breath, then another, until he was breathing evenly. Sienne found she was breathing in time with him. It was a compelling rhythm.

"O most cantankerous Lord," Perrin said in the conversational tone he always used when addressing his avatar, "I beg you to forgive my importunity at such an early hour. I am certain your renowned sagacity and awareness of all that transpires on earth means you know the plight in which we find ourselves, and the urgency of our need."

Sienne glanced at Cressida. Her hands were clasped in front of her tightly, and her eyes were closed and her head bowed. Her lips were moving soundlessly, making Sienne wonder if she was even listening to Perrin's prayer.

"I ask for your guidance in the blessings I receive today, that your wisdom, so much greater than my own, will provide me with direction and aid as you see fit," Perrin went on. "And, o Lord of pestilential bad humor, if I might trouble you for more specific guidance. I ask only that you confirm the direction I intend to—"

Perrin's eyes flew wide open, and he gasped as if he'd been struck, arching his back against some unseen force. His breathing became rapid and shallow. His hands, which had curled loosely over his knees, clenched so tightly on the arms of the chair Sienne could see the tendons standing out on their backs, white against his normal tan. Sienne's hand closed on Alaric's arm. "Is he all right?" she whispered.

Alaric stepped forward. Perrin didn't flinch, didn't blink. He seemed not to notice Alaric at all. Cressida continued her silent prayer, if that was what it was, but tears had begun trickling down her face to drip unchecked from her chin. "I'm afraid to interfere," Alaric said in a low voice.

"But what if it's like when he tried to see as God sees?" Sienne whispered. "What if he's dying?"

Alaric hesitated. Then he took another step closer, putting himself within arm's length of Perrin, and reached out to put a hand on his shoulder. Before he could touch him, Perrin let out a long breath and sagged, his head drooping so his hair curtained his face. "O Lord," he whispered, "I beg your forgiveness for my audacity. You are more generous than I deserve."

Alaric let his hand fall and looked back at Sienne. Sienne shook her head. She didn't know what to say, either.

Perrin looked up and brushed his hair out of his eyes. All his attention was on Cressida, who had stopped crying but hadn't wiped the tears away. "How did you know what he would say?" he asked in wonder.

"Averran asks us to use our own judgment and in that way gain wisdom," Cressida said. "You told me that, months ago. Perrin, you have changed so much in ways I could never have imagined. Your companions are key to that change. You cannot abandon them now, however noble your intentions."

Perrin rose from his seat, not at all stiffly, and went to stand in front of Cressida. His black eye had vanished. "I abandoned *you* once," he said. "And suffered tremendously for that choice. I cannot do it again."

Cressida took his hand. "It is not abandonment, because you will return. I am certain of it. Please, Perrin. Finish this task. And come back to me."

Sienne was sure neither of them remembered she and Alaric were in the room. She tugged on Alaric's arm and backed away toward the door. Alaric glanced at her once, startled, then opened the door and followed her through.

"That was...dramatic," Sienne said when the door was shut. "Do you think Averran spoke to him?"

"I can't imagine anything else that would strike him so hard," Alaric said. "But I wish he'd received blessings. We need to be on our way."

Sienne punched him lightly on the arm. "They're reconciling! That's so much more important."

"We're in danger of losing the Delucco children again. How is that more important?"

"It's...all right, we need to get out of here, true. But don't you hope they've finally resolved their differences? *I* think they're kissing."

A door opened farther down the hall, and Dianthe appeared. "I must have coffee," she moaned. "I hate this time of day. Nobody sane is awake."

"I love mornings," Sienne said.

Dianthe squinted at her. "And you're clearly insane. Is Perrin conscious? We barely have enough time for coffee."

"Perrin and Cressida are making up," Sienne said.

"They are? I don't suppose he's changed his mind."

"Averran seems to have changed it for him," Alaric said.

Cressida's door swung open. "I am thoroughly humbled," Perrin said. "Let this be a reminder to me not to be so certain what Averran's answer to a question will be."

"So you're going with us?" Alaric asked.

Perrin nodded. "I must petition Averran once more for blessings, and hope he is not so thoroughly sick of me he ignores my request. But I think he will not." He held out a hand, which quivered. "Being touched by God leaves a mark, and I believe Averran will know I do not approach him frivolously."

"I will ready the children and their possessions, few as they are," Cressida said. "And I think—"

Steps sounded on the nearby staircase, and a girl no older than Delphine Delucco, dressed in the green and gold of the Verannus family, came into view. "Mistress Delucco," she said, bowing, "you're wanted downstairs. There are men at the door looking for you."

Cressida blanched. Perrin put his arm around her and drew her close. "They cannot prove the children are here," he said, "and you are fierce in their defense. You have nothing to fear from my father."

Cressida nodded, looking up at him. She didn't look certain. Swift as thought, Perrin kissed her. "Go," he said, "and be as distraught as you may."

That brought a smile to her lips. She squeezed his hand once, then followed the girl down the stairs. Perrin watched her go, smiling himself. "Blessings," he said, "and perhaps Sienne and Dianthe might help the children pack?"

Sienne found she was grinning like a madwoman and didn't feel like controlling herself. "Alaric, find Kalanath, I'm sure he's awake," she said. "Cressida may be able to deter those men, but we should leave quickly."

She and Dianthe found the children stirring and assured them their parents were there and no, Grandpapa would not take them away ever again. They helped the two stuff their clothing into a knapsack—Cressida was right, there wasn't much—and got Noel dressed with a minimum of fuss. When they emerged from the bedroom, the hall was empty. Sienne rapped on Perrin's door, hoping she wasn't interrupting his prayers. Alaric immediately opened the door. "We're ready," he said. "Perrin is prepared to scry for you."

"Papa!" Noel shouted, racing past Alaric to jump on Perrin, who was seated cross-legged on the floor this time. Perrin laughed and scooped the boy up. "Papa, Grandpapa took us, and Lady Sienne made us jump here. It felt like being hooked like a fish! Can we do it again?"

"Indeed we can, and will do so shortly," Perrin said. He set Noel down and rose, letting out a deep breath. "But now you must be still. Perhaps you might sit on the bed."

"I have my shoes on. Mama says not to jump on the bed with my shoes on."

"Sit quietly, and it will be all right," Perrin said, helping Noel up. He had a handful of slightly crumpled squares of rice paper in his left hand and tucked most of them away, retaining only one. "I do not know Esthold, so I cannot choose a location. We will have to use our best judgment."

"I don't think any of us have been there," Sienne said, and felt a twinge of doubt about their plan.

The door opened again. "They are gone," Cressida said, somewhat out of breath. "They will return when they have legal grounds to search for the children. I do not think the duke will allow it, but we should not take risks."

"Agreed," Perrin said. He held the blessing paper at arm's length and murmured, "O great Lord, have mercy on me, and grant this blessing."

The paper burst into blue fire that coursed down Perrin's fingers without harming him, turning his tanned skin yellow. The air thickened in front of his face, rippling like glowing blue water. Slowly, angular shapes, dark like a charcoal drawing, emerged from the ripples, until with a jerk the thickened air became an oval window on a city. The view was of a street lined with squat stone buildings whose dark green roofs were steeper than any Sienne had seen before. Doors as heavy as the never-closed gates of Fioretti gave the buildings a forbidding look, though there were signs over each one painted with words in Ansorjan: tailor, chandler, baker. She'd be afraid to shop in any of the stores.

"Should I move the vision?" Perrin asked.

Sienne examined the street. It was busy, but not crowded, and she didn't think there would be any trouble taking herself through. "It's fine," she said. "Give me a minute."

The stones the shops were made of were small, no bigger than her doubled fists. How long would it take to build a store with stones that size? They were multicolored, too, mostly pale gray, but also charcoal and midnight blue and a mossy green that matched the roofs. Paving stones as big as she was made a sharp contrast to the stones of the buildings. Thick blades of grass grew up here and there between the cracks, defiant against the shoes and hooves that trod them down.

The nearest shop sign read *Lassten. Hats.* Sienne studied it, noticing how the pale blue lettering was faded around the edges. There was a light patch near the N that suggested the sign painter had blotched his work and had cleaned it imperfectly. She closed her eyes, holding that sign in memory, and chanted the syllables of *jaunt.*

The now-familiar jerk near her midsection pulled her a few stumbling steps through a world that blurred past her eyes. She blinked, and the blurriness solidified into the street she'd seen in vision. The sounds of carts rolling past and the low murmuring hum of men and women speaking in curt, abrupt Sorjic filled her ears.

Esthold smelled nothing like Fioretti, where the warm southern sun heated the ocean waves and filled the air with the bitter-tart scent of brine. Though it was still the end of true summer, there was a chilly nip in the morning air, which smelled deliciously of baked goods and hot fruit and made Sienne look forward to winter's delights. She breathed in deeply, then had to take a few quick steps out of the way of a cart drawn by two plodding horses enormous enough to match Alaric's unicorn form. She didn't need to be run over at the start of this adventure.

She turned and backed up against the wall of the hat shop, surveying the street. A few people were staring at her, but they turned away when she smiled pleasantly at them. So wizards appearing out of nowhere weren't the kind of rarity that started a riot. She hadn't expected rioting to be the case, but it was a risk she'd had to take.

What the scrying vision hadn't revealed was that the streets were filthy with animal waste and mud. It looked as though rain had fallen the night before, but hadn't left the streets swept clean and fresh the way it would in Fioretti. But the smell of baked goods overpowered the nearer stink, so where...

The bakery turned out to be just across the street. Twice the size of the hat shop, it had an enormous plate glass window, far bigger than anything she'd seen in Fioretti, displaying its wares. That made sense, since Esthold was famed for its glassworks, even in the south. Sienne's stomach rumbled. Bring everyone here, and then, breakfast.

She crossed the street and walked a short distance away from the bakery, looking for an alley wide enough for several people to fit. Esthold might not care about strangers popping into existence in the middle of the street, but horses spooked easily, and Sienne didn't want to cause a scene.

She found what she wanted three doors down: an alley more than wide enough to admit a night soil cart, though it didn't smell any worse than the rest of the street. She ducked into it and, walking its length, discovered it let out on a quieter street where the shops didn't have signs. Maybe they weren't shops, though they lacked the liveliness a household would have had at this hour. Not important.

She backed up to the center of the alley and focused on the stones of the wall, whose varied colors made a pattern like the toothy maw of Doom from a hazard deck. Very easy to remember. She focused on it until her sense of the place surrounded her, and cast *jaunt*.

Cressida's bedroom was crowded with people and their belongings. Noel shrieked with excitement when Sienne popped into existence beside him. "I want to be a wizard when I grow up!" he shouted. "Can I be a wizard, Mama?"

"I'm sorry, Noel, but no, it is something you must be born to do," Cressida said. Noel's face fell. Looking at him, Sienne wondered as she had before whether the ritual that had unlocked her potential as a wizard might work to give an ordinary person magical abilities. It was one more thing she had no answers for. She loved being able to do wizardry, and the idea of giving that capability to someone like Noel thrilled her. But it would have to wait until later. Much later, probably.

Alaric tapped her on the shoulder. "You forgot this," he murmured, handing her her spellbook. Sienne looped the harness over her shoulder—and went briefly numb with shock. She'd cast *jaunt* without the spellbook. In front of Cressida. Giving away her secret without even thinking about it.

She found her hands had settled the book without conscious direction from herself. Cressida didn't look as if she thought anything was out of the ordinary. In fact, she was occupied with fastening the children's knapsack around Delphine's shoulders. Sienne bit her lip nervously, then decided to say nothing to draw attention to herself. Who would Cressida tell, after all? And for all Sienne knew, it wasn't a secret worth keeping...oh, but that was so false she couldn't believe it herself. Being able to cast spells without a spellbook was a development that would turn wizardry on its head. But that, too, she would have to deal with later.

"*Transport* can only manage five people at a time," she said, "five people and whatever they're carrying. I want to take all the Deluccos on the second trip, and Alaric, you'll have to carry Leaf." She eyed Leaf, who stood near the door looking like an ordinary dog, for signs that the Pekkanen objected to this idea. Leaf looked back at her with an impassive gaze. Well, it was unlikely Sienne was going to win her over.

Kalanath slung his staff across his back, thrusting it through his belt, and held out his hand to Sienne. "This is a way of travel I like," he said with a smile. "It is not as exciting as carpets, but it is like Alaric says, it is a...rush."

"It is infinitely preferable to carpets," Perrin said with a shudder.

Dianthe put her hand on Sienne's right shoulder as Sienne balanced her spellbook in the crook of that elbow. "What should Alaric do?"

"Hold Kalanath's hand, and Dianthe, you put your other hand on Alaric's shoulder. It's not like *transport* actually goes anywhere—you're one place, and then you're another—so you can't get...flung off, or lost, or anything. If you break the circle, it just doesn't work. So physical contact is the important thing." She waited for the others to settle, then pretended to read *transport*. Kalanath was right; the feeling of being tugged and the world zipping past was fun.

The alley was empty when they arrived. Doom's toothy maw and fleshy tongue gazed down at them. "Wait for us at that end of the alley," Sienne said. "It will just take a moment."

Alaric drew in a deep breath. "I smell food," he said. "I didn't know how hungry I was."

"Ansorjan pastries," Sienne agreed. "This day is already looking up."

8

It turned out one major difference between dogs and Pekkanen was that the latter were omnivorous. Watching Leaf make short work of hot bread stuffed with blueberries put Sienne in greater charity with the creature. Maybe she was short-tempered because she'd starved for so many months. Maybe she would come around to Alaric's way of thinking. It was unlikely, but having brought the Deluccos safely out of Beneddo, Sienne felt inclined to optimism.

She wiped her mouth with the back of her hand and let out a delicate burp. "Now what? We find a place for Cressida to stay?"

"And outfit ourselves for a journey," Alaric agreed. "*Leaf, can you lead us to the wizard's valley?*"

Do you still mean to save Genneva?

"*We'll free the Sassaven and destroy the wizard,*" Alaric said. "*And save Genneva.*"

The Pekkanen let out a long mental sigh that sounded like wind over new grass. *I will help you. But I do not know what you can do.*

"Why did you come if you had so little faith in me?" Alaric exclaimed, sounding exasperated.

It was Detlenda's idea. Your mother has faith enough for thousands.

Alaric smiled. "*She wouldn't have believed I was dead.*"

She did not. I know she prays to God every night for your survival.

Sienne, looking at the others' uncomprehending faces, said, "Leaf will be our guide. But we need to find a Rafellish neighborhood first."

"You'd better do the talking, Sienne," Alaric said. "The Sorjic they speak here is difficult for me to understand."

"I wish I could take you to Stravanus," Sienne said. "You're a living example of phonemic drift."

"I'll assume that's not as horrible a thing as it sounds," Alaric said. "Lead on."

Sienne discovered almost immediately that Esthold and Fioretti had more in common than it seemed on the surface. For one thing, people weren't at all interested in conversation with strangers, even strangers who spoke their language. It took Sienne ten minutes to find someone interested in stopping to talk, and another ten to find someone who knew anything useful. But by the end of that twenty minutes, she'd learned what she wanted to know: there was a neighborhood where many Rafellish had settled, north near the docks.

"I dislike the sound of that," Perrin murmured when she'd conveyed this information. "Docks are traditionally environs for hardened criminals and the coarser element of society."

"We have to start somewhere," Sienne pointed out. "And it's unlikely any Rafellish neighborhood is going to be wealthy."

"I am not afraid of living among the poor, Perrin," Cressida said. "At the moment, I am of the poor myself. But I have skills I can turn to supporting our family, and I feel certain Averran will watch over us."

"It's not far from here, if I understood that woman's directions," Alaric said. "Let's investigate. At worst, they'll tell us of some other neighborhood of Rafellish, and we'll do some more walking."

They'd left the shops behind and were now passing through a neighborhood of wooden houses with stone foundations taller than Alaric. The wooden upper stories were all painted in what had been bright colors five years before, before time and weather had scoured them pale, but Sienne liked the effect better than if they were still vividly red and blue and yellow. Every house had glass windows that anywhere in Fioretti would have meant wealth, but glass was so common in Esthold even poor people had well-polished, gleaming casements.

Here, the narrow cobblestone streets were clear of dirt thanks to the many women wielding brooms and scrub brushes. They smiled and waved at the companions, friendly as their other countrymen were not, and Sienne smiled and waved back. Children playing a ball game in the well-scrubbed street stopped to stare at Kalanath, whose dark skin was such a contrast to their fairness. One ball escaped its minder and came rolling toward Noel, who stopped it with his foot, then looked as startled as if his foot had acted on its own.

"Kick it back," Alaric said when the Ansorjan children didn't approach.

Noel glanced at his father for approval, then delivered a surprisingly accurate kick that sent the ball flying straight back to the others. A tentative smile crossed his face. "I want to play," he said.

"Some other time," Perrin said. "Perhaps there will be children where we are going."

But as they passed through the neighborhood, the houses grew smaller and dingier, their colors muted not by time but by disrepair. The streets narrowed and became hard-packed earth, rutted from the last big storm. No women swept the steps, and the only people visible were hard-eyed men loitering on corners, hunched into their collars as if it were a stormy day and not a pleasant morning. Sienne eyed the sagging roofs and the cracked windows and felt less sanguine about her plan.

Noel and Delphine drew closer to their mother. "Are we going to live here?" Delphine said, sounding as if she hoped the answer was "no."

"This is just the part nearest the docks," Cressida said, but she didn't sound very certain either.

"Let's ask," Alaric said, and crossed the street to where three men stood around a lamp post from which hung a lantern missing half its glass. Sienne and the others drifted after him.

"Is this where the Rafellish live?" Alaric asked.

One of the men, whose scruffy brown hair looked in need of a wash, eyed Alaric and clearly came to the conclusion that harassing someone his size was a bad idea. "Ayep," he said.

"We're looking for lodging for a family," Alaric went on. "Where should we go for something like that?"

His companions looked them all over. One of them smiled in an unpleasant way. "For these lovely ladies? I'm sure we can find...something."

The third man elbowed him hard in the ribs. "Don't be a jackass, Tymmon," he said, straightening and slicking his hair back with one grimy hand. "Look, this ain't no place for families, 'cause there are way too many like Tymmon who think they're a laugh riot. And these children here, they don't deserve to be brung up around the likes of him."

"But—" Cressida began.

"You are quite right," Perrin said. "Thank you for your candor."

"Plenty of inns where the keeps speak Fellic," the first man said. "Expensive, but better'n what's here."

"We'll try that," Alaric said. "Thanks."

They walked back the way they'd come in silence for a dozen yards before Perrin said, "I do not wish to thwart the will of Averran, but I think it unlikely I have enough money for an extended stay at an inn where they speak Fellic."

"They were honest with us," Cressida said. "Do you not think—"

"*No*," Perrin and Alaric said at the same time. "There would be enough like that man Tymmon that you would not be safe," Perrin went on. "Perhaps we should try Aldmerrow."

"We're running out of time," Alaric said. "We can't afford to *transport* all over Ansorja looking for a safe place."

They'd reached the street full of sweeping women once more. A gaggle of children, all shouting and running after the ball, split to rush around them as if they were a rock in a stream. Sienne saw Noel's gaze follow them, somewhat longingly. "I have an idea," she said, and crossed the street to where a stout middle-aged woman plied her broom. "*Excuse me*," she said in Sorjic. "*Do you speak Fellic? Or have a friend who does?*"

"*Jula's husband is Rafellish. She speaks it some,*" the woman said. She put two fingers to her lips and whistled two earsplitting notes, high-low. Every woman within fifty feet of her stopped sweeping and looked up. "*Jula! The strangers want a word,*" the woman called out.

Three houses down, a flaxen-haired young woman, likely no older than Sienne, propped her broom against the wall and approached. She was slim enough to be called skinny, and her blue eyes looked enormous in her thin face. She brushed imaginary dirt off her immaculate apron as she neared, and said, "*Yes?*"

"*Do you speak Fellic?*" Sienne asked.

"I do," Jula said. "Not of the best, I think, but it is my husband is Rafellish. You have need?"

Sienne took Cressida by the arm and pulled her forward. "My friends and I are scrappers, and we're about to head out on a job. But this is my friend Perrin's wife, and she and her children need a safe place to stay while we're gone. They can't afford an inn, but I was thinking, maybe someone here has a room they're willing to rent?"

Jula cast a quick look up the street toward the Rafellish enclave. Her thin face took on an expression of distaste. "They cannot stay in there," she said. "They are not all of the good, there."

"Yes. Can you help? They have money to pay for room and board, if it's not too dear."

Jula eyed Sienne. "Why do they not in Rafellin stay? Do they bring trouble?"

Jula was smart. "No," Sienne said. "There was trouble, yes, but they left it behind in Rafellin. It won't follow them here."

"My children and I would be so grateful," Cressida said.

Now Jula turned her keen eye on Delphine and Noel, and her expression softened. "Thordis has a room now that her daughter is married," she said. "We will ask her."

"Thank you," Sienne said fervently.

"I am willing to help with chores, whatever is necessary to ease the burden," Cressida said.

"Thordis will not say no to that," Jula said with a grin that transformed her thin face. "It is that her daughter did much, and she misses the company. And a hand to wash dishes." She pointed a ways down the street, back toward the center of town. "She is here, if you will come."

Cressida immediately followed Jula, who strode off as if the matter were already settled. Sienne and the others trailed off after her. "That was inspired," Perrin said.

"People are generally the same wherever you go," Sienne said. "These are women with families. They understand what it means to care for others. I think Cressida will find the language barrier not so difficult to overcome."

"Where did Noel go?" Dianthe exclaimed.

Perrin swore and turned rapidly to scan the street behind him. He took a couple of steps, but halted before he got very far. "I think Noel is another for whom the language barrier matters little," he said with a smile.

Noel had joined the ball game and, laughing, kicked the ball to one of the shouting children. "Has he ever played foot-the-ball before?" Alaric asked, watching the children with amusement.

"It is not a Rafellish game, is it? I do not think he has even seen it played."

"He's a natural." Alaric looked as if he itched to join the game himself. Sienne took his hand fondly and squeezed it.

Perrin glanced over his shoulder at where Jula and Cressida were speaking to a very short woman with two blond braids coiled over her ears like Ansorjan pastries. "Let him play," he said. "I think he is as safe as we can make him."

———

SIENNE WATCHED PERRIN AND CRESSIDA AS THEY STOOD CLOSE together near the door of Thordis's house, speaking quietly. "Now I almost wish they hadn't reconciled," she said. "It must be so hard to have to separate after that."

"Harder if they were still at odds," Dianthe said. "And he'll probably still have that communication blessing. I'm more worried about what happens when this is all over."

"You mean...he might leave us?" Sienne shivered despite the warmth of the air and the bright sunlight. "He wouldn't. Would he?"

"Scrapping can be dangerous work, you know that," Alaric murmured. "Perrin might think he owes it to his family to do something where he's not risking his life all the time."

"I do not know what that is," Kalanath said. "He is smart, but does not have skills that are outside what his father's business does. And I do not think he can do those skills now."

"Yes, and priests of Averran are travelers," Sienne said, feeling more cheerful. "He wouldn't do that to the children, give them an itinerant lifestyle. Staying with us is a much better choice."

"Let's not worry about it now," Alaric said. "We have plenty of other things to worry over. Like finding the valley. I've never approached it from the north, and I'm not sure Leaf has either."

"Didn't she say she'd help?" Sienne asked.

"Yes, but Pekkanen don't see directions the way humans do." Alaric crouched to put himself closer to Leaf's head. "*Do you know how to reach the valley? How far is it?*"

I do not know far. I took the southern route when I left. But I know when I am near the Pekkanen.

Alaric relayed this to the others. "That doesn't sound promising," Dianthe said. "We might wander a long time if we're dependent on Leaf sensing her fellows."

Sienne glanced at Perrin and Cressida, who were kissing as if nobody else in the world existed. Sienne reached for Alaric's hand and leaned against his shoulder. They hadn't told anyone their intention to marry because the morning had been so busy, and now Sienne felt awkward about bringing it up out of nowhere. *That's us in ten years*, she thought, and happiness bubbled up inside her.

Perrin and Cressida separated, and Perrin hugged first Delphine, then Noel, who looked impatient to get back to his game. Then he took Cressida's hand one final time and said something Sienne couldn't hear that made Cressida laugh. With a smile, Perrin released her and strolled toward his friends. "I feel more sanguine than I did this morning," he said. "Thordis is a talkative woman. I half expect my family to speak nothing but Sorjic when I return."

"And Noel to be captain of the foot-the-ball team," Dianthe said, laughing as the crowd of children rushed past them again.

"So, what next?" Perrin asked. "Shopping?"

"We were discussing how to find the valley," Alaric said.

"Oh, that is nothing," Perrin said. "I need a map and a quiet corner, that is all. Though my assessment of this blessing—" He held up the handful of blessings he still hadn't stitched together—"suggests that it is not terribly accurate in the sense of directing us to a specific place. We may still have to search for the entrance to the valley."

"That's something Leaf can help with. We just have to get close enough." Alaric scanned the street. "Let's see if we can't leave here before nightfall. I want to be on our way as soon as possible. Sienne, you go with Perrin to find a map, and the rest of us will buy supplies."

"We don't need horses, do we?" Sienne asked as they walked back toward the center of town.

"Not even a pack mule, if we can get away with it," Alaric said. "I don't want to worry about an animal when we might end up having to sneak through Barholt—that's the village where the wizard's tower is. So everyone's going to have to carry a little extra weight."

"I can manage a heavier load now with invisible fingers," Sienne pointed out.

"True, but we shouldn't depend on that. If you have to cast spells, you don't want your attention divided."

It was noon, and the streets of Esthold were busier than they'd been that morning. Sienne fell into her usual position behind Alaric and let him break the crowds. The air still smelled of food, but now the aroma of hot roasted meat joined the delicious yeasty smell of fresh bread. She liked Ansorjan cuisine even though it mostly consisted of bread stuffed with a variety of foods: fruits for a morning meal, meat or potatoes for the afternoon. It was perfect for eating as you walked, and she said so, prompting Alaric to veer off toward a store front where people stood crowded around, eating and talking loudly. They made room for him without doing more than glance upward at his tall, muscular frame.

Alaric returned to hand out hot, aromatic pastries that smelled of beef and fresh herbs. Sienne bit into hers and had to suck the juicy gravy off her fingers. Alaric nodded off down the street. "There are booksellers that way," he said, "and they'll have maps. Let's meet back here in two hours."

Sienne nodded, her mouth too full to speak. Munching companionably, she and Perrin headed off in the direction Alaric had indicated.

"Booksellers" turned out to be an understatement. Esthold was a modern city, true, younger than Fioretti and not as large, but it didn't have a university and Sienne had had the notion this meant it wasn't a place for scholars. The street they were on, though, appeared to be the center of Esthold's publishing industry. Every other building was a publishing house, and the rest of them were booksellers or stationers. Carts in the middle of the street held used books, some of them so battered their spines were illegible.

And the patrons were so varied Sienne had the momentary illusion that she was back in Fioretti at the great marketplace, where beggars might rub elbows with nobles looking for a good price on artifacts from the before times. Voices speaking all the continental languages filled the air, making Sienne feel even more cheerful. It was hard to believe in failure on a day like this.

Asking around led her to a store whose wares overflowed its bounds. Carts filled with books in Sorjic and Fellic sat to either side of the doorway, untended. Sienne couldn't help wondering why the owner wasn't concerned about theft—and yet no one took anything, not even the people who stopped to browse.

The store itself was as crowded with books as the carts on the street suggested. Bookcases crammed full of fraying leather-bound books formed aisles barely wide enough for one person to pass at a time. The aisles were made even less passable by wooden crates overflowing with more books, wedged against the bookcases where anyone could trip over them. Sienne breathed in the scent of old leather and dusty paper and a hint of glue. It almost didn't matter whether the books themselves were interesting; the smell alone made up for it.

A tall, fair-haired man with rosy cheeks greeted them when they entered. "How can I help you?" he said in Fellic.

"You speak Fellic," Sienne said, surprised.

"I do business with Rafellin all the time. Imports, exports...mostly I resell Fellic novels." His accent was strong, but intelligible. "Did you see the sale carts? I need to make room for new inventory."

"Actually, we need a map of Ansorja," Sienne said. "Of the area around Esthold, really."

A genuine smile crossed the man's face. "That's my passion, maps. Come with me."

The maps were stored beyond the aisles, in a space barely wide enough to be called a room. Deep shelves about two inches high lined two of the walls nearly to the ceiling, past where Sienne could reach. Scroll cases filled cubbies on the other two walls, most of them of hardened brown leather, a few made from skinny, hollowed-out tree trunks. None of the cases were sealed.

The shopkeeper began hauling out flat trays just deep enough to fit the narrow shelves. "One that shows the Pirinin Peaks, please," Perrin said. The man nodded and spread parchments and papers on the square table occupying most of the room. Sienne examined the scroll cases. Each had a tag dangling from it, but she didn't think the shop owner needed those reminders.

"This one," Perrin said.

"I'll make you a copy," the shopkeeper said. "Just let me get my spellbook."

When he was gone, Perrin said, "A spell to make a copy of a map?"

"It's called *draw*," Sienne said. "I don't know it, but it's a useful transform for people who work with maps or notices. It makes a perfect copy of a single page. Not cost-effective for making a book, but if you had a flyer to put up, or needed a map—"

The shopkeeper returned holding a book bound in dark blue flexible wood. It was slimmer than Sienne's and bore no decorations, a working man's spellbook. "One copy, yes?"

"Yes, and if you don't mind, may I use this room to study it when you are finished?" Perrin said.

"I'm going to browse," Sienne said. "Let me know when you're ready to leave."

She wandered the aisles for a while, trying not to get caught up in any of the titles. If they weren't taking pack animals with them, she'd have to haul more of a load than she usually did, and adding books to that weight was a bad idea. But there were *so many* books...she wasn't a scholar like Alcander, but she loved epic poetry about the before times, and some of Dianthe's favorite romances appealed to her. She reached high to pull an interesting-looking book off the shelf and paged through it. Maybe just *one*...

"Probably not a great idea," someone said.

Sienne looked up, startled. A man was approaching her along the narrow aisle. His long, greasy gray hair framed a fleshy face with a bulbous nose shot through with broken blue veins. He wasn't tall, barely taller than her, but he walked like someone accustomed to breaking a path wherever he went. A whiff of unwashed body and the faint hint of sour milk reached Sienne's nose, and she almost pinched it shut before remembering her manners. The man's clothing was stained and travel-worn, his jerkin looked more patch than original fabric, and a threadbare dark green cloak covered the lot. Sienne realized she was clutching her book close to her chest as if to protect it, or protect herself, she wasn't sure which. "I beg your pardon?" she said, discomfort ratcheting her response several steps up the social ladder.

"You'll read it in two days and then have to keep carrying it," the man said. "Not the best strategy for a scrapper."

"How do you—that is, I'm not sure it's any of your business," Sienne replied, feeling shaken. His casual attitude of superior knowledge made her change her mind about putting it back, even though his words echoed what she'd been thinking.

"Probably not," the man agreed. "But wisdom is wisdom wherever you find it, Sienne Verannus."

A jolt of fear went through her. "I don't know you," she said, very conscious that she was at least nominally in public and uncertain as to whether she was in enough danger to justify casting spells with or without her spellbook. "I think you should leave."

The man smiled. "I'm no danger to you. But I think you know that."

"I can take care of myself."

"So I hear." The man ran a hand through his greasy hair and picked...something...out of it, crushing whatever it was between his fingers. "Would you like to know who told me about you?"

Footsteps drew near, filling Sienne with relief that she wouldn't be alone with this horrible man anymore. "Sienne," Perrin said, "are you ready—dear Averran." The man had turned to face Perrin, who stopped, his eyes wide and his mouth hanging slack.

"Perrin," the man said. "It's been a while."

"It has." To Sienne's surprise, Perrin smiled and took the disgusting man in a powerful embrace. "Is it coincidence, or...no, likely not."

"I was just making Sienne's acquaintance," the man said, pounding Perrin on the back the way men do to show affection. "Introduce us."

"Of course," Perrin said, releasing him with no sign of distaste. "Sienne, this is Evander Galli. My mentor."

9

"You're a divine of Averran?" Sienne said, then wished she could sink into the floor when Evander burst out laughing.

"Not what you expected, eh?" Evander said. "That's all right. You're a smart girl—tell me why I look like this."

Sienne looked him over. "I imagine you're a living test of other people's wisdom," she said. "And I failed."

"Not really," Evander said. "I admit I pushed you harder than I normally would, and it's natural for a young woman to be... concerned...when a strange man who knows her name approaches her for Averran knows what purposes. You were polite and you didn't attack me, though you could have. Without your spellbook."

"You know about that."

"I know a lot of things," Evander said. "Most of which I'll share with you and your companions."

"Is that why you are here?" Perrin said.

"I'm here," Evander said, "because Averran booted me in the ass several times over the course of the last three months to get me here before you left. Why he couldn't just talk to you directly, I don't know, but the divine mind is more than usually inscrutable these days and I don't argue with him."

"That is not true," Perrin said.

"All right, it's not true. More accurate to say I don't argue with Averran when the stakes are this high. And now young Sienne is looking at me like I've grown a second head, so that's all I'll say until I can speak to all of you at once. Are you finished here?"

"I have the map, and Sienne has her book," Perrin said.

"I—" Sienne looked at the book in her hand. It wasn't all *that* big. "I will take this, after all," she said, not meeting Evander's eyes.

"See if the shopkeeper will take trade instead of coin," Evander said. "You'll want every advantage you can take."

"You mean, swap spells?" Sienne's eyes narrowed. "Did you have something in mind?"

Evander shrugged. "It's just a thought."

"I would heed his advice," Perrin said. "Evander is the wisest man I know."

"You don't know enough people," Evander said.

When they reached the front of the store, the shopkeeper said, "Found something interesting?"

"Yes, and I was wondering if you were open to a trade," Sienne said, holding up her spellbook.

The shopkeeper's eyes gleamed. "I never say no to new spells. What do you have?"

"Take a look." Sienne handed over her book and received his in exchange. Almost immediately she regretted listening to Evander. The shopkeeper had little she didn't already have. *Draw,* yes, but how useful was that likely to be where they were going? And he wasn't a scrapper, so he didn't have anything in the way of offensive spells.

She caught Evander looking at the book with a peculiar amusement in his eyes. It irritated her. If he was so wise, why couldn't he just tell her what Averran had in mind for this little encounter? Impatient, she held the book open flat across both her palms and closed her eyes. *You pick,* she thought, and willed the pages to riffle first one way, then the other, so they fell open at random. She opened her eyes and managed not to groan. *Bubble.* A basic, short evocation that produced a pocket of clean, clear air around someone's head. Useful, yes, but under very limited circumstances. Even so...

"*Pri'inista*," the shopkeeper said, tapping a page in Sienne's spellbook. "What do you say?"

Convey was worth far, far more than *bubble*. Sienne sighed. "The map, this book, and *bubble*—I mean *dusek*, and we'll call it a fair trade."

"You want *dusek?*" The shopkeeper glanced down at Sienne's book as if assessing the number and complexity of the spells she already had. "I think I might be cheating you."

"I'm...following my instincts," Sienne said. "But we need to do this quickly, because my companions are waiting for me."

Sienne had never been so impatient to scribe a spell in her life. Her normal pleasure in writing the sharp, hard-edged lines of an evocation was dulled by her awareness of Perrin and Evander standing nearby, conversing in low voices. She made herself slow down and focus on the shopkeeper reading out *bubble*, careful not to blotch the lines. They were in no hurry. Evander wasn't going anywhere, and Alaric and the others would wait if they were late. Even so, after drawing one final line, she set her pen on fire with more than usual haste.

"Our Lady of Darkness," the shopkeeper breathed, watching the fire. "I've never seen a spark that big."

Too late Sienne remembered how much greater her small magics were than before. "I, um, practice a lot," she said. "Thank you."

"My pleasure. Stop by on your way back, if you wish, and I'll give you a good deal."

The street was still busy with shoppers picking over the wares on the carts and going in and out of shops. Sienne dropped her destroyed pen on the ground and crushed it under her heel. "I have got to be more careful."

"You'll find people are in general so absorbed in their own business they don't think to worry about anyone else's," Evander said. "Except for those who care about nothing but their neighbors' business, of course. And how many people know enough about wizardry to know yours is unusual?"

"If I go around casting spells without a spellbook, someone will eventually notice," Sienne said, following Perrin down the street toward the rendezvous. "I don't know if that's good or not."

"What would you do if you decided to share your knowledge with the world? Offer that ritual to others?"

Sienne decided to stop being astonished at the things Evander knew. "I'd approach some of my former teachers at Stravanus, or maybe someone at the University of Fioretti. Someone who knows me and knows my reputation. I'd show them what I'm capable of and offer them the same. And then we'd work out how to tell others."

"And you're not afraid of the wrong person getting hold of this power?"

"Of course I am. But I don't see how I can prevent it short of never telling anyone."

"I confess to being more concerned about only a few of Sienne's peers having her ability than about all wizards having it," Perrin said. "As things stand, wizards who abuse their powers are policed by their peers. What can an ordinary wizard do against one like Sienne?"

Sienne considered this. "Not much. I counted the other night and I know forty spells. Forty-one, now. That's a lot for any wizard. And without the limitations of a spellbook and a high reserve of power, I could defeat almost anyone I went up against. It's frightening."

Evander nodded. "Would you like my opinion?"

"Of course."

"You should consider," he said, "the ultimate end of the ancients. They destroyed their civilization with magic impossible for us to comprehend, let alone use. If their wizards were as powerful as Averran says you've become, maybe that's a power that should stay buried."

The idea that Averran knew her, knew what she was capable of, felt...well, of course she believed God knew everyone by name, and she gave her devotion to Averran, so naturally he'd know her, but it still felt uncomfortable, like there were depths to her she wasn't aware of. "I hadn't thought about it that way," she said. "Do you think abuse of power is inevitable?"

"I think you're safe from that. But not everyone is like you. Even so, that's just one perspective. You'll need to consider it as you travel. Maybe encountering Kyros will change your mind."

"Kyros?" Perrin said.

Evander shot him a quick glance. "The name of the wizard you intend to kill."

"I didn't think he had a name," Sienne said. "Alaric always just calls him 'the wizard.'"

"Averran wasn't happy about revealing it," Evander said. "Names have power, and that name...the fact that it's been buried for five hundred years suggests to me it might be a weapon. A two-edged one, based on Averran's reaction to mentioning it. I'd be careful how you use it."

Alaric, Dianthe, and Kalanath were waiting for them, standing against a short wall where two streets intersected. Bags and packs surrounded them. Leaf sprawled across two of the bags, her head resting on her front paws. "You found the map?" Alaric said. He eyed Evander suspiciously. "And this is..."

"Evander Galli, my mentor in the worship of Averran," Perrin said.

Alaric's eyes widened, but he said nothing. Dianthe said, "That can't be coincidence."

"It is not," Perrin said. "Let us find a place to sit and talk, because Evander has messages for us."

The pack Alaric handed Sienne clanked as if it contained cook-ware, but it weighed less than she expected. Rather than hoist it onto her back over her own personal gear, she used her invisible fingers to tow it along beside her. There were plenty of other wizards doing the same thing, so she didn't worry about drawing attention to herself. She watched those other wizards as she followed Alaric through the streets. People in Esthold were even more overt about wizardry than in Fioretti. She saw wizards casting confusions and transforms as casually as talking about the weather, changing the color of their clothing or creating mirrored surfaces to see themselves in, and it seemed every other person used spark to light the long-stemmed pipes so popular in Ansorja.

The casual use of magic made her again wonder what would happen if every wizard went through the conduit-opening ritual. Suppose you could cast transforms with only a few memorized words. Would human anatomy mean anything if a person's lungs or heart or limbs could be shaped to beyond peak performance? Who needed a ladder when *float* could be cast at will? Or confusions—suppose someone committed crimes by fooling the eyes of the city guard? *But people can do that now,* Sienne thought, *and most people choose not to.* So the real question was, would increasing a wizard's power decrease their inclination to do good?

She realized they'd come through the mercantile district into a plaza wide enough to fit her parents' ducal palace. Six marble fountains formed a circle around the center of the plaza, which boasted a statue of someone wearing a crown. Probably a long-dead king of Ansorja; there had been a time when Ansorja was littered with them. Alaric made for a fountain at the far side, which turned out to depict Averran in his most common guise of crusty old curmudgeon, leaning on a walking stick and scowling at the world.

"This seems fitting," Alaric said, setting down his much larger pack. "And there aren't many worshippers today."

"Probably there aren't ever many worshippers," Dianthe said, pointing at the next nearest fountain, which was crowded with people dipping their hands in the water and taking drinks from brass cups. Atop it, a robed Lisiel appeared to be whispering to an unseen listener. "I don't think Averran is very popular in Ansorja."

"Averran is an uncomfortable avatar, true," Perrin said. "Even for his priests."

"Well, I don't intend this to be more uncomfortable than it has to be," Evander said, "so take a seat, all of you."

Leaf immediately lay on the ground as if the day's walking had tired her out. Sienne sat on the wide rim of the fountain next to Alaric, who put his arm around her. Perrin and Dianthe settled on the ground. "I will stand," Kalanath said, leaning on his staff in his usual way.

Evander lowered himself heavily to the ground and sat cross-legged before them. "I told you Averran booted me in the ass to get me here," he said. "He says you've been valiant servants, and you deserve to know why he's guided you this far."

"Not to be rude, but I'm not a servant of Averran," Dianthe said. "And Alaric worships Sisyletus."

"That's an interesting point," Evander said. "When God takes an interest in something, it doesn't much matter to Her which of Her faces guides Her children. In this case, well, Kitane had her chance once before, and Sisyletus doesn't interfere in the affairs of humans beyond granting the blessings his priests ask of him. None of you worship Delanie or Gavant, and they're both interested in abstract justice anyway. And Lisiel's plans are too convoluted to be much use in this case. So worshippers of Averran or not, you've been guided by him since Alaric first decided to approach Perrin to join your merry band."

"What do you mean, Kitane had her chance?" Dianthe asked.

Evander held up a hand. "Let's take this in order. Eleven years ago, Alaric fled his home to avoid being enslaved by the wizard who created his people. He hoped to find a way to free them. Move forward ten years. A typical scrapping job led to Alaric breaking his own rule about hiring wizards. How'd that work out for you?"

"You're taking your own sweet time getting to the point," Alaric said.

"Let's forget about the personal aspect for the moment. You ended up with a wizard who thinks outside the box, a warrior born to be God's mouthpiece on earth, a thief who's more honest than a divine of Gavant, and a priest whose conversion to Averran came at a tremendous cost. And you thought it was just coincidence you all became a team?"

"Alaric's right. You're being far too cryptic. And insulting," Dianthe said.

Evander looked each of them in the eye. His scrutiny gave Sienne an itchy feeling between her shoulder blades, as if he'd positioned a knife there. "You couldn't do this alone," he told Alaric, who looked more annoyed than before. "And pardon my bluntness, but it took ten years for you to learn patience and endurance to the point that you'd be ready to accept help."

"All right, it took me a while to overcome my childish habits," Alaric said. "What does that have to do with Averran?"

Evander ignored him. "You all had things to learn. Sienne needed to understand how to use her magic in ways she hadn't been taught. Dianthe grew brave enough to face her past. Kalanath had to come to terms with his birthright. And Perrin...well. You all saw him undergo his trial. And all that time, Averran watched you change, following your progress. There was always a chance one of you would fail."

"But fail at what?" Sienne asked. "And why didn't we know any of this? It's not as if Perrin wasn't in communication with Averran for all that time."

"Fail at what? Nothing." Evander smiled. "You weren't being tested. You were given the chance to become something extraordinary. Failure just meant God would try again some other time. But you all, individually and together, did just as Averran hoped. You became one. And you became the tool he could use to free the Sassaven."

Sienne's mouth fell open. Everyone else was silent. "You probably know God gives humans the power to choose even when those choices damage others," Evander went on. "That wizard, whose name, as I told Perrin, is Kyros, used his power to create the Sassaven. That should have been a remarkable, wonderful creation. But he chose to warp it by enslaving them and using them to keep himself alive far longer than he deserved. That's not what God has in mind for Her children. But for God to reach out and destroy a man—that would invalidate everything that makes Her God."

Evander cleared his throat. "This isn't the first time someone's tried to free the Sassaven. About two hundred and fifty years ago, a group of holy warriors under Kitane's guidance assaulted the wizard's valley in an attempt to kill him. I don't know what happened, but I do know they failed. Well, obviously they failed, or we wouldn't be here. Kitane took the failure hard. She's used to relying on strength to carry her to success, and when her warriors failed...at any rate, it was a debacle."

"And now Averran intends to try," Perrin said, "using us as his hands."

"More accurate to say Averran has an interest in something you all decided to do." Evander scratched his hair and wiped his finger on his shirt. "And isn't opposed to giving you a little boost here and there. Or did you think it was normal for Perrin, a mere beginner of a priest, to be granted Averran's power to use without the need for prepared blessings?"

"So he's willing to grant Perrin greater power," Dianthe said.

"That, and give you assistance in his own idiosyncratic way," Evander said. "Which is why I'm here. You're heading off into what will be the greatest challenge of your career, and while Averran won't intervene directly, he sees nothing wrong with giving you a few hints."

"Because he expects us to use our own understanding and wisdom to figure them out," Alaric said dryly.

"You catch on quick, mountain," Evander said with a wink. "So, here's a reminder, and a warning. You already know you're stronger together than you are apart, but you should remember that's literally true. But if you are separated, your strengths will endanger each other. And...try not to be the first through the door."

"That's...more cryptic than I'd imagined," Alaric said.

"It will make sense eventually," Evander said. "Or not. It's possible you'll never know what it means. But I think it's more likely to help than not."

"Do you intend to come with us?" Perrin said. "You would be very welcome."

"My adventuring days are long over," Evander said, shaking his head. "I'm heading south to Onofreo to spend the winter. Hope I make it before the first snows fall."

On a whim, Sienne leaned down and hugged him. He smelled

even worse up close, but she found she didn't mind. "Thank you," she said. "For everything."

"Averran watches over you," Evander murmured, "and you'll learn soon enough what that means. Never take it for granted."

"I won't."

Evander stood and stretched. "Good luck to you, and God's blessing," he said. "And mine as well, for what it's worth." He bowed his head and muttered a few words Sienne couldn't make out. Immediately she felt suffused with light, as if the afternoon sun were a tangible thing that she breathed in with the air. Her bones hummed with it.

She looked at Alaric, whose eyes were closed in an expression of profound pleasure. His skin glowed a radiant warm yellow, prompting her to look at her own arms and discover they, too, glowed. She laughed; she couldn't help herself, she felt so wonderful. Alaric opened his eyes and took her hands in his. Where their skin met, a tingle flooded through her, warm and comforting. She laughed again, and Alaric's deeper laugh harmonized with hers.

"Will it last?" she said, and marveled at how her voice sounded like chiming bells.

"It will fade, and sink beneath the skin," Evander said. "No telling what else it will do for you, but I imagine it will bring you courage at the time you most need it."

Sienne looked at the rest of her friends. The glow was fading, but even Leaf had been touched by it. She noticed the people gathered at the fountain of Lisiel gazing in their direction and whispering. A few of them drifted in their direction, moving cautiously. Sienne let go of Alaric and said, "We should probably move on. I don't want to be the misplaced center of devotion to Averran."

"I have marked our route on the map," Perrin said, handing it to Alaric, "and I judge we have several days' walking to do."

"Then let's get started," Alaric said.

10

Sienne had traveled far the last fourteen months, from the great oak forests of western Rafellin to the pine woods nestled into the base of the Bramantus Mountains and beyond that to the deserts of Omeira. None of it had prepared her for the sheer vastness of the wilds of Ansorja. She had the feeling that the great firs were the true inhabitants, and humans had merely cleared away tiny specks of open land that were constantly under threat of being swallowed again.

Esthold had been circled by a protective stone wall like the city of her birth, but half again as tall, and trees grew right up to its base as if no one had considered basic principles of military defense when they designed it. Or maybe she was right, and the trees were the real enemy. It made her nervous, and when they'd left the city she'd considered idly how she might fight a tree. What if they could uproot, and amble over the ground, an unstoppable foe impervious to sword or arrow? Axes, or fire—she imagined casting *scorch*, and turning a tree into a torch, and shuddered.

Ahead of her, Alaric's comforting bulk blocked her view, not that there was much to see: fir trees, casting a cool shade and blocking out the sun's rays, and rare undergrowth, low-growing shrubs or ferns.

They'd been walking through the forest for five days and hadn't seen anything more dangerous than the occasional deer or fox. Sienne could almost tell herself they were on a pleasure trip.

She opened her spellbook to *rainbow* and read the syllables silently, then snapped the book closed and let her mind's eye bring the spell to memory. Of her new spells, *rainbow* was the one she felt least confident of, which made sense because of its complexity. Technically, it was seven different spells, and though her new ability meant she could cast each variant with ease, she still had to memorize them. Her memory of Carys scoring the surface of her table with *rainbow* made her reluctant to try it for real. So she went over it in her head, again and again, and hoped that would be enough.

To the left, a moving shape low to the ground resolved itself into Leaf, trotting toward them. *We are near*, she said. *The valley is ahead.*

"How far?" Alaric asked.

A confusing impression of trees and needle-covered ground came to Sienne's mind. *I do not know far*, Leaf said. *Before nightfall.*

"Gather up," Alaric said. Kalanath and Perrin drew near, and moments later Dianthe returned from where she'd been scouting ahead. "We have to make a decision. Entering at night has benefits and drawbacks, mainly that they won't see us and we won't see them. Also, I don't know the territory here. I think we're better off camping for the night and scrying out the land for entering tomorrow morning, early."

"I have two more scrying blessings," Perrin said, "which should give me an aerial view of the valley and provide us with a map of sorts. And for the second, I will try to see the interior of the tower well enough to *jaunt* to."

"Waiting until morning will give us time to conceal our things well," Dianthe said.

"I think we can have one more fire," Kalanath said. "Once we are in the valley we must not be noticed by smoke."

Alaric nodded. "It's another hour until sunset. Let's see how far we can get in half an hour. If Leaf's assessment is right, we'll see the pass by then."

They picked up the pace, making it difficult for Sienne to concentrate on practicing spells as she had to pay attention to her footing. The ground was mostly clear of anything but dry, fallen needles, brown and giving off a crisp scent when she trod on them, but its unevenness caught her off-guard on occasion. She ran through the contents of her spellbook without practicing them, just to count. Forty-one spells. *Forty-one.* Add to that her vastly enlarged reserves and the ability to cast without a spellbook, and she might be the most powerful wizard in the world. Except, of course, for the one they intended to kill.

It was a humbling thought, a terrifying thought. Back at school, she hadn't ever competed with her classmates for the biggest or most powerful spellbook because she'd never cared about such things, and now...if her teachers could see her now, what a shock they'd have.

Thinking of her teachers reminded her of her conversation with Evander. "I was thinking," she said. "I've been going over spells in my head this whole time, memorizing them."

"Do you think you'll be able to leave your spellbook behind if you have to?" Alaric said.

"Yes. But that's not what I was thinking about."

"You think of the conduit," Kalanath said.

"How did you know?" Sienne half-turned to look at the young Omeiran, who walked behind her.

Kalanath shrugged. "It is what I dream of, every night since we leave Esthold. You have power. It is not an easy thing."

"What did you dream?"

He shrugged again. "A stream of running water I knew was the conduit. First murky, then clear. That, I do not understand. Then you are unharmed at the heart of *fury*, and it means the power that fills you now. And—" He closed his mouth into a tight line as if holding back terrible words. "The rest is...it is when a thing makes no sense because it will not come together."

"Incoherent," Perrin said. "It sounds prophetic indeed. To stand at the heart of *fury*...it is, or was, an impossibility. A glimpse of the future—or, perhaps, a reminder of the past?"

Sienne nodded. "That's exactly it. If what I am is what the ancients were, if it's what they took for granted about magic, should I reveal this knowledge to the world? Restore what we've lost? It's what we do as scrappers, more or less."

"I'd be worried about people misusing that power," Dianthe said. "*You're* trustworthy, but think of someone like...like Lysander Delucco wielding your power. It might be why the ancients destroyed themselves."

"But evil men and women will always find a way to exert influence, whatever power they do or do not have," Perrin said. "You spoke of my father—he has done untold damage despite not being a wizard, or anything but a man with extensive financial resources. Were he nothing but a merchant, he would still be capable of evil, and inclined to do so."

"I'm more scared of someone who can cast *fury* at will than I am of your father, though. Maybe that's just me."

"No, I think wizardry can be frightening," Sienne said. "And what happens if we provide this ritual to all wizards, and the ones who secretly know the charm spells are able to use them the way that carver wizard did? No one would be safe from *dominate*."

"Again, I suggest that however more dramatic wizardry might be, it is not different in the essentials from any other form of power," Perrin said. "Civilization is founded on the give and take between the powerful and the powerless. King Derekian has tremendous power, but we trust that he will not misuse it, and if he does, there are those prepared to remove him from power. Wizards—not you, Sienne, but your fellows—have power, and almost all of them choose to use it responsibly. Those who do not are policed by their peers. As I believe I told Evander, I am more worried about only a few wizards possessing your ability than I am about all of them having it."

"That raises a different question," Dianthe said, "and one that's troubled me since we came north. Why hasn't this wizard, this Kyros, made a play to take over the world? Or even just Ansorja? If he's got power like Sienne, only more of it, why is he content to stay in this little valley doing...I don't even know what he does all day, if it isn't persecuting the Sassaven."

"I don't know," Alaric said. "Like I said, we try to stay out of his way, because he tends to think only about what's immediately in front of him. I know he writes a lot, because papermaking employs many Sassaven, but I don't know what his subject is. And he—" Alaric went silent for a few paces. "He breeds the Sassaven like horses. Forces us to mate so we'll produce the right kind of offspring. And when he's not doing that, he treats us like servants when he isn't ignoring us. I suspect we're an ongoing project to him. That creating us was only the beginning of what he had in mind. Sisyletus knows what will happen when he's through."

No one spoke. Sienne blinked away tears. Alaric had sounded so bleak, for a moment she'd lost hope. How could they expect to defeat someone so powerful and so evil? "How do the Sassaven not fall into despair?" she said. "Five hundred years of slavery...how can anyone hold onto hope for that long?"

"Because the wizard's grip on us doesn't extend to our minds." Alaric's fist clenched once, then relaxed. "And I think it's evidence that God hasn't deserted us that we defy the wizard as best we can, every day. We worship in secret. We make our own alliances. My mother and father kept their love secret successfully my whole life—I refuse to believe that's changed."

"And had three children," Dianthe said.

"Two children. My older brother was the result of one of those forced unions." Alaric let out a heavy breath. "That's misleading. Osten and my mother were required to produce offspring, but they fell in love. Then Osten became the wizard's host and died of it. My father was Osten's cousin, and he supported Mother in her grief— and that led to them falling in love secretly."

"So Karlen is your half-brother," Sienne said.

"Yes, but Sassaven only count the female parent when it comes to siblinghood. So any child born to my mother is my sibling, regardless of who their father is." Alaric let out a low chuckle. "Karlen and I certainly fought like full siblings, growing up. It took me coming into my full growth as a Sassaven unicorn to stop him tormenting me."

"Does that mean he is not unicorn?" Kalanath said. "I think it is that all your family is unicorn, is that not right?"

"We don't understand what makes some of us unicorns." Alaric cast a quick glance over his shoulder at Kalanath. "It's not as simple as who your parents are. Osten was a unicorn, my mother is not, and Karlen isn't one. My father isn't either. So with me and Gen, that's two unicorns born of two non-unicorn parents. Maybe the wizard understands how the pairings work. It might be why he makes some of us mate—how he makes that decision."

"And you said all the Sassaven unicorns, in their human selves, are as big as you," Sienne said.

"More or less. There are some bigger. The women aren't any smaller than the men, on average."

"I'm picturing an army of giant Sassaven women screaming for our heads," Dianthe murmured.

"I'm picturing Genneva as a female version of Alaric," Sienne said.

Alaric laughed. "She's much prettier than I am. And her unicorn form is all white except for the black horn."

"Now we have to save her," Sienne said, "because I bet she knows all sorts of stories about you, and you'll never tell them."

"Is that what you want? Because I'm sure your parents have stories about *you*—"

"Shut up, mountain."

The ground gradually sloped upward as they walked, and the trees thinned until there was plenty of space for the travelers to spread out. Sunset came early in the forest, what with the trees blocking the sun, but there was still plenty of light when they came out of the forest entirely onto the slopes of the foothills. Ahead, the foothills stretched eastward as far as they could see, and the mountains rose beyond them, south and east. Though the day was warm, snow touched the tops of the most distant peaks, and Sienne shivered with cold. Climbing that high was not, she hoped, on the agenda.

Kalanath came up beside her. "There is another thing I see," he said in a low voice. Sienne glanced at Alaric, walking just ahead of her, but he didn't react. "It is a thing I do not wish to say, because it frightens me in the dream."

"If it's something that might mean danger—"

Kalanath shook his head. "I do not know what it means, only that when it happens, I am afraid. More than I should be." His voice went even quieter. "I see you with a knife in your hand, dripping blood. Your knife."

Sienne's skin crawled at how matter-of-factly he said the words. "And it frightens you?" *It terrifies me.*

"As if you kill something precious. I fear..." Kalanath let out a deep breath. "I fear it is one of us you kill."

Another shiver ran through her. "Maybe this is something you should tell everyone. If there's danger, knowing about it can only help."

"I feel it is for you to know," he said. "Not for them. I do not know why." He bit his lip, a gesture that made him look very young for a moment. "I hope it is not true."

"But you always know when your dreams are true, don't you?"

He hesitated, then nodded. "But it is a glimpse of a moment, and maybe that is why it is for you alone—your moment. I do not think we should try to guess the path that will take us to that moment so we can avoid it. That will certainly bring us to it." He took a few steps away, resuming his place at the rear of the group.

Sienne realized she had her hand on her knife hilt and released it. She'd never killed anyone with a blade in her life—wasn't trained for it at all. But Kalanath's visions were never false, and his reassurances, if that was what they were, that they revealed only moments in time and not the events leading to them didn't make her feel more comfortable. And a vision only for her...what could that mean? She almost wished Kalanath had kept it to himself.

Leaf trotted past, startling Sienne out of her reverie. *The pass,* she said. She ran on ahead, as she had often done on their journey, and was soon out of sight.

Ahead, where the foothills rose to meet the mountains, a dark crease beyond two hills sank like a knife's edge between the peaks. In the sharp shadows of twilight, it looked almost as if the mountains were folded in on themselves. "Is that it?" Sienne asked, though it couldn't be anything else.

"That's it," Alaric said. "We'll camp here tonight. Leaf will scout it out for us." He lowered his pack to lie at his feet. "I'm ready for a hot meal."

Sienne took extra care building the fire, gathering big handfuls of dry needles to pack in around the branches and setting them alight with her spark. They gave off a fresh, resinous scent she inhaled deeply, welcoming how it cleared her mind. In the gloom of twilight, the fire was a welcome light, solid and comforting.

She summoned her spark again, this time in midair above the fire. The name was almost ridiculous. The "spark" was the size of her fist and burned for several seconds without fuel. She summoned another and watched it blaze and quiver and then vanish. It filled her with such joy she felt, again, a flicker of doubt. If this were available to any wizard...was it right to withhold the coming of age ritual when this was the result?

Dianthe squatted beside her. "That's amazing," she said. She drew her belt knife and went to work stripping the meat from a skinned rabbit. "You could almost use that as a weapon."

"That's an uncomfortable thought, but you're right." Sienne hauled the cookpot over the flames and summoned water in a neat glob to fill it. "I might even be able to boil water without wizardry, just using small magics."

"That is a good thing," Kalanath said. He dropped another skinned rabbit to lie next to Dianthe. "If we do not need a fire that makes us noticed in the valley, we can still have hot food."

"You could clean that," Dianthe pointed out.

"I will catch one more first. And—" Kalanath went still, lifting his head as if listening to the wind. "Something comes."

Sienne got to her feet. "What is it?"

He shook his head. "It flows like water. I do not understand the sound." He took a few steps away from the fire. "Wait here."

Alaric, kneeling beside his bedroll across the clearing, looked up as Kalanath approached. "I don't—no. I hear it too." He rose and followed Kalanath. "Where's Perrin?"

"I am here," Perrin said, emerging from the shadows. "What is it?"

"Something big," Kalanath said.

Sienne became aware of a sighing sound, like the wind in the branches. But the air was perfectly still, the fire burning steadily, and the sound was too deep for wind. As it grew louder, more sounds emerged: the pattering of rain on hard earth, a high twittering like distant birds, a rhythmic swishing as if a river suddenly flowed nearby. Sienne remembered what she'd thought about animate trees and had the sudden feeling that the natural world had come to life and was advancing on them, intent on wiping them off the face of the earth.

She found Alaric had moved to stand beside her, sword drawn, his shape backlit by the fire. "Kalanath, don't get in the way of *shout*," he said. "Sienne, are you ready?"

"I can't see anything." Her voice shook. "I could cast *scorch*."

"You'd set the forest on fire."

"That might not be a bad thing."

The noise had grown until it filled the evening air. Shadows shifted beneath the firs, and then a wave of darkness swept toward them across the forest floor, flowing around the tree trunks in an onslaught that made Sienne cry out in fear. She instantly felt stupid. She'd faced worse things than darkness.

Stepping forward, she began casting *shout*. Maybe it wouldn't do any good against shadows, but Alaric was right, she shouldn't set the forest ablaze with *scorch*. The harsh syllables of the evocation echoed more loudly than the shadows' advance, building to an almost painful pressure in her chest.

"No!" Alaric shouted, grabbing her arm. Startled, she pronounced the last syllable wrong and felt as if she'd been stabbed by the spell lashing out at her. She gasped and clutched her chest, and Alaric put his arms around her, holding her up. "Sorry," he said, "but it's—they're no danger to us."

Sienne blinked, and squinted into the dimness. Dark shapes moved beyond the firelight, as if shadows had come to life and surrounded them. Nearer the fire, bright eyes caught the light and reflected it back at them like a cat's. Then a dog twin to Leaf stepped forward, followed by another, and another, until their circle of light appeared to be holding a wave of shadows at bay.

"It's the Pekkanen," Alaric said.

The first Pekkanen continued to advance until it stood five feet from Alaric and Sienne. A new voice, one deeper than Leaf's, said in Sorjic, *You bring trouble. We want no part of it. Go, and do not return.*

11

Sienne held still. The Pekkanen quivered with pent-up energy, as if they were half a breath from bolting. Alaric released Sienne and faced them. "*Trouble for the wizard,*" he said in Sorjic. "*Not for the Pekkanen.*"

Trouble for the wizard makes trouble for us. The coal-black creature nearest Alaric shifted its weight, lifting its nose as if scenting the air.

"*We don't intend to leave the wizard alive to make trouble.*"

Others have tried. The Pekkanen remember. The wizard cannot be defeated.

Alaric took a step forward. The Pekkanen remained still. "*I say he can. My friends and I have learned the secret of the binding and we intend to free the Sassaven.*"

You must kill the wizard. He will not allow his creation to go free. The wizard cannot be killed.

"*Storm. You never used to be this fearful.*"

When you spoke of fighting the wizard, you were young. It was a child's dream. I should not have listened. The Pekkanen, Storm, sounded as weary as Leaf had.

"*I've spent the last eleven years looking for a way to make that dream a reality.*" Alaric stepped away from Sienne, forcing some of the shadowy wave back. *"Look at me. I'm not a child."* He shivered, and in the next breath, the unicorn stood there, his brown flanks nearly black in the firelight. He lowered his head to touch his horn to Storm's head.

Storm sat on his haunches and tilted his head so the horn grazed his cheek without cutting him. *You are full Sassaven. How is it possible?*

"We discovered the original ritual," Sienne said, aware that Alaric couldn't speak in unicorn form. *"It transformed Alaric without subjecting him to the binding."*

Storm stood and walked toward Sienne. *And you,* he said. *You were transformed as well. You are like the wizard.*

She wanted to protest she was no such thing, but took the creature's meaning. *"I had the conduit opened, yes. I don't know everything that means yet."*

Storm looked from Alaric to Sienne and back again. *I will listen—for now,* he said, and sank down to lie on the ground, his head held alertly up. A wave of motion rippled outward as the rest of the Pekkanen followed his example. Sienne took a few steps toward Alaric just as he transformed from his unicorn shape. He lowered himself to sit cross-legged before Storm, and Sienne knelt beside him. Behind her, she could feel movement as the others did the same. It felt like the opening moves of a ritual she could barely imagine.

Fir-scented wind swept across them, stirring her hair and chilling her once more. The fire behind them chuckled as the wind whipped it higher. Alaric rested his hands on his knees and regarded Storm. *"We have a long way to go to reach the wizard, across territory full of Sassaven who could alert him to our presence. We want your help in moving invisibly across the valley, and in locating my family, who will support us."*

You want us to ally ourselves with you, Storm said. He sniffed the air and added, *A storm is coming.*

"Better for us if it drives the Sassaven indoors."

Worse if it slows your progress.

"I choose to see it as an advantage."

Storm sniffed the air again. *You intend us to scout for you? Guide your path?*

"Yes. If you will."

If you fail, and the wizard learns of our help, we will suffer.

"We won't fail."

You cannot know that.

A quiet hum, pitched high enough to be called a whine, rose up from the massed Pekkanen. It echoed the cry of the rising wind and raised the hair on the back of Sienne's neck. Alaric shifted his weight and leaned forward. He and Storm might have been the only ones in the clearing. "You're slaves, just as much as the Sassaven are," he said. "You're only safe because the wizard has his attention on the Sassaven. When he notices you, he kills you. You live rough in caves and burrows that freeze in the winter, and there's never enough to eat. What I propose will free your people just as it will mine. You don't have to help us. We'll do this with or without you. But it's time for you to make a decision—continue to live in fear, or take a chance on freedom."

The whine grew louder. Storm barked twice, and it cut off abruptly. He gazed at Alaric with liquid black eyes that flickered with reflected firelight. *What is your plan?*

"Sneak into the tower. Force the wizard to restore his host's heart. Kill the wizard."

Genneva is lost. You should not risk your plan on saving her.

"Then she's still alive." Alaric let out a deep breath. "I won't fail her."

She will fail you. You know how a host is transformed. She will fight you.

"Then I'll knock her unconscious and do it anyway."

Storm raised his head in a defiant gesture. *We will not help if you are a fool. Swear you will not let your love for your sister keep you from your goal.*

Alaric's expression hardened. "I won't—"

Swear it. Or we will not help.

Alaric unfolded his legs and made as if to stand. "Then—"

"Alaric," Sienne said, laying a hand atop his. "He's right. We don't know if we can make the wizard reverse what he did to her. Would she thank you for sacrificing your entire race just to save her?"

Alaric turned swiftly to look at her. "You don't know what you're asking."

"Yes, I do. And I'll do everything in my power to restore Genneva. All Storm wants is for you to promise you won't let your love for her interfere with destroying the wizard. That might...mean her death. I *know*, Alaric, that's not what we want. But—"

"That's enough," Alaric said. "Gen was as much a part of this plan as I was, back in the beginning. She would want me to see it through. Whatever that means." He turned back to Storm. "*I swear I'll do whatever it takes to free both our people. Even if that means sacrificing my sister.*"

Then we will help. Storm got to his feet, sending a ripple of movement through the massed Pekkanen as they did the same. Alaric remained seated. Storm took a few steps that put him face to face, nose to nose, with the Sassaven. They regarded each other for a moment. Alaric's face lay in shadow, preventing Sienne from seeing his expression. Then he let out a long, deep sigh and laid a hand on Storm's head. Storm butted against his touch as if he were a cat instead of a dog. *We thought you were dead,* he said. *I told Leaf she was mad to hunt for you. As mad as Detlenda, to send her.*

"*Mother always had faith in me past reason,*" Alaric agreed. "*It's good to be back.*"

But not home?

Sienne, too, had caught Alaric's unusual phrasing. Alaric glanced at Sienne and smiled. "*My home is where my friends are. And my family. Did they move to Barholt when Gen was taken?*"

Detlenda and Ellard did. Karlen is with the Niskanen.

"*Leaf told me. How long?*"

Three years. It is not what you think.

"*I don't see how I can think anything else. Why else would Karlen join the Niskanen? Or was he forced?*"

He chose. It drew attention from your parents. The wizard came close to discovering their union. You know what that would mean.

"So Karlen sacrificed himself."

Storm was silent.

Alaric scratched Storm's head. *"He wanted to go."*

It was an excuse. You know he dislikes feeling weak.

"I wish I could say this surprises me." Alaric's hand fell away, and he tilted his chin back to look up at the sky. Somewhere to the west, beyond the forest and the hills, the sun had set, and clear white stars dotted the velvet canopy of night. Sienne followed his gaze, but saw nothing except the constellation of the Boat, pursuing the Lovers in an eternal course across the sky. This far north, the Lovers' feet were obscured by the horizon, but enough of them remained that it was clear why someone centuries ago had drawn that particular pattern in the stars.

"We intend to camp here tonight, and hide what we can't carry with us," Alaric said. *"Then we want to take the shortest route to Barholt that will avoid the Sassaven. Can you help?"*

We can scout. We do not see everything. Storm settled back on his haunches and let out a faint whine. It brought two more Pekkanen to his side. They all looked identical to Sienne, but she kept that thought to herself. *Gleam and Ember will go now to locate the Niskanen. They ride in the plain north of Barholt for the most part, but the wizard might send them anywhere. Avoiding them is essential.*

"I remember," Alaric said with a grimace. *"Has anything else changed since I left? Anything I should know?"*

All is as it was. The wizard learned you left only when it was time for your binding. He questioned your family, but Genneva lied well, and the others were bound to tell the truth and of course knew nothing of your escape. The wizard believes you died in the mountains. Your return will be a surprise. Storm let out a strange coughing sound Sienne belatedly recognized as a Pekkanen's laugh. Alaric chuckled with him.

"I certainly hope so," he said. *"I'm sorry it took so long. Though according to Averran, it's how long I needed to master my impatience."*

You are not the same. Bolder. I see self-mastery in you. Storm stood and shook himself as if he'd come out of a deep pool. *We will return in the morning. Sleep well.*

The flood of shadows ebbed away, flowing into the night, until only Leaf was left. Alaric stood and stretched. "Sorry you all couldn't understand that," he said. "The short version is that the Pekkanen, somewhat reluctantly, agreed to be our eyes in the valley, to help us evade the Niskanen."

"Good," Kalanath said. "It is like being invisible to their eyes."

"Only without the risk of losing track of each other," Dianthe said. "What else did they tell you?"

"My parents moved to Barholt to be closer to Genneva. If we can make contact with them, they may be able to help us. Provide us shelter in the village, at least." Alaric bent to sniff the soup pot. "I'm suddenly very hungry."

"It will be a while yet," Sienne said. "The Pekkanen interrupted me."

"Don't worry about it. This may be our last chance for a leisurely meal. We'll set watches tonight and conceal the camp in the morning."

"I have finished scrying," Perrin said, "and I believe I have an understanding of the valley's geography and the route we should take. Though with the Pekkanens' guidance, that route may need to alter. Unfortunately, my attempt to scry the wizard's tower failed. He has precautions in place to prevent such divinations."

"That was always a long shot," Dianthe said. "We could try to *transport* into the village instead."

"Barholt is a busy place, and someone would notice us popping in out of nowhere," Alaric said. "We're better off taking the long route."

"Then that brings me to another matter." Perrin stood and brushed himself off. "I have in mind to petition Averran for a blessing that will allow us to speak Sorjic as the Sassaven do. If nothing else, it will allow us to communicate with our Pekkanen allies, and if we are separated, that might be vital."

"I hadn't thought of that, but you're right," Alaric said. "How late should we start tomorrow, for you to get blessings?"

"I believe Averran will be responsive rather earlier than is usual for him. He is as crotchety as ever, but I sense underlying the crotchetiness is a desire to see us succeed. But after dawn is still wisest."

Sienne returned to the fire and began chopping vegetables small enough to cook quickly. "Someone bring me more carrots," she said. "I need to do something that isn't running around in nervous agitation."

She prepared the soup in silence, and sat stirring the pot and staring into the fire until the aroma of rabbit and cooked vegetables woke her stomach to hunger. When they'd all eaten, she volunteered to wash dishes and was rebuffed by Kalanath, whose turn it was. So instead she leaned against Alaric and they sat together by the fire, holding hands in silence, until Sienne's pocket watch told them it was time for bed.

Sienne wished for the first time on one of these journeys that she could share a bedroll with Alaric, and never mind their mutual decision not to sleep together while on a job. She wanted the comfort of snuggling up with him on this night. Was it too superstitious to acknowledge the chance that it might be their last night? She lay on her back listening to Dianthe snore and let fear and anxiety fill her heart. She hated going into a situation where she knew so little. There was no help for it, so she didn't feel right about sharing her doubts with the others, but she couldn't stop herself churning over possible horrors—the wizard knew they were coming, the Sassaven would know her *imitate* wasn't the real thing, the Pekkanen intended to betray them—until they drove her to exhaustion.

She woke to Alaric shaking her foot in the pre-dawn blackness. She'd been dreaming of the wizard's tower, which in her dream was even taller and thinner than in reality, and his touch dissolved it into a chaotic, swirling mass of images and sensations. She blinked away the feeling that the tower walls were closing in on her and sat up. "What an unsettling dream."

"What did you dream?"

Sienne crawled out of the tent and put her arms around him. "About the tower, and how strange it is. If you hadn't woken me, I think I would have started counting steps."

Alaric stroked her hair. He smelled of wood smoke as well as the unicorn musk, and the dream withdrew a little farther. "There aren't any steps in that tower," he said. "It's solid stone, remember?"

She tilted her head to look at him. "Right. The walkstone. Are you sure you remember how to operate it? What if you're wrong, and we can't get into the tower?"

He hugged her closer. "Then you'd figure something out. Between your magic and Perrin's scrying...but really, sweetlove, I think getting into the tower will be the easiest part of this plan." He put a finger below her chin and tilted her head farther back. "For now, I'm not interested in the wizard, or his tower, or the plan."

Sienne smiled at him. "Oh? What are you interested in, then?"

Alaric smiled in return and lowered his head to kiss her, sliding his hands down her back to rest on her hips. She drew him closer and kissed him back. Her previous night's desire to have a private space to share with him returned, more powerful than before. Alaric lowered them both to sit on the ground and pulled her into his lap. "I wish we were home," he murmured.

"This is enough for me."

"I don't believe that."

Sienne traced his earlobe with one finger. "You're right. I wish we were home." A thought crossed her mind, and before she could stop herself, she said, "What will your family think of me?"

"That you're amazing?" Alaric kissed her more firmly, sending a rush of desire flooding through her and almost distracting her from her question. She drew back and put her hand over his mouth, stilling his next kiss.

"They won't be happy about me, will they?" she said.

Alaric took her hand away from his mouth and held it clasped in his. "No. You represent an ending, as far as my life with the Sassaven is concerned. With Gen...where she is, and Karlen with the Niskanen —who knows how long that will go on?—my parents will see you as a distraction from my duty to make more Sassaven children. Grandchildren, to be precise. They won't understand how I could possibly give my heart to someone not of my race."

"Maybe...we shouldn't tell them. I don't want to hurt them when Genneva's fate is so uncertain."

"I will never conceal what you are to me, Sienne. They'll accept it, or not, but I'm not going to pretend I don't love you just to keep them happy." He kissed her again, more gently, then nipped her lower lip, drawing a gasp from her. "Though it's not something I intend to bring up until we've killed the wizard. It's not relevant, and you have a point that it will be a distraction. So—" He tugged her shirt free from her trousers. "I intend to take advantage of you, while we have time."

"Alaric, we are not going to make love in the open on bare ground."

He slipped his hand beneath her shirt. "There are plenty of things we can do that stop short of actual sex."

She gasped again, then giggled. "I love your cleverness. Show me more."

12

They entered the valley an hour after dawn, when pale mist still shrouded the ground. Storm had been right; leaden clouds massed on the eastern horizon, low enough to obscure the tops of the Pirinin Peaks, and a stiff, cool breeze that smelled of dying leaves ruffled Sienne's clothes and hair as they walked. She wished she had a heavier shirt, or a cloak like Dianthe's, though probably the weather would become warm again once the storm passed. Besides, there was only one cloak like Dianthe's, which was an artifact that concealed a multitude of surprises.

She'd almost left her spellbook behind on purpose. After five days of walking, she knew all the new spells as well as she did the ones she'd had for years, and they hovered at the edge of her consciousness, ready to be drawn on at will. Now the spellbook felt like an old friend she'd gradually drifted away from: fond memories kept her from discarding it entirely, but losing it wouldn't break her heart. In the end, she kept it, reasoning if by some remote possibility she had the chance to scribe more spells, she'd need the book to store them. It banged against her hip as she trotted along after Alaric, a comforting sensation. Maybe she wasn't as ready to get rid of it as she thought.

They traveled westward, moving at a steady, not-quite-running pace that nevertheless covered ground quickly. Sienne had never felt so exposed as on the open plains south of the foothills. Fine, short grass covered the fields as far as she could see, burned straw-pale by the true summer sun. On this chilly day, it looked as dead as it would come winter—no, come winter the snows would turn these plains blinding white.

Far to the south, the horizon thickened and darkened as if even blacker clouds hovered there. She squinted. "Is that another storm?"

"That's the forest," Alaric said. "We'll go another hour and then turn south, once Storm's people join us. They'll be able to direct us more accurately."

"And the forest is north of Barholt," Kalanath said.

"Right. Barholt's on the river, and the tower's on the south side, so we'll need to cross."

"That's when I'll cast *imitate* to make us—the rest of us—look like Sassaven," Sienne said. "It's not much, if the Niskanen turn out to know everyone who's supposed to live in Barholt, but it should give us an edge if there's a confrontation."

"And I will cast the language blessing at that time," Perrin said. "While I believe we could enter the village unnoticed, I confess to feeling relief at the prospect of not going into it ignorant of Sorjic and in a position to give us away by my ignorance."

"Me too," Dianthe said. "I hated not being able to speak Meiric when we were in Omeira. I felt so embarrassed having to depend on other people speaking my language."

Perrin patted his jerkin, over his heart. "I do not know how long it will last, so I will err on the side of caution."

"Even so, we'll stay out of sight as much as possible," Alaric said. "There are all sorts of cultural cues people don't even think about that they respond to instinctually. Even I might not behave like a Sassaven, after eleven years away."

"Do you think much has changed in that time?" Sienne asked

Alaric shook his head. "The biggest shock to me, in leaving the valley, was seeing the really old places in Rafellin, the abandoned ones—I don't mean before-times ruins, just old construction—and realizing it's how we Sassaven still build our houses. It's like the wizard has kept us suspended in time, all these centuries. Growth, because our population increases, but no change. And innovation isn't encouraged unless it's the wizard's."

"And I bet his innovation is bent toward his own desires and not the comfort of the Sassaven," Dianthe said.

"Oh, it trickles down to us eventually. I said papermaking was important—he's introduced all sorts of improvements to the process, and even the poorest Sassaven have access to as much of it as they want. But that's typical of the benefits we get. Not much use for paper when you're struggling to eat." Alaric slowed and pointed toward the southeast. "That's Gleam and Ember now, I wager."

They stopped and waited for the two dark specks to approach, growing larger and sleeker as they came until they were clearly a pair of Pekkanen. They came right up to Alaric and circled him, bumping up against his legs and begging to be petted. Anyone who didn't know better would think they were ordinary dogs.

We followed the Niskanen in the night, one of them said. *They ride north and east of Barholt. Smaller groups go in all directions. One headed this way, but not fast and farther north. You will reach the forest before they do.*

"*Were they headed for the forest?*" Alaric said.

We do not know, the other one said. *We did not hear their orders. But they rarely enter the forests because there are no villages there.*

"*True.*" Alaric rubbed their sleek, short fur. "*All right. We'll continue as we've been going. Will you stay with us, or do you have elsewhere to be?*"

We will stay, the first one said. Sienne wished she knew who was who. *We will run ahead and to the sides and be your eyes. There are others roaming wider, and they will report to us as well.*

The second one left Alaric and padded to Leaf's side, sniffing her. *You were gone long,* he said.

The seasons passed faster than I expected, Leaf said. *I am sorry, Ember.*

I am more sorry that I chose not to go with you, Ember said. *But the child could not travel so far.*

Leaf shivered all over, and her tail drooped. *I am home now.*

Ember turned to look back at Alaric. *Is it true you will kill the wizard?*

"It's true." Alaric scratched Gleam's head again.

Ember's head dipped in a nod. *It is what I want to see, in my lifetime. In our child's lifetime. If I can help, I will.*

"Thank you."

Sienne closed her mouth on a million inappropriate, prying questions, chief of which was *You and Leaf have a child?* Maybe if she knew them better, she could ask that, but for now, she bottled up her curiosity and hid it far away.

The Pekkanen circled one another, nosing up against each other's faces, then turned and ran off in three directions, rapidly becoming black specks in the distance. Alaric led the way, following the third speck.

They ran on in silence, to conserve breath as much as because there was nothing to say. The broad plains might have been as frozen in time as Alaric suggested the Sassaven were: nothing moved, not even small wildlife, and even the birds flew in pairs rather than flocks, high as if they were afraid of nearing the ground. Sienne told herself it was a good thing that they saw no movement, which might indicate the presence of Sassaven. How well could the Sassaven deceive the wizard, if they couldn't lie to him? Best for all concerned that her team remain unseen.

This led her to think about Alaric's family. Her initial eagerness to meet them had faded almost to nothing after what Alaric had said the previous night. She had no doubts about Alaric's feelings for her, and was just as certain he meant to spend his life with her, but at what cost, if it meant alienating his parents? It wasn't something she wanted to test, but that confrontation definitely lay in their future. She refused to entertain the tiny spark of doubt that said she was being selfish.

The Pekkanen returned occasionally, but ran beside them

without comment. Sienne assumed this meant there was no danger. After a time, Alaric signaled a halt, and they all gathered around, breathing heavily but not painfully so. "This is where it gets dangerous," he said. "We've got ten miles of open ground to cover before we reach the forest. There are no villages within miles of here, and you've probably already noticed the absence of game, so we can't pass as a hunting party even if Sienne makes you look like Sassaven. All of which means we're in danger of being exposed if we run across any Niskanen patrols."

"That's true, but we have to cross this ground somehow," Dianthe said. "I think we should disguise ourselves and take our chances. We can say we're...exploring new hunting grounds."

"Sassaven are discouraged from exploring. But there are mines throughout the mountains. I don't know how close they are to here, but we can say we're returning from our assigned shift—miners work for six months, then get a month off." Alaric grimaced. "I'd say it was generous of the wizard if I didn't know he just wants to maximize productivity. You can't work someone who's dead."

"Then it's time for *imitate*," Sienne said.

"It's earlier than I planned," Alaric said. "How long will it last?"

Sienne shook her head. "Before my transformation, it lasted six hours. It might last longer than that now."

"Let's plan on six hours, then. We should reach the forest in no more than three."

"Give me a minute." Sienne reached into memory and brought the image of the confusion *imitate* to mind. The tangle of letters wavered in and out of focus, just as they would on the page of her spellbook. She faced Dianthe and began reading from that mental image, picturing the Ansorjan woman, Thordis, they'd left Perrin's family with in Esthold nearly a week ago. As she neared the end of the spell, Dianthe's form shivered just as the letters did, and in a blink, Thordis stood there wearing Dianthe's clothes. Dianthe looked at her arms, whose skin was now much paler.

"I'll never get used to this," she said.

"Perrin next," Sienne said, and repeated her confusion for Perrin, then Kalanath, and finally herself. She had to cast a different confusion to create a mirrored surface she could see herself in before doing the last. But finally the blue-eyed, fair-haired Jula blinked back at her. She dismissed the mirror confusion and said, "What about language?"

"That, I am afraid I should not help with," Perrin said. "I have only one such blessing, and as I said, I do not know how long it will last. I believe we should reserve it for use within Barholt."

"It's another chance we'll have to take," Alaric said. "Let's move."

Crossing the plains, with Alaric's broad back before her as always, Sienne wished she could imagine this was just another scrapping expedition. It certainly resembled one. But the mountains hemmed them in on all sides, even to the distant south, and it was hard not to feel the peaks were watching her. It was impossible that the wizard could see them, even if he knew they were there; that sort of magic was a priest's province. But with no shelter for miles and an absence of other life, she couldn't help feeling they'd stepped back in time four hundred years and more, to when civilization had all but collapsed after the magical wars and the plagues that followed. Then, most of the continent had been Empty Lands. This land felt as if it, like the Sassaven, had gone unchanged for half a millennium.

She'd grown strong over the last fourteen months of scrapping, but Alaric set a pace fast enough to leave her with no breath for conversation, even if she'd had anything to say. She trotted onward with her eyes fixed on the dark "cloud" on the southern horizon. The distant forest never seemed to grow closer as she watched it, but if she looked away for a few minutes, when she looked back it was bigger by the width of a fingernail paring. She alternated between watching Alaric's back and observing the horizon. It didn't soothe her anxieties.

They ran, then slowed to a walk, then ran again, over and over. The Pekkanen continued to scout ahead and to the side, returning at times with nothing to report. Sienne lost track of time and didn't want to dig out her pocket watch. That was something no Sassaven would have. Maybe she should have left it behind. *No, no one's going to search me.* The lowering gray clouds obscured the sun, but she thought it was an hour or so before noon. No rain had fallen, and Sienne hoped the storm would hold off until after they reached the sheltering trees.

Gradually, the forest loomed before them, dark and to Sienne's eye menacing despite being oaks rather than the terrible firs she'd imagined walking on their roots like giants. It spread before them to left and right as if reaching to embrace them, fold them into its leafy arms and swallow them whole. It should have looked welcoming, a protection against the storm, but instead it unnerved her. But it was their only hope for shelter.

The wind gusted, and cold rain spattered her, just a few drops. She wiped her face and looked once more at the oncoming storm. Now she really could see the rain falling in great sheets, advancing across the plains. "Alaric!" she shouted.

"I know," he replied. "We're almost there."

The forest was close enough to make out individual trees. The Pekkanen raced ahead, and Alaric broke into a run. Sienne followed him, though there was no way she could keep up with his long-legged strides. Thunder rumbled, and the rains came, going from a sprinkle to a full-out downpour in seconds. Sienne shrieked and threw herself beneath the shelter of the trees. The rain fell hard enough that some of it penetrated the forest canopy, so she backed farther beneath the trees and swiped at her shoulders and hair, ridding herself of rainwater.

"That was bracing," Perrin said, sounding out of breath. Thunder rumbled again, more loudly, and he added, "Are we safe here?"

"Likely not, but it's a chance we have to take," Alaric said. He looked less damp than the others. "Let's eat as we walk. We don't have much time."

Dianthe handed out small, skinny loaves of bread and hunks of yellow cheese. Alaric broke his loaf in half and handed half to Sienne. It was five days' stale and hard to chew, but filling. The cheese, sharp and redolent of distant dairies, crumbled as she bit into it. Alaric gestured to her to precede him. "Due south," he said.

Sienne worked the small magic that told the direction, oriented herself, and strode deeper into the forest.

Despite the sheltering branches of the oaks, the rain gradually soaked them, turning Alaric's blond hair light brown and forcing Perrin to tie his newly-blond hair out of his face, where it dripped down his back. The forest floor, thick with the humus of last year's fallen leaves, squelched underfoot, sending up waves of rich, loamy scent with every step Sienne took. Running was out of the question, here between the wide boles, and she trudged in front of Alaric and tried to keep ahead of his long-legged strides. As on the plains, the forest was still, empty of life save for the eight of them. Without the rainfall, it would have seemed a dead place, long abandoned and home only to ghosts.

She finished her meal and wiped her hands on her trousers. It was still startling to see pale skin where she was used to seeing tanned, or to look around and see strangers rather than her friends. "How far is Barholt?" she asked.

"I'm not sure. I don't know where we'll come out on the river," Alaric said. "Maybe another five hours through the forest, then however long it takes to follow the river to Barholt. We'll be there before sunset."

Sienne nodded. "I hope the rain lets up before then."

"It's early for fall rains—you would say late true summer, but in Ansorja we have four seasons instead of three." Alaric swiped a hand through his hair, making water droplets fly. "It gets rainy just before winter, and then the snows fall. But generally it doesn't rain like this until after the harvest."

"I don't know why I never pictured the Sassaven as farmers," Dianthe said. "But if you don't trade with the outside world, the food has to come from somewhere."

"Farming, goat herding...we provide all our own food, yes. We have to be self-sufficient or we die."

Sienne shivered. "You make it sound so bleak."

"It's not so bad. This valley is good for crops, and there are enough of us to make industries like metalsmithing and weaving work. But being able to leave for the outside world, or sell our goods elsewhere..." Alaric's voice trailed off. Sienne was about to ask another question when he said, "I wonder if they really want to be free."

"Why would they not wish to be free?" Perrin asked.

"They want not to have the wizard breathing down their necks, and they want to be able to make romantic alliances and worship in the open. But leaving the valley might be too much. I know I was overwhelmed by Concord when I was sixteen. Maybe it's not the same, but suppose they find the world too big a place for the Sassaven?"

"You do not mean not to free them," Kalanath said.

"Of course not. I'm just saying maybe I should have thought past the goal of breaking the binding."

"I think it might be a little early for that," Dianthe said. "Nobody's going to hustle them out of the valley the minute Kyros is dead."

A shiver passed through Sienne at the sound of the wizard's name. "Dianthe is right," she said, ignoring her sense of unease. "With winter coming on, the Sassaven have months to decide what they're going to do."

"But we only have a few hours," Dianthe said. "I hate that we don't have more of a plan than 'sneak into the wizard's tower.' How big is it? What kind of defenses does he have? What if killing him doesn't break the binding—have you thought about that?"

"I have," Alaric said. "I know I said killing him was just as good, but I've come to believe we can't take the chance that the binding won't persist past his death, however that will look. We need him paralyzed, which means *shout*—"

"Which means we can't do this quietly," Sienne pointed out. She ducked under a low-hanging branch and added, "But I feel confident about reversing the unbinding after all the work we did on the way here. We just need a bound Sassaven to stand in symbolically for all Sassaven, perform the binding, and break the chain. And Genneva will be right there."

"We can't use Gen," Alaric said. "The wizard controls his host to defend him against would-be attackers. She will have to be subdued as well."

"Well, another of your relatives, then. We sneak into the tower, I cast *shout* on the wizard and Genneva, we do the unbinding, and then..." Sienne's voice trailed off. "I don't see how we can make him reverse what he did to Genneva if he's paralyzed."

"Once the paralysis wears off, I'll take care of that," Alaric said grimly. "I'll be at my most persuasive."

Sienne shivered again. Alaric sounded like someone relishing a challenge. She could hardly tell him not to save his sister, but she wished she didn't feel so uncomfortable about his eagerness to threaten the wizard.

"So it is a plan," Kalanath said. "And I think it is a good plan that will collapse when we meet our enemy."

"Just like always," Alaric said. "But it's comforting to imagine it all working out our way, no?"

13

The heavy rains diminished to a light shower after forty-five minutes, long enough to leave them all thoroughly soaked despite the sheltering branches. Sienne trudged through the sodden masses of dead, mostly disintegrated leaves, grateful for the waterproofing on her trusty boots. The rain left behind a fresh, wet scent that mingled with the darker, loamy smell of the forest floor and made her think of late true summer storms and bonfires to drive away the chill in the air.

As the rains dwindled, the wildlife emerged from hiding: tiny red squirrels and gray chipmunks skittering from one tree to another and kicking up wet leaves as they went, robins and jays and some black and white birds Sienne didn't recognize fluttering through the branches and calling to each other with unfamiliar songs. If they hadn't been walking toward a potentially deadly confrontation, it would have been a pleasant afternoon's ramble, though an odd one, with three black dogs who didn't chase the squirrels.

She adjusted the *silence* wand strapped to her left thigh. It would be a powerful weapon against the wizard, making it impossible for him to cast spells, but if he also had artifacts at his command, it wouldn't make him helpless. Still, she intended it to be her first attack. She had no idea what to expect from a five-hundred-year-old wizard who presumably didn't need a spellbook. How many spells could you learn, how fast could you be, with half a millennium of practice? She refused to let it frighten her. People could only speak intelligibly so fast, and there was no reason to think Kyros could cast spells just by thinking them. He could be defeated. It was Genneva's fate they had to worry about.

Hours passed. They walked in silence, as much, Sienne thought, because the forest compelled it as because they were afraid of being overheard. The forest felt more ancient than any place Sienne had ever explored, older and more vast than anything she and her friends had ever seen. Only the twittering of the birds and the scampering of the woodland creatures kept it from feeling like an immense, alien being, tolerating their presence out of curiosity. Sienne twice tried to put up the hood of the cloak she wasn't wearing to block out her sense of being watched. "We *are* alone here, aren't we?" she said, then repeated it in Sorjic for the Pekkanen.

We sense no one near, Gleam said.

"The Sassaven don't live in the forests," Alaric said. "We like wide open spaces. We hunt in the forests, cut down trees, and plant new saplings. It's as if the forests are a kind of domesticated animal, like a herd of goats. Though they aren't all that domesticated. People get lost in the woods on occasion, and some of them never find their way out."

Sienne reflexively checked her sense of true north. "That's frightening."

"That won't happen to us."

"I know. I was thinking more of how it would feel to wander around this place in circles, getting farther and farther from home with every step. The forest isn't small."

"I do not like that we cannot see the sky," Kalanath said. He used his staff to push aside a low-hanging branch. "It will be very dark when the sun goes down."

"We'll reach the river before then," Alaric assured him. "Only an hour or so more, now."

Sienne dug in her belt pouch for her watch. Nearly five o'clock. It felt later, thanks to the dimness beneath the trees. She put her watch away and walked a little faster. Sunset came around eight-thirty to Esthold, but wouldn't it be earlier in the mountains? She wanted to be out of this forest well before the sun set, even if it meant exposing themselves to sight.

The trees grew too thickly to cast shadows, but the light dimmed gradually, prompting Sienne to speed up again until she was nearly jogging. A hand fell on her shoulder. "We're not in that kind of hurry, sweetlove," Alaric said.

"I know. I'm sorry. This place has me on edge." One of the black and white birds swooped past her head, making her cringe and then laugh unsteadily at herself. "Somebody tell a story or something. The silence is driving me mad."

"I've just forgotten every story I've ever known," Dianthe said.

"I know stories of the pictures in the stars," Kalanath said. "They are what my mother teaches me when I am young."

"Are they the same as the stories we tell?" Sienne asked.

"I do not know. But we see the same pictures—they are older than your civilization. So you will have to judge."

"What story do you tell of the Lovers?" Perrin said. "They are the brightest constellation in our skies."

"To us, they are the Twins. My mother called them Jugal and Jaiva," Kalanath said. "She said they are two friends who grow up together, play together, fight together—always as one. Then Jugal is accused of a crime against the *rakhyan,* killing the *rakhyan's* most beloved horse, and sentenced to death. Jaiva begs the *rakhyan* for his friend-brother's life, saying Jugal is innocent. The *rakhyan* refuses to spare Jugal, but tells Jaiva he will give Jugal the chance to prove his innocence if Jaiva agrees to take his friend's place and be executed if Jugal cannot return in one year. And Jaiva agrees."

"That's brave," Alaric said.

"Jugal goes out into the world, looking for the one who killed the horse. He has many adventures—they are each a story themselves and I will not tell them now—and in the end he finds the killer and captures him. But he returns one day and one year after leaving, and the *rakhyan* has killed Jaiva."

Sienne gasped. "That's terrible!"

"The *rakhyan* is sorry, but not very sorry, and he executes the killer. But Jugal's heart is broken, and he pleads with God to take him to Herself so he can be with Jaiva again. And God takes pity on the friends, and sets them both in the sky, where they can be together forever." Kalanath shrugged. "I do not know why it is my favorite, because it is sad."

"I like it better than ours about the Lovers," Sienne said. "That one is just boring. Two young people from feuding families fall in love secretly and come up with this overly complicated plan to flee together that ends up getting them both killed. I don't think stupidity is romantic."

"That's not the way we tell it," Alaric said. "We call them the Lovers, yes, but the story goes that the two young people fell in love without ever seeing each other, speaking to each other through a gap in the wall between their houses. Harvalt, the young man, arranged to attend a dance where Audny, the young woman, was celebrating her union with another man—"

"A wedding? I thought Sassaven don't marry," Dianthe said.

"It was one of those forced unions the wizard loves so much, but that's how you can tell the story is older than the Sassaven, because we don't throw parties or dances for that. Just listen. Harvalt sneaked in and claimed a dance with Audny, who didn't know he was the one she fell in love with. He tested her with a series of questions that ultimately revealed the truth, and they decided to run away together. So that night, she sneaked away from her home and they met outside the village and headed south toward the mountains."

"I believe I know how this story ends," Perrin said.

"Probably not. It has two endings. The one we tell in public is that the two of them were pursued by the Niskanen until they reached the mountains, where they died trying to cross. But the version mothers whisper to their children has Harvalt and Audny finding a secret passage south and escaping the wizard's grasp. That's the one I always wanted to believe. It's what gave me the idea to try to flee."

"So why are they a constellation?" Sienne asked.

"The first version says it's to serve as a warning never to try to escape. But my mother told me and Genneva it was God's promise to the Sassaven that someday we'd all be free."

"I like that version," Dianthe said. "But I still can't think of any stories. Perrin? What about all those anecdotes of Averran you allude to?"

"There are many, and as I believe I have said, it is likely not all of them actually happened to him," Perrin said. "There is one, however, that has been on my mind these last days. I do not know if it has meaning, or if it is simply random whim on the part of my memory, but I will share it with you."

A wind blew across the tops of the trees, scattering raindrops that had clung to the leaves and spattering them all. Sienne, who was still damp, shivered. Perrin chuckled. "Wind features in this story. Perhaps it is a sign." He drew in a deep breath and let it out. "One day Averran was walking along a road that ran near a stream. Tall rushes grew along the shore, and lone oak trees grew at intervals along the road's far side.

"Averran came to a place where the road passed near the stream and heard a deep voice call out to him. 'Traveler,' it said, 'we seek a judgment.'

"Averran looked all around and soon discovered that it was an oak tree that had spoken. 'What judgment?' he asked.

"The oak tree said, 'The rushes and I have been arguing over which of us is superior in strength. I say I am obviously stronger, because when the wind blows, I stand firm, but the rushes blow about with every gust because they are weak.'

"The rushes cried out with their tiny voices, 'We bow before the wind. That does not make us weak.'

"Just then, a terrible storm came up, and Averran cast about for shelter. He considered what the oak and the rushes had said, and after a moment's hesitation, he found a depression in the stream bank where he could settle, hidden by the rushes. The storm blew, and the rushes flew wildly with every gust, and the oak tree laughed. Then a tremendous, booming crack shattered the sky. When the storm passed, and Averran emerged, he found the oak tree split in two and lying on the ground.

" 'It is as I thought,' Averran said. 'It is better to yield than to resist, when resistance would bring destruction.' And he took a piece of the oak and carved it into the shape of a water drop, to remind him of the storm and what came of it."

Everyone was silent when Perrin came to the end of his story. Finally, Kalanath said, "It is a good story. Very wise."

Alaric said, "What I want to know is, how do you know when to bend and when to resist? Because lying down and being walked over isn't how I want to live my life."

"That is the task of wisdom," Perrin said. "Recognizing when the wind is too strong. And you have already done so. Did you not choose to leave your home rather than attempt to fight the wizard when he would force you to submit to the binding? That, to me, is quite rush-like."

"I suppose that's true." Alaric shrugged. "But we're past the point where bending will get us what we want."

"I believe so, yes," Perrin said, "but the story has been on my mind nevertheless. As I said, it is perhaps nothing but a whim."

"The wind's picking up again. Maybe that's why you thought of the story," Sienne said.

Dianthe took several steps ahead of her. "That's not the wind. That's the river."

Sienne hurried to catch up. Ahead, the trees thinned, and now that Sienne knew what she was hearing, she could easily make out the sound of running water. A few more minutes' walking brought them to the edge of the forest. They stood at the top of a rise that descended gently to the steep riverbank, which dropped away sharply to the surface of the river nearly two feet below the shore. Rushes just like the ones Sienne had imagined in Perrin's story waved gently with the wide river's flow, bobbing their heads in welcome.

Sienne took a step toward the river and was arrested by Alaric's hand on her shoulder.

"Let Dianthe go first," he said. "There doesn't seem to be anyone around, but let's not take chances."

Sienne stood and watched Dianthe descend the hill in a few graceful catlike bounds, barely disturbing the short grasses that covered it. She knelt at the river's edge and looked down at the water for a minute. Then she turned and beckoned to the others. Sienne followed Alaric to where Dianthe stood. "Nobody's been here in the last few days," Dianthe said. "That suggests we're far from Barholt. Any idea how far?"

"None," Alaric said. "I've never been this far east along the river. We always took the road south of here." He looked off down the watercourse eastward and shook his head. "I guess we walk."

Sienne glanced westward. The sun hung low in the sky, about a finger's breadth above the distant peaks. "Coming into Barholt after sunset is good for us, right?"

"Assuming Gleam or Ember knows where my parents' house is," Alaric said. "*Does one of you know how to find my family?*"

I know, Ember said. *We are somewhere west of Barholt. We will reach it before sunset.*

"Then let's walk," Alaric said, "and in half an hour, I want Perrin to invoke that blessing."

Sienne took up her accustomed place behind Alaric, grateful for his broad shoulders between her and whatever lay ahead. The fierce river flowed ahead of them, wide and fast enough that anyone swimming across would be swept several dozen yards downstream before reaching the other side, if they reached it at all. No trees encroached on the river's far side; it was plains stretching southward as far as Sienne could see, though there were dots here and there at the limit of her vision that might be lone oaks or maples. Frogs hidden in the rushes croaked, their voices unexpectedly high and sweet. Sienne watched a couple of long-legged white birds stalk the shallows, one of them bobbing its head abruptly and coming up with a small lumpy shape it swiftly swallowed. Sienne wasn't sure whether to be glad for the bird or sorry for its froggy meal.

They walked for several minutes along the uneven ground of the riverbank while the intermittent gusts of wind dried what was left of the rain's dampness. Sienne rubbed warmth into her arms. It definitely didn't feel like true summer anymore. The sun's final rays cast their long shadows ahead of them like gray fingers pointing the way to Barholt. Then the shadows were gone, and dim purple twilight filled the world. Sienne almost made light, but remembered in time that it would mark them as outsiders. Better to be careful, even if they were the only ones around.

Just as she thought this, Alaric slowed to a halt and she almost bumped into him. "Gleam is coming, and she's in a hurry."

The Pekkanen raced toward them, low and dark against the ground. *Someone is coming,* she said. *A Niskanen patrol.*

"Can we hide?" Dianthe said.

Alaric shielded his eyes. "They've seen us. Perrin?"

"Let us hope this has no visible effect," Perrin said, removing his riffle of blessings from within his vest. He tore one free and, cradling it in his hands, murmured an invocation. Rose-pink flames filled his hands, and one sharp pain stabbed through Sienne's head before fading gradually. Nothing else happened. Well, it was likely Sienne wouldn't notice a difference, since she already spoke Sorjic, even if it wasn't the Sorjic the Sassaven spoke. Or would that matter?

Alaric resumed walking. Sienne stepped to one side so she could see around him, almost tripping over Leaf as she did so. The three men approaching them, two of them enormous and therefore unicorns, wore red woolen vests. The Niskanen uniform, perhaps? She wiped her sweaty palms on her trousers and wished her spellbook would stop banging against her hip. Beside her, the stranger who was Perrin looked perfectly calm, but Sienne suspected it was a façade.

"Hoy!" the Niskanen in the lead shouted when he was about ten yards away. "Where have you come from?" He spoke Sorjic without a trace of an accent, completely intelligible, and Sienne sent up a prayer of thanks that Averran had included her in the blessing.

"Rantzau," Alaric shouted back. "Is there a problem?"

The three men approached closer. "Why didn't you take the road?"

"We felt like doing some hunting in the forest," Alaric said. "Nothing wrong with that."

The three men stopped again, this time only about ten feet away. The Niskanen said, "So you were in the forest earlier." His companions put their hands on their sword hilts in a way that said violence was an option if they didn't like Alaric's answer.

"We were. Again, is there a problem?" Alaric didn't shift his position at all, but Sienne was sure he was ready to go for his sword in an instant. Leaf and Ember sat to either side of him, their eyes fixed on the stranger. To Sienne, they quivered with pent-up energy. She hoped the Niskanen wasn't as observant.

"Not for you, friend," the Niskanen said. "Our master has informed us there are strangers in the valley. Have you seen any foreigners in your journey?"

14

"We've seen a few people we didn't know," Alaric said. "Is that what you mean?"

"People who weren't Sassaven," the Niskanen said. He was enormous, bigger than Alaric across the chest and an inch or two taller. He didn't have his hand on his sword the way the other two did, but Sienne was sure that didn't make him harmless. Her heart was pounding painfully hard. How could the wizard possibly know they were here?

"No one like that," Alaric said. "Why would strangers enter the valley?"

"That's what our master would like to know. He's interested in meeting them." The Niskanen examined Alaric closely. "Where are you from? Rantzau?"

Alaric nodded.

"Long journey. You have business in Barholt?" the Niskanen went on.

"We do."

The smaller man—smaller in comparison; he was still as tall as Perrin—who stood behind the huge Niskanen said, "What family?"

"My mother is Gerda." Alaric shifted his weight, and the sword hilt bobbed behind his neck. The Niskanen's attention snapped to it. Dread filled Sienne. She should have hidden his sword.

The smaller man drew his sword. "I'm from Rantzau. There's no Gerda there."

"You're no Niskanen," the big man said, drawing his own sword. "You're not allowed to go armed. On the ground, all of you."

The third man, who'd been staring at Alaric with the air of someone working out a difficult puzzle, suddenly said, "By God's own name. You're Alaric, Detlenda's son."

The big Niskanen swung around. "Who?"

The third man pushed his way past his companions. "I remember you. The one who ran away. You died in the mountains. Our master said so."

"Do I know you?" Alaric said.

"You won't remember me," the man said with a smile. "I'm Dag, Hildrun's son. I was just a boy when you disappeared—"

"By Sisyletus," Alaric exclaimed, "I do remember you. You used to follow Karlen around pretending—"

"—to be a Niskanen, yes." Dag smiled again. "I've grown since then."

Dag wasn't as big as Alaric, but he was still clearly a Sassaven unicorn. The smaller man lowered his sword. "*This* is Alaric?" he said.

The big Niskanen didn't back down. "What are you doing here?"

Alaric said nothing. Leaf stood, baring her teeth.

The big man raised his sword. "I said on the ground. All of you."

"But, Gunndar—" Dag protested.

"He's not here for innocent reasons. He means our master harm. And I don't know any of his companions." Gunndar's sword never wavered. "We're taking them back to Barholt."

The smaller man raised his sword again, threatening Sienne. She held her hands where they were clearly visible and thought furiously. Alaric and Kalanath were both too close to the Niskanen for *fury* or *shout*, disarming them with *grease* would be temporary if they changed to their other selves, *rainbow* might be too powerful... She settled on *force,* conscious of what Alaric had said about not wanting to hurt the Sassaven if they could help it.

"You don't know why we're here," Alaric said. "You don't know we're a threat. You don't have to take us in. Step aside, and go on with whatever you were doing."

Dag said, "Are you here to kill the wizard?"

Once again, Alaric said nothing. Dag's face was a mask of indecision that hardened into resolve. "I can't let you do it," he said.

"You don't want to stop me," Alaric said.

"What I want doesn't matter. You know that." Dag drew his sword. "Drop your weapons and we won't hurt you. I swear, Alaric, he just wants to talk to you."

Alaric drew his sword. "I've seen what happens when all he wants is a talk," he said. "We're here to put a stop to it."

Sienne began murmuring the syllables of *force,* drawing her target's attention. "What did you say?" he said, taking a step closer. Sienne backed up, letting the spell roll off her tongue, and *force* erupted from her and knocked him off his feet. The two Niskanen unicorns recoiled.

"Magic," Gunndar breathed. Alaric charged him.

Kalanath leaped after Dag, followed by Dianthe. The Pekkanen circled wide, clearly unwilling to interfere and possibly distract their friends, but just as clearly wishing they could. Sienne backed away, looking for a clear target.

She'd never seen Alaric fight anyone his own size before, and it was terrifying to watch the two men going at it, their enormous swords clashing with a sound like a hammer striking an anvil. Gunndar pressed the attack, forcing Alaric back a step before Alaric parried and shoved his opponent away. They circled each other, each looking for an opening. Alaric found his first and feinted at Gunndar's head, then drove the blade toward his unprotected midsection, a move Gunndar only just avoided. Gunndar stepped back and drove his blade at Alaric's side, scoring a line across Alaric's jerkin. He grinned savagely. "Take care, traitor," he said.

Alaric grinned back. "You'll thank me later," he said. Sienne realized he was carefully working his way around to put Gunndar's back toward Sienne. She rapidly chanted *force* again and caught Gunndar square in the back of the head. The big man dropped. She felt a moment's guilt at having effectively stabbed him in the back, but suppressed it. She'd spared his life, really.

A cry from Dianthe pulled Sienne's attention away from Gunndar. Something struck her in the chest, knocking the wind out of her and sending her flying, then falling, then crashing into the river.

She sputtered and thrashed, flailing wildly to get her head above water. The current buffeted her along, sweeping her downstream as she swam for the bank. She couldn't get her well-fitted boots off to make her struggles more effective, couldn't see anything but white foam, and as she went under a second time, she wished she could cast spells by thinking. *Gills* would be useful now.

The river tumbled her heels over shoulders, dizzying her, numbing her with its icy chill. She had no idea which way was up until her head broke the surface once more. She gasped, sucked in waterlogged air, and struck out again for what she hoped was the riverbank. She ached with cold and tiredness. Her stupid brain insisted on presenting her with magical options for her escape that all required her to have breath to speak: *gills*, of course, but also *float* or one of the many transportation spells. Even *summon companion*— no, a dolphin probably couldn't function in fresh water, or were there dolphins that could? It could tow her to shore. She was so light-headed that sounded like a rational option.

Lightheaded. Lighter than air.

She went under again. Three times, wasn't that the magic number? Desperate, she thrashed her way to the surface and with her last breath gasped out the three syllables of *bubble*.

Sweet, fresh air surrounded her head, and as she slid beneath the surface once more, the water pressed in around her without touching her face, as if a film separated her from it. Her brain cleared, and she felt a momentary hope that vanished almost immediately. She was so tired, and her arms ached from fighting the current, but she wasn't giving up. All she could see was black water and pale foam churned up by the current. She closed her eyes and tried to roll onto her back, float to the surface, but the water buffeted her in all directions, and she kicked her legs and found they wouldn't respond.

Averran, she thought, but something large and dark rose up in front of her. She slammed into it, her head exploded with sharp pain, and the rest of the prayer was swallowed up in darkness.

———

THE SOUND OF THE WIND ROARED IN HER EARS, RISING AND FALLING like...no, it wasn't the wind, it was the rushing tide off Fioretti. She fought the heavy hand weighing down her eyelids, but saw only charcoal darkness, too black even to be the dead of night. Someone held her upright by the shoulders, and she struggled away, or tried to; her body felt as limp as if she'd been beaten, and the hands restrained her easily.

The blackness was lightening to a pale gray, just the color of Perrin's shield, but opaque and dull. Sienne sucked in a deep breath untainted by water. Fioretti, how had she gotten back to Fioretti? She'd lost time—there'd been the Niskanen, and the river, and the lifesaving *bubble*, and she'd gone under three times...but the sound was fading, replaced by the murmur of voices. She strained to hear them.

"...not until after..."

"...don't want to carry..."

"...hair like that..."

Feeling was returning to her numb body, which tingled as if it had been entirely asleep. Her confusion faded. This wasn't Fioretti, it was the valley. Something had knocked her into the river. She jerked against the restraining hands, and the voices went silent. Sienne raised her head. The gray haze was no more than a film over her vision now, but she still couldn't see much. Full dark had fallen since she landed in the river, but did that mean minutes, or hours, that she had been unconscious? The trees were gone, and she caught glimpses of low stone buildings with thatched roofs, dimly lit by torchlight. Barholt. She hoped it was Barholt, anyway. The alternative was too confusing to contemplate.

Several blond Sassaven in red vests, two of them big enough to be unicorns, surrounded her. "Let me go," she said. It came out as a hoarse whisper. She cleared her throat. "I said let me go."

"What are you?" said one of the women. "You're a foreigner, aren't you?"

"Don't be stupid, Ellois, of course she's a foreigner," the female unicorn said. "We need to take her to our master immediately."

Ellois's jaw tightened. "What if he kills her?"

"Why would he do that? She's hardly a threat."

"He might. And her death would be on our heads." Ellois stepped forward to take Sienne's chin in her hand. Sienne jerked away, but Ellois's grip was firm.

"All right," the unicorn said, "suppose we don't turn her in. What do we do with her then? We can't leave her to roam free in Barholt, and I for one am not taking her to the border and setting her loose there."

The picture of herself as a squirrel set free from captivity irritated Sienne. "I don't need your help. Let go of me."

Ellois and the unicorn both examined her. "Such dark hair, and dark skin," Ellois said, touching a hank of Sienne's hair. It was still wet. She hadn't been unconscious long. "Where are you from?"

"South," Sienne said. "Far south. I'll go back there if you let me go. No need to turn me over to the wizard." Either the buffeting of the river had dispelled *imitate*, or it had worn off on its own, but either way her disguise was gone. She shivered, and couldn't stop shivering.

The two women looked at each other. The hands of the unseen Sassaven gripping her tightened. "We didn't say he was a wizard," the unicorn said. "How would a stranger know that?"

Sienne groped for an answer, but was overridden by Ellois saying, "Maybe I was wrong, and our master needs to see this one, Olega."

"No—"

"Are you going to give us trouble, stranger?" Olega said. "Because I'd rather treat you as a guest than as a prisoner."

Sienne glared at her. "I'm a prisoner no matter what you do, since I don't want to go with you."

"Walk, then," Ellois said. Sienne glanced up at the two men holding her. Only one of them was big enough to be a unicorn, but the other was still a lot bigger and stronger than her. They started walking, and Sienne stumbled over her feet before matching strides with them, scuffing the hard-packed earth of the road. Stone houses, their windows covered with oiled paper, crouched in rows to either side. Warm light leaked from most of the windows, which couldn't be much protection against the winter winds—

She squeezed her eyes shut briefly. What was she thinking? As if windows mattered when she was a captive. Fear filled her, numbing her brain briefly. She could not be taken to Kyros. Where were her friends? If she'd been swept downstream to the town, they might be miles away. It would take one of Perrin's blessings to locate her.

That last thought calmed her. She would eventually be reunited with the others—she just had to stay free until then. Which meant getting away from her captors. But how? *Force* and *fury* wouldn't work on anyone this close to her, *shout* had the same problem, and if she cast *rainbow* on one of the men holding her, the other would have time to subdue her. But maybe she didn't need to attack. She just needed a distraction.

Lowering her head, she muttered the syllables of *glow* under her breath. "What was that?" the man on the left said. Then he gasped and yanked his hands away from her. "Secret name of God," he breathed.

His companion let go of Sienne's shoulder, and exclaimed, "She's glowing!"

Sienne didn't wait to hear what Ellois and Olega thought. She shoved past them and ran. *Jaunt* rose to her lips, and she suppressed it. She might *jaunt* away, escape these Sassaven, but she had no memorized location nearby, and she would be unable to return anywhere closer than Esthold—six days' journey from this place. One more spell that was useless to her now.

"Wait!" Ellois shouted. Sienne kept running. The road curved slightly, though not enough for her to lose her pursuers. She needed to find a side street.

Just as she realized she didn't hear any sounds of pursuit, someone shouted, and a force like a sledgehammer took her square in the back, knocking the wind out of her. She stumbled, fell to her knees, and collapsed face-first onto the street. *Force*, except it couldn't be, because the Sassaven weren't wizards, but what...? She tried to force air into her starving lungs, blinked away the spots filling her vision, and scrabbled at the hard ground, trying to get up.

Footsteps approached, slow and measured. "You should have known running was a bad idea," Ellois said, crouching beside her. "We don't want to hurt you."

"We're going to be in trouble for hurting her," a man said. Sienne couldn't see which of the two had spoken. "If she's a wizard like our master, maybe he knows her."

"She would have said," Ellois said. "What I want to know is why she thought she could outrun our magic. She—oh, she's awake." Ellois rolled Sienne onto her back, which hurt as badly as if it had been a real sledgehammer. "Olega was gentle with you."

That was gentle? Olega had vanished. In her place stood a bright bay unicorn with a black horn that gleamed like oil in the lamp lights. "Sassaven...unicorn?" Sienne managed. First the blow that had knocked her into the river, now this. Probably she should be grateful the Sassaven had to be in unicorn form to use magic, but her back hurt too much for gratitude.

"You know about our master, but not about us? Strange." Ellois helped Sienne sit. "You really should see our master. Will you cooperate, or do we need to gag you?"

Sienne concentrated on breathing and thought furiously. Dianthe would have bound and gagged her no matter what promises she made, but these people were clearly not as suspicious and devious as

Dianthe. Sienne had to remain free if she wanted to escape. "I'll cooperate."

One of the men, the smaller of the pair, offered her a hand up. Sienne accepted it, though it was tempting to spurn his help, demonstrate some small measure of defiance. But that would have been stupid, not to mention that these Sassaven seemed genuinely kind and not interested in hurting her. She rubbed the small of her back. Well. Not interested in *permanently* injuring her.

Olega, still in unicorn form, stepped forward, dipping her horn in a gesture that clearly meant "after you." Sienne followed Ellois through the torch-lit streets, painfully aware of Olega's razor-sharp horn within stabbing distance of her throat. Surreptitiously, she brushed her fingers across the wand, still securely sheathed at her thigh. The wand was there, her pack was still strapped to her back, her spellbook—

She almost stopped walking. Only her fear of Olega overrode her closer, sharper dread. Her spellbook was gone. She made herself breathe calmly. It didn't matter. She didn't need it anymore. But her heart cried out at its loss, the book that had been her close companion for nearly ten years. It would probably fetch up against the bank somewhere, to be found by some Sassaven who wouldn't know what it was, and then—the thought of Kyros pawing over it drove away her fear, filling her with fury.

No. It doesn't matter. Stay focused. What mattered was that she was going to face the wizard, alone and unsupported, with no plan and no idea where her friends were. If she'd ever been in a worse spot, she couldn't remember it. She breathed out again, drew in a breath of cool night air scented with the resinous smell of torches and the fainter stink of animal waste. She'd just have to do her best, that's all, and hope the others found her soon. She tried not to think what a weak and forlorn hope that was.

15

Sienne tried to keep track of the turnings, but fear made that impossible, distracting her with thoughts of what might be happening to her friends and what the wizard might do to her. Barholt reminded her of the tiny villages on the outskirts of Rafellin, west near the border with Wrathen, places where people scrabbled for survival. The little thatch-roofed houses were built of small stones haphazardly arranged, not quarried stone, which told Sienne none of the mines Alaric had mentioned provided stone. It seemed like an oversight, and made Sienne even more angry with the wizard. Surely someone as powerful as he could provide *some* measure of comfort to his slaves. For a moment, anger displaced fear, and then fear came creeping back like water seeping down a rock wall, quiet and inexorable. Almost she resorted to *jaunt*.

They walked for several minutes without Sienne seeing anything that might be something other than a house. Did that mean they didn't have businesses like bakeries or taverns, or that all the buildings really did look alike? Nobody was abroad in the streets but the five of them, and if not for the lighted windows, Sienne would have imagined the village abandoned. She smelled the aroma of cooked meat wafting from some of the houses, but it didn't rouse her appetite. Her wet clothes chafed her, and she rubbed her arms, wishing she could heat the water in her clothes as she walked. But doing that to clothing she was wearing was, she'd learned months ago, a very bad idea. So she rubbed her arms, and shivered, and tried to think of anything else.

They made one more turn, and the tower loomed up before them. It had been absurd in her dream. In person, it looked intimidating. The white stem of the tower rose hundreds of feet in the air, impossibly narrow and tall. A cylinder of a room, much wider than the tower, topped the stem like a fat bud waiting to open. Its round cap of a roof, dark-tiled and perfectly conical, still looked like a hat, but of no kind Sienne had ever seen before. She watched the tower as they drew closer, half expecting the fat cylinder to topple off its perch and roll unstoppably across the houses. It looked so unreal she pinched herself.

They came out suddenly from between the houses to a vast open field—not a field, she realized, but a plain of the same packed earth that made up the roads. Beyond the plain, a gray stone wall rose between them and the tower, made unearthly by the bluish light of the moon rising over the mountains. The wall was of dressed stone, which rearranged Sienne's ideas about how the Sassaven built things. Apparently if it was for *Kyros*...

Without the tower's presence, Sienne would have thought the wall impressively tall. As it was, it was comfortably human sized—or would have been comforting if Sienne weren't so tense. Towers rose at the corners of the fortress, with specks of torches burning atop each one. More torches lit the door, which wasn't large; it looked like an ordinary front door, if a bland one. The wind's cold fingers made Sienne shiver and set the torches dancing. It was all so primitive Sienne felt angry again, and this time the anger stayed, filling her heart with the warmth her body couldn't feel. She clung to it like a lifeline.

Sienne's guards guided her across the plain toward the door, never touching her, but making it clear with their bodies that fleeing was not an option. As if she had anywhere to flee to.

Ellois strode ahead of their little group and rapped firmly on the door, then pushed it open. Sienne, following her, couldn't see the point of knocking if the door wasn't locked—until she passed through it and saw men with crossbows standing atop the towers, their weapons lowering from where they'd been pointed at the door. Ellois ignored them. Sienne calculated her chances of hitting one of them with *force* or *rainbow* before the others shot her. Not good.

Beyond the door lay a stone-paved courtyard, empty of any outbuildings. The corner towers were reached via wooden beams embedded in the fortress wall like stair steps without rail or risers. They looked incredibly unsafe. Sienne's gratitude at not being expected to climb them faded as Ellois made straight for the tower door. This one did look appropriately big and menacing, made of solid iron as black as Kyros's heart no doubt was. Sienne remembered where that heart currently resided and wished she hadn't come up with that image. Would she see Genneva as well? Crazy plans for defeating the wizard on her own, freeing Genneva, and escaping to find her friends clamored for her attention, and she crushed them. Freeing herself was about the limit of what she was willing to plan for.

Ellois didn't knock at this door, just pulled it open. It swung as freely as if it weighed nothing. Ellois held it open, and the male unicorn put his hands on Sienne's shoulders, holding her back while Olega and the other man went inside. She thought about asking again to be let go, decided it would just make her look pathetic, and instead tried to see into the dark interior of the tower.

Olega, still in unicorn form, couldn't have carried a torch with her, but the second man hadn't had one either. Whatever they were doing, they could do it in darkness, but Sienne felt frustrated at being unable to watch them. She'd need to know how to operate the walk-stone if she wanted to get back in once she'd escaped. She clung to that optimism along with her anger and wished the unicorn would let go of her; his hands were heavy and made her still-damp shirt cling uncomfortably to her shoulders.

The other man emerged from the tower. "It's ready."

Sienne followed Ellois into the tower, but hesitated on the threshold, counting her breaths and giving her eyes time to adjust. The room smelled sharply of mildew and damp, making her want to pinch her nose shut. After five breaths, the darkness had receded enough that she could make out lumpy shapes, though not the dimensions of the room. It might be ten feet deep or ten times that for all she could tell. The lumpy shapes made no sense—chairs, tables, furniture she'd never seen before? They were all so much nonsense in the darkness. She took three more steps forward—

—and was immediately elsewhere. She winced at the bright light filling the space and covered her eyes with her arm, blinking hard to clear pained tears from them. "Keep walking," Ellois said, so she took a few more steps, hoping she wasn't about to run into anything. She lowered her arm, blinked again, and bit back a scream at being face to face with a monstrous gray face that snarled at her. In the next second, she realized it was a carving of some hideous creature, and let out a shaky breath of relief.

She turned to survey the rest of the room, madly storing details away. If she could *jaunt* anywhere, she would want it to be this place. The room was a funny trapezoidal shape with two curved walls and two straight ones, exactly the shape one might expect of an outer room in a round building, like a wedge of pie whose tip someone had bitten off. One window in the longer curved wall, flanked by two wrought-iron sconces, looked out on darkness. More of the awful carvings stood mounted on mannequins along the other windowless walls, none of them the same. That some sculptor had been able to imagine multiple unique monsters struck Sienne as more horrible than the monsters themselves.

The male unicorn blinked into being at the center of the room, startling Sienne, then Olega, once more in human form, appeared behind him. The two moved to stand in front of two of the room's three doors, opposite each other. Sienne stared at each door in turn, filling herself with the knowledge of how far they were from each other and from her, where they stood in relation to the window, which gruesome carving was nearest which. She'd never learned a location faster in her life. Just a few more minutes...

Ellois went to the third door. It was bigger than the others, ornately carved with an abstract design of rings within rings, directly opposite the window. Sienne focused on the rings. The pattern dizzied her, but she clung to it, praying as she did that her mind would make the connection necessary to let her *jaunt* back to this room. She felt her growing awareness of the space building within her, an uncomfortable pressure like a full bladder. Almost there.

Ellois rapped on the door with the iron ring attached to it. "Sir, we have the intruder," she said.

The door swung open noiselessly. Ellois gestured to Sienne to follow her. Sienne gritted her teeth with frustration. So close... She stood her ground and shook her head. Ellois rolled her eyes and nodded to the male unicorn. "Bring her," she said. He grabbed Sienne's shoulders and marched her forward. Sienne contemplated the wisdom of fighting, stalling him just long enough to finish her memorization. But his grip was implacable, his stride compelling, and Sienne felt her mental construct fall apart around her as they passed through the door into the room beyond.

Instantly she knew they were elsewhere—not just in a different room in the tower, but somewhere else entirely. The space was far too vast to fit into the tower, for one, and for another, it was bright daylight, and the perfectly circular room was much warmer than the antechamber had been. The windows were another clue; if this room were truly the tower's interior, it couldn't have had windows at all. The Sassaven seemed not at all disturbed by this.

Sienne immediately set about memorizing this room for *jaunt* and found her concentration slipping. She cast her eyes on the room's scant furnishings—an ebony cabinet with inlaid mother-of-pearl stars, a couple of ladderback chairs, a cluttered table—and made note of their relationships to each other, but as she did so, her mind slipped away from them as if someone had cast *grease* on the memories.

A man stood by the window, looking out at whatever lay outside.

He was darker blond than the Sassaven and, to Sienne's surprise, dressed much as they did. He didn't turn when they entered. Ellois took a few steps toward him. "We fished her out of the river, sir," she said. "She has magic of some kind. We thought—"

The man turned around, and Sienne was again surprised to see he was young, no more than mid-thirties. She'd expected someone ancient and bent and...evil-looking. This man looked no different than anyone else, neither handsome nor ugly, and at the moment his expression was quizzical. "A wizard?" he said. "She can't possibly be here alone."

Sienne stayed silent. The male unicorn said, "She was the only one we found."

"Search upriver," Kyros said. "There will be others."

"I'm alone," Sienne said. "There's no one else."

The wizard smiled, raising one eyebrow as he did. "That's not a chance I'm willing to take. Search. Bring me any strangers you find."

The four Sassaven nodded and left the room, shutting the door behind them. Sienne once again tried to learn enough of the room for *jaunt*, but her concentration shivered and dissolved after only a few moments. The wizard walked toward her, still smiling. "Don't bother," he said. "*Sammanjati* makes it impossible to use the tower or this room in a transportation spell. I'd rather have your full attention, anyway." He waved at the two chairs. "Will you sit? Or are you going to be tedious and make yourself uncomfortable in a futile act of defiance?"

Sienne eyed him. He sounded amused, not angry, and she felt no sense of menace from him. That didn't mean he wasn't a threat. She sat and folded her hands in her lap. "That's better," Kyros said, taking the other chair. "Now, I'll tell you what I told the last outsiders who entered the valley." A curious blankness crossed his face. "How strange," he said. "I can't remember how long ago that was. It seems like only a year or so ago, but that can't be right." He shook his head, dispelling memories. "At any rate—oh, yes. I don't mind you roaming the valley so long as you don't interfere with me or mine. Try to kill me, or hurt the Sassaven, and I'll destroy you."

His pleasant tone of voice made his words more terrifying, as if destroying her would mean no more to him than swatting a fly. "What if I *jaunt* away?" Sienne asked. "Bring an army?"

"Who would supply you with one? My valley is isolated, and no one cares about this territory. And what would you say, anyway? That there's a community living in the Pirinins that...oh, I don't know, doesn't pay taxes? None of the Ansorjan kings would be willing to commit resources to bringing me under their control, not for the pittance our economy would bring them." Kyros crossed one leg over the other and leaned back. "I don't understand why people keep coming here to kill me. Do you think I have treasure, or something?"

"The Sassaven," Sienne said. "They deserve to be free."

Kyros's eyes widened, and he laughed. "I wonder if that's what the last ones wanted, too," he mused. "They didn't get this far. Freeing the Sassaven. That's unexpected. And a waste of your time, because they don't want to be free."

"Of course they do," Sienne shot back. "You oppress them, you force them to mate against their will, you won't let them worship—"

"The Sassaven are little better than children. Freedom is too much for them to endure. And, frankly, it's none of your business." Kyros regarded her steadily. "What I would like to know," he said, "is how you learned my name."

Startled, Sienne said, "Your name?"

"I haven't heard my name spoken in hundreds of years. Then, just hours ago, it rang in my ears like a chiming bell. It's how I knew you were here. How did you learn it? I doubt you have any idea what it means, but I'm curious."

"Averran told—me." At the last second, Sienne remembered not to reveal that she had companions.

Kyros looked puzzled. "Who's Averran? Some priest? I suppose a priest might have divined what I keep hidden, since I've heard God knows us all by name."

"...Yes. A priest." Kyros really had been isolated these five hundred years not to recognize the name of an avatar. "He said it was a weapon."

"And one you don't know how to use, or you'd have done so already." Kyros tapped his short, stubby finger against his lips in thought. "So what was your plan? Sneak into my valley, kill me with your magic? That would have been hilarious to watch, though granted if I were dead, I wouldn't be in a position to watch your consternation at the failure of your plan."

"Killing you would solve everything," Sienne said.

"You think so?" Kyros's pleasant demeanor vanished, and a malevolent smile touched his lips. "Kill me, and every single adult Sassaven dies in that instant."

16

"You lie," Sienne said, clinging to defiance as a shield against the horrible dread that filled her.

Kyros's smile broadened. "Go ahead," he said, spreading his arms wide to expose his rather narrow chest. "Take your shot. *Rasapadi* will do the trick nicely."

Sienne's hands shook. "It wouldn't kill you. You're protected. Your own heart is elsewhere."

The smile vanished. "You know more than I believed. All right, it's true. Attacking me won't do you any good. But destroying my heart, if you were able to find it, would take my life at the cost of every Sassaven bound to me. Ten thousand lives, young wizard. Utter failure for the cause you hold so dear. Is my life worth that to you?"

Sienne clasped her hands tightly together to still their shaking. "You're a monster," she said.

"Me, a monster? I'm just interested in protecting my research. Without me, the Sassaven have no purpose." Kyros leaned forward and lowered his voice as if imparting a great secret. "I've learned so much over the years. The Sassaven are the greatest triumph of magic in the history of the world. Through them, I will make it possible for every human to be born a wizard. Think of it, young—I beg your pardon, I didn't ask your name."

"Sienne."

"Sienne, can you imagine it? Everyone born with the ability to work magic. Would not that be glorious? You know what it's like—you can't help but want that for your friends. Your family."

"I—never thought about it. I guess I never believed they were lacking in any way." Sienne's mouth was dry, and she licked her lips to moisten them.

"Of course they are!" Kyros put a hand over Sienne's clenched ones. "This is a gift greater than they can imagine. Greater than some of them deserve, no doubt. I've almost worked out how to make wizardry breed true. The Sassaven—do you mind if I share my discovery with you?"

"Can I stop you?"

Kyros laughed. "I like you. You're spunky. Sienne, the Sassaven have no wizards. Instead, any of them who would normally have been born wizards are born with unicorns as their other selves. I've bred them, over the last several hundred years, to increase the number of unicorns born. But it's not just that. I've watched very carefully the breeding pairs that produce more unicorns, and identified the characteristics they bear. Another, oh, fifty or sixty years, and I'll be able to alter all Sassaven to produce nothing but unicorns. And then it's a simple step to being able to do the same for humans. Isn't it marvelous?"

"It's disgusting," Sienne said, cursing the tremor in her voice. "Changing people to make them into what you want—only a monster would think that was a good idea."

Kyros sat back and withdrew his hand. "You keep using that word. I—" His chin jerked up, and his eyes went distant, as if he were listening to something Sienne couldn't hear. "Someone spoke my name. I was right—you aren't alone." He stood and paced to the door, raising the medallion he wore to his lips. "He's in Barholt, and if—"

Sienne whipped the silence wand out of its sheath and willed it active. Kyros turned and flung up a hand, his lips moving in the smooth sounds of a transform. The wand went bright, Sienne brought it up to point at Kyros—and it shattered.

Sienne cried out and dropped the splintered remnants. Kyros strode back across the room and grabbed Sienne's chin. "You're too spunky," he snarled. "And more resourceful than I imagined. I was going to kill you, but I think I can use you instead."

He began murmuring, a soothing, soporific sound like a lullaby. Sienne blinked, trying to keep her eyes open. It wasn't so much that she felt sleepy as that her brain was wrapped in cotton wool, fuzzy and dull. Once again, concentration eluded her. There was something important she had to remember, something about Kyros. She tried to speak, but between the numbness of her brain and the hard hand gripping her chin, her words came out mushy.

"You don't want to fight me," Kyros said. "You will submit to my commands. Do as I tell you, and everything will be well."

Dominate. Kyros was casting *dominate* on her. Fear shot through her like lightning, and she fought back against the cotton wool. It surrounded her, stuffed up her ears and her eyes so she saw and heard everything through a gray blur. Wherever she struck, the wool faded only to rise up elsewhere. She racked her memory for a spell that would counter it, but nothing came to mind—literally nothing, as she found herself incapable of even remembering what the spell languages looked like, let alone how to cast a spell. Even the small magics eluded her. Tears welled up, trickled down her cheeks. Kyros ignored them.

"There," he said. "You'll find it's for your safety as well as mine. I don't want you hurting yourself in your attempts to kill me." He switched his grip from her face to her arm. "Let's find you a place to wait while I locate your friend. Is he another wizard, by chance?"

Sienne felt an answer growing inside her. She clenched her lips together, but heard, to her horror, her own voice saying, "They're not wizards. I'm the only one."

"'They'? So there's more than one. How many?"

"Four."

"Interesting. The last incursion—really, it disturbs me that I can't remember how long ago that was—was a whole regiment of highly trained knights. They were no match for a squadron of unicorns, of course, but I expected, if someone tried again, it would be an even larger army. I suppose even I can lack imagination."

Kyros opened the door and pulled Sienne along behind him. The antechamber was empty. "Ellois, throw up a cordon around Barholt," he said into the medallion. "No one enters or leaves. You're looking for four strangers—are they all southerners like you?" he asked Sienne. Sienne, hating herself, shook her head. "Some of them may look like Sassaven. Detain anyone you don't recognize and bring them for questioning."

He dropped the medallion to hang around his neck and guided Sienne to one of the other doors. Beyond was a hallway that curved to follow the contours of the tower. The walls were of white, unblemished stone, lit by more lamps in wrought-iron sconces. Kyros pulled Sienne to walk beside him. She tried to fight, but the more her mind struggled, the tighter Kyros's will bound her. She couldn't even wipe away the hot tears of anger and despair that spilled over her cheeks.

They passed two doors and a window that looked out over, Sienne hoped, Barholt—she wouldn't be any less trapped if they'd once again traveled a great distance, but it made her feel less off-balance. Kyros opened the third door, which was unlocked, and gestured for Sienne to enter. "Now, stay here until I come for you," he said, and closed the door on her.

In her dream-like state, Sienne surveyed the room. It was a bedroom, and it looked unused; at least, it lacked any of the personal touches that said a room was inhabited. There was a narrow bed covered with a dark blue blanket, a clothes press, and a chair the twin of the ones in Kyros's chamber. No art hung on the walls, there were no windows, and it smelled of dust and disuse. Sienne sat on the chair and stared at the door. Deep down, she raged at Kyros and at herself and fought to recall a spell, any spell, that might break free of his compulsion. Fighting made her mind cloud over more, and after a long gray moment she realized she'd passed out and was lying on the floor.

She pushed herself to a sitting position and leaned against the bed, pressing her face against the scratchy blue blanket. Despair washed over her again. This was it. The end. She couldn't fight *dominate*, she couldn't leave the room, she couldn't warn Alaric and the others... She stopped herself crying again and felt slightly less despairing that she had control in this one small thing. It wasn't going to be enough.

The door inched open, and Sienne jerked upright, reaching instinctively for the spellbook that wasn't there. An old woman poked her head through the gap. She regarded Sienne with unexpectedly acute blue eyes, sharp enough that Sienne felt as if the woman could see through her skin. "Did you try to kill him? It wouldn't have worked."

Her directness shook Sienne further. "I know," she said without thinking, "because he keeps his heart elsewhere."

"How do you know that?" The old woman advanced into the room, shutting the door behind her.

"We...it's a long story." Sienne got heavily to her feet, feeling as old as the woman, and sat on the bed. "Are you the housekeeper? Because I can already tell you there's nothing you can do to make me comfortable. I want to get out of this place."

"Then leave."

"I can't. He cast *dominate* on me."

The old woman closed her eyes and swore softly. "Then you're no good to me."

"I'm sorry—what on earth could I possibly do for you?"

The old woman's eyes met Sienne's. "Kill me," she said.

"I'm not—" Sienne's shocked exclamation cut off mid-word. "Wait. Are you...you're not Genneva, are you?"

"How do you know my name?" the old woman exclaimed. "Who are you?"

"I'm Sienne. I'm with your brother Alaric—"

"*Alaric?* He's alive?" Genneva grabbed Sienne's shoulder. Her grip was much too strong for the old woman she appeared to be.

"He's alive. We came to rescue you and destroy the wizard and free the Sassaven." It was impossible that this was Genneva; she ought to be younger than Sienne, but she looked in her eighties. But the eyes...Sienne had heard somewhere that eyes never changed no matter how old someone got, and the family resemblance to Alaric around the eyes was striking.

Genneva raised her eyebrows. "You plan to do all that? Ambitious."

"Not really." Genneva looked at her even more skeptically, and Sienne's cheeks warmed. "All right, I suppose if you put all that together, it's a lot. But we did have a plan!"

"A plan that required you to be captured and put under a spell?"

Sienne blushed harder. "That was an accident."

Genneva shook her head, her lips pursed in thought. "You can't save me. I'm lost. But maybe there's still a chance." She flicked the blanket free of the end of the bed and began picking at the hem. "Maybe if you can tear this, you can strangle me."

"I'm not going to strangle you!" Sienne stood and took a few steps away, holding out her hands in a warding gesture. "I probably couldn't even if I wanted to."

Genneva sighed and dropped the blanket. "And I'd have to fight you if you tried. It wouldn't matter. I think it has to be a knife through the heart. I hold his heart—but it sounds like you know that."

"Yes. But you don't understand. I can't. He's linked himself to the Sassaven somehow. If he dies, all the Sassaven bound to him die too."

"That can't be true."

"I don't think he was lying. And it's not something I want to risk, do you?"

Genneva blanched whiter than she already was and sank onto the bed, her hands fumbling as if she'd gone blind. "I almost succeeded," she whispered. "I almost found a way around his compulsion just three weeks ago. I would have..." She covered her mouth with a hand. "I can't believe it."

Sienne sat next to her. "There has to be a way. Alaric is not going to let you die."

Genneva laughed, a short, bitter sound like the bark of a dog. "It's not up to him. I don't care what he thinks, the only way to kill the wizard is to destroy his heart, and that means killing me. And that's a price I don't mind paying."

"Don't give up. We've gone through so much to get to this point. Figuring out the real coming of age ritual, learning how to break the binding—we can free the Sassaven, I promise. And Alaric won't kill the wizard until you're safe."

"Right now you can't even free yourself. Forgive me if I'm not filled with confidence in your plan." Her words were as bitter as her laugh.

"They'll come for me. But I want to be free before they do."

"There's no way to break that spell. I've seen him work it a dozen times since he took my heart. The victims are lucky if they figure out how to kill themselves to get free."

"I've done a lot of impossible things in the last fourteen months. This is just one more of them." Sienne stood and paced between the bed and the door. Brave words. She'd never heard of anything that would break *dominate*. She put her hand on the doorknob, and her vision clouded again, tunneling away to nothing. She sank to her knees and focused on breathing slowly until the lightheadedness passed. She couldn't even leave the damn room.

Gradually she became aware that Genneva was crouched next to her, saying, "Are you well?"

"I'm fine," Sienne lied. "I just...can't leave." Her heart ached too much for tears; she felt numb, and her skin was too tight, and the gray cotton wool hovered at the edges of her perception, ready to swallow her if she thought the wrong thing.

"Well, I can," Genneva said. "Do you know where Alaric is?"

"No. I mean, we were upriver, and I was knocked into it and swept downstream where they captured me. He could be anywhere now." If he was looking for her, he could be going into terrible danger. She didn't know what to pray for—that he was, or that he wasn't.

"I have to find him." Genneva stood. "He has to understand that freeing our people is the only important thing."

"He won't listen. Genneva, he did all of this for you."

"He was supposed to do it for our people. I'm the least important Sassaven in the world right now." Genneva let herself out, shutting the door with a barely audible click.

Sienne looked at the doorknob. If she could open the door—if she could do one thing to counter the wizard's command—*dominate* would be broken. She closed her eyes and concentrated on breathing, in through the nose, out through the mouth, until her whole body resonated with the sound. Slowly, she reached out, feeling for the knob. Its cool metal surface brushed her fingers—

—and dizziness swept over her, making her knees tremble before they stopped supporting her entirely. She smacked her elbow on the door as she fell, but even that sharp pain didn't dispel the gray wool filling her mind. Sienne pressed her face against the rough grain of the door and finally wept.

Eventually the hard floor pressing against her knees forced her to rise and return to the bed, where she sat and tried to think of ways in which this wasn't a total disaster. She wasn't in the central chamber, wherever in the world it actually was; if Perrin scryed her out and learned she wasn't in the valley, who knew what her friends would think? So at least Perrin would know she was in the tower. She wasn't dead, that was good. Probably. If the others came charging to the rescue and were killed because of her...all right, she would do the same for any of them, but it felt like such a waste. She searched for a third positive thing and came up empty. Helpless captivity made it difficult to maintain optimism.

The door opened, not tentatively as Genneva had done, but as if the opener expected to be preceded by a fanfare. "Still here? I apologize, that was unworthy of me," Kyros said. "You've already failed—I shouldn't taunt you."

"You're evil," Sienne said, but it came out weakly, with no force behind it.

Kyros gave her the kind of smile indulgent rich women give their lapdogs. "Come with me."

Sienne rose and followed Kyros from the room. She didn't bother fighting; it was pointless, but she also wanted to know what he had in mind.

He led her back along the curving white corridor to the antechamber filled with grotesque masks. No Niskanen waited there. "We're quite alone, I assure you," Kyros said as he held the door to his central room open. "The Niskanen aren't necessary at this stage."

"Stage of what?" Sienne asked, and hated how pathetically happy she was at being able to speak.

"This drama that's playing out with you and your friends." Kyros shut the door behind them and waved Sienne to a seat on one of the ladderback chairs. He paced to one of the windows and looked out. "What a marvelous day. Don't you love these translocated rooms? This one is tied to a place twelve hours offset from my valley, so I can have sunlight almost twenty-four hours a day if I want."

"We don't have anything like that," Sienne said.

Kyros's brow wrinkled. "What do you mean? There must be a hundred of these places scattered throughout the continent."

"Not anymore. Not since the wars."

She suddenly had his full attention. Kyros grabbed a chair and dragged it around to face her, his eyes never leaving hers. "What wars?"

Could he really be so isolated? On the other hand, who would have told him? "Over four hundred years ago," she said. "Countries fought with magic and with steel, and civilization was nearly destroyed. All the world you remember is gone."

Kyros's jaw hung slack. He blinked several times like someone emerging from deep water. "All gone," he said, his voice faint. "Senegyra? Papaleire? Strusk?"

"I don't even know what those words are." They sounded like Ginatic names, but she didn't feel compelled to tell him that, and so long as she wasn't compelled, she wasn't going to give up what little freedom she had.

"But—" Kyros sounded like a child denied a treat. "But—this was for them! To show them what was possible! How can they be gone?"

"It's been five hundred years. Even if there hadn't been war, wouldn't they be dead anyway? Unless they're like you, siphoning the life from innocent creatures—"

The slap came out of nowhere, cracking Sienne across the face and knocking her head back. "You understand *nothing*," Kyros snarled. "The lives of a few Sassaven over the years are a small price to pay for knowledge."

"Except *you* aren't paying the price, they are," Sienne shot back.

"They wouldn't even exist without me. They owe me far more than they can ever repay."

"They're independent, thinking beings! Maybe they owe you—though I don't think they owe you any more than any child owes a parent—but that doesn't mean you can take lives in payment."

Kyros shoved the chair back as he stood. "You're too young to understand what's at stake. Powerful, maybe, but immature and self-centered as all young people are. You probably think you owe society to use your magic on its behalf, too. Let me tell you something, young Sienne." He grabbed her chin again and forced her to look at him. "Everything we do is for the sake of magic. Society—my society; who knows how yours is different—society depends on magic to run smoothly, but magic doesn't need society for anything except perhaps a foundation to draw wizards from. *That* is why it matters so much that all humans are wizards. Only then can magic truly fulfil the measure of its purpose."

Sienne made herself stare fearlessly back at the madman. "We know your people used magic for everything," she said, fighting the grip of his hand. "We don't live like that. And nobody seems to mind."

"Then you're all fools," Kyros said, thrusting her chin away from him. "I've changed my mind. I was going to talk to your friends, maybe learn why they care so much about freeing the Sassaven, but now I think that would be a waste of my time." He grabbed Sienne's arm and hauled her up. "Stand here."

"Why?" Sienne asked. He'd positioned her directly in front of the door, so she would be the first thing anyone entering would see.

"Because you're going to kill them," Kyros said.

His matter-of-fact tone, as if he were again commenting on the weather, made his words incomprehensible. "I'm what?"

His smile curled up at the corners, lighting his eyes with unholy mirth. "It will be so beautifully tragic. Our brave adventurers, racing to the rescue, cut down by their own companion...do you think they'll have time to realize what's happened? How fast are you?"

"Fast," Sienne said without thinking. Then his meaning sank in, and she sucked in a horrified breath. "I won't—you can't—" *Make me* hung at the tip of her tongue, scalding her lips.

"Oh, I can," Kyros said, his smile broadening. "Let's see. You said four, yes? That seems an even fight, four against two. I'll let you attack first. *Jenogla* would be excellent—I assume you know that one? Burn all of them at once, soften them up for individual attacks. Or *zamphogla*, if you'd prefer."

"I won't," Sienne cried. She fought his control, but this time she welcomed the gray wool choking her vision and her mind. Desperate, she tried to bring to mind any spell, not because she intended to cast it but because she hoped for blessed unconsciousness.

She swayed, and Kyros caught her. "Oh, none of that," he said. "Stop resisting my control."

His words dragged her back from the brink, another slap to the face, but this one an intangible frozen hand that jerked her into consciousness. She felt herself stand up straight and face the door as if someone else were moving her limbs. "No," she sobbed. "Please. Don't make me do this."

"You forget, I'm evil," Kyros said. "Your tears only make this sweeter. Now. I've made some suggestions, but I think this will work better if I simply command you to attack as if these people were your worst enemies. You seem clever, and you're certainly confident enough. And when they're dead, well, we'll just see what else I can make you do. Now, stop crying. It's an embarrassment."

Sienne wrapped her arms around herself, trying to control her sobs. How had Alaric been able to live with himself after enduring this spell? She felt, not humiliated, but thoroughly abased, dirty and used and helpless. She managed to calm her breathing, but tears still flowed from her eyes. She clung to that small thing as a reminder that not all of her was under his control. It didn't help.

Kyros held up a finger in a "wait there" gesture and raised his medallion to his lips. "Give them a fight, but not too much of a fight," he said. "We want them to think they're winning. And signal me when they reach the walkstone." He smiled at Sienne again, a friendly expression that made her want to gouge his eyes out. "You'll attack the moment that door opens, and make it your most powerful attack. Don't stop fighting until all of them are dead."

"If they die, I swear I'll kill you," Sienne snarled.

"Bravado. You really are incredibly spunky. Fortunately for you I find that endearing." He raised the medallion to his lips again. "Good. Let them through, but set up a defensive position around the entrance. Just in case."

Sienne stared at the door, memorizing its whorls and grain. There was a pattern near the top where the carpenter hadn't fully smoothed out a knot, and it looked like a tiny face seen in profile: one long curve forming the back of the head all the way to the chin, another making a tiny snub nose, and a third outlining hair pulled tightly back from a wooden forehead. If she cast *scorch,* the door wouldn't burn at first, because it was age-hardened oak—she could tell by the shape of the knot-profile. But it would alert anyone on the other side that a wizard was present. She rolled the first acidic syllables of *scorch* around on her tongue and found them slipping away from her. She tried again and succeeded only in filling her mouth with the taste of bile. She felt too numb to cry, even if *dominate* had let her.

"They should be just outside," Kyros said. "Now, remember. You will protect me from our enemy. They will kill us if they can." He murmured a spell, an evocation she didn't recognize, and a faint red glow sprang up, outlining his body.

Gray cotton fog swelled up in her mind. Enemy? But they weren't her enemy...or were they? They wanted to kill Kyros. Kyros was...

The fog filled her brain, driving out every thought. She looked at Kyros. That's right. He was her friend. He didn't want her to be hurt. She had to defend him against the enemy. She had the vaguest notion that something was wrong with that idea, but it slipped away into the fog, and she didn't try to retrieve it.

The door rattled as if someone had tried the knob. Sienne's memory of *scorch* returned. This time, slow and perfect, the syllables of the spell took shape in her mind and emerged from within her. A glowing orange mass formed in the air in front of her face, hot and dense and smelling of sulfur. It grew, thickened, grew again until it was nearly five feet across. She hadn't cast *scorch* since her transformation, and she marveled at its size and power.

The door rattled again. Then it flew open.

Sienne launched *scorch* at the figure standing in the doorway.

17

S *corch* engulfed the figure, which stood still and took the full force of the fire. Whoever it was didn't scream or fall to the floor. Confusion shook Sienne, and *dominate* retreated slightly. Then four people streamed through the door, knocking over the burning figure. They spread out and advanced on Sienne and Kyros.

Instinctively Sienne cast *fury*. Six bolts of magical energy burst from her, flying toward the foe. The woman dove and tumbled out of the way of one bolt, another burst harmlessly on a pearly gray shield surrounding one man, and a third figure simply twisted to let a bolt pass by him, inches from his nose. The fourth, a giant of a man, flattened himself on the floor, then rose with a roar and charged Kyros, drawing his greatsword.

Sienne began casting *fury* again. She couldn't cast it in Kyros's direction without hitting him, but the other three were still vulnerable. In the next moment, someone bore her to the ground and put a hand over her mouth. "How do we break it?" the woman shouted.

Break what? Sienne bit down hard on the woman's hand, making her shriek and yank her hand away. Sienne spat out the bloody syllables of *castle* and hit the floor several feet away as the shielded man cried out in pain from beneath the woman. Without getting up,

Sienne cast *mirror*, and three more of her popped into existence scattered throughout the room.

She glanced at Kyros, praying he was safe. As she watched, the blond giant swung his sword at Kyros's head. Kyros didn't try to dodge. The blow struck him, and red light flared. The sword rebounded with equal force, nearly flying out of the giant's hands. Kyros didn't so much as flinch. His lips moved in another spell, and three duplicates of him appeared, the four of them shifting so even Sienne couldn't tell which was the real Kyros.

The slim man wielding a staff went after one of Sienne's duplicates, striking it in the chest and making it pop like a soap bubble. Inexplicable relief flashed through her, not that the duplicate had taken a blow that would likely have felled the real Sienne, but a more nebulous feeling that the slim man had done something right. She shook it off and began casting *fury* again. Again she had the distant feeling that this was somehow wrong, but it made no sense.

The slim man took out another duplicate of Sienne. The woman moved to where she could attack Kyros from behind, and Sienne wanted to shout a warning, but that would ruin *fury*, so she chanted faster, hoping—yes, the woman had struck a duplicate Kyros. Then the slim man was in Sienne's face, and she shrieked in astonishment. *Fury* fell apart as she dodged the staff. She backed away from the man, who snarled as he attempted to kill her.

Black metal surged up between her and her opponent, spiraling toward the ceiling. The man's face froze in astonishment, and then a *wall* of metal surrounded him in a cylinder that went from floor to ceiling without a break. The metal was rough and pitted like ore hewn from a mountain and looked unbreakable. Sienne breathed out relief and circled around him, looking for another target.

Someone grabbed her from behind, pinioning her arms with one hand and pressing his other hand to her forehead. "O Lord, have patience—" he began, and Sienne slammed her head backward into his nose, cutting him off. It hurt, but her enemy was the worse off. Alaric had taught her that—

Alaric.

She jerked away from her captor and ran for the other side of the room, breathing heavily. Alaric. Not a stranger. That was Alaric fighting the wizard, and Dianthe, and Kalanath was trapped in the metal cylinder, and she'd probably just broken Perrin's nose. They weren't the enemy, they were her friends. Terror struck her, and she once more desperately fought *dominate*. She couldn't kill them. It would destroy her.

The gray cotton fog swelled as she struggled against it, and then the compulsion not to fight returned. As she watched, tears spilling down her face, Kyros half-turned, holding up a hand to block Alaric's blow, and lightning struck Dianthe in the chest, making her spasm and then fall. Sienne couldn't even cry out in anger or despair, couldn't force herself to the breaking point to keep from hurting her friends.

The thought triggered a flash of memory, something about breaking. The oak in Perrin's story. The storm came, and shattered the tree, but the rushes bent with the wind and stood tall when it passed. Desperate, she clung to that image. Suppose she stopped fighting *dominate*. Suppose she let herself fall into it. *Bend like the rushes...*

Kyros's red glow had faded, and from across the room she saw his lips moving in another spell. Perrin stood near the metal cylinder with his palm pressed flat against it, invoking a blessing. Sienne felt herself begin to cast *rainbow* at Alaric. For a moment, she fought it, then forced herself to relax and let the syllables flow through her. A flicker of thought that if she failed at this, she might kill her lover, passed through her, but she let that flow through her too. The gray fog of *dominate* receded slightly. She embraced it, told herself *This is what I want*, and a spear of rainbow light shot away from her.

It struck Kyros square in the chest.

A green flash of light blinded Sienne briefly. She blinked away afterimages and drew in a great breath. Then someone tackled her and again put a hand over her mouth. "I will knock you out if I must," Kalanath said in her ear.

Sienne shook her head and struggled, but his grip was implacable. She tried to tell him she was free, but it came out as a mumble.

"Let her up," Alaric said. "She's not *dominated* anymore." He was kneeling beside Dianthe. "Perrin!"

Perrin ran to his side. "She is not dead."

"What of Kyros?" Kalanath asked. He released Sienne and helped her up.

"Paralyzed—for now," Alaric said. "But—"

With a roar of fury, Kyros sat up from where he'd been lying in a frozen heap. "That's *enough!*" he shouted. He sprang to his feet and backed away from Alaric.

Sienne started chanting *force* as Kyros went into another spell she didn't recognize, something smooth and soporific. Another charm. Who would he try to *dominate* next? Sienne's mouth went dry at the thought of fighting Alaric again.

She blasted Kyros with *force* before he could finish his spell, knocking him backward. He hit the wall with a dazed groan, but to her horror did not fall unconscious. "We have to get out!" she shouted. "I can't stop him."

Perrin, kneeling beside Dianthe, said, "She needs more than one healing. There is no time."

Alaric scooped Dianthe up in his arms and headed for the door. "Sienne!"

Sienne raced ahead of him, tripping over the masked mannequin she'd cast *scorch* on, and flung open the door. She recoiled at the sight of several Niskanen filling the chamber, weapons ready. Her abrupt appearance startled them enough that she had time to cast *shout*. Amid the falling bodies, she weaved her way to the window and looked out over the tower grounds and the torchlit streets of Barholt. "There's more Niskanen at the bottom," she exclaimed. "We can't go out that way."

"*Transport*," Alaric said. "Get us out of here."

"I don't know anywhere closer than Esthold!"

"Line of sight, Sienne. Take us into Barholt."

She looked out again. "It's too dark. It could kill us."

Alaric hitched the unconscious Dianthe higher. "We're going to die if we stay here. Just do it!"

Sienne grabbed Perrin and Kalanath's hands and turned so she could see out the window. She had no attention to spare to see if they'd made a circle with Alaric. She focused, not on Barholt's poorly lit streets, but the forest beyond that gleamed in the moonlight, and began speaking *transport*.

She heard Kyros moving around in his tower chamber, and then the sound of him casting a spell. She couldn't tell which one thanks to her own words echoing in her ears, but it sounded like an evocation. If he knew *scorch*, they were all dead, grouped so nicely to all be caught in its effect. She made herself speak, not slowly, not rapidly, but at a steady pace, blood filling her mouth from the sharp-edged syllables, despite the panic that threatened to overwhelm her.

Heat washed over her, the leading edge of a fire spell, her face burned, and then the welcome jerk of *transport* tugging her sideways landed her somewhere cool, with fresh air that smelled of green growing things. She dropped Perrin and Kalanath's hands and crouched, breathing deeply to rid herself of the dizziness that threatened to overwhelm her. It wasn't the dizziness of having reached her limit—she still felt as if she could cast spells for days—but a weakness in the joints of pure relief at still being alive.

"Perrin," Alaric said, "she's not breathing."

Sienne's head jerked up. They were at the edge of the forest, with Barholt a smudge of light on the horizon, and the sheltering branches blocked the moonlight so Sienne could barely see her friends' faces. Alaric had laid Dianthe down beneath the trees and knelt beside her. Perrin knelt on her other side and pressed a blessing paper to her forehead. "O great Lord," he said, a trifle breathlessly, "have mercy on me and on this woman, and grant me this blessing."

Green light flared, bright as sunlight in the darkness, and Sienne flung up a hand to shield her eyes. She heard Alaric say, "It's not working," and Perrin reply, "It will. Everyone gather round and lay a hand on Dianthe."

Sienne scooted closer and put her hand on Dianthe's knee. Perrin didn't use another blessing paper, but instead rested both his hands on Dianthe's forehead and closed his eyes. "O most recalcitrant and gracious Lord," he cried, "you gave us your power, and we beg of you to aid us now."

A faint yellow glow sprang up on Sienne's hands and arms, growing to a rich gold. Once again she felt a tingle go through her bones until she hummed with power. All the others, even Dianthe, glowed as brightly as she did. The despair that had been her constant companion for hours faded away, as if it was ashamed to share space with the avatar's touch. Sienne let out a long, thin stream of breath and it misted away from her with the faintest sparkle of gold.

Dianthe breathed in deeply and then coughed long and hard. Alaric supported her head as she struggled for breath. "Try to relax," he said.

Dianthe nodded amid her coughing spasm. "Did we win?" she asked when she was breathing clearly again.

Despair struck Sienne in the face like a *force* bolt. She jerked her hand away from where it rested on Dianthe's knee and rocked back on her heels. The golden glow still lingered on her skin, but it was fading away, and Sienne felt as cold as if she'd taken another dip in the river.

"We're alive, and that's what matters," Alaric said. "And Sienne is safe."

Sienne rose without meeting anyone's gaze. Turning her back on her friends, she walked a short distance into the forest until she was shrouded in comforting darkness. *Dominate* wasn't her fault. Probably none of them blamed her for attacking them—though how they'd known she was compelled to serve the enemy, she couldn't understand. But the memories of not recognizing her friends, of wanting to see them dead, burned inside her alongside the humiliation of having had her will shredded to nothing by the spell.

Heavy footsteps crunched through the undergrowth, and a large hand rested on her shoulder. "I know," Alaric said. "And I wish I could tell you it's all right."

She turned and flung herself into his arms, sobbing, and let him bear her up. He was warm and solid and held her without saying anything, and some of the bleak despair melted away in the face of his love. "I didn't have a choice," she wept. "I wanted to. He made me want to kill you."

"I'll see him dead for that," Alaric whispered. "You looked so different I hardly knew you."

"How did you know I was *dominated?*"

"We didn't." Alaric chuckled. "It was a guess based on what Evander told us, that separate we were a danger to each other. So we shoved that mannequin through the door first. You really are deadly, sweetlove."

Sienne stiffened. "I don't find that funny right now. It's only luck that K—the wizard was the one who struck Dianthe and not me. If I hadn't figured out how to break *dominate, rainbow* would have killed you."

"I'm sorry." He stroked her back. "You did figure it out, and we all escaped."

"But we can't defeat him. Even without me on...on his side, he's too powerful. I didn't even know it was possible to shield yourself with wizardry and not a priest's blessing. And lightning—"

Alaric stopped her words with a kiss. "Come. We need to talk this out together."

Dianthe was sitting up when they returned. Sienne couldn't stop staring at the black spot on her shirt, directly over her heart. "Don't say anything," she warned Sienne. "It wasn't your fault. If anything, I blame that unicorn Dag for blasting you into the river. We left him unconscious by the riverside, though I'm sure he woke up and ran for Ky—"

"*Don't* say his name!" Sienne exclaimed, cutting her off. "He has some wizardry that lets him know when his name is spoken, and it tells him the exact location of the speaker. It's how he knew we were in the valley."

Dianthe's eyes were wide. "That's...unexpected," she said.

"I suppose it is what Averran meant by its being a two-edged sword," Perrin said. He dropped down to sit beside Dianthe and added, "Now if only we could work out how to wield that sword to our benefit."

"He did say it was a weapon, and if we knew how to use it, we would have done that already," Sienne said.

"Sit," Alaric said. "What else did he tell you?"

She'd almost forgotten her first conversation with Kyros. "That killing him will kill all the bound Sassaven. I don't think he was lying."

Alaric went still. "That can't be," he said, but in a way that told Sienne he knew the truth. "So we definitely have to break the binding before killing him."

"Yes. But we can't even subdue him, Alaric. You saw him! He has that *force* shield, he shrugged off *rainbow*, *force* bolt barely touched him...I don't know what else to do!"

"If we *transport* back in at a time he is not expecting us..." Perrin suggested, but he sounded unsure.

"I can't even do that," Sienne said. She was starting to hate herself again for how pessimistic she sounded. "He cast a spell on the tower and on that inner room to prevent anyone using a transportation spell to get in."

"There are many Niskanen below the tower," Kalanath said. "We break ourselves on them before we even reach the tower."

Alaric took a few steps back toward Barholt and stood very still, his head raised to catch the scent of the wind, his shoulders taut. "I don't know what to do," he said quietly. "Even if we could get into the tower, the wizard is more powerful than we are. I'm not going to risk your lives on a fool's gamble." He turned around. "Sienne, I want you to cast *vanish* on me."

Sienne gasped. "You aren't going to try this alone, are you? That's madness!"

He shook his head. "I'll sneak past the Niskanen and take the wizard by surprise."

"But he cannot be killed unless his heart is destroyed," Perrin said.

"And that will kill all the Sassaven. Alaric, you're not thinking straight," Dianthe said.

"Then what else can we do?" Alaric shouted. "Go home? Let

everything run on the way it has been for five hundred years? How can we have done so much and have it count for so little?"

No one replied. The wind picked up and whistled around Sienne's ears like a child calling for his lost dog. That reminded her of something. "Where are the Pekkanen?"

Alaric looked at her as if he didn't understand what Pekkanen were. Then he blinked and said, "We sent them away before we assaulted the tower. I didn't want them hurt. They were supposed to return to the rest of the Pekkanen and wait for word. But now I don't know how to reach them any more than I can see a solution to this."

Again Sienne couldn't think of a response. Alaric bowed his head as if he couldn't support its weight anymore. "We should sleep," he said. "Maybe things will look better in the morning."

"Will not the Niskanen find us?" Perrin asked, standing and dusting himself off.

"Right now I don't care if they do," Alaric said. "But no, I don't think they'll roam this far tonight. We're safe, for now."

He strode into the forest without waiting to see if they followed. Sienne muttered *cat's eye* under her breath, and the world brightened as if the moon had suddenly grown to five times its usual size and seeped past the thick canopy of leaves. She could see clearly how Alaric's back was hunched and despondent, and her heart ached for him. "I can cast *cat's eye*," she said.

"I can see well enough," Alaric said, not stopping.

"Not me," Dianthe said. "Alaric, we can wait for this."

Alaric sighed and came to a stop, but didn't turn around. Sienne quickly cast the spell on all of them, ending with Alaric. When she finished, she put a hand on his arm. "Alaric," she said.

"There isn't anything left to say, Sienne," he said. "Please, let's just get through the night."

She could see clearly how dull his eyes were, how deep lines that hadn't been there before dragged down the corners of his mouth, and she nodded. When they continued, she walked beside him rather than behind him, thinking obscurely that if he could see someone he cared about, he wouldn't fall quite so deeply into despair. Whether or not that was true, she didn't know, but it was all she could do for him.

They walked for about half an hour before Alaric said, "This looks good." It was a clearing about fifteen feet on a side where an ancient oak had fallen thanks to—Sienne shuddered—a lightning strike. Moss grew over its bole, which crossed the clearing, discouraging saplings. Ferns still dripping with rain from the earlier storm grew along its sides and at the bases of the living trees. Alaric scuffed up damp, dead leaves that made a thin film over the earth. "It's better than nothing, anyway," he added. "Let's each watch for an hour, just in case."

Sienne lowered herself to sit on the ground. She felt as weary as if she'd walked a thousand miles without stopping. The shivering had started again, and she wrapped her arms around herself and tried to still it.

"Are you cold?" Alaric asked. He knelt beside her and put one hand on her cheek. His touch burned. "Your skin feels like ice."

"I never got really warm after the river."

He scooted closer and drew her into his arms, then lay them both down in the shadow of the dead tree's trunk. "I don't think it matters anymore where we sleep."

He radiated warmth better than the noonday sun, and she began to relax almost immediately. "Thank you."

He laughed quietly, and a little bit of her despair vanished. "As if I needed thanks for holding you. I can't tell you how frantic I was to see you disappear down the river. I nearly broke Dag's neck, poor fellow. He wants to be on our side."

"Interesting, because I would think *force*-blasting me is a sign he doesn't."

"He could have done something far more fatal. Not all the Niskanen are blindly obedient. We just can't afford to assume any of them aren't." Alaric wriggled into a more comfortable position, not that the hard ground was comfortable. "If we had their support—the ones who side with us—that would be some help."

"There must be *something* we can do. I don't want to give up."

Alaric kissed the side of her face. "All I want right now is to hold you while you sleep, and let go of this problem for a few hours. At the moment I see nothing but failure."

She turned in his arms to face him. "It will pass. You'll figure it out. I know you will."

His smile was sad, but it was still a smile. "I love you," he said. "You have such faith in me."

"Earned faith."

He kissed her, his lips lingering on hers until she tingled with something other than cold. "I hope I live up to that."

"Of course you will. I love you, and we'll get through this, and go back to Fioretti and get married." That thought made the despair retreat further. Married. It was so far in the future she could barely see it, but knowing that future awaited her gave her another tingle.

"You really do have faith." Alaric kissed her again, then tucked her into his chest and tightened his arms comfortably around her. "Try to sleep. No matter what the morning brings, we'll need it."

She was already drifting off, and heard his last words in a haze.

Sienne dreamed of the wizard's tower again. It was still impossibly tall, but this time it was impossibly thin as well, no fatter than the stem of a tulip and as flexible. It bobbed in the wind, dodging her hand as she tried to grip it. In the dream, she was fifty feet tall and stepped over the surrounding wall with ease, and the crossbowmen plinked at her with their bolts that glanced off her thick skin with no effect. If she could grab the tower, she could drag the room perched atop it to her and reach inside to pull out the wizard, who stood at the window and laughed at her.

But he should cast spells, she thought, and immediately her dreaming mind tried to force reality into the dream. Kyros waved his arms and shouted nonsense words that streamed fire and ice, filling her with fear so she backed away and tripped over the wall. The fire and ice grew and grew, the fire a *scorch* big enough to engulf even her enlarged body, the ice freezing arrows with lethally sharp tips that weren't melted by *scorch*.

Just as the ice caught fire and reached her face, someone shook her awake and the dream faded. "Someone's coming," Alaric said.

She rolled away from him and got to her feet. The night was still dark, and *cat's eye* lingered, so she couldn't have been asleep for more than a couple of hours. Memories of the dream lingered enough that when Alaric put a hand on her arm, she jerked away from him. "Sorry," she said to his startled face. "Bad dreams."

He nodded and put a finger to his lips, urging silence. Beside them, Kalanath and Perrin rose, brushing away damp dead leaves and dirt. Dianthe stood at the edge of the clearing, leaning forward in a listening pose. "One or two people," she said. "We should hide. They might pass by, if they're hunters or something."

"Into the trees," Alaric said. "Attack only if they see us."

Sienne found a large oak to shelter behind. Its rough bark scraped her cheek where she pressed her face and body close to it. If only she could melt into it, disappear completely...but she didn't even know the name of a spell for that, let alone have the ability to cast it. Kyros might know. She hated feeling so...so *inferior* to him. She was a powerful wizard. He was just more powerful.

Now she could hear the strangers' approach. Whoever they were, they weren't trying to be stealthy, and the third time one of them stepped on a fallen branch, making it crack, she wondered if they were doing it on purpose. She closed her eyes and breathed in the resinous smell of the bark, bitter and dry despite the heavy rains. The strangers continued to approach. Sienne commanded her heart to be still and ran through wizardry options. *Force* was still her most powerful targeted spell, even if it hadn't worked on Kyros.

The footsteps stopped. A soft voice whispered, "Alaric?"

Alaric, hiding behind a tree near Sienne's, tensed. His eyes were wide and startled. Without drawing his sword, he stepped into the open. Sienne quickly followed him. Even if the stranger knew his name, this could still be a trap. Her fingers went to her side and fell away as she remembered her spellbook was gone. She didn't need it. She still wanted it.

A lone woman stood at the far side of the clearing. She wore a simple wool dress with short sleeves, cinched at the waist by a leather belt too masculine to match the dress. Her pale blonde hair fell in loose curls past her shoulders, a youthful style at odds with the lines on her forehead and at the corners of her eyes. Sienne guessed her to be in her forties. She stared at Alaric as if she'd forgotten, now that she'd summoned him by his name, anything else she might say to him.

Alaric took a few more steps forward and said, *"Mother."*

18

"I know I sent Leaf after you," the woman said, "and I knew she would find you. But that's not at all the same as seeing you in person." She walked forward, holding out her arms, and Alaric went to meet her, gathering her up and holding her close. She was tall for a non-unicorn, tall enough that the top of her head came past Alaric's shoulder. Sienne revised her estimate of the woman's age.

Leaf came to Alaric's side. *Gleam and Ember went to join the Pekkanen,* she said in that hollow mental voice. *I chose otherwise. I apologize if I chose badly.*

"No. Thank you. It's..." Alaric released his mother to arm's length and studied her face. "You look just the same."

"You don't," she said with a smile. "You grew into your height. And you look so much like your father I can hardly believe it."

"Where is he?"

"Providing a distraction. Did you attack the wizard? He recognized you and sent Niskanen to my house. He thought you would go there for a refuge. Karlen insisted on staying against the possibility you might still appear."

The smile vanished from Alaric's face. "Karlen."

"Don't be angry. He did what he had to do."

"What he always wanted to do."

"He's protecting us the only way he knows how." Alaric's mother hugged him again. "It's not important. Who are these people? I've never seen anyone as dark as they before."

"These are my friends. My scrapper companions. Dianthe, Kalanath, Perrin...and Sienne. Everyone, this is my mother, Detlenda."

"It's nice to meet you," Sienne said. "Alaric has told us stories of his family. We're glad you're all still safe." She managed not to burble anything about how she hoped Detlenda would welcome Sienne to her family. Now was not the time.

Detlenda nodded politely. "I don't understand what scrapper means."

"It's what I've been doing for most of the time since I left. We search for ancient ruins and artifacts. They've helped me in my quest to free our people." Alaric took Detlenda's hand and drew her to sit on the fallen tree.

"You attacked the wizard, but you had to flee." Detlenda's tone was carefully neutral, the sound of someone who wanted to criticize but was restraining herself.

Alaric closed his eyes briefly before replying, "He was too powerful, and he had Sienne in his thrall. Two wizards against us...we were barely able to escape with our lives."

Detlenda looked at Sienne. "You are a wizard?"

Sienne nodded. "I couldn't...I barely broke *dominate* in time to get us all out of there." The memory still burned with residual humiliation and fear.

"I didn't think there were any other wizards." Detlenda returned her attention to Alaric. "What will you do now?"

"I...don't know." The admission sounded like it cost Alaric a lot, and Sienne's heart went out to him. "Maybe nothing. I don't think we can do this."

Detlenda raised an eyebrow. "You're giving up? One defeat and you're giving up?"

"I can't ask my friends to die for nothing. Even if we could get past the Niskanen guarding the tower, we don't have a way to defeat the wizard."

"He's not omnipotent, Alaric. There has to be a way to defeat him."

"Mother, we've already discussed this, my friends and I. Not only do we have to reach him, we have to subdue him long enough to reverse the binding between him and the Sassaven or every one of them dies with him. *And* he's immune to harm unless we kill Genneva. It's just not possible."

Detlenda rose and paced a few steps away, passing Sienne closely enough to brush her clothing. Detlenda didn't seem to notice Sienne even when she stepped back to avoid the Sassaven. "Then you *have* given up," she said coldly. "I didn't realize I'd raised a coward."

Alaric's head snapped up. "What?"

"You heard me. You're not thinking clearly, Alaric. All those things you mentioned, they're difficulties, yes. Enormous ones. But they all have solutions. You survived a trip through dangerous mountains by yourself and you've stayed alive for eleven years under God knows what kind of conditions. If anyone can find those solutions, it's you. But only if you don't give up before you've even tried."

Alaric shot to his feet. "Inspirational talk won't win this battle, Mother!"

"Then what will?" Detlenda shot back. "Tell me what you need from me, and I will give it to you. We are in grave danger now. The wizard won't stop looking for you, and he is unlikely to believe I didn't help you escape. It is only a matter of time before someone thinks it's their duty to tell him who your father is, and that will put Annegret and Viveka in danger as well. He might even decide Karlen is tainted and put him to death. We have to strike soon, before he strikes at us."

Alaric turned away, his jaw clenched. Sienne risked laying a hand on his arm. "She's right," she said. "We're committed now. We have to do something."

He looked at her, his eyes haunted. "I won't put you at risk."

"Me personally, or all of us?" She shook her head. "Alaric, we're at risk every time we head into the wilderness. Every one of us has nearly died at some point. This is only different because the stakes are so much higher. And you promised me you wouldn't do stupid things to protect me. Don't break that promise, or I'll make you regret it."

He smiled, and the distant look faded a little. "Does Sienne speak for all of you?" he said.

"She has the right of it," Perrin said. "This is a cause worth risking our lives for."

"You have a family, Perrin."

"Cressida and I know the risk, and she agreed to what I chose to do." Perrin shrugged. "But Averran is on our side, and that is no small thing."

"We already agreed to this, Alaric," Dianthe said. "We didn't agree only to go until it got hard. We're not children."

Kalanath just nodded and leaned on his staff in the position he could maintain for hours. Sienne said, "We can do this. Just show us how."

Alaric clasped Sienne's hand. "All right," he said. "We're not giving up. So what next?"

"You said three things had to happen to defeat the wizard," Detlenda said, eyeing their joined hands. "Tell me again what three things?"

Alaric held up a finger. "We can't *transport* directly to the wizard's tower, so we have to get past the Niskanen stationed in front of it," he said, ticking the point off. "We have to break the binding between the wizard and the Sassaven. And we have to get him to reverse what he did to Gen."

Detlenda's expression went cold and hard. "Can you do that?"

"I don't know. But we have to try."

"Genneva went into Barholt to look for you," Sienne told Alaric. "She's not in the tower, or wasn't when we left."

Alaric rounded on her. "You saw my sister?"

"She...doesn't look good. It's like the wizard's heart has leached away all her youth. She..." Sienne hesitated. "She said she doesn't want you to save her. That your people are more important."

"It's not up to her," Alaric said flatly. "I *will* save her. It's no more impossible than any of the rest of this."

"The only thing we're certain we can do is break the binding," Dianthe said. "If we can find the chain."

"It was hanging on the wall of the central chamber," Alaric said. "So you're right, that part should be easy."

"If we can subdue the wizard long enough," Sienne said. "And I can't guarantee that."

"It just has to be long enough to gag him," Alaric said. "He won't break my hold if he can't do wizardry."

"But we cannot go through the Niskanen," Kalanath said. "There are too many. And even the ones who do not like the wizard will die to protect him."

"Yes," said Detlenda. "You need an army. And I think I can get you one."

They all stared at her. "An...army?" Dianthe said.

"The citizens of Barholt far outnumber the Niskanen," Detlenda said. "The only reason the Niskanen can keep them in line is that they choose not to fight back. If they are united, the Niskanen can't stand against them."

"But aren't they bound not to harm the wizard?" Sienne asked. The image of hundreds of maddened horses and unicorns charging the tower wall captivated her despite herself.

"The Niskanen aren't the wizard," Detlenda said, "and the proscription doesn't extend to them. It's a precaution in case a Niskanen goes bad—tries to beat someone up, or rape someone. We're allowed to defend ourselves against them. We just don't take it any further than that. And the Niskanen...they're trained to keep the peace, yes, but they're not fighters the way you all appear to be. I believe determined Sassaven could defeat them."

"But you don't have weapons," Alaric said. "And you might have determination, but that's not always enough."

"You let us worry about that," Detlenda said. "You worry about convincing Lothar to help."

"Who's Lothar?"

Detlenda took a seat on the log again. "He's Barholt's headman. If you want all the villagers to help, you need his support. Otherwise you'd have to spend a week convincing each person separately, and you don't have a week. Lothar and Arris and Brigit...get them behind you, and they'll build you an army."

Alaric released Sienne and started pacing. "How soon?"

"Just after dawn. But we have to be able to reach them, and there are Niskanen patrols in the streets and a cordon around the village." Detlenda said this matter-of-factly, as if these obstacles were nothing.

"And we need to find Genneva," Sienne said. "She may still be in Barholt. No one will touch her, so the patrols won't matter to her."

"That, to me, sounds very much as if we are in need of scrying," Perrin said. He withdrew his tattered riffle of blessings from within his jerkin and flicked through it. "I have one left, and will pray for others after dawn has come."

"We need a safe place to *transport* to within Barholt, so we can bypass the cordon," Alaric said. "I'd prefer not to take the risks associated with *vanish* when none of us know the village well enough to find a rendezvous. Your home, Mother?"

Detlenda shook her head. "Karlen is likely still there, waiting for you to return. I pray he doesn't learn that Ellard concealed my absence, or Ellard might be in danger. But Annegret's home is a possibility. I don't think she and Viveka are being watched."

Alaric turned to Sienne. "You can't cast *transport* from a scryed image?"

"Not *transport*. I can *jaunt* anywhere I can see, and build up an image to *transport* to once I've *jaunted* there." This might actually work. Sienne tried not to become too excited. There were also many ways in which it could fail. If she *jaunted* into a stranger's home and caused an alarm, she might have more than Niskanen patrols to worry about.

Alaric's lips drew into a thin, hard line. "I don't like the risks there. If you startle Annegret or Viveka—"

"That's a very small risk." Privately Sienne decided if she woke the two women, she'd *force*-blast them before they could raise an alarm. "And if we go now, they won't even be awake. Who are they, anyway?"

"Oh. Annegret is my father's sister and Viveka is her daughter. My cousin. Relations we can't openly acknowledge because they're through my father."

Sienne remembered what Leaf had said about Viveka waiting for Alaric and decided not to ask any more questions. If Alaric and Viveka had a history, that was none of her business.

Perrin had already settled himself on the leaf-strewn ground. "Sit with me," he invited Sienne. Sienne sat cross-legged opposite him as he held out a square of rice paper midway between them. "O great Lord, have mercy on me and grant this blessing," he said.

Blue flames consumed the paper and spread, flowing across the air as if an invisible sheet of oil hung vertically before him. As quickly as they had spread, they vanished, and the air thickened and shimmered in a perfect circle that bled heat like a true summer day. Colors swam across it, gradually shrinking and becoming more defined until, with a snap, dim blue shadows touched with gold hung there like a window on another place. Sienne resisted the urge to reach into it.

"It's not lit well enough," she said. "Hang on. I want to try something." It wasn't supposed to be possible, but maybe that just meant no one had ever tried. She focused on one corner of the "picture" and summoned a magic light, not where she was, but within the image.

A cold white light appeared, shivered, blinked a couple of times, then began to fade. Sienne focused her will on it. The light hesitated, halfway extinguished, then glowed more brightly. It illuminated a room whose size was hard to judge in the hard white light that gave everything sharp edges and crisp shadows. "Can you pull back?"

Perrin nodded. The image widened at the edges until it looked like she was standing in one corner. A stone hearth, its fire banked, filled one wall. Opposite it stood a table with a couple of chairs, both of them rough-hewn, but in a way that suggested it was intentional. A round braided rug in green, red, and cream covered the center of the floor, its colors arranged at random. A glow warmer than her light's tinged one side of the image, suggesting there was a window on that side.

She took a few moments to anchor herself in the clearing, give herself a memory to return to, and then focused on the rug. Even if the colors were popular, their arrangement here had to be unique. She followed the non-pattern, taking it into her, committing it to memory, and as the rug filled her vision, she chanted the syllables of *jaunt*.

A jerk, a stumble, and she was on her knees on the rug. She managed not to trip into the table or knock over a chair and immediately began committing the room to memory for *transport*. She idly wished she had time to check her pocket watch, to give her some idea of how much time they had before dawn, but it didn't really matter. What mattered was getting everyone into this house before one of its occupants got up for a drink of water or something and discovered Sienne.

She was used to the noises of Fioretti, which never truly slept. Even Master Tersus's quiet neighborhood always murmured with the sound of small nocturnal animals prowling or the wind disturbing the leaves of the ash or cypress trees that grew along the street or in people's gardens. Barholt, by contrast, was eerily still. Sienne felt as if she'd gone deaf, or that she hadn't *jaunted* into a place, but was trapped inside Perrin's silent scrying. She almost would have welcomed the sound of Niskanen boots tromping along the street.

The window with its oiled paper made the light outside a bright smear. If the lamps burned all night, that seemed a waste of fuel. She scanned the room, noting the two doors that didn't quite fit square in their frames and the metal vase of flowers that had just begun to wilt. Her memory of the small room settled deep into her bones, to be called up when necessary.

With a final deep breath, she *jaunted* back to the small clearing. "It will take two trips," she said. "Alaric, Leaf, and Detlenda first."

It was hard to remember she'd only had *transport* for a week, given how easily she'd taken to it. That, she thought, was her natural ability with spells and not her enhanced powers. Sienne found that satisfying, knowing she had skills that hadn't been given her by accident. When she arrived in the tiny front room a second time with Kalanath, Perrin, and Dianthe, Detlenda was gone. "She went to wake Annegret," Alaric whispered. The room was incredibly crowded with all of them in it. Sienne thought about sitting, but decided that was presumptuous. They were guests, after all, and uninvited ones.

Yellow light flared beneath one of the doors, and Sienne heard muffled voices. She stilled her toe, which had begun to tap nervously, and sidled up to Alaric. "You do trust your aunt, don't you?" she asked.

Alaric nodded. His attention was fixed on the door. "Some paternal relations don't keep up the connection. Too dangerous. But Annegret, after Viveka's father died, said she didn't want to lose what little family she had left."

"That sounds brave."

"It is." Alaric looked down at her. "Sienne. About Viveka—"

The door swung open, flooding the front room with a warm light that outshone Sienne's cold magical one. A strange woman stepped through, followed by Detlenda and another woman. The first woman had blonde hair darker than usual for a Sassaven and was considerably shorter than the other two. She showed no surprise at the foreigners filling her house. "Alaric," she said in a deep, commanding voice that seemed the wrong size for her body. "We thought you'd died."

"I never did," Detlenda said.

"You were a fool. Or at least that's what we thought. Not so much a fool, apparently." The small woman came forward to clasp Alaric's hands. "It's good to see you."

"Thank you, Annegret," Alaric said. "I apologize for invading your home."

Annegret's mouth curled up at the corners in a wry smile. "It seems you had no choice."

"Even so," Alaric said. He looked past his mother to the third woman. She was younger than Annegret and Detlenda, and beautiful, with a heart-shaped face and pale blonde hair curling loose to the small of her back. "Viveka. It's good to see you."

Viveka walked toward him, moving as if in a dream. "Alaric," she said when she stood next to him. Then she took his face in both her hands and kissed him full on the lips.

19

A spark of jealousy, white hot and burning brighter than her magical spark, shot through Sienne. All her resolve about letting Alaric's past stay in the past, her certainty of how he felt for her, was scoured away by that one kiss. She firmly told herself *She kissed him, it doesn't mean anything* and refused to let her inner turmoil show.

Alaric had gone very still when Viveka kissed him, his eyes wide and astonished. When she released him, he said, "Ah. I'm...glad to be back."

"I knew you'd return," Viveka breathed. Her eyes were bright and adoring, and her smile was brilliant. "Someday, you'd come back with the secret to freeing us."

"Ah...yes. That's why we're here. Annegret, Viveka, let me introduce you to my companions. Kalanath, Perrin, Dianthe, and... Sienne." He indicated each of them in turn, lingering over Sienne's name just enough to make Viveka's expression grow confused. Sienne couldn't decide if she wanted him to kiss her in public or go on pretending she was nothing to him.

"Together, we've worked out a way to release the Sassaven from the wizard's control," Alaric went on. "But it means getting to him, and there are too many Niskanen in the way."

"I intend to take them to see Lothar," Detlenda said. "He can convince the citizens of Barholt to fight on our side."

Annegret laughed, a derisive sound. "Fight? Against the Niskanen? You're mad!"

"Hardly that," Detlenda replied. "This is our chance, Annegret. We have to seize it or be forever slaves."

"Lothar is practical, and what's more, he's conservative," Annegret said. "He won't want to risk his people—"

"They are already at risk," Alaric said. "The wizard controls you utterly. Just because he doesn't exert that control doesn't mean he doesn't have it. We will never have this chance again."

Annegret looked from Alaric to Detlenda and back again. "It's your choice," she said. "I just think it's a fool's errand. Especially since there are still Niskanen patrols about. How do you plan to get to Lothar's house, crossing the river and all?"

"We have magic," Alaric said, nodding at Sienne. Sienne smiled and tried to look confident, though she was having trouble looking anywhere but at Viveka.

"A wizard?" Annegret exclaimed. "Doesn't that make her—"

Someone pounded on the outside door, making it shake in its frame. "Annegret!" a male voice shouted. "I know you're in there."

Detlenda said, "Karlen. He must have discovered my absence."

"Quick," Annegret said, "into the bedroom."

The door flew open and a man entered. He was no unicorn, but was still fairly tall, with broad shoulders and blond hair cut very short. His gaze immediately locked on Alaric. "Secret name of God," he breathed. "I didn't actually believe I'd find you here." His voice sounded uncannily like Alaric's, if not quite as deep.

"Karlen," Alaric said. He shifted his weight in a way that told Sienne he was ready for a fight. "I'm glad the wizard didn't punish you when he found out whose brother you are."

"He's not punitive like that," Karlen said. Alaric let out a short bark of laughter, and Karlen frowned. "You know he's not."

"I know he keeps our people enslaved with the help of Sassaven like you," Alaric said.

Karlen's frown deepened. He took a few more steps into the room. Another man followed him, this one shorter and stockier. One glance was enough to tell Sienne this was Ellard, Alaric's father. Detlenda was right; they looked like twins born twenty-five years apart. Alaric saw him and froze. "Father," he said.

Ellard pushed past Karlen and put his arms around his son. "It's so good to see you," Ellard whispered. "You've grown."

Alaric smiled. "A little."

Ellard pounded him on the back and released him. "I apologize," he said to Detlenda. "I kept up the ruse as long as I could."

"I guessed, when I learned Mother had slipped away, that she might come here," Karlen said. "I didn't know how good my luck would be. Alaric, you and these strangers are coming with me."

Alaric took two steps that put him face to face with Karlen. "How, exactly, did you plan to enforce that?"

Karlen looked up at him without a trace of fear. "I'm asking, Alaric. You're endangering the Sassaven by remaining at large. I swore to protect them."

"You swore to keep them enslaved," Alaric said. "What's the point of being alive if you're not allowed to truly live?"

"Romantic words," Karlen said, "and pointless ones. We'd be dead if not for the wizard. He protects us."

"Some protection." Alaric took a step forward, towering over his brother. "I escaped him once tonight. I'm not going back there and I'm certainly not turning my friends over to him."

"Karlen, don't you see that Alaric can give us a chance to live in freedom?" Viveka said. "You don't have to serve the wizard. Step aside."

Karlen looked at Viveka, and his expression softened. Sienne's heart sank. Karlen, in love with Viveka, as was painfully obvious even to her. And Viveka in love with Alaric. What a coil. "You know what I'm sworn to do," Karlen said. "Alaric brings nothing but death."

"That's up to you," Alaric said. "I won't kill you, but I won't give myself up to you either."

"The Niskanen will be here soon," Karlen said, tapping the medallion he wore that was the twin of Kyros's. "I don't want anyone hurt. Come with me willingly, and it doesn't have to come to a fight."

"You'd have to *force* me," Alaric said, laying a peculiar emphasis on the word "force." Sienne, still watching Viveka, startled. Slowly she took a step to the side, then another, until she was out of reach of Karlen and had a good view of him. She probably should have done this the moment Karlen made his first demand. Stupid, stupid!

Muttering under her breath, she began reciting the syllables of *force*. Karlen's attention immediately snapped to her. "What is she saying?" he said. He reached for her, and Alaric stopped him. "It's magic!"

"Wizardry," Alaric said, and *force* erupted from Sienne and struck her target. Karlen jerked and folded at the knees. Alaric caught him and gently lowered him to the ground, though Sienne knew Karlen couldn't feel anything in that state.

"We have to get out of here," Alaric said. "If he summoned the Niskanen—I'm sorry, Annegret. We've put you in danger."

"If you're right, this danger is the least of our worries," Annegret said with a wry smile. "Let's go to Lothar, and move quickly."

"Just a minute," Dianthe said. She unlooped the medallion from around Karlen's neck and pressed it to the inside of her cloak. It blurred, seemed to melt, and turned into an irregular cloth patch of blue and silver. "You never know," she told the others. "And this will slow him down."

"Lead on, Mother," Alaric said.

Detlenda opened the door, allowing Leaf to slink out before her. The Sassaven checked both directions before slipping out and gesturing to them to follow. Sienne winced at how long it took all of them to leave. Five scrappers, four Sassaven, one Pekkanen...it would be a miracle if they could reach this Lothar's house without being noticed and no doubt starting another fight.

Leaf trotted before Detlenda, followed by Ellard and Annegret.

Sienne took up her usual position behind Alaric as they hurried through the midnight streets of Barholt, their footsteps muffled by the hard earth. The longer she stayed in the village, the more questions she had. How many hundreds of feet over hundreds of years were needed to pack this ground hard as rock? And why did the streets curve the way they did, not sharply, but just a little bit out of true? It was hard for Sienne to imagine a village that hadn't changed at all in five hundred years except maybe to expand as the population grew. Which was another question—how hadn't it expanded into a town or a city in all that time?

Viveka stayed close beside Alaric as they ran. Her proximity irritated Sienne. The woman was a fool not to see Alaric was indifferent to her. Not that he'd done much to dissuade her. Sienne reminded herself that there hadn't been time for anything like that, but she couldn't stop wishing Alaric had been more overtly dismissive of his cousin. Not shove her away, of course, but...Sienne mentally slapped herself. She was being stupid. There was nothing to be jealous of, and she ought to feel sorry for Viveka, who'd nursed her grand passion all these years for nothing. Too bad she couldn't be attracted to Karlen instead. That would solve all manner of problems.

She realized she could hear rushing water and smell the dark, silty wetness of the river just before Leaf turned and harried them back. "Someone's coming," Dianthe whispered, and Sienne and Alaric ducked out of sight, with Viveka following. Sienne prayed the others had found hiding places. They did not need another encounter with Niskanen as they were trying to reach Lothar.

She heard footsteps and held her breath as if that would make her invisible. Too late to cast *vanish*, as whoever it was might hear her speaking. Was it a mistake not to have made everyone invisible? No, because that was the fast path to losing contact with each other. All of them stumbling around, unable to see the others...she closed her eyes so their gleam wouldn't give her away and pressed her face into Alaric's arm.

The footsteps paused. "Left," a woman said. "And be careful. If they're on the streets, they might be able to ambush us. These people, whoever they are, are dangerous."

"Against all of us?" a man said, sounding incredulous. "They're not God."

"Watch how you blaspheme," the woman said, but without rancor. "And our master was very clear that they have magic like his. You want to face that alone?"

"No," the man said. The footsteps receded into the distance. Sienne, feeling dizzy, took in a breath. Alaric's arm tightened around her briefly before releasing her.

"Let's move," he said quietly.

Viveka hadn't noticed how Alaric had put his arm protectively around Sienne. "That was close," she said. She took Alaric's hand. "I'm glad you're here."

Alaric gently extricated his hand from her grip. "We have a lot to talk about," he said.

Sienne winced. *She* knew what he meant, but even in the dim light Viveka's face glowed with happiness, as if she'd understood his words differently. "Later," she said. "I see the others."

They regrouped near the river's edge. A wooden bridge on stone pilings crossed it, lying close enough to the river's surface that it was dark in places with water. Like the streets, it curved, not in an arch like an ordinary bridge, but in a flat, angular series of zigs and zags as if it were following a foundation they couldn't see.

They trotted across it, not trying hard to stay silent. The four Sassaven wore the same soft-soled leather boots Sienne had seen on the Niskanen, and Leaf moved as silently as her namesake, but the rest of them in their hard-soled boots sounded like a cattle stampede, with Alaric their heavy-footed leader. Sienne winced every time her foot came down on the bridge and made a complicated noise, part thump, part creak. When they were finally across, she couldn't stop herself running a few more steps to dissociate herself from the tremendous din.

They ran on, Detlenda taking turns at what seemed to Sienne random. Most of the houses were dark, and few lights burned outside them. She thought about making everyone stop for *cat's eye*, but her sense of being watched, of the wizard's baleful gaze on them all, made her eager for the shelter of a house and disinclined to waste time. It was silly, she knew, because the wizard had no magic for perception, but the memory of *dominate* wouldn't leave her.

Detlenda came to a stop in front of a house half again as large as the others. Its thatched roof gleamed silver in the moonlight, and its windows were thick, bubbly glass slabs instead of oiled paper. No light shone behind them, though a lantern burned above the door. It flickered as if low on oil. Detlenda opened the door without knocking and gestured for the others to enter.

The unlit room beyond smelled of wood smoke and tallow candles, a smell that would have been comforting if Sienne hadn't felt so tense. What little light came through the thick windows showed only that it was mostly empty, and despite how many people there were, it didn't feel cramped. She felt around until her hand landed on a candlestick, then summoned her spark and lit the candle. Despite her care, the fist-sized flame made a quarter of the waxy length run like water down the candle and painfully over her hand. She dismissed spark and used the candle to light its neighbors. The light would be visible outside, but they couldn't stand around in darkness.

She turned to see Viveka watching her. The woman's eyes were wide and her jaw slack. "You do have magic," she whispered. "It's astonishing. Why are you not on the wizard's side?"

"Because what he's doing is wrong. Having wizardry in common isn't enough to overcome that," Sienne snapped, more hotly than she'd intended.

Viveka recoiled slightly. "I'm sorry. I meant no offense. I just meant—I thought magic was what made him the way he is."

"Maybe. I think he'd try to control people even if he didn't have magic." Sienne saw Alaric watching the two of them. He had the look of someone whose two worlds were colliding and who was powerless to stop it. Despite herself, Sienne had to admit that from a certain perspective, it was pretty funny. She wished, irrationally, that Alaric had told her about Viveka—though why would he, if he no longer felt anything for his cousin and likely hadn't made her any promises? She made herself smile at Viveka and then set the candlestick on the table.

The light from the candles confirmed that they were in a large, mostly empty room. A chair more finely crafted than the ones in Annegret's house was pulled up behind a table, also ornate, at least by Sassaven standards. A shelf on the wall behind it held a handful of tattered books with worn leather covers. Sienne stood next to the only other furniture in the room, a narrow table that ran the length of the wall from the door to the corner. In addition to the many candlesticks, the table held stacks of paper and writing supplies. The paper, fine and white and neatly trimmed, looked out of place in this rustic environment.

Detlenda stood next to the interior door and knocked loudly enough that Sienne wanted to shush her. She moved closer to Alaric and said, "Is this all because he's the village headman, or whatever you call him?"

"You mean, the size of the house?" Alaric nodded. "The house goes with the office. This room is where he sees people to make judgments. If he resigns, he moves out."

"I thought you'd never been here before."

"I haven't. This is just how it works. There's a house like this in Rantzau where I grew up where the village chief lives."

The door opened. "It's well after midnight," a petulant voice said. "What in—"

A tall man, the biggest Sienne had ever seen, emerged from the dark room beyond. His blond hair was in disarray and he wore a nightshirt Sienne would have found comical if he weren't so muscular and solid. Nothing about him made her want to laugh, though he had to duck his head to avoid cracking it on the lintel. He stopped just inside the room and stared at them all. "This couldn't wait until morning?" he said. His querulous tone didn't suit him at all.

"Take a better look, Lothar," Detlenda said. "You'll understand why it couldn't wait."

Lothar scanned the room. His eye immediately stopped on

Kalanath, who regarded him calmly. "Strangers," he said. Then his eyes widened. "The strangers our master is after!"

"That's right," Alaric said.

Lothar turned on him. "Who are—wait. You look just like..." His gaze flicked from Alaric to Ellard and back. "You're the son who fled. We thought you died in the mountains."

"I survived to make it south," Alaric said. "Now I'm back, and my friends and I intend to destroy the wizard and free my people."

"Free..." Lothar put a hand on the door frame. His stunned expression didn't suit him either. "Detlenda, you brought them here? Why?"

Detlenda glanced at Alaric and nodded to him to continue. "We need the Sassaven's help," he said. "We can't reach the wizard's tower because it's guarded by the Niskanen. We want you to fight."

Lothar's eyes widened. Then he laughed. "Us, fight? We're not trained for that! The Niskanen will scatter us like goats in a storm."

"This is our chance to free ourselves," Alaric said. "I think the Sassaven can stand strong if those are the stakes. And my mother believes you're the one who can convince them to fight."

"I can't convince them to take up a fool's quest," Lothar said. "They're not stupid."

"I'm no fool," Alaric said. "I've spent the last eleven years searching for a way to free the Sassaven, and with the help of my friends, I've found it. Look at me. Take my hand. What do you see?"

Lothar, with some hesitation, took Alaric's confidently proffered hand. His brow furrowed. "You've been through the coming of age ritual," he said. "How is that possible? You're not bound!"

"It's one of the things we found, the original version of the ritual," Alaric said. "We know how to separate the binding from it, and that means we know how to reverse it. All we need is to reach the wizard. We can release the Sassaven and kill him. I wouldn't make that promise if I weren't sure."

Lothar let go Alaric's hand. "Then you don't know," he said. "Your sister—"

"Is his host, yes," Alaric said. "We'll free her too."

"I don't see how. He doesn't give up what's his."

"You let us worry about that."

"You've been gone too long if you don't remember what he's like," Lothar said, shaking his head. "Let's say for the moment I convince the people to rise up against him. I'll even grant you your absurd belief that we can defeat the Niskanen. What then? We're incapable of attacking our master directly. And he won't allow us to go on living once we've shown our disobedience. We'd just stand there and meekly be slaughtered. I won't be party to that."

"That won't happen," Alaric said. "The wizard will be too busy fighting us to have any attention to spare for you. And I promise you we'll defeat him."

"How can you make such a promise? I've seen no evidence that you have the kind of power that would take."

"Anything I show you to demonstrate my power would draw attention to this house," Sienne said, startling Lothar into turning his gaze away from Alaric. She summoned a spark and encouraged it to burn for several seconds. Lothar flinched. "I'm a wizard too. And I'll be honest, I'm not as powerful as he is. But the five of us have taken on challenges as great as this and survived. We wouldn't ask this of you if we weren't sure we could make good on our word."

Lothar looked at Alaric again. "And if he controls your will? No one can fight that."

"Sienne has," Alaric said, nodding at her. "She knows how to break free of *dominate*, and none of us will be caught by it."

Lothar's lips twisted, and his eyes went distant as if he were thinking hard about something. Turning away, he said to Detlenda, "And you support this?"

"We'll never have a better chance," Detlenda said. "And before you make your next objection, my son and his friends will be in even more danger than we are."

Lothar closed his mouth. He shook his head. "I can't order the Sassaven into danger."

"Then give them a choice," Alaric said. "Tell them what's at stake and let them decide. There aren't many Niskanen, and the Sassaven can overwhelm them if even a fraction of the population rises up. We can't do this without them."

"Then what will you do if I refuse?" Lothar said, his voice once again petulant.

Alaric tilted his head to look up at the big man. It made for the oddest illusion, that Alaric was, for once, normal size. "Then we'll attack directly," he said, "and many people will die. But one way or another, we *will* do what we came for."

Lothar regarded him steadily. Something changed behind his eyes. "I see," he said. "When do you want this attack?"

"As soon as you can gather everyone." Alaric gave no overt sign of relief, but Sienne knew him well enough to recognize a loosening of tension in his shoulders.

"That will take a few hours. I assume you can't wait until dawn."

"It's a tradeoff. The longer the Niskanen go without someone to fight, the less alert they'll be, but the more time they'll have to prepare a counterattack." Alaric ran his hand through his short hair. "What can we do to speed things along?"

"Nothing. The Sassaven don't know you. They need to hear this from people they trust." Lothar sighed. "I hope I don't regret this." He turned and went back into the other room, shutting the door behind him.

Alaric let out a long breath. "And now," he said, "we wait."

20

Awkward silence fell. Ellard finally broke it by saying, "This is not how I pictured our reunion, Alaric." He laughed. "I didn't picture it at all. I can't believe you're alive."

"I'm sorry I had no way of contacting you," Alaric said. "When this is all over..." His voice trailed off. Sienne could guess he didn't like making plans when the future was so uncertain.

She eyed Viveka, who'd moved to be close to Alaric again. "I knew you'd return," Viveka said. "I never believed otherwise."

"I didn't think..." Alaric cleared his throat. "We've both—we've all changed in the last eleven years."

"I haven't," Viveka said, and Sienne closed her eyes. This was just too awkward for words. If Viveka's next action was to declare her undying constancy, Alaric would have to say something, and publicly embarrassing the woman was not something Sienne wanted to see.

"I think I can do something with this," Dianthe said. Sienne opened her eyes to see Dianthe picking at the blue and silver patch. It shrank into a silver medallion as it peeled away from the cloak lining. "We saw a couple of the Niskanen using them when we assaulted the tower the first time. It clearly receives responses, but inaudibly. I might be able to at least make those responses audible."

"But we do not want them to hear us," Kalanath said. "Do the Niskanen speak to each other or only to the wizard?"

"I'm not sure." Dianthe walked to the table and examined the medallion by the marginally brighter light of the massed candles. "Sienne, can you make a brighter light?"

"It looks different from firelight, and I don't want to draw attention to this house any more than we already have."

Dianthe pursed her lips. "I guess I can make do."

"How are we doing for resources? Perrin, how many blessings do you have left?" Alaric asked.

"Only three," Perrin replied. "One healing blessing, which thank Averran we did not need, a shield, and one that has puzzled me all day. It is a memory blessing, and I have no idea what we might need it for. And I cannot pray for more blessings for several hours yet. Alaric, we may need to wait until dawn."

"It's going to take—" Alaric said. He was interrupted by the door opening and Lothar emerging. He was fully dressed and his hair was combed.

"We'll need the rest of the council here," he said. "Then they'll pass the word. Detlenda, Ellard, Annegret, will you contact them?"

"Can I ask how they'll pass the word?" Alaric said.

Lothar smiled grimly. "We have a passphrase in case of emergency. If the wizard decides to send the Niskanen after us, for example. The councilors will tell the citizens that Harvalt and Audny summon them to a certain meeting place, and when they're gathered, they'll give the citizens their instructions. So you'd better have a plan for them to pass on in an hour."

"Just get them together, and I'll have a plan," Alaric said.

Lothar nodded and gestured to the other Sassaven, giving them instructions in a low voice. Detlenda gave her son one last look before disappearing into the night, following the other four. The door closed, and Viveka said, "You didn't kill Karlen, did you?"

"My spell just knocked him unconscious. He might even sleep this out, if we work fast enough," Sienne said.

Viveka shook her head in astonishment. "Are you as powerful as the wizard? No, you said you weren't."

"I'm not," Sienne said, suppressing irritation, "but I don't have to be so long as I can take him by surprise." But that wasn't true, was it? She remembered *dominate*, and anger and humiliation rose up within her again. She might be able to subdue Kyros long enough to reverse the binding, but without *dominate*, how could she force him to free Genneva? Too bad she couldn't cast the spell from memory without writing it out, not that she had been paying close attention—

She ran back over what she could remember. There were big gaps, but...well, it was worth trying, wasn't it? "Perrin," she said, "what kind of memory blessing is it?"

Perrin had been studying the books on the shelf and turned at her words. "Just the ordinary kind," he said. "Like the one we used to allow Alaric to remember the wizard's ritual last year."

"I want you to invoke it on me. I think I might be able to recall *dominate*."

Alaric, who'd taken a few steps toward Viveka, also turned. "I don't want you using that spell," he said. "You've had it used on you. You know how evil it is."

"We need *something* to force him to release Genneva. Besides, I don't even know if this will work." She tried not to notice how Viveka had drifted close to him as he spoke.

Alaric's lips thinned into a taut line, but he only shook his head and turned away. Sienne found a pen and ink and settled herself at the table, paper drawn up neatly before her. "I just focus on the memory I want, right?" she said.

"That is correct," Perrin said. He pressed a square of rice paper to her forehead and muttered an invocation. Pink light glowed above her eyelids momentarily and was gone. Sienne called to mind Kyros's face, close to hers, murmuring soporific syllables she could barely make out. It felt as if she were living through it again, anger and fear pulsing through her, and she had to concentrate not to stand up and flee the immaterial grip of the wizard. She let the memory run to its end, wiped tears away, and went back to the beginning. This time, the sounds were clearer, and she caught a few of them. She scribbled them down, not caring about her penmanship—that could wait.

Again and again she relived that agonizing moment, her heart pounding, sweat slicking her temples and neck. There were so many things she hadn't noticed at the time because she'd been too busy fighting: Kyros's smile, a parody of tenderness, his thin lips barely touched with pink. The way his eyebrows met above his nose. The way his palms gripping her wrists were faintly moist and soft, not the hands of a man who worked for a living. And the smells, ripe and rancid in memory, the sour smell of unwashed body and the unmistakable scent of too much magic in one place. By the time she wrote down the final syllable, her vision was smeary with tears and her hand and her back ached with exhaustion. She dropped the pen and covered her face with her hands, weeping.

Arms went around her, lifting her up. "If I'd realized how bad it would be, I wouldn't have allowed you to do it," Alaric murmured in her ear. She clung to him, desperate for his comfort.

"I don't let you *allow* me to make my own decisions," she sniffled, and heard him laugh.

"You know what I mean," he said.

"I do. Thank you for caring. I'll survive."

"The question is, did it work?" Alaric said.

Sienne wiped her face on his shirtsleeve and picked up the paper. It was a blotchy mess of scribbles. "I'll recopy this, and then we'll see," she said. "I don't have any way to make blood ink, but I've been thinking that may not matter. The idea is to make a connection between yourself and the written word, but I have a feeling I don't need that connection anymore."

"Then try it on me," Alaric said.

"No," said Kalanath. "That is wrong. You already endure it once, and I think it is bad you endure it again. It is me you will try it on."

"I'm not—"

"Alaric, stop being stoic and let someone else stand up for you," Dianthe said.

Alaric scowled. "It probably won't work," Sienne said.

She caught sight of Viveka, who was now standing in the corner nearest the front door. Even in the candlelight, Sienne could see her cheeks were rosy and her eyes red-rimmed. She glared at Sienne as if she wished she had a dagger pointed at her heart. Sienne glanced at Alaric, whose attention was on Kalanath. What had passed between him and Viveka while she was in the throes of memory? Suddenly her wish for Alaric to put a stop to Viveka's fantasies felt cruel. And yet what else could he do?

"Let me write this out properly, and then..." she said, letting her words trail off. She half hoped it would fail.

Scribing the spell took only a few minutes. Sienne took her time. It was the first charm spell she'd ever written, and it had been years since she'd learned the charm language. Fortunately, the spell languages were the sort of thing that stayed with you, like knowing how to climb stairs or ride a horse. The lines of the charm language were languorous, relaxing, and at one point she found herself drifting toward slumber and had to shake her head to wake herself. That cheered her, because it had to mean she'd done something right.

When she finished, she read it over silently. It was the right spell, she could tell. Whether it would work, she had no idea. But she had to try.

"All right," she said, letting out a deep breath. "Kalanath?"

"Should I relax?" Kalanath said. He looked not at all afraid.

"I don't think it matters. I fought, and it...anyway." Sienne took one last look at her friend's dark eyes, suppressed momentary self-loathing for what she intended, and began reading the spell.

Immediately she felt as if she were being drawn out of herself, as if an unseen hand had plucked a thread from her chest and wound it on a spool. It wasn't painful, just a steady pressure drawing her toward Kalanath. Kalanath closed his eyes and twitched, and she felt the movement as if she'd done it herself. He twitched again, and then Sienne felt his consciousness writhing to get away from her. She could see the gray fog swelling up around him, blocking his attempts to flee, and she almost stopped reading. *I have to see this through*, she thought, and bore down on him with all her might.

She read off the last sleepy syllable, and Kalanath's eyes opened. They'd lost their usual brightness, and his mouth hung slack, but otherwise he looked just as always. Sienne found herself speechless. She felt in her bones it had worked, but what now?

"Drop your staff," she said.

With a clatter, the staff hit the floor. Kalanath looked surprised, as if his hand had opened of its own accord. He bent to pick it up. "Leave it," Sienne said. Kalanath froze. All his muscles quivered as he strained against the compulsion. He looked up at her, terror contorting his handsome face, and Sienne's heart lurched. Frantically, she searched for a way to dismiss the spell. The thread was still bound to the spool, and in desperation she snapped that delicate connection and saw the gray fog vanish. Kalanath dropped to his knees and clutched his staff to his chest, which heaved in desperate gasps for breath.

Sienne knelt beside him. "I'm sorry," she babbled, "I shouldn't have done that, I don't care if it helps us—"

Kalanath shook his head, which he kept carefully averted from her. "It is what we need, and I will live," he said. "I do not know how you and Alaric endured it longer, and from an enemy."

Sienne wanted to hug him, but she had a feeling the last thing he needed was her touch. Instead, she stood, and said in a shaky voice, "If we can get the wizard to hold still long enough, that will be...effective."

No one spoke. Viveka now looked frightened as well as angry. "Then here's the plan," Alaric said. "We'll have the Sassaven coordinate an attack. Lothar made it sound as if they'd gather in smaller groups, so we'll need to give them instructions and timing. Sienne, you'll disguise the non-Sassaven so our group can move freely within the crowd. We'll work our way to the tower, activate the walkstone, and take the wizard by surprise."

"You make it sound easy," Dianthe said with a grin. "Any ideas for taking him by surprise?"

"Well, *that*—" Alaric flicked the medallion she held with a finger—"will make us look like a bunch of Niskanen reporting in, so we won't stand out. We'll set up an ambush. Sienne, you'll hit him with your most powerful paralysis, and the rest of us will subdue him before that wears off. Then we'll work the unbinding —oh."

"Oh, what?" Perrin asked. "That does not sound promising."

"We need a Sassaven to stand in as proxy for the race," Alaric said. "I'll have to ask my mother or father—but they'll likely be needed in the attack—"

"What is a proxy?" Viveka said. "I mean, I understand the concept, but what do you need a proxy for?"

"You remember your coming of age ritual," Alaric said. He didn't sound as if he felt the least bit embarrassed having a normal conversation with his cousin. "You were bound to serve the wizard. We can't perform the ritual ten thousand times to free each Sassaven individually. Instead, we've come up with a variation that will allow one bound Sassaven to stand in for all of them, and free every Sassaven at once."

"I'll do it," Viveka said.

Alaric blinked. "You?"

"Why not me? I've been through the wizard's ritual, so I qualify. And I'm not much of a fighter." Viveka's expression lacked the animation and passion it had held just half an hour before, and Sienne finally felt genuine empathy for her.

"Well...yes. It's dangerous," Alaric warned.

"No more than any of the rest of this," Viveka said. "And I'm not going to sit back and watch others free me. I want to help, even if you —" Her mouth closed sharply on the rest of her words, and Alaric reddened slightly.

Dianthe took a startled step back and held the medallion out in front of her. "It twitched," she said in a low voice.

"*Karlen, report,*" said Kyros, his voice taking on a metallic echo as it emerged from the medallion.

No one spoke. Dianthe gestured wildly to Alaric. "I...haven't seen them, sir," Alaric said. "Did you capture them?"

"*They're at large in Barholt,*" Kyros said. "*Where are you?*"

"Still at my mother's house," Alaric said. "I think this may be a waste of our time. Should I take up the search?"

"If they haven't gone there yet, they likely won't. Join your squad and proceed to the north gate. No one enters or leaves, understand? They could look like anyone."

"Understood, sir," Alaric said.

Dianthe lowered the medallion. "It's inert again," she said. "Good thing you sound like your brother."

"How does the wizard know where we are? We haven't said his name," Sienne exclaimed.

"I think he's guessing," Alaric said. "He knows we aren't likely to give up after one setback, and we'd have to be in Barholt for another attack. But it doesn't matter. The problem now is there's a Niskanen patrol expecting Karlen to join them, and if he takes too long, someone's going to go looking for him, and when they don't find him at my mother's house, they'll raise an alarm. That's if he didn't summon a bunch of Niskanen to *Annegret's* house, and they've found him already and just haven't reported in yet. We're running out of time."

As he said those last words, the door opened, and Detlenda entered, followed by a man and a woman. Both were older than she and had the look of people dragged out of bed unexpectedly at far too early an hour. "This is Arris and Brigit," Detlenda said. "My son, Alaric, and his friends from the south."

Arris peered nearsightedly at Alaric. "Quite an unexpected arrival," he said. "And you intend to overthrow the wizard?"

"It's madness," Brigit said. She was as tall and heavily-built as Alaric, but wore her hair in a long braid that at the moment was in disarray. "But I promised I'd listen."

The door opened again, admitting Ellard and a petite blonde woman who looked younger and more alert than either Arris or Brigit. They were followed almost immediately by Annegret and Lothar, trailing three more strangers, two of them unicorns. The third was a lanky woman with prominent front teeth who shut the door behind them all and said, "We were nearly caught. I want to know what's so important I just risked being harassed by Niskanen well after I should be safe asleep in bed."

"Freda, this is Alaric," Lothar said. "Everyone, I want you to listen to Alaric's proposal. Then we'll talk."

Sienne backed away toward the wall to make more space in the crowded room and found herself next to Viveka. Her awareness of the Sassaven woman felt like spiders crawling over her skin, spiders whose legs burned and prickled. She didn't know what to say, if anything. Alaric had begun speaking, but with her whole attention focused on Viveka, she couldn't keep her mind on his words. It didn't matter. She wasn't the one he needed to convince.

Viveka shifted her weight. "You and Alaric," she said in a murmur that barely carried to Sienne's ears. "Has it been long?"

"Half a year," Sienne replied in the same low voice. "I didn't..." *He never mentioned you* seemed unnecessarily cruel, and *I'm sorry* was both untrue and condescending.

"We were close as children, and he promised he'd return for me," Viveka said. "I suppose he didn't really mean it."

Again Sienne couldn't think of anything to say. Viveka almost certainly didn't want her sympathy.

Viveka sighed. "It doesn't matter now. In twenty-four hours we might all be dead. I just feel like a fool."

"You're not a fool," Sienne said. "People change. It's not your fault if you were faithful enough that you didn't."

"Sorry, but that's not much comfort." Viveka shifted, and Sienne turned her head to find the woman looking at her. "You realize you're condemning him to childlessness?"

"It was his choice. I offered to step aside."

Viveka pursed her lips. "Generous."

Her sarcastic tone irritated Sienne. "I love him," she retorted, "and that means I want him to be happy on his terms, not on mine."

A muscle twitched in Viveka's jaw. "There's nothing I can—"

"And I say it's impossible!" someone shouted, cutting Viveka off. Sienne's attention jerked back to the conversation Alaric was having with the Sassaven elders. One of the male unicorns had stepped up to be right in Alaric's face. "You place us all in jeopardy for some impossible fantasy!"

"We can do it," Alaric said, unmoved by the man's aggressive stance. "I'd prove it, but we can't afford any of you to be incapacitated by *force*."

"I don't know what that is. You're talking nonsense."

"It's a refined, more potent version of the magical attack unicorns can do," Alaric said. He gestured to Sienne. "Sienne is more than capable of facing down the wizard, and with her companions' help, she'll knock him out long enough for us to reverse the binding and free you."

"Some of us are likely to die," Brigit said. "Do you have an answer for that?"

Alaric looked past his antagonist to where she stood, lounging in a corner as if none of this mattered to her. "I have no guarantee that everyone will make it out of this alive," he said. "But I've already risked my life repeatedly to get us to this point, and you should remember that my friends and I will be in more danger than anyone. I'm willing to risk death for the sake of Sassaven freedom. I hope it matters enough to my people that they're willing to do the same."

Brigit's eyes narrowed, but she said nothing. Alaric returned his attention to the unicorn staring him down. "I'm not a fool," he said. "I wouldn't ask this of you—of all of the Sassaven—if I didn't believe it would work. But we can't do this without you."

The man continued to glare at Alaric for a moment. Then he took a step back. "It's a risk," he said, "and I'm taking your word for it that the boy is capable, Ellard."

"He is," Ellard said.

Silence fell as all the Barholt elders turned to Lothar. "We need complete agreement on this," he said, "or it won't work. Does anyone still have an objection?"

"Are you sure the people will respond? We haven't had to use the emergency passphrase since I was a child," said Freda.

"The names of Harvalt and Audny represent the promise of freedom," Lothar said. "Invoking them will tell the people this is serious."

Freda nodded. "Then I'm in."

The others all nodded or murmured assent. Sienne realized she'd been holding her breath and let it out slowly so as not to draw attention to herself. "Alaric, what is your plan?" Lothar said.

"Am I right that you are each responsible for a portion of the citizenry?" Alaric asked. When they nodded, he went on, "Then you'll each gather those people to wherever your predesignated location is, and tell them it's time to rise up against the wizard." He took a deep breath. "And here's what I want them to do."

21

Sienne stood concealed between two of the low thatch-roofed cottages at the edge of the plain surrounding the tower with Alaric's heavy hand resting on her shoulder. The black sky shaded to gray in the east, and the stars there had faded. "Be careful," Alaric said. "You could still be caught."

"Everything depends on this," Sienne said. She put her arms around his waist and buried her face in his warm chest. "I'll be fine."

He returned her embrace before kissing her lightly and letting her go. "If you're caught, make a racket so we'll know to come charging to the rescue."

"Of course." Neither of them had to say if Kyros did the catching, she might not be allowed to make any noise at all.

She stepped away from him and cast, first *vanish*, then *float*. Viveka gasped when Sienne disappeared, but said nothing else. She'd been silent the whole way from Lothar's house to this watch point. It wasn't as if there were anything to say, but Sienne wished perversely that the woman would throw a screaming fit, or attack Sienne, anything to show a normal reaction to finding out the man she loved was in love with someone else. That could wait until later.

"I'll be back in fifteen minutes," she said, and took a couple of running steps out of their hiding place, rising higher with every step. *Float* was nearly as good as flying, or so she guessed; she'd never had *fly* cast on her, but this sailing, swooping motion through the air took her breath away and left her feeling exhilarated and utterly free. She pushed off the hard earth again and gauged the distance to the wall. She'd aimed at the northeast side, midway between the gate and the corner tower, and one more leap should put her...*there*.

She sailed over the wall with nearly a foot to spare and touched down lightly, rebounding off the ground without giving herself an extra push so she'd decelerate quickly. Even so, her final step caromed her gently into the tower wall, where she clung, heart racing, and listened madly for any sound that someone had noticed. Nothing moved. Distantly she heard the guards on the towers shouting to each other, but the sound lacked the urgency that would mean the Sassaven assault had begun.

She inched down the wall and walked at a fast shuffle to the tower door, careful not to bounce. The solid black iron was as intimidating as ever. This was the dangerous part, getting inside without drawing attention. Even the most stolid, unimaginative Niskanen warrior would wonder at the door opening seemingly by itself. More Niskanen filled the space between the tower and the wall, crossing the ground in pairs or groups of three, some of them entering or leaving the tower at unpredictable intervals. She hugged the wall next to the door, and the next time it opened, she gave the Niskanen time to exit, then slipped inside.

The room smelled even more strongly of mildew than she remembered. Probably she'd been too terrified the first time to pay attention. This time, it was lit by torches that flickered in the breeze caused by the opening door. She'd been right; the room was full of cast-off furniture, tables and chairs and a sheet-draped vertical oblong that was probably a mirror. Why Kyros would fill the base of his tower with such prosaic things, she couldn't guess. From what she could see, the room filled the entire base of the tower, and the junk crowding it made that space cramped rather than expansive. Sienne almost felt claustrophobic.

She swiftly set about memorizing the space for *transport*. The clutter made the job easier, defining the unique space well, but she felt twitchy the whole time, half her attention on the door so she could get out of the way if anyone came through the door or used the walkstone. She let the space fill her, concentrated on the relation of sofa to table to mirror until her awareness snapped into place around her. She stood for a moment breathing in the smelly air and relaxing her tense shoulders. Then she concentrated on *jaunt*, and with a jerk, she was back in the alley between houses.

The others all stood where they could clearly see the wall, their backs to Sienne. "—almost time," Perrin said. Sienne dismissed *float* and caught herself as she dropped an inch to stand on the ground. "I'm back," she said as she dismissed *vanish*. Everyone turned, startled. She smiled and said, "We're all set. We just need a distraction."

"I was just saying it is nearly time for that," Perrin said. "I wish to give us the language blessing before that happens. It may not matter, as I believe it lasts for twenty-four hours, but I choose not to risk it."

"I agree," Alaric said. "But hurry."

Perrin held up the blessing and murmured an invocation. A sharp pain stabbed through Sienne's head and was gone with the last of the pink flames surrounding Perrin's hand. They matched the rosy streaks touching the eastern sky, setting the shadowy mountains into stark relief.

She watched Perrin bind a fat bundle of blessings together at one corner with needle and thread. He'd never received so many at once, which frightened and reassured her. Averran was on their side. She just wished she knew how that would look in the heat of battle.

"Something happens," Kalanath said. He stood at the mouth of the alley and beckoned to them, his attention on the distant gate. "I think they ready an attack."

Sienne crowded around Kalanath with the others. It was still dark enough that the mass of people gathering at the edge of the plain was indistinguishable as individuals, but it was large and growing by the moment. She looked toward the gate. A handful of Niskanen stood there, their red vests dull maroon in the pre-dawn light. The guards atop the corner towers had their attention on the crowd, but Sienne didn't think their crossbows were at the ready. The Niskanen at the gate huddled together, looking like a tiny flock of red sheep consulting on whether the animal in the distance was a dog or a wolf. She found she'd clasped Alaric's hand, which was dry and warm rather than slightly sweaty with anxiety as her own was.

A couple of Sassaven detached from the crowd and walked forward, striding with confidence. This made the Niskanen draw closer together briefly before coming to meet them. The light wind, which gusted chill and brisk on occasion, carried to Sienne's ears flashes of conversation she couldn't comprehend. She tried to read their body language, but aside from the Sassaven—two unicorns, male and female—standing like they weren't afraid of anything, she made nothing of it.

The Niskanen leader, or at least the woman in front, gestured at the crowd. Sienne guessed it meant something like "what do they all want?" More snatches of conversation, and then the Niskanen leader strode past the two Sassaven and put her hands to her mouth. "You should all go home!" she shouted, though it was faint to Sienne.

The Sassaven crowd murmured something Sienne couldn't make out. Then they shouted, almost with one voice, "*Freedom!*" It was ragged as some spoke later than others, but still readily comprehensible.

The Niskanen leader recoiled. She once more shouted, "Go home! We don't want to hurt you!"

Laughter rose up from the crowd. The Niskanen leader returned to the two Sassaven, gesturing madly. One of the Sassaven shrugged, and they both turned and strode back toward the crowd. Sienne held her breath. "When will they attack?"

"Soon enough...just watch," Alaric said, gripping her hand tightly.

The two Sassaven reached the others. The man shouted something that prompted an answering shout from the crowd. It made the Niskanen, who'd been cautiously retreating to the gate, pause where they stood. The man shouted again, the crowd roared, and something like a ripple passed over it, transforming the humans into their equine counterparts. Ranks of gleaming hide and proud, tall heads shifted until they became an orderly mass of horses and unicorns. The first rank, all unicorns of every conceivable color, reared up, screamed a challenge, and thundered toward their enemy.

The Niskanen were fast. All ten of them transformed and took up defensive positions. The unicorns in front lowered their horns to point at the oncoming Sassaven. Blasts of yellow-white *force* energy shot away from them to strike their foe. Some of the unicorns stumbled and fell, but the remaining ones closed ranks and the horses coming up behind leaped over their fallen comrades to maintain that intimidating juggernaut. The Niskanen blasted them again, and then the Sassaven were upon them, shooting out blasts of *force* themselves and slashing with horn and wickedly sharp hoof.

Sienne realized she was still holding her breath and it wasn't just the magic in the air that made her dizzy. "I can't believe that worked," Dianthe said. "Not that it's over yet."

The high, shrill sounds of animals in pain filled the air as the crossbowmen on the towers shot into the crowd. After one volley, they dropped their crossbows and turned to climb down from their posts. Clearly they'd realized shooting into a crowd where they could injure their own people was stupid. Sienne hoped it also meant they didn't really want to hurt or kill the Sassaven. Her secret wish was that the Niskanen would all decide to turn on the wizard...no, the binding made that impossible. But if they chose not to fight, that was possible, yes?

The gate opened, and more Niskanen, these still human, streamed through, swords drawn. Sienne's heart beat faster. She didn't know which was more deadly, a Niskanen in human form or one transformed, but the swords looked dangerous and the Niskanen moved like they knew how to use them. It was light enough now that she could see them shouting, though she couldn't hear anything over the noise of the horses and unicorns. Some of the Niskanen sheathed their swords and transformed, but the press near the gate was too close to allow much room for more enormous bodies. Even the non-unicorns were bigger than most of the horses Sienne had ever seen.

Something in the melee flashed, and Kalanath said, "That is a medallion. I think they are overwhelmed."

"Get ready," Alaric said. Everyone joined hands except him. Viveka stood next to him, her expression tight and unhappy. Well, this was the only way to get all of them inside at once, and Sienne wasn't inclined to coddle her, given that she'd volunteered for this. She clutched Dianthe and Perrin's hands and tried to see past Alaric, who stood watching the fight.

The air above the gate quivered, and Kyros floated there as casually as if he stood on solid ground. "*Now*," Alaric said. He picked up Viveka and slung her over his shoulder, then took Dianthe and Kalanath's hands to complete the circle. Sienne chanted the syllables of *transport* as rapidly as she dared, felt the familiar tug, and they were inside the base of the tower. The torches burned merrily, casting their flickering light over all six of them.

Alaric set Viveka down and ran to the shrouded mirror. He lifted the cloth, revealing not a mirror, but an obsidian surface with a jagged crack running from top right to lower left. He traced the line of the crack with his forefinger, breathed heavily on a spot above it, and drew a couple of symbols in the remaining mist. Then he gestured to Sienne. "Hurry, we don't have much time," he said. He pointed at a square stone embedded in the packed earth of the tower floor. It was about three feet on a side and worn as if generations of feet had trodden it.

Sienne hurriedly stepped onto it—

—and was suddenly in the tower antechamber, confronting one of the grotesque masks. She stepped forward to make room for Dianthe, who followed her. Dianthe immediately went to the door and examined it. "No traps, not that I expected any," she said, "and it's not locked. He was in a hurry."

"So are we," Alaric said. "Let's see where we can hide."

He flung open the door and shooed everyone inside. Sienne

examined the room. It was as bare as she remembered. "It'll have to be *seeming*," she said. "Tell us where to stand, and I'll hide us."

"Half here, half over there," Alaric said, gesturing to either side of the door before shutting it. "When he comes through the door, Sienne, hit him with *force* or *rainbow*. That will be the signal for everyone else to attack. Perrin, where is Gen?"

"Still in the tower," Perrin said, his eyes going briefly unfocused. "The locator scrying continues strong."

"We'll worry about her later," Alaric said. "Good luck, everyone."

Sienne cast *seeming* twice and watched her friends' images blur and twist until they blended with the gray walls of the central chamber. She could still see Dianthe and Perrin, who stood beside her, but Alaric, Viveka, and Kalanath were invisible. She calmed her breathing and brought to mind *rainbow*. The green paralysis ray hadn't lasted long the first time, but she'd been trying to break free of *dominate* and had a feeling she could do better now. She breathed, in through the nose, out through the mouth, and watched, and listened.

She wished the door weren't quite so sturdy, so she could hear Kyros's approach. Though it was possible, since this room was displaced from the rest of the tower, no sound would come through regardless. To keep from becoming too tense, she scanned the walls, looking for—there. A slim silver chain, its links half her pinky finger in length, hung near one of the windows, which showed the sky fading toward sunset. It looped once around the peg it hung from, and she guessed it to be about five feet long. Seeing it relieved her mind. They just had to subdue Kyros, and from there, the unbinding would be easy. *As if anything about this has been easy*, she thought, and had to stifle an inappropriate giggle.

The door opened, and she tensed again. She heard Kyros speaking and recognized *scorch* just as Perrin tore off a blessing and swiftly murmured an invocation. Then *scorch* shot through the doorway to fetch up against the far wall, expanding hotter and brighter toward them—and coming up against a pearly gray barrier that went up just inches from Sienne's nose.

Without giving herself time to think, she stepped into the doorway, the syllables of *rainbow* already filling her mouth. Kyros had started in on a new spell, one she couldn't recognize, but it didn't matter because she was faster than he. A bolt of green light like new grass shot away from her and struck him, not in the chest, but in the shoulder as he tried to get out of the way. His momentum carried him a few more paces before he fell, landing on his face.

"Quickly," Alaric said, pushing past Sienne. He picked up Kyros and carried him into the central chamber, dropping him roughly on the floor. Kalanath knelt to securely gag the wizard as Alaric unlooped rope from around his chest. "Perrin?"

"Genneva is moving," Perrin said. He shut the door and pressed a blessing on it. Yellow light like melted butter seeped up through the grain, spreading across it and then vanishing as if the wood had soaked it up. "That will hold her. You are certain—"

"She's bound to protect him," Alaric said, "and I don't care how old she looks, she's strong, and unicorns don't get weaker with age. We can't let her in here."

Kyros suddenly convulsed, thrashing to get away from Dianthe and Kalanath's restraining hands as they thrust a bag over his head. Alaric bound his arms to his side and looped more rope around his legs, tying it off at the ankles. "Sienne, get the chain," he said.

Sienne held out a hand and let her invisible fingers whisk the chain off its peg into her grasp. She slung it around her neck and beckoned to Viveka. From her waistband she drew her belt knife. "It's just a prick of the finger," she said when Viveka hesitated. "There's nothing to fear."

Viveka nodded and held out her hand. Sienne poked her finger, squeezed it to make the blood flow, and said, "Hold his hand, Kalanath." Kalanath forced Kyros's hand open, and Sienne pricked his finger as well. Sheathing the knife, she took hold of Kyros's bloody finger and drew a shaky, rough symbol on Viveka's palm, struggling against how he fought her. "Same thing," she grunted, and Viveka drew a more steady symbol on Kyros's hand. A hand-sized flame erupted in the air before them, making Viveka shy away before it went out without igniting anything.

"Now—clasp hands," Sienne said. Viveka needed both hands to hold Kyros's still as he jerked and strained away from her, despite Kalanath's restraining grip. The room grew darker as the sun set, but Sienne didn't have time or attention to create lights. She drew the chain from around her neck and wrapped it three times around Viveka and Kyros's joined hands, binding them tightly. Viveka looked frightened, but her jaw was set.

Kyros bucked against Alaric's confining arms around his chest and shoulders. "Hurry," he grunted.

Sienne covered the chain-wrapped hands with hers. "Hand to hand, heart to heart," she gabbled. If they'd guessed wrong, it was all over for the Sassaven, and for them. "We two are one until death, Kyros and Viveka." As she said the wizard's name, a pulse of power ran through the clasped hands and into her, like a brush of a *force-bolt*. She felt his name sink into the binding, drawing him down into it far more deeply than she'd expected. A two-edged weapon indeed.

She drew in a steadying breath. "Let this chain bind us, in body, in heart, in mind, in spirit. As the chain persists, so does the binding."

Something struck the door that sounded like a battering ram. Sienne swallowed to moisten her dry throat. "Do you speak for the Sassaven?" she asked Viveka.

Viveka nodded. Sienne glared at her. "Yes," Viveka said hastily.

"Through you are the Sassaven bound," Sienne said, and recited the syllables of *change*. Viveka gasped. Her eyes went from bright blue to glossy black. The battering ram hit the door again. Sienne ignored it. Now all the Sassaven were bound, not just the adults. Their greatest risk, with the greatest promise of reward.

"With this breath, I break the chain of the spirit," Sienne went on. She breathed heavily in Viveka's face. Viveka, her eyes still solid black, inhaled sharply. Kyros twisted, nearly wrenching free, and Sienne gripped his and Viveka's hands more tightly. "With this spark, I break the chain of the mind." She lit her spark inches from Viveka's face, but Viveka didn't flinch.

One-handed, she wrested the knife from her waist again and drew it along the back of her other hand. "With this blood," she gasped, "I break the chain of the heart." She dropped the knife, switched hands, and smeared the blood across Viveka's forehead. The pounding was irregular now, and loud enough that it shook the door with every blow.

Sienne put both hands over the chain. "With this blow, I break the chain of the body," she said, and began speaking the honey-sweet syllables of a transform. *Break*, even for her new capabilities, wasn't powerful enough to break metal, but within the spell she'd seen the possibilities for something greater. Now, she let *shatter* emerge from within her, a powerful pressure that built and built until she could hardly bear it. With a final prayer that it wouldn't take Kyros and Viveka's hands with it, she loosed the final syllable.

The chain shivered. With a crack louder than the pounding, it shattered, every link breaking at once as if made of ice rather than silver.

Viveka yanked her hand free, crying out in pain. "I'm sorry!" Sienne said.

The Sassaven shook her head. Her eyes were once more blue. "I'm fine. Just surprised." There were fine cuts all over the back of her hand, which was white from gripping Kyros's.

"Sienne!" Alaric shouted. "*Dominate!*" The muscles on his arms stood out from fighting Kyros's attempts to free himself. The wizard kicked, and Dianthe fell back before diving to pinion him again.

Sienne cursed, yanked the bag off the wizard's head, and took Kyros's face in her hands. Swallowing fear and disgust, she let the soothing sounds of *dominate* slip from her lips. Tension fell away, leaving her weary from everything she'd done. She fought sleepiness and concentrated on the thin thread connecting her with the wizard.

He was far more skilled at evasion than Kalanath. His consciousness darted this way and that, slipping away from the gray fog and concealing itself for a time. Wary as a predator, Sienne hunted him down, blocking him in and hedging him up until his movements became cautious, then tentative, then frightened. His fear was a palpable thing, battering at her and making her want to weep despite her knowledge that he was simply playing on her emotions. She played out her thread until she had, not one connection, but many, a web linking her to Kyros, and finally she tugged on one thread and saw him twitch, blink, and stop fighting.

She sat back. "It's done," she said.

The door slammed open and Genneva burst through. She was in unicorn form and barely fit through the door, and Alaric had been right, she was beautiful, pure white flanks and ebon-black horn. She screamed a challenge and pounded the floor with enormous hooves.

Alaric released Kyros and stood. "Gen, it's me," he said. He held out a hand to her, unafraid of the possibility that she might bite it off. Genneva shook her head, and then she stood before them in human form. Alaric's eyes widened as he took in her wrinkled face, her shaking hands. "Gen," he said again, his voice rough. "It's not too late, is it?"

"You broke the binding," Genneva said in her creaky voice. "I thought it was impossible." She stepped forward. "Kill me now, and it will be finished."

"I'm not going to kill you," Alaric said. "We're going to make him reverse what he did to you." He began untying Kyros as Kalanath, with a look for confirmation at Sienne, removed the gag.

Genneva looked down at where Kyros lay sprawled on the floor, breathing heavily but otherwise motionless. "It's impossible," she said, but in a voice filled with wonder.

Sienne felt as if she were waiting for something, though she couldn't imagine what. "Kyros, stand up," she said. Kyros jerked when she said his name, but stood. Sienne realized the sense of waiting came from him, and in the next moment saw that he was breathing in time with her. It unnerved her, as if their lives and not their wills were entwined. "How do we reverse the exchange of hearts?" she asked.

Kyros worked his mouth a couple of times before replying. "*Spana,* and *spremba. Tragoven.*"

"*Sleep, change,* and *castle. Sleep?* How can you do it if you're asleep?"

"*Spana* for the host. *Spremba* for me. *Tragoven* for the exchange." His conversational tone was as unsettling as their synchronized breathing. Sienne had never guessed it was possible to turn *castle* on something other than yourself.

She let out a deep breath and saw Kyros do the same. "All right. Do it."

Kyros beckoned Genneva forward. Dianthe and Perrin stepped out of her way. Kalanath hovered near Kyros, his staff at the ready. Sienne didn't tell him it was unnecessary. She didn't trust Kyros, even under the influence of *dominate*. She retrieved her knife and sheathed it with unnecessary force.

"Lie down," Kyros said. Genneva looked at Alaric, who nodded. She got heavily to her knees and then lay on the floor. Kyros squatted beside her and put his hand flat on her chest, between her breasts. He began speaking the slow, soporific syllables of a charm spell.

Suddenly the web of connections binding Kyros to Sienne vanished, shriveling like burning thread. Kyros's words became harsh and acid-etched, the sound of an evocation.

Sienne screamed, "Stop him! He's free!"

Alaric dove forward, lunging not for Kyros, but for Genneva.

An arc of white-blue lightning shot away from Kyros to hit Alaric in the face.

22

The impact knocked Alaric on his back, his arms flung wide as if trying to embrace Kyros. The lightning split four ways, arcing toward the others. Sienne screamed and hurled herself backward. The bolt grazed her foot, sending a shock through her and making her see double for a minute. Her eyes watered, and her legs wouldn't support her. From where she lay, she saw Dianthe fall, saw Kalanath spin out of the way not fast enough, saw Perrin go down with an unused blessing in one hand.

Kyros stood. "Impressive," he said, dusting himself off ostentatiously. "You almost succeeded. I had no idea you were so competent. 'You' meaning all of you, of course. The power of friendship." He laughed, a nasty sound. "Don't worry, they're not dead. I wouldn't waste such tremendous human resources as you are."

Trembling, Sienne made herself look at Alaric. Where his face had been was a black, contorted smear. He wasn't breathing. "You lie," she whispered. "You killed him."

"Hmm?" Kyros glanced at Alaric. "I suppose I did. Unfortunate, since I'm sure he would have bred impressive children. That's the trouble with *obluska*; it's gentler with its secondary targets than the first. But—" His eyes widened. "You didn't *care* for him, did you? How terribly tragic."

Sienne screamed. Her rage and pain gave her invisible fingers more strength than she'd ever known. She lifted the ebony cabinet and hurled it at Kyros. He sidestepped, but it clipped his shoulder, making him cry out in pain.

"No more of that," he said. "I've said I won't kill you. I'm just going to make you slaves. And then...you're not Sassaven, true, but I'm sure I can think of something you'd be good for."

Sienne glanced at Viveka, who stood unmoving, staring at Alaric's body. So, no help from that quarter. And Genneva...she lay motionless on the floor, though Sienne was sure the wizard hadn't completed the *sleep* spell. Her eyes were open and she appeared to be following the conversation. Even so, what could she do?

She looked at her friends, who'd all begun to stir. Get everyone out? They'd have to leave Alaric's body behind, and *transport* took long enough Kyros could destroy them all easily. Attack him? Nothing she could do would last. Desperate, she dug deep within herself for *change*. It might slow him down long enough to free the others.

Kyros smiled when she began casting the spell. "You haven't given up. Really, you're remarkable," he said.

The spell fought Sienne as Kyros's will opposed hers. She envisioned him turning into a frog, saw his outline shimmer, and his smile wavered. Behind him, Kalanath got to his feet, staggering toward them. Without looking, Kyros gestured and sent Kalanath flying into the far wall. Sienne focused harder. It felt like moving through gluey mud that oozed back wherever she pushed it aside. Then, with a snap, her concentration shattered, and she leaned over, breathing deeply to dispel the dizziness that threatened to engulf her.

"I know what I'll do with you!" Kyros exclaimed. He sounded not at all out of breath or discommoded. "It's obvious. I don't really want children, but you and I—really, it would be a shame not to take advantage of the opportunity. And I find myself eager to see what kind of match we'd make. Our children ought to be incredibly powerful."

Shaking, Sienne stood upright and spat at him.

"It's too bad I can't convince you to come to me willingly," Kyros said. "*Prafladuo* takes some of the spirit out of its victims. But you'd knife me in my sleep—though that wouldn't work, would it?" He leaned over and gave Genneva his hand. "Stand up, my dear."

Genneva got to her feet and didn't snatch her hand away as Sienne would have. "I'm afraid," Kyros said, musing, "my experiment has gone somewhat awry. I'll have to do something about that. You've broken my death binding, but that wasn't the only way I was connected to the Sassaven—you didn't know that, did you? Well, why would you? It's a very low-level awareness, but more than enough to track down all those who rose up against me."

"The Niskanen won't kill them," Sienne said. "And the Sassaven will fight back."

"They can't fight back against *obluska*," Kyros said. "I'll send it out along that awareness and...probably it won't kill all of them, but enough to make an example. Genneva, hold her." He spoke a handful of syllables, and *silence* enveloped Sienne. She shouted, screamed, threw herself at Kyros, who shoved her toward Genneva, and heard nothing. Genneva grabbed her by the arms and drew her close to her chest. Sienne fought, but as old as Genneva looked, she was far stronger than Sienne.

Tears streamed down her face as she watched Kyros begin speaking. She had no idea what he was saying, whether it was *shock* or the beginnings of whatever he did to make the connection between himself and the Sassaven, but it didn't matter. She was helpless. She struggled again, and Genneva shook her into stillness.

Dianthe moved, but only enough to push herself upright once before collapsing again. Sienne wasn't sure Perrin was even breathing. Kalanath didn't look conscious. Viveka knelt beside Alaric, crying uselessly. Sienne turned back to Genneva, who was staring at her intently as if willing her to read her thoughts. *Not possible*, Sienne thought, *not without the right blessing*, and laughed silently and hysterically.

Genneva slapped her. It rocked her back on her heels, silent and painful. Genneva fixed Sienne with a fierce blue gaze that hurt for being so familiar. Sienne glared back. Then Genneva's gaze slid down over Sienne's body to focus on a point at her left hip. Sienne lowered a hand to touch it and found the hilt of her belt knife. Kyros hadn't disarmed her. Why bother, when she was helpless?

She met Genneva's eyes again. Genneva was breathing heavily, and her hands on Sienne's arms were rigid and painfully tight. She held herself as still as if she were in the grip of *shout*. Sienne reached across and pulled the knife from its sheath. She glanced at Kyros, who was still chanting and had his eyes closed. The silence shrouding her made it all feel like a terrible nightmare, one from which she would never wake.

Genneva's grip loosened, and her hands fell to her sides. She closed her eyes and mouthed the words *Do it.* "It's not what he wanted!" Sienne cried, her lips moving soundlessly. "I can't!"

Once more she was caught up in an implacable grip, but one she couldn't see. It wrapped her in a warm, powerful embrace too strong to be comforting, holding her up and filling her with power. Peace like she'd felt a handful of times before touched her heart, pushing aside the numb agony she felt when she looked at Alaric's broken body.

Save them, a voice said. It shook her body all the way to her center. *You are my hand.*

Her hand on the hilt felt steadier than the rest of her. She raised it high and, with a silent scream, drove the blade home.

Genneva jerked, and her eyes flew open. Sienne let go, leaving the knife embedded in her chest. Black liquid too thin and dark to be blood seeped from the wound, staining Genneva's shirt and her hand where she pressed it against the hilt and the half-inch of blade still protruding from her chest. Sienne staggered back and spun to face Kyros, ready to attack him with her hands. They were the only weapon she had left to her.

Kyros had stopped speaking. He had a peculiar look on his face, an expression of bewilderment as if Sienne had asked him an impossible question. He raised one hand to touch his chest lightly, just a brush of the fingertips over where his heart would be. With the other hand, he made a strange sweeping gesture in front of his face as if brushing away cobwebs. He said something Sienne couldn't hear, his lips moving slowly enough that he might have been casting another charm spell. Then he fell, his knees buckling, and didn't try to catch himself.

Sienne turned away in time to see Genneva go down. Instinctively, she reached for the woman, who was big enough to take Sienne down with her. Black liquid smeared Sienne's chest and face as she landed atop Genneva. "We can finish the exchange," Sienne babbled, not that anyone could hear her, not even herself. "He's right there. He said *castle* would do it—" And she didn't know how. Weeping, she slammed her fist against the floorboards and tried it anyway, realizing before she reached the end of the summoning that she was incapable of casting spells while she was *silenced*.

Genneva grabbed her hand with one blackened one and shook her head. Her lips moved. "I can't hear you," Sienne said. Genneva shook her head again, and smiled. Then her blue eyes took on a distant expression. She said something else, and went still.

Sienne held Genneva's lifeless hand cradled to her chest and rocked silently back and forth. Someone touched her shoulder, and she startled. Dianthe stood over her, tears pouring down her cheeks. She spoke, and halfway through the sentence, sound flowed back into Sienne's world. "—still alive," Dianthe said.

"Alaric's dead," Sienne said. It was an absurd, impossible sentence. This had all been his quest. He couldn't be dead.

Dianthe dropped to her knees and put her arms around Sienne, sobbing too hard for words. Sienne clutched her arms, but no tears came. Maybe she'd cried them all out already.

"Who else is dead?" she asked. Really, it was ridiculous how normal she sounded.

"No one," Dianthe said. "Well, Kyros, of course, and Genneva, and

A—" She choked on another sob. "Perrin's tending to Kalanath, who hit his head pretty hard, and Viveka is fine."

Sienne turned her head to look at Kyros. In death, he still looked astonished, his eyes wide and staring, his mouth hanging open. She'd half expected him to turn to dust. "Did he kill the Sassaven?"

Dianthe drew back far enough to give her a funny look. "Sienne, we took care of that. The binding is gone. Viveka would be dead if that hadn't worked."

"No, he...he had a less powerful connection, one he had to consciously use. He was going to punish the Sassaven who rioted."

"I don't know anything about that." Dianthe released her and wiped her eyes. "What do we do now?"

That struck Sienne as the funniest thing anyone had ever said. She choked on a laugh, put her hands over her mouth to contain it, and more laughter poured out of her. It didn't sound like laughter; it sounded like a sick bird coughing. "Sienne, stop," Dianthe said, alarmed. "Sienne!"

With some effort, Sienne got herself under control. "I don't know," she said. "I don't know what to do. We have to take care of...of the bodies. Detlenda and Ellard...oh, by Averran, they're going to mourn two of their children today, Dianthe!"

Dianthe's face crumpled into tears again. She brushed them away and took a deep, calming breath. "All right. We have to be strong now. Someone needs to tell the Sassaven the wizard is dead. That should happen first, because they're probably still fighting. We need to show them his body as proof. Kalanath, are you all right?"

Kalanath looked up from where he sat beneath the window. Drying blood coated the left side of his face. "I am not dead," he said. He looked at Alaric, and added, "I wish I do not say that. My heart is breaking."

Perrin, who crouched beside Kalanath, stood and said, "He is as well as healing can make him." He crossed the room and knelt beside Sienne. "Look at me."

Obediently Sienne looked into his eyes. He tilted her chin one way and then another, examined the long scorch mark across her boot, and held her wrist briefly. "You were luckier than we," he said, indicating the boot. "Though we were likely all luckier than we deserve."

"There has to be something you can do," Sienne exclaimed. "He can't be dead. He's too strong for that."

"All healing has its limits," Perrin said softly, laying a hand on her knee. "He died instantly, if that helps—"

"Of course it doesn't help!"

"No, it doesn't. Forgive me."

He looked so crushed Sienne put her arms around him. "I know what you meant," she whispered. "It's just that...if it were me lying there, he wouldn't give up until he'd exhausted every possibility."

Perrin tensed. She pulled away from him. "What did I say?"

He shook his head, but slowly, as if working through a puzzle. Then he stood and walked to where Alaric lay. Viveka had straightened his limbs so he wasn't sprawled anymore, and if not for the black, charred ruin of his face, he might have been asleep. Sienne followed Perrin. She'd been avoiding looking at Alaric, feeling that if she didn't see him, it wasn't real. Now she stood at his side and made herself look. He was unmarked except for the point where the lightning had struck him, but now that she was paying attention, she couldn't see him as sleeping anymore. He was too still for anything but death.

Viveka knelt beside him. She held one of his hands pressed to her chest, and tears rolled silently down her face to drip on his arm. Sienne turned and strode to the window, suppressing fury. How dare the woman act as if she were entitled to grieve for Sienne's lover? She wanted to fling spell after spell at Viveka until she was unrecognizable as human, but she was still sane enough to realize that was her grief talking. She gripped the windowsill. Wherever this room was really located, it had an ocean view, but full dark had fallen, and an overcast sky gave Sienne the illusion that she was looking into a void, the movement of the waves barely visible.

"O Averran, most gracious and all-powerful Lord," Perrin said. Sienne turned around. He sat cross-legged near Alaric's head with his eyes closed and his hands resting on his knees. "I am grateful beyond measure for your assistance. We have freed the Sassaven and rid the world—" He went still, his head tilted in a listening pose. "Of course Kyros was as deserving of justice as anyone, and I will not usurp your authority in that matter, but you cannot deny he did much that was evil."

Again Perrin went silent. "Very well," he finally said. "Let us agree that the Sassaven deserved freedom, and we were pleased to be your agents in the matter. But did you not say no man is a fool who reaches beyond his grasp? My Lord, I have a request in which I am reaching so far beyond my grasp my hand stretches across the continent." He smiled. "I realize it is a metaphor."

Sienne drifted toward Perrin, fascinated. Viveka had dropped Alaric's hand and scooted back a few paces. She, too, watched Perrin, though she looked more frightened than amazed. "I ask a boon," Perrin went on. "A kindness, if you will. You are God's face to mankind and you have power beyond mortal comprehension. If it is your will, you can restore the life of our companion. He died in your service, and I do not believe it is so—"

Perrin went rigid, his face suddenly tight with concentration. "No, I am aware no man nor woman has ever returned from God's embrace to mortal life," he grated through clenched teeth. "I do not wish to set a precedent, though—yes, I realize that is precisely what I ask, but—" He gasped, and his eyes flew open, though Sienne didn't think he saw her or anything else in the room. "I do not understand. What cost? I assure you we are all willing to sacrifice to restore Alaric to life."

Sienne slowly knelt beside Alaric and took his lifeless hand in hers. She couldn't look away from Perrin, but she gradually became aware that Dianthe and Kalanath had joined her, loosely grouped around Alaric's body. The pressure she'd felt just before stabbing Genneva built again, growing until she felt swollen with power and ready to burst. She closed her eyes and clung to Alaric's hand as the one solid thing she could be sure of in this nightmare.

A voice filled her head, making her bones hum. *What will you give?*

She was sure she spoke, but she couldn't hear her own words. "Everything. Anything you want, I would give for him to be alive again."

Your memory of your family?

Instantly her knowledge of each of her siblings, her mother and father, came to mind and as instantly dissolved, leaving her groping for the memory of something precious she'd forgotten. "Yes. For his sake."

Your magic?

All her memories of the spell languages deserted her. She felt hollowed-out and empty, a shell of Sienne with nothing left but scraps of magic to remind her she'd lost something. She swallowed. "I would give up magic for him."

He matters so much to you?

"My lord Averran, he is everything to me."

Then I will bring him back—but at a price. Your companionship will be at an end. None of you will remember the others as anything but shadows. He will live on, will rejoin the Sassaven, will find a mate and have the children he desires, and you will be nothing to him. Is that what you are willing to give?

For a moment, Sienne saw Viveka's face and imagined Alaric looking at the woman in love. The thought burned in her heart. Yet, if it meant seeing him alive again? Even if they wouldn't be together? She wouldn't even know they'd loved each other, so what loss would it be? She let out a deep breath. "No," she said.

Too high a price?

"I could give up his love if it meant he lived. That's not it." Sienne breathed out again, desperate to loosen the band round her lungs and heart. "We went through this together. We became your tool in freeing the Sassaven. To give that up—to have it be nothing, to have been nothing —that would make a mockery of what we accomplished. Alaric would be the last to accept life at that price. So, please, my Lord, set a different one."

The bone-humming presence pressed down on her, hurting her, but she held herself tall and prayed she hadn't made a terrible mistake. *Very well,* Averran said after a long, long pause in which Sienne thought she might be crushed. *Have faith, Sienne. Faith beyond reason.*

The pressure released her so suddenly she sagged. She drew in a deep, unfettered breath and opened her eyes. Alaric still lay motionless, his face still a blackened wreck, his hand limp in hers. All around him, her friends were sitting up from where they'd fallen, blinking and breathing as heavily as she was. "No," she gasped, then screamed, "*No!*"

"Sienne—" Perrin said.

"He said he'd bring him back!" Hadn't he? Her memory of her conversation with Averran slipped away, leaving only those last words —*faith beyond reason*—and a sense of powerful immensity bearing down on her. Sienne flung Alaric's hand away and shot to her feet. "He promised!"

"Sienne," Perrin said again, more forcefully. "Look." He gestured, drawing her eye.

Green pinpoints of light sparkled near Alaric's head, spreading outward and multiplying until the lights were a solid sheet lying over Alaric's body, completely concealing him. The sheet drifted downward until it rested on him, outlining his powerful frame and concealing the mess his face had become. Sienne returned to her place, kneeling beside him. She was seized with a desire to take hold of the edge of the sheet and flip it away from him, see what the lights had done. She clasped her hands in her lap against the impulse so tightly they went white.

The light glowed brighter, and the tantalizing edges of the sheet curled beneath Alaric, tucking themselves in so no part of him was visible. Sienne realized he was floating just as Dianthe gasped, "Look!" and scooted back a pace. Horror filled her. He didn't look alive; he looked like a body wrapped for burial. A tear slid down her cheek. *Faith beyond reason.*

The light had grown so bright it burned Sienne's eyes. She

squinted, wanting to close them but afraid to take her eyes off Alaric. Then it flashed white, making all of them cry out in pain, and Sienne couldn't help herself—she flung up her arms to protect her face. The light vanished as quickly as it had appeared, and Sienne rubbed sight back into her eyes and blinked several times to dispel the afterimages of the flash.

The first thing she saw when the blindness passed was Alaric's body, floating back to rest on the floor where it had lain. His face was perfectly restored and still in the repose of sleep, not death. As she watched, Alaric's eyes fluttered open. He worked his mouth a few times as if his jaw was stiff. His head turned to look at Dianthe, kneeling near his shoulder. She looked as stunned as if she'd been hit by *force*.

"Dianthe," he said. "What happened?"

Sienne let out a sound somewhere between a shriek and a moan and flung herself atop him, sobbing tears of relief and joy. A large hand came to rest between her shoulder blades, holding her steady as Alaric sat up. Then he took her by the shoulders and held her away from him. Sienne looked up at him through teary eyes. He had the oddest expression, part curiosity, part astonishment, and he appeared to be searching her face for something. He looked back at Dianthe, then at Kalanath, who crouched near his feet. His puzzlement deepened.

He let go of Sienne's shoulders. "Dianthe," he said again, "what is this place? And—" He looked at Sienne. "Who are you?"

23

Once more a terrible pressure engulfed Sienne, but where Averran's presence had filled her with peace and hope, this felt as if someone were trying to crush her under a giant thumb. "Alaric," she said, and couldn't think of anything else to say.

"I don't know you," Alaric said, scooting away from her in a movement that broke her heart. "I don't know any—*Viveka!*"

Viveka crept forward, going to her knees and tentatively hugging her cousin. His arms went around her with no hesitation. Sienne felt as if she were going mad. This was all a terrible nightmare, and she would wake soon—

"Sienne. Don't worry," Perrin said. "No one has ever returned from the dead before. Averran assures me it will be a complete recovery."

"*Will be*? As in, it isn't now?" Sienne clenched her teeth to keep her words from coming out as a shriek.

"Ah...he did imply there would be temporary...impairments. I believed he meant physical ones." Perrin gripped her forearm. "This is a mere setback."

"But—it's ridiculous! Why wouldn't—I mean, if he's going to go to all the trouble of bringing him back, why not make it a perfect restoration?" Sienne tried to control her breathing, which was growing rapidly out of control.

"I don't know, Sienne. Alaric was hit in the head by a bolt of lightning. That might be related."

Viveka chose that moment to look past Alaric's shoulder at Sienne. She smiled a terrible, triumphant smile, and Sienne let out a shriek and dove at the woman, ready to claw her eyes out. Kalanath restrained her. "Have faith," he murmured.

Sienne gripped his arm and breathed slowly. Temporary. Any minute now. *Faith beyond reason.* This was definitely beyond reason. That Averran might want her to endure this struck her as ludicrous. Hadn't she already suffered enough?

Alaric released Viveka and didn't take her hand even though Sienne could see Viveka wanted him to. It cheered her slightly. "Dianthe," he said. He put a hand to his head as if it pained him. Blinking, he said, "How did we get from—" He groaned and closed his eyes. "The cockatrices. We were fighting cockatrices."

"That was three years ago," Dianthe said. "We've been a team for the last fourteen months. Try to remember."

Alaric staggered to one of the chairs, which creaked under his weight. "I don't—damn it, everything is coming too fast. I remember —wait." He focused on Sienne. "You're the wizard. The babe in arms. You can barely walk a full day's journey without collapsing."

Sienne nodded, then shook her head. "That was fourteen months ago. Our first job. What else do you remember?"

"The drunk priest—no, you were under chastisement for drinking. Perrin. Perrin!"

"You do remember," Perrin said with a smile.

"It's all in pieces," Alaric said. "I feel...by Sisyletus, it hurts. All those memories...what happened to me? Where—" His eyes flew open and he shot to his feet. "*Sienne,*" he said with feeling. "I forgot you. How could I—"

Sienne threw herself at him and let him fold her into his embrace. "You were dead," she said into his chest. "And now you're alive. Everything is going to be all right."

"I still feel I'm missing pieces," Alaric said. "But I can remember not remembering, if that makes sense." His arms tightened on her. "Sweetlove, I'm sorry."

"It's not your fault."

"It feels like it is." His breathing was slowly returning to normal. "I remember a voice, asking me what I would give—oh. I was dead." He said the words in a tone of astonishment. "I was dead, and Averran brought me back to life. I told him his price was too high."

"What price?" Dianthe asked.

"Forgetting all of you. All of this." He kissed the top of Sienne's head. "It was too much to give up."

"It's what he asked of me, too," Sienne murmured.

"And I," said Perrin. "I feared I had made the selfish choice."

"It is too much for me too," Kalanath said.

"I'm afraid I was ruder than the rest of you," Dianthe said, "but I wonder what would have happened if we hadn't all been in agreement?"

"I hope God doesn't play games like that," Alaric said. He suddenly went rigid. "Genneva," he said, and released Sienne. She glanced up at him; he was looking past her at Genneva's body, lying where she had fallen that final time, at Sienne's knife protruding from her chest. His arms fell away from Sienne. "You killed her."

Fear once more filled Sienne. "She asked me to," she said, feeling desperate. "Alaric, there was no other way. He was about to start killing the Sassaven, he would have turned us all into slaves...look at me!"

Alaric ignored her. He took a few steps and knelt beside his sister, took one of her black-stained hands in both of his and bowed his head. "It's not too late," he said. "We could—what did you say he needed? *Castle,* and *change*?"

"Yes, but I don't know how," Sienne said.

"Try," Alaric said, looking back at her. His eyes were fierce on hers. "*Try*, Sienne. It can't be too late."

Sienne closed her eyes and reviewed *castle* in memory. Like all summonings, it was spiky and sharp, with staccato lines and dots that would make her mouth bloody. She remembered altering *break* into *shatter*. That had been a matter of enhancing what was already there, but this—this meant finding the heart of the spell and rewriting it, and that...if it wasn't impossible, it was damn close.

She traced the lines of the spell until her head ached as if they'd stabbed her. This syllable determined distance, this targeted the other person, so *this* must identify the wizard casting the spell. If she could disconnect it from herself, give it some other point to latch onto... Tentatively, she spoke the first syllables, licking blood away from her lips. It hurt, going so slowly, but she only barely knew what she was doing, feeling her way along the spiky lines one sound at a time.

As the last syllable left her lips, she felt the spell snap away from her and heard gasps. She tried to open her eyes, but they felt too heavy, weighed down by enormous weariness. Lowering her head, she tried again, and this time they opened. Blinking slowly, she looked at Genneva. Perrin crouched over her, a blessing pressed to the wound in her chest. Alaric's gaze was fixed on her unblinking blue eyes. Sienne held her breath, willing the woman to blink or twitch or sit up.

Green light flared, but weakly, pulsing twice like a heartbeat and then fading to nothing. "No," Sienne breathed. "It worked. I know it worked."

Perrin sat back on his heels. "Something happened," he said, sounding breathless. "We all saw her convulse, as did Kyros. But I tried to heal the wound and the healing failed."

"Try again," Alaric said.

"I—" Perrin subsided when Alaric glared at him. He tore another blessing free and pressed it over the black wound. "O most gracious Lord," he said, "have mercy on me and on this woman, and grant me this blessing."

Nothing happened. "O Lord, I beg of you, heal her!" Perrin shouted. The blessing lay inert and pale against the black stains.

Alaric gripped Genneva's hand tighter. "She's changing," he said. "She doesn't look as old as she did."

Sienne was afraid to approach him, but even from where she stood, she could see he was right. The wrinkles were fading from Genneva's face and hands, her eyes appeared less sunken, and her fair hair looked more yellow than white.

"It's not too late," Alaric whispered. "Please."

No one moved. Finally Perrin lifted his hand, leaving the blessing where it lay. "I am sorry," he said. "Healing will not work on the dead."

"Then bring her back," Alaric said. "She didn't deserve to die."

"Few people do," Perrin said. "But Averran has already intervened once, restoring you to life. I dare not petition him again for such a blessing."

Alaric swore viciously and thrust Genneva's hand away. He rose to his feet and strode to the window, gripping the sill with both hands like he wanted to tear it away from the wall. Sienne felt as if the lightning arc had come back to strike her again, her heart pounding, her eyes aching with unshed tears. He needed her, and she was the last person he ought to see right now. What if he couldn't forgive her? What if it didn't matter that Genneva had sacrificed herself, that Kyros had been going to destroy all of them?

Someone put an arm around her shoulders. "Go to him," Dianthe whispered in her ear. "It's what he needs."

"He hates me."

"He doesn't hate you. He just needs to come to terms with what you did for her. For all of us."

Sienne swallowed. She walked slowly toward Alaric, passing Perrin and Kalanath, who looked like they wanted to speak but didn't know what to say. She looked out over the gray void, which moved slowly as the almost invisible waves crept in toward the shore. "I'm sorry," she said. "Maybe if I'd been faster—"

"She was always a self-centered brat," Alaric said. "I guess eleven years changed her, too, if she was able to think of the Sassaven rather than her own life."

"It took tremendous willpower to hold still and let me...she had to fight Kyros's compulsion as well as her own instinct for self-preservation." Sienne wiped away a tear. "He *silenced* me, or I could have—no. Even if I'd figured out *castle*, he would have killed all the Sassaven who helped us before I could make the change, and there wasn't anyone close enough to kill him once it was done. I can't think of any way this could have ended other than it did."

"Me either," Alaric said. He put his hand over Sienne's. "But I hoped—"

"You always do," Sienne said. "It's how you got us this far. Faith beyond reason. That's what Averran told me I needed. But I think it's something you've always had."

Alaric let out a deep, shuddering breath. "I wish I could have said goodbye."

"I wish I knew what she said, at the end. I couldn't hear her because of *silence*."

"Maybe—"

Heavy footsteps sounded in the antechamber, and Sienne and Alaric turned in time to see several Niskanen burst through the door, led by Karlen. They came up short before tripping over Kyros's body. "Stop!" Karlen shouted, though Sienne couldn't tell who he was talking to, because he looked as if he had more to say and thought better of it. He stared open-mouthed at Kyros's body. "Then it's true," he breathed. "We all felt something change. Who killed him?"

"Gen did," Alaric said, "with Sienne as her hand."

"Who—"

Alaric put his arm around Sienne and drew her forward with him. "This is Sienne, Karlen," he said. "The woman I intend to marry. And these are our friends who worked with us to make freeing our people possible. Dianthe, Perrin, and Kalanath."

Karlen didn't react to "marry." Sienne wondered if the Sassaven even knew what marriage was. His gaze swept from one to another of them and ended up back on Alaric. "You..." he said, and once more lost his words.

"What happened to him?" one of the Niskanen exclaimed. He prodded Kyros with the toe of his boot. "He looks...decayed."

Kyros looked worse than decayed, though he didn't look five

hundred years dead. His dark eyes were sunken and rimmed with black, his thin lips had curled in on themselves, and he looked as wrinkled as Genneva had been before the final exchange. Fortunately, he was still recognizable as himself. Sienne didn't think anyone would argue that Kyros was still alive just because his body was aged beyond recognition, but the possibility of having to fight that argument wearied her.

Karlen had stepped around Kyros and gone to stand beside his sister's body. "I don't understand," he said, almost plaintively. "Viveka, what happened?"

Sienne had almost forgotten Viveka was still in the room, she'd been so motionless in the corner she'd backed into. Her face was unusually pale and her eyes looked dull. "She killed Genneva," she said, pointing at Sienne. "That's all I saw."

"And destroyed the wizard's heart," Karlen said. Viveka's expression grew even more wooden, and Sienne felt mixed relief and exasperation. If Viveka had intended to turn the Niskanen against her for killing Genneva, it hadn't worked. What did she think, that Alaric would fall in love with her if Sienne was forcibly removed from the valley, or executed for murder?

"Yes," Alaric said. "Genneva fought the wizard's compulsion long enough for Sienne to destroy the heart. We..." His voice became husky. "We couldn't save her."

"Of course not." Karlen crouched beside Genneva and closed her eyelids, then folded her hands over the wound in her chest. "She was always the bravest woman I ever knew."

His stoicism angered Sienne. What kind of a brother— Then Karlen stood, and Sienne regretted her anger, because silent tears leaked from his eyes and his mouth quivered with the effort of holding them back. Alaric released Sienne and went to his brother, embracing him tightly. Sienne wiped away her own tears and felt her friends gather around her.

The other Niskanen shuffled uncomfortably in the doorway until Karlen and Alaric separated. Karlen swiped a hand across his face and said, "We need to spread the word. Lothar needs to be told so we can gather the people in Barholt and then send messages to the other villages. Some of you, take the wizard's body. Alaric and I will carry our sister. I don't want to leave her in this place." He focused on Sienne for the first time. "I remember you. You blasted me with magic."

"We couldn't have you following us," Sienne said, feeling a flash of inappropriate guilt.

"I'm trying to feel grateful you didn't kill me." He smiled, an expression that so transformed his face Sienne could finally see the resemblance to his brother. "I guess not all wizards are evil. What does it mean that Alaric is going to marry you?"

"That's...a discussion for another time," Alaric said. "Let's go. We need to tell everyone they're free." A smile crept across his lips. "They're free."

———

SIENNE COULDN'T REMEMBER EVER BEING SO TIRED. IT HAD BEEN...SHE couldn't remember how many hours since she'd last slept, but enough that her brain felt fogged and her eyes ached with tiredness. The roast chicken Ellard had made for all of them was delicious, though it tasted of unfamiliar herbs, but she chewed it without really thinking about the flavor. Weariness blunted her hunger.

Detlenda and Ellard had reacted to Alaric and Karlen bringing Genneva home without wild displays of grief. Sienne had guessed they might not, having seen the brothers' reaction to her death. She also wondered if they hadn't already grieved Genneva's death when she was first taken as Kyros's host, and this was just the end of long days of sorrow. Even so, she stayed away from them, not wanting to intrude.

There hadn't been much for any of the companions to do. Perrin had used the last of the many, many healing blessings he'd been given on the Sassaven wounded in the attack on the tower, and the other three had helped treat those not seriously injured enough for divine healing. Alaric had been gone most of the day, talking to people, explaining what had happened, answering questions. Sienne hadn't seen Viveka and was just as happy not to. If she had a way to tell the woman to turn her affections toward Karlen, it would have been different, but at the moment, Sienne's exhaustion wouldn't let her care.

She washed her last mouthful down with fresh spring water that, like the chicken, tasted odd, of strange minerals, and thought about laying her head down on the table and falling asleep there. "Thank you for the meal," she heard Dianthe say.

"It was my pleasure," Ellard said. "If you want, there's an empty house where you can rest. You look asleep on your feet."

"It has been a very long day," Perrin said, rising from where he'd sat on the floor to eat—the table wasn't big enough to accommodate all of them. "We are grateful for your hospitality."

"The house will fit three," Detlenda said, "so, perhaps Sienne might use our spare bedroom?"

Sienne was alert enough to hear Detlenda's hesitation over "spare bedroom," and wondered at it as her friends said goodnight and followed Ellard out of the house. It wasn't until Detlenda opened the door to the room that Sienne realized it wasn't so much a spare room as Genneva's old bedroom. She froze in the doorway, guilt and sadness sweeping away the fog. "I can't," she began.

"She hasn't slept here for months," Detlenda said. "She wouldn't mind you using it."

"I—thank you." Guilt still took up space in her heart, despite her knowledge that there was nothing for her to feel guilty about. She suspected it was going to be a long time before she could think of Genneva without wanting to shrivel up inside.

"When will you be leaving?"

Sienne pretended she didn't hear the eagerness in Detlenda's voice. "I don't know. As soon as Alaric thinks he's done enough."

"Alaric will stay here, with us."

"I...suppose that's possible." They hadn't actually discussed what they'd do after it was all over. Sienne had assumed they'd go back to Fioretti, but there was no reason they couldn't stay with the

Sassaven, help them figure out what they wanted to do with their new freedom.

"No. A fact. Alaric belongs with his people." Detlenda's certainty sounded carved of granite.

"I think that's up to him, don't you?"

"Once he's free of your influence, he'll see where he belongs."

Sienne bit back a sharp reply. "You're his mother," she said instead. "You ought to know better than anyone how hard it is to make Alaric do anything he doesn't want to do. And I offered to step aside. He wants children and we can't have them together. He made his decision and I wouldn't insult him by forcing him to do what I think is best for him."

"He was supposed to join with Viveka."

"Well, somebody failed to tell him that plan." Sienne felt her temper rising and once more got it under control. "Detlenda, you can't make him fall in love to suit you or Viveka. Don't you want him to be happy?"

Detlenda's eyes narrowed. "You killed my daughter," she said, "and now you're taking away my son. He will never be truly happy with you, particularly if you make him live far from his people, denying his nature. All he has with you is temporary pleasure. How can you claim to love him and still refuse to do the right thing?"

Sienne's jaw clenched. "You're not listening. I haven't made Alaric do anything."

"You seduced him. He isn't thinking straight." Detlenda's hands shook, and she gripped the door frame with one, stilling it. "*Please.* See reason."

Weariness returned, making Sienne's bones ache. Was there ever going to be a good time for this conversation? Probably not. She pushed past Detlenda. "I can't stay here tonight," she said. "I'm sorry for your loss. Both of them. But I'm not going to leave Alaric just to suit you."

She was on the street and heading west before she realized she didn't have anywhere to go. Inertia kept her feet moving, one in front of the other, until she reached the dirt plain stretching from the edge of the houses to the wall surrounding the tower. Or, rather, where the wall had been. Teams of unicorns were busy dismantling it even at this hour, working by the light that radiated from their horns with a glow warmer than that of her magic light.

She walked until she was about ten yards from where the construction—deconstruction?—continued. The unicorns were either too busy to notice her, or thought she wasn't worth noticing by comparison to the importance of their activity. That suited her fine. After Detlenda's attack, she longed for invisibility, though not literally. Casting spells felt too much like work in her present condition.

A bay unicorn lowered her load and came trotting toward Sienne, transforming midway into an enormous, heavily-muscled woman with her long blonde hair pulled back in a tail. "Hello," she said. "Were you looking for Alaric? He's on the north side."

It hadn't occurred to her that Alaric might be there, but he was a unicorn and as capable of working magic as any of them. "I just felt like watching," she said. "It's going fast."

"Don't take it personally, miss, but I won't ask for your help even though I know you're probably more capable than we are," the unicorn said. "This is something we need to do ourselves."

"I know," Sienne said, though that also hadn't occurred to her until the unicorn said something. "I'm not offended. Good luck." She nodded to the woman and headed north, giving the flying stones a wide berth.

There were at least four unicorns on the north side as brown as Alaric, but she knew him instantly. It was surprisingly easy to tell the unicorns apart, even for someone like her who was generally indifferent to horses. Alaric didn't seem to notice her, so she stood and watched him and his team for a while. The unicorns had a rhythm to their work: work a stone free, send it sailing toward one of the piles, steady it in place. Sienne wanted to ask what they meant to do with the stones now, but didn't think she should interrupt.

It was full dark, and Sienne was nearly asleep on her feet, before some unseen signal went through the workers and the stones stopped flying. The wall was gone, replaced by piles of quarried stone. Here and there, unicorns were transforming into their human selves. They didn't look tired at all, though they were quieter than a group of humans would be after a day of hard labor. Some of them glanced at Sienne as they passed, but said nothing to her. Did they know what she'd done? They had to know, at least, that she was one of the foreigners who'd defeated the wizard. She felt as conspicuous as Alaric must in Fioretti, though at least there he wasn't the only one who looked Ansorjan.

Alaric finally finished the conversation he was having with a couple of Sassaven women, turned, and saw Sienne. He smiled, and it warmed her despite the chill in the night air. He came toward her and put his arm around her. "Were you waiting for me? I meant to tell you I'd join you at my mother's house."

"I...couldn't wait there."

"Why not?" They followed the stream of Sassaven back into Barholt. *Now* everyone was staring at them, at the Sassaven man walking inappropriately close to the foreign woman. Sienne suppressed an urge to step away from Alaric and snuggled closer under his arm instead.

"I, um, had a discussion with your mother. She's not happy that we're together."

"Well, she'll have to get used to it." Alaric squeezed her gently.

"I don't think she will. She thinks I've entrapped you and you don't know your own mind."

Alaric's arm stiffened. "Is that so? Then the two of us will have to have our own discussion."

"Alaric, I'm exhausted. Can we find a place to sleep and deal with this in the morning?"

"That's why we're going to her house, sweetlove. You look dead on your feet."

Sienne looked up at him. "I'm not sleeping there. She managed to stop short of calling me a conniving slut, but just barely."

"Oh." Alaric's jaw hardened. "I see. I...didn't realize it was that bad."

"That reaction was always possible."

"She'll change her mind when she gets to know you." He didn't sound certain. Sienne chose not to respond.

He led the way to Lothar's house instead. Sienne heard his conversation with Lothar in a daze, trying to keep her eyelids open. "...not sure you want..." she heard Lothar say.

"...any of your business..." Alaric replied. "...explain about marriage..." So maybe the Sassaven really hadn't ever heard of marriage, even in stories. It seemed the sort of thing Kyros would have wanted to conceal from them, as part of keeping them under control. If Lothar was going to raise a stink about Alaric sleeping with the unsuitable foreign woman, Sienne might blast him and then... well, no, she wouldn't blast him, but she might make threatening noises until he produced a bed.

Finally, Lothar showed them the door, and Sienne was about to protest that she didn't want to walk any farther until he led them a few yards down the street and pushed open the door of an unlighted house. Sienne instinctively made a light, revealing a front room similar to Detlenda's. Alaric said, "Thanks. We'll talk in the morning," and steered Sienne to one of the interior doors, hanging ajar.

She sent the light ambling ahead into the new room—making it fly faster was beyond her—and saw, to her relief, a bed big enough even for a Sassaven unicorn covered in a pieced quilt in navy and rose-red. She sank onto it immediately and tugged her boots off. "Who did we evict?" she said.

"No one," Alaric said, removing his own boots. "Sassaven don't own more than the most basic personal property. This is waiting empty for the next bound Sassaven to take possession. Which will never happen again." He sighed and lay back on the pillows. "The longer I think about it, the more I realize what a difficult transition this will be. Private property, the worship of God in the open, marriage...that's just the beginning of what a free society needs."

Sienne curled up beside him and closed her eyes. "They'll figure it out," she murmured, and yawned.

"They're going to need a lot of help," Alaric said, but that was all she heard before falling into a blissful sleep.

24

She woke before dawn as usual. It was too dark to see, but she could feel the space surrounding her, that it was the wrong shape to be their room in Master Tersus's house, and it took her a few moments to orient herself. It helped that Alaric slept peacefully beside her, his quiet breathing the same as it always was. Then she remembered him lying too-still on the tower floor, and her heart lurched. She flung her arm over him and buried her face in his shoulder.

"Sienne?" he said. "What's wrong?"

She shuddered, unable to stop crying. "Just remembering," she said between sobs. "He killed you."

Alaric put his arms around her and stroked her hair. "I can't remember being dead, but I remember…it's odd, but I know there was more than what few memories I have. Like, I know I was somewhere, but I can't remember it. And I know Averran spoke to me, but I don't remember what he looked like." He chuckled. "Perrin wanted details, but I had to disappoint him. I think God doesn't want us knowing too much about our ultimate destiny."

Sienne sniffled. He was warm and solid and his heart beat as rhythmically as ever. "I'm just glad you remembered *us*. That was almost as terrifying as you being dead."

"It frightened me. I felt I'd lost myself—my last memory was of screaming at Dianthe to move out of the way of the cockatrice queen, and then I was tackled by a beautiful stranger who looked at me like I should know her. Nothing made sense. And then it was like being rained on by memories, none of which were connected to each other."

"You thought I was beautiful, even as a stranger?"

"I always have, sweetlove. Even when I only knew you as a young wizard who didn't appreciate the magnitude of her power." He kissed her lightly, wiped away a few tears, and kissed her again, slowly and intently. She kissed him back, then pulled away.

"We have to talk," she said.

Alaric groaned and worked his hands beneath her shirt. "I died," he said, "and I'd like to celebrate the fact that I'm alive again. And this house is completely empty, though I want you badly enough that I'd make love with you in my mother's house with my parents sleeping next door."

"That's what we have to talk about." Though she didn't wriggle away from what his hands were doing. "What do we do next? I thought we were going back to Fioretti, but from what you were doing yesterday, I wondered if you wanted to stay for a while. Help the Sassaven understand their freedom."

His hands stilled. "I'm...not sure. There's so much we can do here. And I want to give my parents time to get to know you—"

"Alaric, I don't think that's going to change their minds. You said it before—I represent an ending as far as their hopes of grandchildren go. And your mother wants you to join with Viveka."

He groaned again, more quietly. "I never did tell you about Viveka, I know. I'm sorry."

"I assumed it was because there was nothing to tell. I know you don't love her and I could see her reaction to your return was a complete surprise." Her first jealous reaction seemed years in the past.

"It was, though in hindsight it shouldn't have been. We were close as children and I was fond of her, but nothing serious. Even when I promised her I'd return, I didn't mean it in a romantic way. If I'd loved her, there's no way I'd have left her behind when I fled."

"That's what I thought. And now she hates me, too."

Alaric was silent for a while. Sienne held her peace, giving him time to work through whatever he was thinking. "I don't want to give up my family," he finally said. "I always assumed I'd be able to settle back here...though, granted, that was before you came into my life. Would you be willing to live here? If my parents could come to terms with you?"

"Of course," Sienne said. "My home is wherever you are. But... shouldn't we discuss this with everyone? We'd be breaking up the team."

"I think that's already happening. Perrin will want to be with his family, and I don't know how long Cressida and the children can bear the strain of him constantly going into danger. I know Kalanath wants to reunite with his parents. And Dianthe..." He let out a breath. "She said, while you were scouting the tower room for *transport*, that nearly dying from that lightning bolt made her realize she couldn't bear to risk her life again, especially far from Denys where he might not ever learn what happened to her. I think she's reconsidering Corbyn's offer to make her Derekian's spymaster."

Sienne drew in a sharp breath. "But—"

"I don't know how serious she is. But I think she's done scrapping, no matter what she decides."

The thought made Sienne feel empty, as if the future had become a great empty hole like the void outside the tower window. "Then... that's it," she said. "We did what we set out to do, and it's over."

"I guess so," Alaric said. He removed his hands from beneath her shirt. "Let's get something to eat, and then I want to have a serious talk with my parents. And then...I don't know what next."

He sounded so uncertain the emptiness yawned wider. "We'll figure it out," she said. "We always do."

———

DETLENDA GREETED THEM AS CHEERFULLY AS IF NOTHING HAD PASSED between her and Sienne. Alaric, for his part, ate the porridge she offered without complaint. It was gluey and bland, and suited Sienne's stomach well, but she knew Alaric well enough to recognize when he was being polite.

Perrin, Kalanath, and Dianthe, who joined them around the table —standing, because there still weren't enough stools—were as subdued as they were, with Perrin speaking only to invoke the translation blessing. It wasn't until the end of the meal, when Kalanath was collecting bowls, that Dianthe said, "So. Should we..." She bit her lower lip and didn't finish the sentence.

"Mother, Father, I'd like to talk to you. There's so much we haven't said," Alaric said. It was an excellent excuse for Sienne to leave the awkward silence. The others followed her outside.

The street in full daylight was more depressing than it had been in darkness. The age of the houses was more visible, and Sienne saw how the streets were lower than the houses as if generations of Sassaven feet had worn them into a deep groove. Sleek black Pekkanen wandered between the houses, some of them scratching on doors to be let in. Now that they were in no danger from Kyros, Sienne wondered how their lives would change. No more sleeping in cold, dank caves, for one.

The Sassaven passing by gave the companions strange looks, but said nothing. Sienne felt in sympathy with them. She tilted her head toward the rising sun and closed her eyes, soaking up its warmth. She didn't know how cold it got this far north, in winter, and couldn't imagine the streets clogged with snow. Beneddo got snow, not much of it, but Alaric had told her stories of being snowed in as a child that Sienne found almost incomprehensible.

"I wonder what they are discussing," Perrin said.

"Probably how he's not giving up his foreign lover to make babies with his cousin," Sienne said.

"How awkward," Dianthe said. "So...what *is* he going to do?"

"I don't know."

Silence fell again. "I suppose there is nothing left for us to do," Perrin said.

"I feel we are in the way," Kalanath said. He waved at a small child tagging along after its parent. The child shied away from him and clung to the adult's legs, prompting the woman to pick the child up and put it over her shoulder. Kalanath's smile vanished.

"I could...I mean, if we're done, I could...take you all where you want to go," Sienne said. "Esthold. Chirantan. Fioretti. Denys has to be worried about you, Dianthe."

"I told him we'd be gone for several weeks," Dianthe said. "But I do miss him."

"And I do not wish to be parted from my family longer than is necessary," Perrin said. "We have yet to decide what we will do about our permanent home."

"I told my mother I would return. I do not know for how long," Kalanath said.

Sienne felt suddenly as if time had turned on itself, putting her back at the outpost where they'd stopped at the conclusion of their first job together. The impulse she'd had then returned, the desire to shout at them all, reminding them that what they had together was greater than anything they could do separately. But this was different. They'd achieved their purpose, and now...what? Go back to taking small jobs? Nothing could possibly top what they'd done for the Sassaven.

Detlenda's door slammed open. "Let's walk," Alaric said, slamming the door shut behind him. He strode off down the street without waiting to see if they'd follow. Sienne hurried after him, surrounded by her friends. Alaric took up the center of the street, forcing everyone else to make way for him. His shoulders were hunched and taut, and if it had been a wood floor and not one of earth he would have shaken the ground with every hard-booted step.

They reached the river, and Alaric veered to one side and stopped at the riverbank. He stood motionless, looking into the rushing water that foamed along the bank, his hands clenched into fists. Sienne found herself afraid of what he might do if she touched him. "Did it... not go well?" she asked.

Alaric's jaw tightened. "They want everything to be the way it was eleven years ago," he said. "Pretend I never had a life outside this valley, that all my desires should fall into line with theirs. And, damn it, they have a point."

Fear flashed through her. "Oh?" she said, trying to sound neutral.

"We need to build our people up. That means children. I don't have a right to withhold that if I really care about the Sassaven's survival."

The fear returned, lodging in her heart and building to an enormous pressure. "I understand," she said, feeling as if the words might choke her.

Alaric looked her way. "You don't," he said flatly. "They wanted a compromise. They said, if I was so determined to live my life with you, I should at least give Viveka a child before I left."

Fear turned to horror. "No," she breathed. "They didn't."

"As if I were some breeding animal, able to abandon my child to a fatherless existence." Alaric looked on the verge of explosion.

"How could they ask that?" Dianthe exclaimed. "You would never—"

"Not under any circumstances," Alaric said. "I can't believe they'd even suggest it."

"Then..." Sienne finally put a hand on his arm. "What will you do?"

"Talk to Lothar," Alaric said. "I don't want to walk away if there's anything left he needs from us."

"But—"

"But what?"

"Nothing," Sienne said. It felt so wrong, Alaric parting from his parents on those terms, and yet... She knew him well enough to recognize when he needed time to work something through, and what he didn't need right now was her blundering in with comments about how they did love him, after all. He'd never said anything like that when her own parents had presented her with a similar ultimatum, and for all she knew, his parents *didn't* care anything for him except as a father for their potential grandchildren. So she kept quiet as they walked, less aggressively, to the headman's house.

Lothar wasn't there despite the earliness of the hour. "Maybe he went to the tower?" Dianthe suggested.

"They were going to tear it down today," Alaric said. "But they weren't sure what to do about the central room."

"Maybe I can help with that," Sienne said. "At the very least I can tell them if they're going to cause an explosion."

"Is that possible?" Kalanath said, alarmed.

"I have no idea. That's just the worst thing I can think of, when it comes to dismantling a room that isn't there."

"Then maybe we should hurry," Dianthe said.

The tower still rose far too high above Barholt when they reached the plain. Unicorns and horses milled about it, moving stacks of stone to make a more orderly pile. The Pekkanen, Sienne noticed, stayed out of the plain as if it were surrounded by a wall of *force*. Alaric made for a black unicorn stallion whose horn was silvery gray instead of black, though it still gleamed as if oiled. The unicorn stood looking up at the tower and didn't acknowledge them when Alaric led their group to join him. "Lothar," Alaric said. "Is there anything we can do to help?"

Lothar shook his head, then transformed into a towering human figure. "You can tell us if it's safe to dismantle the thing," he said. "We've emptied all but the central chamber."

"It might be possible to disconnect it from the tower," Sienne said.

Lothar glanced down at her. "You can do that?"

"I don't know. I can look at it."

Lothar waved in the direction of the tower. "We're in a hurry."

"Why?" Alaric asked.

"You don't feel it? Nobody wants that thing looming over us one minute longer than it has to." Lothar's lips pinched tight shut briefly. "The sooner we can rid ourselves of his memory, the better."

Sienne suppressed a moment's fear that the unicorns would begin dismantling the tower while she and her friends were inside. "I'll be quick," she promised.

The antechamber was empty of everything, including the horrible masks. "I wonder where they took everything?" Perrin said. "I half expect to see a giant bonfire on that plain."

Alaric pushed open the central door. "I'd be afraid to inhale any smoke from burning Kyros's things. Sienne, what do you see?"

Sienne stepped over the threshold, then stepped back again. "I don't feel anything different," she said. "The only reason we can tell it's in a different place is that there are windows, and it's night."

"So what will happen if it is gone? If they destroy it?" Kalanath asked.

"I don't know." Sienne stepped back into the room. "But my instincts tell me it would be a bad idea for them to simply take it apart. I just don't know any spell that would disrupt the connection."

"That is because such magic is a priest's province, as you may recall from our freeing Jenani," Perrin said. He pulled out his riffle of blessings and plucked one free. "This is identical to the one that disrupted the ashwar's connection to the ring that held it captive. I believe it will do the same for this room."

"I remember that being fairly explosive," Alaric said. "Is it safe?"

"This time, I have a shield blessing that will protect us." Perrin removed a second blessing. "If we are in agreement?"

"Do it," Alaric said.

Sienne hurried back into the antechamber as Perrin placed the first blessing on the floor at the center of the wizard's chamber. She remembered how effective it had been and how it had temporarily blinded her when they'd used it to free Jenani, and gave it a respectful distance.

Perrin returned and held out the other blessing, murmuring an invocation. A pearly gray shield covered, not the destruction blessing, but the entire inner wall in which the door to the chamber was set. Sienne pictured the shield blessing forming a sphere centered on the chamber and hoped the explosion wouldn't take the whole tower down with it. "Um," she said, "maybe we should be prepared for *transport*, in case the blessing is more powerful than we expect."

Perrin rested his hand on the curve of the shield. "Form up around me, then," he said, and the others made a circle that ended with Alaric and Kalanath's hands on each of Perrin's shoulders. Perrin bowed his head and said, "O great Lord, protect us now, and grant me this blessing."

The world went white. Sienne, who'd closed her eyes just in time, felt as if she'd been blinded anyway. A deep rumble shook the floor, nearly knocking her off balance. Alaric's large hand kept her upright, and she clung to him gratefully. Gradually, the light faded, and Sienne blinked away pained tears and opened her eyes.

The pearly shield still covered the wall, but a thick dark fog lay behind it, concealing the door and the chamber. Perrin drew his belt knife and stabbed it into the shield, making it crumple and part like flower petals wilting. The fog faded and then vanished. Where the doorway had been was nothing but blank white stone matching the rest of the walls. Even the wooden door was gone. Perrin rapped on the stone with the pommel of his blade. "I believe it worked," he said.

The tower rumbled again, less loudly this time, but the room shook enough that Sienne had to cling to Alaric again. "Time to go," he said.

They met Lothar at the base of the tower. "It's safe now," Alaric said. "At least, it's just an ordinary tower. No more magic."

"Join in, if you're inclined," Lothar said to Alaric. He transformed once more into his unicorn form and cantered off toward one of the groups.

Alaric watched him go. When it was clear Lothar wasn't interested in them anymore, Sienne said, "Will you join them?"

Alaric startled. "I—yes, I guess I should," he said. "This shouldn't take long. But you all might want to back up."

They retreated to the edge of the plain and found themselves standing where they had the previous morning, waiting for the Sassaven to provide their distraction. In the distance, groups of unicorns and horses milled about. "I find it difficult to believe they can take down something so large," Perrin murmured. "One would think its height would militate against its being so easily demolished."

The tower swayed. Sienne grabbed Dianthe's hand. It reminded her so much of her dream she almost expected to see Kyros looking out at them, plotting revenge. It swayed the other way, and then the top of the tower popped off its stem and came floating down toward the Sassaven. All the unicorns' horns glowed bright gold that made a shimmering fog surrounding them and drifting into the air to enfold the falling tower. A breeze came up at that moment, blowing across the field to where Sienne stood. It didn't disturb the glowing fog, but it carried with it the scent of roses, and Sienne breathed it in and felt some of her tension dissipate.

"Is that their magic?" Kalanath said. He inhaled deeply. "It is beautiful."

The tower's top gently came to rest on the ground about twenty yards from where they stood. Then it shivered, and came apart, like an explosion in a dream, blocks and roof tiles floating away from each other in a slow, contemplative dance. The golden fog caressed each piece, guiding them into neat piles near where the wall's stones had been gathered. In only a few minutes, the tower's top was gone, and the tower itself looked like a beheaded tulip stem, waving in the rose-scented wind.

"Perhaps I should have more faith in Sassaven magic," Perrin said. "That was astonishing."

Now the swaying tower began to come apart in the same diffident manner, stones loosening themselves from the wall and then floating downward, some of them spinning lazily as if they weighed no more than a leaf. The piles of stone grew taller, and new piles formed. "What will they do with it all?" Sienne said.

"Build real houses, I hope," Dianthe said. "Though that's not enough to rebuild all of Barholt."

"No, but it's a start." Sienne started counting stones and gave up almost immediately. "I hope they aren't superstitious about using that material, or about building on this plain."

"They seem rather pragmatic," Perrin said, "at least, that is my conclusion after treating so many of them yesterday."

"They are good, solid stone," Kalanath said. "I think it is good that they use them."

Eventually, nothing was left of the tower but the massive iron door. The Sassaven, for some reason, left it standing until it fell over on its own. Then, with a noise like rushing wind, they all returned to their human shapes. Sienne waited for a cheer, or a cry, or something to acknowledge what they'd achieved, but the massed crowds were silent, most of the Sassaven standing with their heads bowed as if in prayer. After a few moments, they turned and made their way back toward the village, dispersing in all directions. Shortly, Alaric appeared. "We're going to Lothar's home. He wants to talk to us. All of us," he said.

The Sassaven surrounding them as they walked took care not to touch them, as if they feared some kind of contagion from their foreign guests. Sienne tried not to take it personally, though she did feel a little irritated that none of them displayed any sign of friendliness. She and her friends *had* put their lives on the line for them, after all. Then she felt guilty. She reminded herself that they hadn't done it to be thanked, and the Sassaven's lives had just been turned upside down; it was natural they wouldn't be in a cheerful mood just yet. Give them time to get used to freedom.

Lothar was there when they arrived. Instead of sitting in the chair, he stood leaning against the table, which took a few inches off his height so he was no taller than Alaric. If he'd done it on purpose in some attempt to make this a friendly meeting, his neutral expression, more intimidating to Sienne than a scowl for being so unreadable, negated the effect. "Is this yours?" he said, pointing at a book lying next to the candles. "Someone fished it out of the river where it was caught by the bridge piling. We've never seen anything like it before."

Sienne snatched up her spellbook with a gasp. "I can't believe it. I thought it was lost for good! Thank you."

"It's no trouble." He still sounded so neutral, as if none of this mattered to him—well, the spellbook probably didn't matter to him, but given the Sassaven's history with magic, she'd expected him to be less unconcerned about it being left lying around. "You've done more than I believed possible," he said. "The wizard dead, the binding broken…I suppose we should be grateful."

"And yet you're not," Alaric said. His expression matched Lothar's, making them look like a couple of chess players caught mid-game where neither wanted to be the next to move.

Lothar's eyes narrowed. "It's hard to be grateful," he said, "when we've been made to feel like helpless children."

Sienne opened her mouth to protest and Dianthe stepped on her foot in warning. "Maybe it was impossible for us to free ourselves," Lothar went on. "Or maybe we just weren't willing to pay the price. Either way, the plain fact is that a bunch of strangers swooped in and saved us, and most of us are having trouble coming to grips with that."

"You think I'm a stranger?" Alaric said, dangerously calm.

"I think you've been gone a long time, and you don't think like us anymore," Lothar said. He nodded at Sienne. "You've made alliances like a foreigner. I could make a case for that to be a necessary part of your solution, and I'm not going to criticize you for it. But you're still no longer one of us, necessary or not. Which brings us back to the central problem."

"I don't see how it's a problem. We didn't do it to be thanked."

"No, and maybe that makes it worse, that you aren't behaving like conquering heroes. That makes us feel all sorts of guilty about not being grateful." Lothar sighed, and suddenly he looked very tired and surprisingly old. "I don't know what you had in mind, Alaric, whether you wanted to stay. And nobody is going to shut any of you out. But we'd take it as a kindness if you'd leave."

Alaric's hand closed into a fist the way it did when he was trying to control his temper. "So you *are* shutting us out."

"But," Sienne exclaimed, ignoring the increasing pressure of Dianthe's foot, "but there's so much you still don't know! We were going to—"

"You were going to go on being our saviors," Lothar said. "Teach us poor ignorant fools how civilization really works, is that it?"

"Of course not!" She thought better of her outburst halfway through that sentence. "But wouldn't you rather know...I mean, what about the coming of age ritual? We know how to use it without the binding—shouldn't you—"

"We want no reminders of the wizard," Lothar said flatly. "That ritual is irrelevant."

"But it opens your full potential! How is that irrelevant?"

"They don't need it," Alaric said. "They'll still have magic, and that's enough."

Sienne saw his closed-off, remote expression and decided to shut up.

"I understand," Alaric said. "We're too much a reminder of what you believe is your failure, yes? Even though you couldn't possibly—"

Lothar slammed his fist on the table. "All it would have taken was one man or woman willing to give their life in killing the host. We were too cowardly to try it."

"It would have killed all of you," Alaric said. "Kyros had it built into the binding. If he died before it was broken, every adult Sassaven would have died as well."

"Leaving our children free to rebuild. That's not too high a price. Even you ought to understand that."

"Your civilization would not survive it," Kalanath said. "Too much death—who would teach them to live? To build? You were not cowards."

Lothar shook his head. "It doesn't matter. We're free, and all we want is to build that freedom on our own terms. Which means with no outside interference."

"I understand," Alaric repeated. "We don't want to interfere." His hand was clenched so tightly the tendons stood out on its back. He turned and walked to the door without another word.

"Alaric," Lothar said. Alaric stopped, but didn't turn around. "I'm sorry. I know you've already sacrificed much to make this happen."

"Meaning this is just one more sacrifice?" Alaric said. "Don't pretend to understand." He opened the door and left the room.

"You *bastard*," Sienne snarled. "He's thought of nothing but achieving this for the last *eleven years*, and this is how you repay him?"

"Leave it alone, Sienne," Dianthe said, taking her shoulder. Sienne shrugged her off.

"He's right, we didn't do it to be thanked," she said, "but you could at least show that it mattered to you."

"We owe you more than we can ever repay," Lothar said, "except by never taking our freedom for granted. That's not something you can give us. Please. Just go."

Sienne spun on her heel and slammed the door open, not waiting to see if the others would follow.

Alaric stood just outside, his head bowed, his arms crossed over his chest. "Can you take us to Esthold?" he said. "Right now?"

"Oh!" Sienne exclaimed, startled out of her anger. "But...shouldn't you say goodbye to your parents, and Karlen?"

"I spoke with Karlen yesterday. I think, even then, I knew it was goodbye. And I have nothing left to say to my parents."

Dianthe laid a hand on his arm. "You'll regret it later," she said.

"You don't know that."

"I do. Just—don't leave them in anger, at least on your end. You can't do anything about their feelings, but..."

Alaric sighed. "You're right. Though I don't know what I'll say. 'I'm sorry you're bigoted and lacking in human decency'?"

"I'm sure you can think of something less likely to start a war," Sienne said.

They waited for him outside Detlenda's house. Sienne almost cast *sharpen* on herself so she could eavesdrop on the conversation. She knew it was wrong, but that had never stopped her before, and she dearly wanted to know what they said to each other. In the end, she didn't have to; sound carried clearly through the oiled paper of the window.

"You don't have to go," Detlenda said. She sounded like she meant it. Could she really be so clueless as to not realize what she'd offered her son as a compromise was a terrible insult?

"Lothar made it clear I did," Alaric said. "Since I don't intend to stay without Sienne, and she's definitely not welcome anywhere in this valley."

"It's not that we don't like her," Ellard said. "But—"

"Father, we've been through this," Alaric said. "I'm not going to change my mind and neither are you. And *don't,* for the love of Sisyletus, repeat that foul proposal. I would never father a child I intended to abandon."

"But you're not one of them," Detlenda pleaded. "You left before and it broke our hearts. Don't do it again."

"I didn't think I wanted to," Alaric said. "But I begin to believe Lothar's right, and I *am* one of them. I don't know. Maybe in another eleven years I can return. I'll want to see how things have changed. Visit Karlen's children, and Viveka's. Maybe they'll be the same."

"Karlen and Viveka?" Ellard said. His astonishment rang clearly through the window.

"You haven't seen it?" Alaric sounded amused, and that reassured Sienne that he might eventually get over this. "Well, maybe I'm wrong. But—I love you both. I never stopped thinking of you, all those years. I hope, if I do come back, I'll find a welcome here."

"Oh, son," Detlenda said. Sienne strained to hear more, but they appeared to be done talking. Shortly, the door opened, and Alaric emerged.

"Esthold," he said. "And...you were right."

"I usually am," Dianthe said.

25

The alley with the funny Doom-shaped brick pattern was empty again. Sienne wasn't sure what would happen with *transport* if she tried to go someplace that was occupied. Probably the spell would just fail, but it wasn't an experiment she wanted to try. She hitched her spellbook higher on her shoulder. Its weight comforted her, even if she didn't need it.

"It is unfortunate I have no communication blessing this morning, or I might warn Cressida of our arrival," Perrin said. "Though for that matter, I am grateful to have any blessings at all. I prayed at dawn as has become my habit these last few days and received a decidedly icy reply. I believe now that the exigencies of the moment are passed, Averran intends me to return to my previous leisurely mornings."

"I'm in favor of that," Dianthe said. "The Sassaven have never heard of coffee."

Sienne almost said *But you're giving up scrapping* and stopped herself in time. If Dianthe was going to behave as if nothing would change, she wasn't going to jinx that with hasty, unconsidered words.

She found herself relaxing as they strolled through Esthold. Yes, the place was full of blond Ansorjans, and she and her companions were clearly outsiders, but the blond Ansorjans, unlike their

Sassaven counterparts, acknowledged their passing. True, sometimes it was with a scowl or a curt "watch where you're going," but Sienne couldn't help feeling she'd returned home.

The neighborhood of sweeping, scrubbing women looked just the same as when they'd left it a week before. The children were nowhere to be seen, but scraps of laughter and shouting from behind the houses suggested they'd moved their game out of the street and into someone's back garden. Perrin's pace accelerated until he was nearly jogging. "Excuse me," he said, and ran ahead to knock on Thordis's door.

"What now?" Sienne said quietly.

"It's a little early to ask that," Alaric said. "It's up to Perrin now."

Sienne jigged with impatience. What she *wanted* was to convince everyone to return to Master Tersus's house and start looking for the next job. But it seemed unlikely she would get her wish.

Perrin had disappeared inside the house, and the children's shouts were growing louder. Suddenly a horde of them appeared around the side of one of the houses, all of them chasing someone who held aloft a red rag tied to a stick. Sienne spotted both Noel and Delphine in the crowd. The mass of children parted to pass around the friends, then came back together as if they were water divided temporarily by a stone in the brook, just as they had the last time. Delphine waved to them and came trotting back. "You're here!" she exclaimed. "Where is Papa?"

"Speaking to your mother, I imagine," Alaric said. "What game are you playing?"

"Oh, it's follow-my-leader, but mostly we just like running," Delphine said. "Are we leaving now? Can we go home? I like this place, and Beneddo is nice, but I miss my own bedroom."

"We'll see what your parents say," Alaric said, dodging the issue of whether Delphine would see her bedroom ever again.

At that moment, the door opened, and Perrin and Cressida emerged, hand in hand. Delphine shouted for joy and ran toward them. Perrin put his free arm around his daughter and hugged her, saying something they were too far away for Sienne to hear. "...quite as grown-up as you appear," Perrin was saying when they drew near. "Cressida has some unexpected news for us," he told the others. "It changes what I had intended."

"Two days ago I received a mind-to-mind communication," Cressida said. "It was the kind I am accustomed to receiving from Perrin, but in this case it was not one that allowed me to respond, merely to hear. Alcander Verannus commissioned a priest for a blessing to send word that his appointment with the king was inconclusive and that the king told him to return in three days—which is to say, tomorrow. I have been quite distraught not knowing the details, but as I said, I was unable to press him further."

"I think we should return to Fioretti immediately," Perrin said. "If Alcander's suit fails, we need to know immediately how far we should flee. I do not intend to be separated from my family again."

"Of course not," Dianthe said. "There's no reason to wait, is there?"

Sienne felt irrationally as if everything was moving too fast, but said, "None. Except I don't know where Noel is."

"I will gather our things, and say goodbye to Thordis, and we may leave," Cressida said.

Sienne waited by Thordis's front door, idly flipping through her spellbook, while everyone else ran about collecting people or belongings or saying goodbye. It turned out almost every woman on the street wanted to bid the Deluccos farewell. She paused at *bubble* and traced its lines with her finger. Such a small thing, but it had saved her life. Just one more way in which Averran had looked out for her. *O Lord,* she prayed silently, *if it's not too much to ask, couldn't you keep us together?*

She waited for the sense of peace she always had when she felt Averran's presence and felt only dull emptiness and, then, a trace of fear. Suppose, now they'd accomplished what God wanted, She didn't care anymore that they were a team? Suppose God felt She'd rewarded them enough by returning Alaric so they all survived? Sienne blinked hard to hold back tears and flipped pages more rapidly. *Castle. Change. Fury.* So many spells she wouldn't need if she wasn't a scrapper anymore. Of course, she and Alaric could still take jobs, but it would feel so strange to have new companions. What had Carys Bettega said—that she'd be lucky not to lose any? How much luckier if she only lost them to new lives and not to death? In either case, it wasn't the kind of luck she wanted.

"Sienne," Alaric said. She raised her head and let the spellbook dangle free in its harness. "We're ready."

She cast *transport* twice and brought everyone through to their sitting room in Master Tersus's house. When she arrived with the second group—the Deluccos—the other three were gone, but a quick search revealed they'd only gone as far as the kitchen. Perrin sat at the table and began sorting through his riffle of blessings. "Ah," he said, holding one aloft. "With this, I can locate Alcander and perhaps learn more of what has happened than his terse communication allowed."

"I'm going to see Denys," Dianthe said. "I'll be back in a few hours." She was gone before Sienne could ask what she wanted to see Denys for. Probably it was nothing. Maybe it was sex. Sienne hoped it was only sex.

Perrin already had his head bowed over the blessing, which glowed with a blue light before shriveling into a milky blue faceted gem the size of his thumbnail. "I will return shortly," he said before swallowing the locator blessing.

"You will not go alone," Cressida said. "I refuse to wait here not knowing."

Perrin smiled. "My mistake. Of course you should come. But the children—"

"Sienne and I will take them to the park," Alaric said, "and Kalanath—"

"I will go with you to guide your steps, Perrin," Kalanath said with a smile, "because I remember this blessing that it makes you walk into things. And if Master Delucco has what Sienne calls his thugs in the streets, you will need my staff."

"I feel I have given insufficient thought to this plan in my eagerness," Perrin said. A peculiar look crossed his face. "I feel it beginning to work. Thank you all for your help."

When Perrin, Cressida, and Kalanath were gone, Noel said, "Do you know how to play foot-the-ball? Axel gave me one as a goodbye present."

"I do know how," Alaric said, "and I'm sure we can teach Sienne."

"Oh, no," Sienne said. "I only run if I'm being chased."

"Really?" Alaric said, a wolfish twinkle in his eye. Sienne brandished her spellbook at him, and he laughed. "Let's see if we can help you change your mind."

In the end, Sienne amused them all by casting transform after transform, changing the color of the ball and turning frogs into birds that hopped and fluttered their wings before regaining their original shapes. She watched Alaric and Noel kick the ball back and forth—Noel really was a natural—and eventually sat with Alaric's head in her lap while the Delucco children dozed beneath one of the cypress trees dotting the park.

"Do you think Alcander will argue the king around to his way of thinking?" she said. "It worries me that the king made him come back another time."

"I choose to look at it as hopeful that he didn't turn him down flat," Alaric said. "And it makes me think Derekian is taking it seriously. If he wanted, he could just order Perrin's father to stop harassing the family. But that wouldn't solve the long-term problem of the law being on Delucco's side. Derekian may be looking for a permanent, legal solution."

"You're far more optimistic than I am. That's a change, don't you think?"

"I'm optimistic," Alaric said, lowering his voice, "because I have plans for you tonight, and they involve the two of us being naked in our own big wonderful bed. That leaves me feeling in charity with the whole world."

She ran her fingers through his short hair. "You're right. I suddenly feel more cheerful."

When they returned at midday to Master Tersus's house, only Leofus was in the kitchen. He groused less vocally than usual, probably because there were children present, and provided them with a meal that left Sienne feeling full and happy. She was less happy about the prospect of spending the rest of the day tending Noel and Delphine, who were well-behaved but still needed more attention than she enjoyed providing. Would it be different if they were her own? Probably, but she was just as happy not to make the experiment.

She cast *summon companion* a handful of times and gave the children with a pile of puppies to play with, then settled in on the sitting room sofa and watched Alaric join them. He so clearly enjoyed himself she felt a little bad about her mild resentment.

"I sincerely hope I am not expected to adopt all those animals," Perrin said in some dismay. Sienne looked up at the trio gathered in the doorway. Cressida had her hand over her mouth, concealing a smile. Kalanath looked as if he wanted to join in the fun but felt it undignified.

"They'll vanish in an hour or so," Sienne said. "No mess, no fuss. What did you learn?"

"That the king has been quite cagey about what he intends to do," Perrin said. He waded past the melee and sat next to Sienne. "In Alcander's first meeting with the king, he provided his Majesty with all the documentation he has amassed, and by his account it is not an inconsiderable amount. He also recounted the efforts of the Eagle-Eyes—that is the group he contacted who have been pursuing the issue separately—and made what I believe was an eloquent plea for the king to weigh in on the situation. King Derekian listened and then told Alcander to return at a later date. No suggestion as to how he intends to rule."

"I believe the king wanted time to go over the papers," Cressida said. She picked up a puppy and cradled it next to her cheek. "If he intended to rule against us, he had every opportunity to do so during that first meeting."

"Yes, but there is nothing to say he may not still do so," Perrin said.

"It's not as if you can do anything about it," Alaric said. "Did Alcander say you could go along tomorrow?"

"I did not ask, as I believe our presence may simply complicate matters," Perrin said. "But Alcander has promised to bring word here immediately."

The back door banged open. A moment later, Dianthe appeared in the sitting room doorway. She looked windblown and out of breath. "There's a bunch of people in royal livery coming this way," she said. "Want to bet they're coming here?"

Alaric rolled to his feet and handed Sienne the puppy he'd been playing with. "I'd say it's impossible, but Derekian is smarter than he looks and he's got resources I can barely imagine," he said. "Come on. If they know enough to come to the back door, I'll be seriously impressed."

Five minutes later, a knock sounded at the back door. Leofus, who poorly concealed his excitement at being pressed into service as their majordomo, opened it. "A royal summons for Perrin Delucco," Sienne heard the herald say in the distance. "I am enjoined to deliver it personally."

Leofus showed the woman into the kitchen. She looked not at all surprised or insulted at finding herself in such low surroundings. "Which of you is Perrin Delucco?" she asked, her eyes fixed on a point above their heads.

Perrin stood. "I am he."

The herald's gaze came swiftly to rest on him. "My lord and master King Derekian requests and requires a response," she said. She extended a rolled-up piece of paper sealed with yellow wax into which was impressed a stylized F. Fiorus.

Perrin took it and broke the seal. He scanned the paper's contents swiftly. "Is a verbal reply acceptable?"

"I have his Majesty's full faith and honor," the herald replied.

"Then...please tell his Majesty I agree, and we will be there at the appointed hour," Perrin said.

The herald inclined her head to him and turned sharply on her heel to exit the room. Leofus scurried after her to let her out.

Perrin took his seat again. "King Derekian wants to see all of us in his audience chamber tomorrow at nine o'clock. That is, perhaps not coincidentally, half an hour before his scheduled meeting with Alcander."

"Yes, but all of us?" Dianthe said. "We're not even involved. Well, no, we're *involved*, but not in any legal sense."

"Derekian isn't stupid," Alaric said. "He knows if the Deluccos vanished—and you can be damn sure Master Delucco spread the word that they vanished—we probably had something to do with it. I'm just not sure what he has in mind. I doubt he wants to bring us up on charges for kidnapping, or aiding and abetting, or whatever it's called."

"No, he'd leave that to the courts," Sienne agreed. "But I'm too keyed up to be worried. We started the day in the Pirinin Peaks, then Esthold and finally back here. If I weren't so familiar with Master Tersus's house, I wouldn't have any idea where I am now."

"I think we've earned a real rest," Dianthe said.

"I'm too keyed up for rest, too."

"Well, I'm not," Dianthe said, rising and stretching. "I'm going to nap and then I'm going to eat the magnificent dinner I'm sure Leofus intends to prepare, and then I'm going dancing. And if you can't figure out a way to relax, I'll find someone to cast *sleep* on you."

Sienne grinned. "Nobody will. It's forbidden."

"Then you'd better not make me do it," Dianthe said.

26

For once, Sienne slept past dawn, the comfort of her own familiar bed in her own familiar room combining to draw her into a deep, undisturbed slumber. She woke briefly when Alaric rose, fell back asleep, and woke more fully when the scent of sweet porridge, savory bacon, and tangy orange juice roused her nose. She sat up. Alaric had an enormous tray in both hands and was just shutting the door with his rear end. "Oh," she breathed, "you really do love me."

"I wanted to have you all to myself a little longer than usual," Alaric said. He balanced the tray on the end of the bed and climbed up next to her without disturbing it. "And since you're usually the one who makes breakfast, I thought this would be a nice change."

She kissed him, then picked up the bowl and dug in. "It's a very nice change. But I want to know what really brought this on."

"I can't just want to do something nice for you?"

"You can, but not if you have the look that says you've got something unpleasant you're softening me up for."

Alaric helped himself to a couple of slices of bacon and sighed. "You know me too well." He chewed for a while, then said, "We need to figure out what we're going to do when the others leave."

The delicious porridge wasn't sitting so well on her stomach anymore. "Go out on jobs, I assumed. It's not like we have to stop being scrappers."

"No, but don't you think it will feel strange, going with, well, strangers?"

"Our friends were strangers once too. Maybe we'll make new friends." It sounded stupid and facile even to her. "And maybe we'll do like Kalanath used to, take temporary jobs here and there."

"I was thinking," Alaric said, a little too casually, "I might take a job with the city guard."

Sienne's eyebrows climbed almost to her hairline. "You, in the city guard? Working with *Denys*?"

Alaric's cheeks went pink. "It wouldn't be so bad."

"Yes, but...what would I do?"

"Anything you want. Teach. You still haven't decided what you're going to do about the coming of age ritual."

She'd almost forgotten about it in the whirlwind of travel and the king's summons. "I should make a decision, I know." She pushed her mostly-empty bowl away. "Can we discuss it after we meet the king? Maybe we're wrong, and they don't want to leave."

Alaric took her hand and ran his thumb over the back of it. "Sweetlove, they've already made their decision."

She sighed. "I know."

Alaric finished his bacon and started in on the pile of eggs. "I think," he said between mouthfuls, "you're going to end up taking people a lot of different places today."

They met the others downstairs in the kitchen, all except Perrin. "You'd think he'd be an early riser today of all days," Sienne said.

Dianthe smirked. "He and Cressida shared a room last night. *Without* the children. I think he's entitled to sleep in a bit."

"Oh. Well. Even so, we shouldn't be late."

Footsteps sounded outside the kitchen door. "We will not be late," Perrin said cheerfully, "because Sienne will *transport* us straight to the palace. Am I correct?"

He looked so happy her irritation vanished. "You are correct," she said. "Was Cressida included in the king's summons?"

"She was not." Perrin's cheerfulness subsided a little. "I choose to see it as a good thing, despite having no reason to believe it so."

"It will be fine," Dianthe said, casting Alaric, who'd opened his mouth to speak, a warning look. Alaric subsided. "But let's go now. I'm starting to get nervous, and when I get nervous, I pace."

"We know," Kalanath said. He propped his staff against the kitchen wall, next to Alaric's greatsword and Dianthe's smaller weapon. "It makes me itch when you pace."

"See?" Dianthe took Sienne's hand. "It can't hurt to be early."

The comforting jerk above her navel of *transport* was the only comforting thing about the morning. Sienne brought them to a spot in front of the palace's grand front entrance, with the broad, shallow stairs flanked by rows of fluted pillars and the arched doorway flanked by liveried guards holding ceremonial pikes. They didn't look any less deadly than they had the first time she'd come this way, accompanied by her parents and prepared to plead her case with the king. The memory of her failure on that occasion didn't cheer her at all. Just because it had all worked out in her favor didn't mean she wasn't fully aware that the king's idea of justice didn't always include mercy.

Though it was still well before noon, and nearing the end of true summer, the outer court was warm enough that the shady interior of the palace grand hall felt cool by comparison. The murals in shades of blue and green added to the effect, making Sienne feel as if she were underwater, swimming with the fanciful and sometimes mythical ocean creatures depicted there. The only light came from the open doorway and the skylights high above, frosted with invulnerability, and Sienne blinked to accustom her eyes to the dimness.

A man in red and yellow livery, Rafellin colors, approached them. He looked unexpectedly uncomfortable, as if his clothes itched. They were gaudy enough to look like a costume rather than anything anyone would wear voluntarily. "Perrin Delucco?" he said.

"That is I," Perrin said, stepping forward.

The man cast his gaze over them. He appeared to be counting. When he reached a conclusion that satisfied him, he said, "You will all come with me, please," and turned on his heel without waiting for their assent. Perrin hesitated, looking at Alaric, and Alaric gestured for him to lead out.

Sienne took up her usual position behind Alaric. The last time she'd been here, she'd been too nervous to pay much attention to her surroundings. Now she calmed her nervousness by examining the halls. The ceilings were high enough to be shrouded in shadow, with the lights affixed to the walls too low to illuminate them fully, and she amused herself by pretending the palace was a ruin they'd been hired to explore, shadowy and mysterious. Though it would be the nicest, most well-kept ruin ever.

Paintings hung at intervals between the doors that opened off the hall. She'd had instruction in art appreciation at school in Stravanus, but none of it had stuck, so she had no idea how valuable any of the paintings were beyond a vague notion that they were probably originals and not copies. Dianthe would know.

There were sculptures on pedestals now and then, and she liked those better, miniature versions of sculptures she'd seen around the city. How interesting if these were models for those originals, practice sculptures that had been presented to the palace after the final ones went up. She saw a foot-tall replica of the sculpture of the six avatars that graced a fountain in the Plaza of Sighs. The full-size version was ugly, but this miniature appealed to Sienne. It was something she could see herself putting in her own home.

The hall took a few turns and then opened up into a room nearly as large as the entrance. Had Sienne not been here before, she would have thought it was the audience chamber. But it was just the antechamber, designed to make petitioners as uncomfortable as possible. That said something about the king's personality, but Sienne didn't want to think too hard about it.

A few lumpy chairs upholstered in red velvet with over-gilded frames stood under the tall, narrow windows glazed with palm-sized square panes. Some of them contained red or yellow glass through which the morning sunlight shone, casting a random, blotchy pattern on the wall opposite and on the door set in that wall. It looked so ordinary it might have been the door to the linen closet instead of to the king's study. One of the yellow blotches fell on it, blending with the wood.

Sienne turned her back on it and walked to the window. It looked out over a courtyard in which a couple of spindly trees and some blue hydrangeas grew. She couldn't see a door giving access to it, but the blooming hydrangeas were too neatly trimmed not to have someone tending them. It made her feel sad to see the plants trying so hard and their show going unnoticed. That made her feel stupid, getting maudlin over a bunch of flowers and trees, so she returned to her friends, who stood together near the center of the room. The gaudy costumed man had disappeared.

"I hate this room," Dianthe said. "Too many bad memories."

"But we won," Kalanath said. "I think it is good."

"Only because Sienne's parents came to their senses." Dianthe rubbed her arms as if she were cold. "I've never forgotten how Sienne looked when she came out of that room behind the king."

"How did I look?" Sienne asked.

"Like you'd taken a wound to the gut and been shown your insides," Dianthe said.

"That's how it felt, too."

The door opened. A man dressed all in black stepped out. "Perrin Delucco," Benedict Gambrus said. "And friends. Please, come in."

Sienne followed the others, lingering at the rear. She remembered too well how it had felt the first time, walking into the monster's maw. Not that it looked like a maw. It looked just the same as it had the first time: a windowless study with a couple of bookcases, an enormous claw-footed desk, and a globe on a stand. The one change was that the two velvet-upholstered armchairs Sienne remembered were gone. A curved row of smaller chairs was lined up facing the empty hearth and a somewhat larger but still very plain chair. Flame-lit lamps flanked the fireplace, casting their light on the little tableau.

King Derekian Fiorus sat in the large chair, his foot casually crossed over one knee. He was dressed as informally as he had been the last time Sienne had seen him, in a red tunic that reminded Sienne of the Niskanen over a finely-woven white linen shirt and twilled cotton trousers dyed a deep blue. His neatly trimmed black beard framed firm lips that at the moment bore the ghost of a smile. "Have a seat, all of you," he said, gesturing with a hand on which winked the signet ring he'd sealed his summons with.

Sienne sat between Alaric and Dianthe and folded her hands in her lap to keep them still. Alaric's chair creaked ominously when he sat, and Sienne prayed it wouldn't collapse under his weight. That would make everything so much more awkward.

The king surveyed them all without speaking. Sienne waited. She didn't know what to say, and besides, *he* was the one who'd summoned *them*; it was his responsibility to explain himself. Finally, the king shifted his foot and leaned forward slightly. "Perrin Delucco," he said, his voice deep and smooth as always. "I understand you have a petition."

"Alcander Verannus speaks on my behalf. On my family's behalf," Perrin said.

"By law," the king said, "you have no family. But I understand that's the substance of the petition."

"It is."

Derekian pursed his lips in thought. "You ask that I overturn centuries of legal procedure for one man's sake?"

Perrin's hands, resting on his knees, closed into loose fists. "I am not the only man who suffers under these unjust laws. And I ask only that you change those laws to conform to what is just and merciful."

"Just and merciful? Not things that are generally compatible under the law."

Perrin shook his head. "Just, because there is no justice in allowing a family patriarch's whim to dictate the law. Merciful, because permitting families to remain intact partakes of God's mercy and love for Her creations."

"And you claim you have been treated unjustly before the law?"

"You refused Pontus Verannus the right to disinherit his children as he saw fit on the grounds that his whim should not be allowed to disrupt the dukedom," Perrin said. "I do not dispute a patriarch's right to protect his family against heirs who will harm it. What I dispute is the notion that differences of opinion, including a man's choice of what avatar he worships, should be grounds for disinheritance. And I dispute utterly a patriarch's right to annul his children's marriages on any grounds whatsoever."

Derekian tapped his lips with one long finger. "And you claim you are not the only one harmed by these existing rights?"

"You have Alcander Verannus's documentation, which contains evidence of other men and women whose situations are similar to mine. It is, in my opinion, past time to rectify these wrongs."

The king's eyes narrowed. "In your opinion."

"Yes, your Majesty. It is the only one I can lean on."

"Indeed." Derekian's gaze shifted to Alaric. "The Delucco children, according to Lysander Delucco, have been kidnapped. I don't suppose you know anything about that."

Alaric said nothing. To Sienne's surprise, Derekian smiled. "Of course not," he said. "Since I have reason to believe Delucco intended to remove his grandchildren from any possibility of their mother's recovering them, I choose not to pursue the matter other than to *hope* they are quite well, wherever they are."

"So long as they're out of his hands, I'm sure that's true," Sienne said. Dianthe kicked her ankle.

"Ah. Sienne Verannus," Derekian said, smiling again. "And are you happy with your choice?"

"Yes, your Majesty," Sienne said. "Very happy."

"To each his own, I suppose." Derekian let out a long breath. "The law is an unnatural beast," he said. "It has only the power we give it, and is capable of regulating behavior insofar as men and women are inclined to allow it to do so. And yet we speak of law as an immutable force, intrinsically powerful and eternal. I have hopes that Rafellin's laws may yet reflect the character of its citizens, but that day may be far in the future."

He fell silent. Sienne wanted to ask what he meant, but a glance at Alaric told her he was following this very closely and knew exactly what Derekian was talking about. Finally, Derekian said, "It has long been a problem in this country that there are those who believe laws do not apply to them." He was looking at Alaric, and Sienne opened her mouth to protest that they were all law-abiding citizens, but Dianthe kicked her again, harder this time, and she subsided.

Alaric nodded. "That's the case in most countries," he said, his voice neutral as if they were discussing a horse for sale.

"In Rafellin, our issue is that there are those in power who give lip service to the law, but seek to turn it to their advantage," Derekian went on. "For example, there are men who, denied what they believe are their rights, take illegal action to gain what they claim is theirs."

"Of course, they're punished when they're caught," Alaric said.

"Which is small comfort to those they harm," Derekian said.

"Naturally."

"How much better," Derekian said, "if they could be prevented taking such action before the harm is done."

"I agree."

Derekian smiled again. "And here I thought the two of us might never come to an agreement about anything."

Alaric smiled in return, his eyes lit with unholy pleasure. "Miracles can happen. I'm living proof of that."

The king's eyebrows lifted. "Really? Perhaps someday you'll explain that."

"Perhaps," Alaric said, and fell silent.

Derekian surveyed them all again, once more tapping a finger against his lips. "Dianthe Katraki," he said. Dianthe startled and sat more upright. "Corbyn Rameldus speaks highly of you."

"He—I owe him my life," Dianthe stammered.

"But apparently not enough to take his offer."

Dianthe glanced from side to side. "I...haven't made up my mind yet."

"Don't take too long. He's unwell."

Sienne cast a sidelong glance at Dianthe. She didn't look very well herself. "I know," she said quietly. "He said he's not suffering."

"He has the best care the Crown can provide for him." Derekian's gaze shot to Kalanath, who regarded him placidly. "And Kalanath Oushikdali. How are you finding Fioretti?"

"Very well," Kalanath said. "It is not Omeira but it is good."

"The Hierarch tells me you're free to return. Do you intend to?"

Kalanath's eyes never left Derekian's face. If he was disconcerted that the king knew so much, he didn't show it. "I have parents again," he said. "I will see them soon."

"I'm glad to hear it." Derekian once more looked at Alaric. "Still not respectful?"

"You're still not my king," Alaric said. "But I always give respect where it's earned."

Derekian laughed, throwing back his head in pure delight. "And why is it I feel respect earned from someone like you is worth something indeed?" he asked. "Go on. Get. And this time I *really* don't want to see you again for at least a year. How five ordinary people can cause so much unrest is a mystery even Benedict can't solve." He stood, prompting them to do the same. "But then," he added, "you're none of you exactly ordinary, are you?"

This time, Alaric led the way out of the study. "Not a word until we're on the street," he said when Sienne once more opened her mouth to speak. She followed him, bursting with curiosity, through the halls—no one appeared to escort them—and out the entry into the sunny courtyard. "That was unexpected," he said.

"I do not understand what he says about law, except that people break it, and that is not news," Kalanath said.

"He's cannier than I gave him credit for," Alaric said. "And more morally flexible."

"But what did it mean?" Sienne asked, somewhat plaintively. She didn't like being left out of things.

Alaric grinned. "He's going to rule in favor of Perrin," he said. "And he gave us permission to take Lysander Delucco out of the picture permanently."

27

"He wants us to *assassinate* him?" Sienne exclaimed.

"Why don't you say it a little louder, Sienne?" Dianthe said. "And no, he doesn't want us to assassinate him. He's the *king*. He's probably got his own assassins on tap and doesn't need to hire us."

"But—"

"He wants us to set up Delucco, catch him breaking the law in a way that will put him in Derekian's power," Alaric said.

"You got all that from that cryptic conversation?"

"I hate to admit it, but we think more alike than I believed," Alaric said. "Though I still haven't forgiven him for hitting you."

"But how do you know he intends to change the law?" Perrin asked.

"Because of what he said about people circumventing the law in their own favor." Alaric ran a hand through his short hair. "You can't do that unless there's a law to circumvent. And...there's Alcander now."

Sienne waved to her brother, who approached them at a near-run despite the overly warm formal law-speaker's garb he wore. "How did it go?" he asked.

"Well enough," Alaric said. "You'll find out shortly."

"Which means you know something you're not telling me." Alcander hugged Sienne. "Keep your secrets. I want to be able to look suitably surprised at whatever the king decides." He saluted them all with a cheery wave and trotted toward the stairs.

"So, we won," Sienne said, "and now we have to ensure our victory, is that it?"

"That's it exactly," Alaric said. "And I have some ideas already. But we'll have to move fast."

———

The inn Dianthe found for the Deluccos wasn't exactly seedy, but it was well past its prime, the paint peeling from its stucco, rust stains spreading from the drain spouts at the corners of the eaves. It occupied one corner of a quiet intersection and had large windows overlooking the street, begging thieves to break in. "We have to be just stupid enough that they believe it," Alaric had said, "but not so stupid they suspect something."

Sienne watched the building from her room in the inn across the street. Dianthe had told her to assume someone was watching them, so she'd left the inn on foot, walked far enough away to be sure no one was following, and *jaunted* back to her rented room. Alaric passed in front of the other inn, moving furtively, and she laughed at how well he gave the impression of a stupid thug set to guard the building.

The sun had nearly set, and long shadows gave Alaric and, more importantly, Dianthe places to hide. Alaric disappeared beyond the far side of the inn. Sienne couldn't see Dianthe at all, which was the point. She flipped the pages of her spellbook, an idle habit she'd found herself doing more often now that she didn't need the book anymore. It was getting too dark to be able to read the pages, but she didn't make a light. Hopefully all of this would happen so quickly no one would notice.

Alaric emerged from the other side of the inn and ducked back into shelter. He was still obvious to anyone watching, but on this job, he was camouflage. It was the rest of them who would see action.

I still can't see Dianthe, she thought, making an effort to form mental words clearly.

Good, Dianthe's thought came to her. *Have I mentioned how much I prefer this blessing to the other?*

It is far superior, Perrin thought. *I will put the children to bed now, and Cressida and I will turn in shortly thereafter.*

Don't fall asleep, Alaric warned.

I believe that would be impossible, Perrin replied.

Sienne sat and waited. There was a chance Master Delucco wouldn't act tonight. Dianthe was sure they'd gotten his attention, with Perrin and Cressida and the children trailing around in the open all day after receiving the public confirmation of the change in the law, but he might decide he needed more time to plan his attack. But Alaric had said, "He's not a patient man, and he knows we can make them disappear at a moment's notice. It will be as soon as he can make it," and Sienne had to agree with that assessment.

She wished they knew better what resources Master Delucco had. He hadn't had a wizard with him in Beneddo, but now that he knew some of what Sienne was capable of, he might have hired one. And if he had a tame priest, he'd have the same access to instant communication they did, and scrying to reveal the family's location. In the end, they'd planned for the worst, and Sienne had stationed herself to watch for any approach, having memorized the family's rooms for a quick *jaunt* if that was necessary.

The sun set, turning the world misty blue. The magic-lit lanterns that burned all day and all night became visible, lighting the street with their cold white glow. Sienne saw the lamp in Perrin's room across the way flicker and then go out. The streets that had bustled with men and women returning to their homes after a long day of work were quiet now, with only a few people still lingering on the corners. Sienne rose and stood by the window, scanning the street. Nothing struck her as out of the ordinary.

See anything, Sienne? Alaric asked at that moment.

Just you. You could probably pretend to fall asleep now, if you want.

I'll do that. Across the street, Alaric leaned up against the wall and let his head droop. Sienne controlled a laugh.

It's still too busy out there, Dianthe said. *We have another couple of hours before they'll strike.*

Wouldn't they want to blend in? Sienne asked.

If they were smart criminals, yes, but we've already seen Master Delucco doesn't hire smart criminals. Dianthe's mental laugh was the strangest sound Sienne had ever heard, mentally or with her ears.

Minutes passed, turned into hours. Sienne did her best to stay focused. Alaric shifted and slid down the wall to sit at its base with his knees pulled up and his head bowed. The moon rose, its half-lidded eye looking down on them like an avatar curious about their activities. Sienne prayed briefly: *O Averran, it's almost over. Please guide our hands.* The avatar had given Perrin all the blessings he'd asked for at mid-morning, plus a few unexpected ones, and Sienne hoped that meant he wished them well.

The street was entirely empty now except for Alaric "snoring" in the corner. Sienne shifted position to be able to see the other side of the inn's front door. Nothing. Maybe Alaric was wrong, and they wouldn't strike tonight.

Then Kalanath said, *Sienne! They are here!* just as Perrin said, *We are attacked!*

Sienne swore and cast *jaunt* as rapidly as she dared, felt the hook above her navel jerk her sideways, and stumbled into a dark room filled with children's screams. Instantly she flung white lights into the air, illuminating Noel and Delphine sitting up and screaming and a man dressed in black, down to the knit cap pulled low over his forehead. He looked like he was dancing, jerking his arms up and back and letting out whooshes of explosive breath. Sienne began casting *force*, but as she spoke the first syllables, the man's head snapped back as an audible blow caught him beneath the chin. He dropped to lie at her feet, his slim black spellbook hitting the floor with a crack.

"You were right," Kalanath said, his voice coming from a point in the air a few feet away. "They have someone to scry and someone to *jaunt*."

"It seemed reasonable they'd turn my trick against us," Sienne said. She dismissed *vanish* and Kalanath appeared, staff in hand, not at all out of breath from beating the would-be assailant. He rushed past her out the door. "It's all right," Sienne told Noel and Delphine, "he can't hurt you." But she hovered over the man anyway despite her urgent desire to run next door and see that Perrin and Cressida were all right. *Force* would make sure of his unconsciousness, but they needed him alert relatively soon if the plan was going to work.

Heavy footsteps came along the hall, and Alaric poked his head into the room. "Everything all right?"

Sienne nodded. "Is Perrin—"

"What is going on here?" a new voice said. Alaric stepped back to admit Denys Renaldi, dressed for sleep but wearing his boots. "It sounds as if someone's being murdered."

"That's almost true," Alaric said, entering the room and prodding the unconscious man's arm. A double-edged dagger with a wickedly sharp point lay inches from his hand. Delphine saw it and let out a gasp, then began crying again.

"Then it's a good thing I chose to stay in this inn tonight, isn't it?" Denys said. One eyelid drooped in a barely perceptible wink at Sienne, who covered her mouth to hide a smile. "Let's secure this fellow, and then see what's going on next door, shall we?"

"You bring handcuffs everywhere, Renaldi?" Alaric said as Denys produced a pair of manacles from somewhere on his person.

"Have to be prepared, Alaric," Denys said. The assailant groaned as Denys took his spellbook, then wrenched his arms behind his back and slapped the manacles on. "Up you get, man, and stop moaning, you're not hurt."

Sienne, who'd witnessed Kalanath's invisible beating, wasn't sure of that, but she didn't care about the man's condition, so she said nothing. She collected the dagger and followed the three men into the hall, trailed by the children, who clung to her in a way she didn't find unpleasant. The next room was full enough to be crowded, and she ended up standing in the hallway, looking in. Noel and Delphine shoved their way through the crowd to throw themselves on their parents. Perrin and Cressida, fully dressed, sat on the end of the rumpled bed. Another black-clad man lay at their feet, this one dead. Blood pooled around his chest, and his eyes stared emptily at the ceiling. Dianthe stood nearby, cleaning her blade.

"He went for me," she was telling Denys, "and I defended myself. But I didn't want him dead, I wanted him alive for questioning, damn it."

"Self-defense, no doubt," Denys said, putting his arm around her. "I'm glad you're not hurt."

"I'm fine. Just annoyed with myself."

The man Denys had manacled was staring at his partner in disbelief. "You killed him," he said. "I'll have the law on you for that."

Alaric laughed. "And your defense for breaking into a private room intent on killing its occupants?"

The man seemed suddenly to realize he had an audience. "Not tellin' you nothin'," he said.

"Yes, you will," Perrin said, releasing Cressida's hand and rising. He removed his riffle of blessings and sorted through it until he found one he liked. "Captain Renaldi, with your permission I would like to invoke this blessing. It compels anyone within its area of influence to tell the truth."

"Interesting," Denys said. "I've heard of it being done in criminal cases, but never seen it. How can you prove it's true?"

"You will do the questioning," Perrin said, "and may ask verifiable questions of anyone in this room until you are satisfied."

A smile spread across Denys's face. "This I have to see," he said. "Go ahead."

Perrin murmured an invocation, and purple fire sprang up around his fingers, consuming the little square of paper. A purple glow sprang up throughout the room, radiating from the walls and floor and ceiling and turning everyone's faces pale brown. Alaric's face was lilac, and his blue eyes were almost colorless in the glow. Denys looked at his hands, which radiated purple. "Fascinating," he said. He turned to Alaric, who looked impassive. "Are we friends?" he asked.

"We are," Alaric said. A confused look passed over his face, as if the answer had surprised him.

"Did you ever sleep with Dianthe?" Denys went on.

"No. We thought about it once, but you don't sleep with your sister," Alaric said.

Denys smiled. "Does she have your blessing on her marriage to me?"

"Not that she needs it, but...yes. You'll be good for her." The look of distress on his face was almost comical.

Denys looked back at Perrin. "I could get used to this."

"It is limited in time, so perhaps you should continue," Perrin said.

"All right." Denys grabbed the assailant by the collar and hauled him up until they were face to face. "Did you intend to kill the Delucco children?"

"Yes." The man looked as stunned as Alaric at the answer, stunned and afraid.

"Who hired you?"

The man looked like he wanted to hold his mouth shut against any more words. "A man. I don't know his name."

"Do you know where to find him?"

"Yes. We were supposed to report back when the job was done."

"And the job was...?"

"Kill the man and the woman. Kill the children." Cressida clutched her children closer to her, her eyes fixed on her would-be murderer.

Inspiration struck Sienne. "Have you ever seen this man before?" she said, casting *mirage*. An image of Lysander Delucco swam into being, clear and detailed as if the man himself stood there.

The killer gasped. "That's him! How did you do that?"

Sienne realized too late she hadn't used her spellbook. Nothing to do about it now. "Denys, do you recognize him?"

"I'm shocked that Lysander Delucco would do anything so evil,"

Denys said blandly. "Just to confirm—what exactly did this man say to you?"

"He said, kill them all, make it look like a robbery, and I'll reward you well." The man was sweating and breathing heavily like someone running a foot race at the heart of true summer. "I answered your questions! Let me go!"

"I think not," Denys said. "I'm going to want you to tell your story again to the judge. Coincidentally, this inn is just around the corner from the guard station. I'll ask all of you to stay here while I summon some guardsmen to take charge of the prisoner and the body, and then...I imagine you can all go home."

"You will arrest my father?" Perrin said.

"Take him out of his own damned bed is what I'll do," Denys said, sounding extremely satisfied. "And see him locked in a cell for conspiracy to commit murder."

Cressida let out a small gasp. Perrin put his arm around her. "Then it is over," he said.

"Not quite, but as far as you're concerned, yes." Denys saluted him with a nod and disappeared down the hall, trailing a surprisingly tuneful whistle.

Cressida turned and buried her face in Perrin's shoulder, shaking with sobs. "Mama, are you hurt?" Noel said, tugging at her dress. "Mama, that man had a knife!"

"It is all right, Noel," Perrin said. He laid a hand on the boy's head. "Mama is happy."

"I don't understand why she's crying when she's happy," Noel said.

"When you are older," Perrin assured him.

Sienne went to Alaric's side and let him embrace her. "That was a good plan," she told him.

"I'm surprised it worked so well," he said. "I thought we'd have to do this for several nights before we drew him out."

"You did? But you said—"

"I didn't want to discourage anyone. And it all worked out, so that's all right, isn't it?"

"I suppose." She put her arm around his waist. "You know, the blessing is still in force. You have to tell me the truth."

"I always tell you the truth, sweetlove. You don't need a blessing for that."

She thought about asking all her friends the question that burned inside her: *Do you want to stay?* But she had a feeling it wasn't a question she wanted a truthful answer to. "So when I had my hair cut shorter and you said you liked it, you were being honest?"

Alaric's jaw quivered with the effort of keeping it closed. "No," he burst out, "I like it longer. But I didn't want to hurt your feelings."

Sienne took his hand and once more thought of asking the question she really cared about. "Maybe honesty isn't as important as people think," she said.

———

THEY GATHERED LATE THE NEXT MORNING IN THEIR SITTING ROOM, NONE of them inclined to speak. Sienne sat with her head thrown back and felt as exhausted as if she'd walked all night. It wasn't even as if the whole job had taken very long. Though maybe that was the problem. It had been a job. The last one.

Perrin stirred finally. "I feel I should thank you again for your efforts on behalf of my family," he said.

"It's what we do for each other," Dianthe said.

Silence fell again. Finally, Kalanath said, "I wish to see my parents again. Sienne, will you *ferry* me there?"

"Of course," Sienne said, trying not to sound as if his request broke her heart.

"Thank you," Kalanath said.

Sienne remembered the first time they'd sat together, in an outpost on the way into the wilderness. They'd been silent then, too, each caught up in their own thoughts. Alaric had hated her. Perrin had been a drunk. Dianthe was friendly but distant. And Kalanath had seen it as just another job. She couldn't bear to let their companionship end this way.

She opened her mouth to say something and was overridden by Perrin saying, "Alaric. There is something I wish to share with you."

"Hmm?" Alaric said. His head was tipped back and he had his eyes closed.

"It is in regard to a blessing I received this morning, unasked for."

Alaric opened his eyes and sat up. "What blessing?"

Perrin bowed his head so his long hair fell like a curtain across his face. "A blessing to communicate with the dead."

Alaric froze, his blue eyes wide. He worked his mouth a few times as if searching for words. "You mean Gen," he said. "Perrin, I don't know..."

"Neither do I," Perrin said, "but I have prayed much concerning this blessing and have come to the conclusion that it is intended for you. You had no opportunity to bid her farewell, and I believe Averran sees that as an injustice to be remedied."

"I—" Alaric's mouth snapped shut. He looked at each of them in turn. When his gaze fell on Sienne, she wanted to weep at how lost he looked. "I don't know what I'd say."

"Then let her speak, and listen," Perrin said.

Alaric nodded. "What do we need to do?"

"Clear the carpet," Perrin said.

They moved the table and shoved the sofa and chairs back, clearing an open space. "Sit opposite me," Perrin said, seating himself cross-legged on the floor and gesturing to Alaric. Alaric sat more heavily and rested his hands on his knees.

"This isn't like when we summoned the spirit of Pedreo Giannus, is it?" he asked.

"That was necromancy. This is divine power," Perrin said. He withdrew a blessing paper from within his jerkin and held it out before them. "O most recalcitrant Lord," he said, "we seek communion with the spirit of Genneva of the Sassaven. Pray, grant us this blessing."

Pink fire consumed the blessing paper without burning Perrin. Instead of fading and dying as the paper burned, the fire expanded, flowing upward as if it consumed an invisible curtain. Perrin lowered his hand, and the fire hung between him and Alaric, a flickering sheet of flame that grew translucent and then transparent until it was nothing but heat haze. Sienne still wouldn't have put her hand into it.

A gauzy shape formed within the heat haze, pale pink and wavering. As it solidified, Sienne bit back a gasp; it was Genneva, as youthful and vibrant as she'd looked at the end. "Alaric," she said. "You saved us."

"I couldn't save *you*," Alaric said grimly. "I'm sorry I failed you."

"You didn't," Genneva said. "I think, if I hadn't been the wizard's host—if it had been anyone else—you and your friends wouldn't have succeeded. Nobody else would have had so much incentive to allow someone to destroy the heart they carried, if I can be immodest." She laughed. "I'm dead, so it doesn't matter."

Alaric had tears in his eyes. "You weren't supposed to die. You were supposed to rebuild the Sassaven with me."

"I notice you're not with the Sassaven, though. They didn't want your help, did they?"

Alaric's jaw tightened.

"It doesn't matter, don't you understand?" Genneva went on. "What you and I wanted was irrelevant. The Sassaven were all that mattered. You *won*, Alaric. And I think you got your heart's desire anyway. Where is she?"

Sienne, startled, lurched forward to kneel beside Alaric. "I," she said, and couldn't think of anything else to say to the woman she'd killed.

"Thank you for restoring my heart," Genneva said. "I know I left my body behind, but the idea of it continuing to be corrupted by the wizard made me extremely uncomfortable."

"I'm sorry I couldn't make it work."

"Don't be. It wouldn't have been a true sacrifice if you'd hauled me back from the brink of death. And—" She smiled again. "I'm not allowed to tell you anything about this place except that I'm truly happy here. You'll see, in time. A long time from now, I hope."

"But..." Alaric cleared his throat. "Gen, there's so much I wanted to tell you. So many things I've seen."

"I know." Genneva's smile faded. "Life isn't perfect, and neither is death. But someday I'll see you again, and we'll have eternity in which to tell each other everything." Her gaze shifted to Sienne. "Take care of my brother, please."

"I will. I promise," Sienne said.

"Thank you." She looked once more at Alaric. "Forgive yourself, brother."

Alaric smiled, a rueful expression. "Anything for you, sister."

Genneva laughed, a merry sound that faded into the distance. "And stop moping," she said. "Remember when I hid the frog in your bed?"

Alaric burst out laughing. "You brat," he said, sounding more like himself finally. "I'd nearly forgotten that."

"I'd rather you remember me that way." Her voice was growing as misty as her laughter. "I'll see you later—much later, if God is kind. Have a happy life." Her face shivered, became amorphous, and then it was gone.

Alaric wiped his eyes. "Thank you, Perrin."

"Thank Averran. It was his gift," Perrin said. "And I am happy it seems to have helped."

"Frog in my bed," Alaric said, chuckling. "She did a thousand things like that. She used to make me so angry, and yet she'd look at me with those big eyes and pretend to be sad, and I couldn't help laughing. She's right. I'd rather remember her that way." He took Sienne's hand and kissed it. "And life goes on."

"For a long, long time," Sienne said.

28

T *hree weeks later*

Sienne stood with her arms outstretched in front of the mirrored surface she'd created on the wall. The silver and cream gown hung loosely around her. She spoke the syllables of *fit*, and it shrank neatly to fit her, loose around the hips, tight in the waist and bodice. It looked beautiful even if it was uncomfortable. She could bear a few hours' discomfort, especially on her wedding day.

She sat gingerly on the edge of her bed, careful not to wrinkle the silk, and stared at her hands. She'd *transported* her family to Fioretti yesterday and seen them installed in their rented house, she'd arranged for a pavilion at the park north of the Plaza of Sighs three days ago, and she and Alaric had spoken to the divine Octavian last week, asking him to officiate. She would have preferred a divine of Averran, but Evander was impossible to find, and in the end she'd realized what she really wanted was someone who knew how much she and Alaric had gone through to get to this day.

What she hadn't been able to do was find the three people she cared most about witnessing it. She'd *ferried* Kalanath back to Omeira two days after Master Delucco was arrested, and when she had gone there last week looking for him, the Hierarch had told her he'd returned to Abhisok with his parents for an extended visit. Two weeks' journey overland or by ship. Dianthe had left the city the day after her own wedding on mysterious business even Denys wasn't privy to. And Perrin, who of all of them ought to have been easiest to find, had disappeared with his family after receiving the official papers that the law had been overturned and he was a Delucco again. Not that Sienne thought he cared about that.

She held out a hand to make her hairbrush fly across the room and smack into her palm. Brushing her hair helped calm her. The ceremony would be wonderful, everything would go well, and then... she wasn't sure what "and then" was yet. She and Alaric had put off finding a new job, neither of them talking about their reluctance, both of them pretending there was no point until after they were married. But she was sure he felt the same way she did: it wasn't the same without the others.

She returned the hairbrush to the shelf and checked the time. They'd rented a carriage to protect their finery from the hazards of the dirty road, and it should be there any moment. She checked her reflection one last time, dismissed the confusion, and headed downstairs.

Alaric waited, not in the sitting room, but in the kitchen. He looked wonderful in his leather jerkin dyed deep blue to bring out the blue of his eyes and a new pair of boots, shiny and free from scuffs. The linen shirt did nothing to conceal his muscular physique and broad shoulders. He turned away from the window and smiled appreciatively. "You should wear that dress more often," he said. "Not that you aren't beautiful whatever you wear."

"It's not very comfortable." She walked forward to join him at the window and snuggled up to his side. "But I love the way it makes you look at me."

"Are you ready?"

She looked up at him. "Past ready."

"You don't look as happy as a bride should. Is it—"

"We did everything we could to find them." Sienne sighed. "I *am* happy. I didn't think marriage would matter that much to me, but after what Octavian said...I can't help feeling if God insists on being part of the ceremony, it means more than I believed."

Alaric hugged her, then let her go, taking hold of her hand. "Your carriage awaits, my lady," he said, and drew her down the hall and out the door to where an open carriage painted a cream that matched Sienne's gown did, in fact, await.

For the first dozen yards, it made Sienne uncomfortable that people stared at them. What did they imagine the two well-dressed people in the fancy carriage were off to? Could they intuit that Alaric and Sienne were just scrappers, not nobles and not...well, that wasn't true, they were wealthy enough now they could afford to buy the carriage, the horses, and pay the salary of the man who drove them. But Sienne couldn't help feeling conspicuous and out of place.

"Crushing my hand is a bad idea, sweetlove," Alaric murmured.

"I'm not...all right, I am a little." Sienne relaxed her grip. "People are staring."

"Yes, because we make an attractive couple, and all of them wish they were us."

Sienne giggled. "They do not."

"I swear on my life they do." Alaric put his free arm around her and kissed her, slowly, until she relaxed. "And now all the men wish I were dead."

She laughed again and rested her head on his shoulder. "This is a beautiful day."

The carriage rattled along through the streets, crossing the Vochus River by one of its many bridges. Sienne admired the palace, though she found it prettier at night, lit by a thousand red and white lights. Her gaze lingered on the red roofs of the University of Fioretti, gleaming in the noon sun. She still hadn't decided what to do. Evander's words about the fate of the wizards whose society had been founded on the kind of magic she was now capable of had stuck with her. She didn't like feeling responsible for the decision whether or not to share her knowledge with the world. She might be powerful, but that didn't make her wise. She refused to consider that it was cowardice talking.

The Plaza of Sighs was busy at this hour with the noon service to Gavant. Filmy confusions like blue and gold scarves drifted through the air, and the carriage driver took them carefully around the chapel that was big enough to be a temple to any other avatar. The display kept people's attention off Sienne and Alaric, for which she was grateful even if she no longer felt self-conscious. She didn't want to be a distraction from religious observance.

The street curved through the plaza and northward toward the park. Now that the year was wending toward winter, the air even at noon was cool and scented with dying leaves and the smell of the first wood fires. But the park's short, well-kept grass was still emerald-bright, and diligent gardeners had raked away most of the fallen leaves to make it a soft carpet unfurled beneath the cypress trees. Small black and red birds clung to the trees, swaying in the breeze that caught at Sienne's hair and dress and made her skirts flutter as Alaric helped her down from the carriage.

The path to the pavilion had been swept clean of debris, but Sienne carefully lifted her skirts off the ground, picturing damp earth clinging to her hem. That wasn't the kind of reminder she wanted for this day. Ahead, the pavilion was crowded with friends and family: Sienne's parents and all her siblings, including her oldest sister Felice and Felice's lover Violette. The two stood at the opposite side of the pavilion from the rest of the Verannus horde, making Sienne wonder what had passed between Felice and their parents. Surely they wouldn't be unwelcoming of anyone Felice loved? Sienne let out a deep breath. That was a problem for another time.

There was old Master Tersus and Leofus. A handful of scrapper friends—scrappers weren't generally a friendly bunch, but there were some Sienne counted as more than acquaintances. The owner of Alaric's favorite tavern and her husband. Denys Renaldi, sending a pang shooting through Sienne's heart. If Denys was here, why not Dianthe?

"Surprise," someone said in her ear, and Sienne whirled around to see Dianthe grinning at her. She wore her blue dancing dress and looked as if this were the best surprise anyone had ever come up with.

Sienne shrieked, startling Alaric, and flung her arms around her friend. "Where have you been?" she exclaimed. "We looked everywhere for you!"

"That's a story for another time," Dianthe said. "After the wedding. But—" She looked past Sienne, and her eyes widened. "This looks like a day for surprises."

Alaric said, "Kalanath!"

Sienne turned. Kalanath, looking dusty and travel-worn, made his way through the crowd toward them. "I am sorry it is not good clothing," he said, looking embarrassed. "I do not know how to tell you I wish to return, so I must take ship. It is very long and I am almost late."

Sienne hugged him, not caring if it got her dress dirty. Maybe a little dirt wasn't so bad. "I didn't know you wanted to come back. I thought you meant to stay in Omeira. How did you know about the wedding?"

"Perrin tells me. He spoke to me at night," Kalanath said with a grimace. "It is one thing to speak to each other in the mind, and another to have thoughts appear there like flowers for the picking. He says, they will be married, and I took ship that day."

Sienne and Alaric looked at each other. "But how did Perrin know?" Alaric said.

"Perrin knew," a new voice said, "because Averran is a crusty old gossip." Perrin clapped Kalanath on the shoulder and smiled at Sienne. "And Perrin is very sorry he put you in a position where you could not tell him more conventionally. I am afraid we were in Onofreo these past weeks, searching for Evander. I could not think of anyone I would prefer to marry Cressida and me."

"But...the decree was overturned," Sienne said. "Your marriage wasn't annulled. Or—I don't actually know what you'd call it, having a marriage reinstated."

"We have endured enough, and changed enough, that we decided a new ceremony was in order," Cressida said. "Something I am sure you understand."

Sienne cast a glance over her shoulder at the center of the pavilion where Octavian waited. He didn't look at all impatient, but Sienne suddenly felt urgency tug at her. "You're all just in time," she said. "Everything's going to be perfect."

She heard the ceremony in a daze, her whole being concentrated down to her hand in Alaric's large one, his eyes on her as if she was the only thing in his world. Most of what Octavian said, he'd told them already the day they'd come to the temple to ask him to officiate. But she thought she might never forget the moment he asked them to look not at each other, but at him, and said, "Marriage is a sacred bond between two people, and between those two and their God. Whatever face of God you worship, She is present in all your dealings with each other. And I make you a solemn promise that She knows you, and is well pleased by your service."

That feeling of peace Sienne associated with the presence of Averran touched her again, but this time it was accompanied by a swelling feeling of such overpowering love Sienne had to hold Alaric's hand tightly to keep from falling over. She almost didn't hear Octavian pronounce them husband and wife, or his invitation for them to exchange the rings that would remind them of this day, but she came to herself as Alaric slipped a delicate gold band bearing a sparkling sapphire over her finger. "Wake up, sweetlove," he murmured, and she startled, sending a ripple of laughter through the crowd. The heavy ring set with an onyx slid neatly over his finger, and he ran his other thumb over the stylized horse incised on it and laughed. "Not a unicorn?" he said in a low voice.

"I tried, but the design looked stupid," Sienne murmured back.

He put his fingers beneath her chin and tipped her head back. "It's perfect," he said, and kissed her to the accompaniment of loud cheers and applause.

Papa and Mother had laid out a noon meal behind the pavilion, and Sienne laughed and talked and hugged her friends and felt as if she might float away with happiness. Thanking Octavian, she said, "I never would have guessed, from how we met, that we would end up here."

"I consider myself blessed to have made your acquaintance," he said with his customary twinkle. "It's not every day one meets someone touched by God." He nodded at Alaric. "Nor one brought back from the dead."

"Did he tell you that?" Sienne asked, startled.

"Kitane did," Octavian said. "She was equal parts miffed and pleased, mainly because I believe she still regrets being unable to complete the task you and your companions did."

Even after everything that had passed in the last fourteen months, Sienne still had trouble with how casually the divines and priests of God spoke of their contact with their avatars. "I feel blessed, myself."

"I hope you will stop by occasionally," Octavian said. "I find myself eager to learn what you will do next." He touched her forehead with two fingers in blessing and nodded a farewell.

The afternoon wore on. Friends gradually drifted away until the only ones left were the five companions. Cressida had taken her children off an hour before, and the Verannus horde had disappeared back to their rented house. Sienne sat on Alaric's lap on a nearby bench and said, "I'm so glad you all made it."

"So am I," Kalanath said. "Next time I will arrange a time for you to return."

Sienne glanced at Alaric and saw his expression was neutral the way it was when he was concealing a strong emotion. "Next time?" she said, hoping she sounded casual and not over-eager.

Kalanath shrugged. "I love my parents, but Omeira is not home," he said. "I think I will visit them some times. But *ferry* is faster than ship and there are not so many sea monsters." He rubbed his arm as if it pained him.

"That's...nice," Sienne said. Inside, she leaped for joy.

"So, you were gone a while," Alaric said to Dianthe. "Someplace you didn't want to tell Denys about."

"Is there a question in there somewhere?" Dianthe teased, her lips somber but her eyes alight with mirth. "Oh, all right. I was working for Corbyn."

Sienne's light heart went leaden. "Oh," she said.

Dianthe eyed her pensively. "I was helping him find a replacement."

Alaric's eyes narrowed. "I thought you were his replacement."

Dianthe shrugged, mirroring Kalanath. "So did I. Nearly dying at Kyros's hands made me reconsider a lot of things. And I thought, for a time, I owed it to myself and Denys and our eventual children to not put myself in danger." She smiled and dug up a tuft of grass with her toe. "That was before Corbyn sat me down and laid out exactly what responsibilities a spymaster has—and gave me the gory details of the five assassination attempts he's survived. I realized I'd be safer fighting immortal wizards or cockatrices or carvers or...or any of the things we've faced together. But I felt I owed it to him to track down a replacement. He...he's not doing so well." Dianthe rubbed her eyes, reddening them. "I couldn't tell Denys because he's smart enough, if he knew who I'd been talking to, to work out who the new spymaster would be."

"So it's done," Alaric said.

"It is." Dianthe stretched out her long legs. "It won't be the same, not living at Master Tersus's house, but I'm sure none of you will miss the snoring."

"Poor Denys," Sienne said with a smile.

Perrin cleared his throat. "As to that," he said, "I have counseled with Evander, and discussed things with Cressida, and...well, you know that priests of Averran are itinerant, with the temples and shrines tended by men and women who stay only a few seasons and move on again. I do not think I can subject my family to that."

Sienne drew in a startled breath. "But you're not...giving up the priesthood, are you?"

Perrin smiled. "No, I am not. Evander and I discussed the nature of the service Averran's priests give, how Averran himself chose to take light into dark places, and I have concluded that my service is best rendered by my continuing as I have been. By wielding his power on his behalf...with all of you."

Sienne let out the breath she'd been holding and wiped away a tear. "Even if it's just fighting cockatrices?" she said. "Not that I know what those are."

"The unholy offspring of a rooster and a bat," Dianthe said. "Scaly and horrible. Don't let them bite you."

"I won't, thanks." She rested her head on Alaric's shoulder. "So... where next?"

Everyone laughed. "Sienne, you just got married," Dianthe said. "You deserve a honeymoon."

"I'd just be restless," Sienne complained.

"Not if I do it right," Alaric rumbled, making her blush.

"Give it a week," Perrin suggested. "We can search for new jobs in the meantime. Onofreo has still not recovered entirely from the plague of undead loosed upon it by Ivar Scholten's death."

"And I may have some more permanent work lined up," Dianthe said. "I don't know if we want to work for the Crown, but Corbyn said there's trouble out east and they want someone to investigate it. Someone not afraid of werebears."

"I would love to see Swift and Clever again," Sienne exclaimed.

"Even if it means being the king's lackey," Alaric grumbled.

"There is a man on the ship who has trouble," Kalanath said. "He has an inheritance in the north that monsters have overrun. I do not say we will help because I do not know there is a 'we.' But I think monsters run from us now."

Sienne smiled. "Just so there is a 'we' now," she said, "I don't care what we do next."

SHE WOKE EARLY THE NEXT MORNING, DISTURBED BY THE PATTERN OF sunlight in the unfamiliar room. Alaric had insisted they have a real honeymoon, Sienne had refused to leave Fioretti, and they'd compromised by taking rooms in an exclusive inn near the palace, with the intention of making day trips to seaside resorts and wilderness locations. She lay in bed watching the sun travel across the walls and listening to Alaric breathe. That sound wasn't going to get old any time soon.

She'd hung her spellbook in its harness on a peg near the door, directly in her line of sight. The harness was worn across the shoulder and near the edges where the flexible wooden cover of the spellbook rubbed it. She ought to make a new one, but the idea irritated her. What was the point of putting all that effort into something she didn't need?

She got out of bed and hunted for her clothes. It had been a memorable night. It seemed marriage was important for more than just the vows you made. Alaric rolled over and reached for her, opening one eye when he didn't find her immediately. "You could sleep in for once, you know," he mumbled. "The inn will serve us breakfast whenever we want. We're certainly paying enough to ensure it."

"There's something I need to do," she said, realizing as she spoke the words that they were true. "I'll be back in an hour. I love you."

"...love you..." Alaric said, already mostly asleep again. She smiled and let herself out, slinging the harness over her shoulder.

Fioretti in the morning was always fresh and new, even in neighborhoods that weren't as nice as this one. Here, Sienne smelled only fresh air and hot bread, not rotten food and animal waste, but she was in a good enough mood even the latter wouldn't have put her off. It was amazing how peaceful a decision could leave you. Even if she'd made the decision unconsciously.

The cobbled streets leading to the University of Fioretti gradually emptied the nearer she came to the university buildings, which had imposing marble façades that usually made Sienne uncomfortable with how unwelcoming they were. She'd never wanted to be a student there, and the tall buildings with their red roofs seemed bent on making her feel outcast. But today she passed between them without a second thought. She was more powerful than they, and what they represented couldn't hurt her.

The tall doors to the wizardry school stood open, and a few students in light blue gowns strode in and out, most of them in chattering pairs. No one paid any attention to Sienne, though she looked out of place in her ordinary trousers and shirt and scrapper's spellbook. She passed through the rotunda, from which corridors radiated like the spokes of a wheel, and followed one of the spokes all the way to the end.

The private lecture hall was mostly empty, with only a few students occupying the desks aligned at precise right angles to the walls and each other. Sienne recognized Mistress Elodie Givvani's hand in their orientation; the woman was more painfully neat than any professor Sienne had ever had. Thick, bubbly glass in the windows showed the outside world as bright smears, nothing that might distract a student from her work. It reminded Sienne of far-off classrooms in Stravanus, though those rooms had always been bitterly cold.

The students looked up when Sienne entered, assessed her quickly, and returned to their studies. Sienne knocked once on Mistress Givvani's office door and pushed it open without waiting for a reply.

The office was as Sienne remembered it: bookshelves empty of clutter, a desk clear of paperwork, no scraps of paper on the floor and no paintings or drawings on the walls. Mistress Givvani sat behind her desk, spellbook in hand, her lips moving as she read from it. She looked up at Sienne's entrance, and her scowl at being interrupted turned into a smile. "Sienne!" she exclaimed. "It's good to see you. I don't suppose you have another artifact for us?"

"No," Sienne said, "but I do have a puzzle for you."

"Really? How intriguing. I have a lecture in half an hour, so if it won't take long..." She pushed back her chair and stood, her short gray hair the most untidy thing about her.

"Showing you won't take long," Sienne said. "Solving it may take a lifetime." Now that she was here, now that she'd come to this point, her heart hammered in her chest and her palms were covered with a fine sheen of sweat. It wasn't too late. She could still walk away.

"That's...cryptic." Mistress Givvani came around to lean against the front of her desk. "You have my attention."

Sienne removed her spellbook harness from around her neck. It was such a small thing, and yet it represented something that would change the world. "Hold this," she told Mistress Givvani, handing her the book. "And let me show you what I can do."

SIENNE'S SPELLBOOK

Summonings:

Summonings affect the physical world and elements. They include all transportation spells.

Castle—trade places with someone else

Convey—teleport an object

Ferry—teleport with one other person

Fog—obscuring mist

Jaunt—personal teleportation

Slick—conjure grease

Summon companion—summon one of six magical creatures

Evocations:

Evocations deal with intangible elements like fire, air, and lightning.

Barrier—wall of fire or air

Burn—ray of fire

Force—bolt of magical energy, hits with perfect accuracy

Fury—six *force*-bolts, hits whatever is in range

Scorch—fireball

Scream—sonic attack, causes injury

Shout—sonic attack, causes short-term paralysis

Confusions:

Confusions affect what the senses perceive.

Camouflage—disguise an object's shape, color, or texture

Cast—ventriloquism

Echo—auditory hallucinations

Imitate—change someone's entire appearance

Mirage—visual hallucinations

Mirror—creates three identical duplicates of the caster

Shift—small alterations in appearance, such as eye or hair color

Vanish—invisibility

Transforms:

Transforms change an object or creature's state, in small or large ways.

Break—shatters fragile things

Cat's eye—true darkvision

Change—polymorph a living thing

Drift—feather fall

Fit (object)—shrink or enlarge an object; permanent

Fit (person)—shrink or enlarge a person; temporary

Float—levitation

Gills—water breathing

Mud—transform stone to mud

Purge—transmute liquid

Sculpt—shape stone

Sharpen—improve sight or hearing

Voice—sound like someone else

The Small Magics

These can be done by any wizard without a spellbook, with virtually no limits.

Light

Spark

Mend

Create water

Breeze

Chill/warm liquid

Telekinesis (up to 6-7 pound weights) (also known as invisible fingers)

Ghost sound

Ghostly form

Find true north

Open (used to manipulate a spellbook)

Invulnerability

AFTERWORD

I have been playing role-playing games since college, when my boyfriend (later husband) introduced me to his gaming group. They said they knew I was a keeper the day he didn't show up and I did. That group has been going for over thirty years in one form or another, and we've played so many systems and so many characters I'm sure I've forgotten more than I remember.

So, thanks to this history, one story I've always wanted to write is one in which the fundamentals of the fantasy gaming party are a reality. I thought it would be fun to write about a group of adventurers who took on quests because they were paid to do it, who fought monsters and found treasure but also were a step above murder hobos. But it was sort of a passive, that-would-be-cool desire, especially since for most of my life, I have not been a fiction writer.

About five years ago, I was bored on a Sunday afternoon and felt the need to create something. Specifically, I thought it would be fun to create a set of characters for an adventuring party. No game, no campaign—just the characters. I happen to have an excellent book called *Central Casting* that is a resource for generating character backgrounds using dice and a bunch of clever tables. (It's still out there if you can get your hands on it.) So I pulled that out and got started.

I came up with five characters—a fighter/barbarian, a wizard, a cleric, a rogue, and...actually, the fifth character didn't come together very well, and I wasn't sure if he was a bard or a monk or what. But it didn't matter, because I was just messing around. I decided they all had a common background of joining the military, that the wizard was the main character but the barbarian was the leader, and put everything aside with no intention of doing anything more with them.

Some years later, I was talking to my writing partner (who happens to be a member of the same gaming group) and we were joking about the next big thing in YA fantasy. Unicorns, one of us said. Purple sparkly unicorns, the other said. No, *were-unicorns.* That struck us as hilarious, right up until I said, "You know, real unicorns wouldn't be sissy and pretty and delicate. They'd be the size of a Clydesdale and utterly terrifying."

So we got to discussing that. What the human form would look like. What kind of magic they'd have. In only a few minutes, I knew I had my next book. But it couldn't be just were-unicorns; there had to be more to it. And that's when I remembered my party of characters.

Fleshing them out, and creating a world for them to inhabit, came so naturally it felt as if the story had been waiting for me to take notice of it. The world Rafellin exists in has fallen from a golden age of magical technology, and that makes it ideal for adventuring, what with lost troves of magic to find and monsters created by magical wars to fight.

Sienne, as I said, was always the main character, and Alaric was always the force driving the party. That he was the were-unicorn became immediately obvious, and from there, the story arc unfolded.

It's astonishing to me, even after as many books and series as I've written, how one decision leads to another. For example, I impulsively decided the "gods" of Rafellin would be avatars of one God, which led to a brainstorming session in which the avatars emerged. I picked six as a good, manageable number of avatars, but it was my husband who pointed out that six is the number of attributes in D&D-flavored fantasy RPGs (strength, charisma, etc.) and what if each avatar represented one of those attributes? And suppose the worship of avatars wasn't universal? Suddenly I had not one, but two robust religious systems, and two characters to represent them.

(The Worship of Averran is due almost entirely to another friend and gamer who, when I was talking about the need to develop the personalities of the avatars, suggested that one of them could be a crotchety old man whose worshippers had to cajole and wheedle him to get him to give them spells. Thanks again, Bryan.)

Aside from the underlying principles, I had no desire to write up an actual campaign I'd played in. That is beyond boring, because most campaigns don't actually work like novels. The plots are unbalanced due to the nature of players, who like to go haring off on side quests, and not every encounter is interesting. I wanted the trappings of an RPG, but it was always going to be a real fantasy novel. I didn't realize how well I'd done my fundamentals. It was a genuine surprise when early reviews of *Company of Strangers* all said the same thing: it was just like a role-playing adventure, but better. The sense of wonder and excitement I always got from gaming came through.

So here we are at the end of the adventure, with all five companions setting off on new quests together. To me, the story is finished, and I won't come back to their lives again. But I know something of what comes next, enough to know that when, years from now, they're done being scrappers, they remain friends and companions.

PERRIN continues to grow in the worship of Averran until he becomes a divine and takes up a role in the Fiorettan temple to that avatar. He and Cressida have two more children, and when his father dies about five years after the end of this series, he reconciles with the rest of his family, three of whom convert to Averran's worship.

DIANTHE eventually retires from active adventuring to raise a family with Denys, who ultimately is promoted to Commander of the Guard. While she never takes Corbyn's position as chief spy, she occasionally acts as King Derekian's left hand when subtlety and a non-official liaison are called for.

KALANATH divides his time between Fioretti and Chirantan, where he studies with the divines of the temple and teaches his younger sisters the use of the longstaff. As *devesh,* he learns to control his visions and becomes well-known for his wisdom and insight.

SIENNE and ALARIC settle in Fioretti, where Alaric takes a job with the city guard and Sienne teaches those wizards who choose to undergo the coming of age ritual. Though they never have children of their own, they become foster parents to a series of older orphans Alaric encounters in the course of his work, and eventually adopt two of them.

Sienne's decision to reveal the coming of age ritual transforms magic as Rafellin knows it, and the results continue to change the country and its wizards. Where it will end, no one knows.

Thank you for following Sienne, Alaric, Perrin, Dianthe, and Kalanath on their journey, and for helping turn my idle desire into a reality.

—Melissa McShane

ABOUT THE AUTHOR

In addition to the Company of Strangers series, Melissa McShane is the author of thirty fantasy novels, including the novels of Tremontane, the first of which is *Servant of the Crown;* The Extraordinaries series, beginning with *Burning Bright;* and *The Book of Secrets,* first book in The Last Oracle series.

She lives in the shelter of the mountains out West with her husband, four children and a niece, and four very needy cats. Her library has officially overflowed its bounds, which is another way of saying she needs more shelves.

She wrote reviews and critical essays for many years before turning to fiction, which is much more fun than anyone ought to be allowed to have.

You can visit her at **www.melissamcshanewrites.com** for more information on other books.

For news on upcoming releases, bonus material, and other fun stuff, sign up for Melissa's newsletter at http://eepurl.com/brannP

ALSO BY MELISSA MCSHANE

THE CROWN OF TREMONTANE

Servant of the Crown

Rider of the Crown

Agent of the Crown

Voyager of the Crown

THE SAGA OF WILLOW NORTH

Pretender to the Crown

Guardian of the Crown

Champion of the Crown

THE HEIRS OF WILLOW NORTH

Ally of the Crown (forthcoming)

Stranger to the Crown (forthcoming)

THE EXTRAORDINARIES

Burning Bright

Wondering Sight

Abounding Might

THE LAST ORACLE

The Book of Secrets

The Book of Peril

The Book of Mayhem

The Book of Lies

The Book of Betrayal

The Book of Havoc (forthcoming)

COMPANY OF STRANGERS

Company of Strangers

Stone of Inheritance

Mortal Rites

Shifting Loyalties

Sands of Memory

Call of Wizardry

THE CONVERGENCE TRILOGY

The Summoned Mage

The Wandering Mage

The Unconquered Mage

THE BOOKS OF DALANINE

The Smoke-Scented Girl

The God-Touched Man

The View From Castle Always

Emissary

Warts and All: A Fairy Tale Collection

www.ingramcontent.com/pod-product-compliance
Lightning Source LLC
Chambersburg PA
CBHW070534260626
47161CB00002B/383